I0714916

Pretty Dudes

the novel

Read all the books in the *Pretty Dudes* series

Pretty Dudes: The Novel
Pretty Dudes: The Sequel
Bravo Double Delta
The Ungodly Hours
The Walls of Jericho Kim
Sired (Magna Edition)

More books by C.S.R. Calloway

The Adventures of a Laguna Witch
The Gay Man's Guide to Heterosexual Weddings
Lost: A Never Novella
Natty Girl Saves the World
Peculiar, INC
Purgatory's Children

Pretty Dudes
the novel

written by
C.S.R. Calloway

based on the digital series
Pretty Dudes
created by Chance Calloway

Pretty Dudes: The Novel
Copyright © 2020 by C.S.R. Calloway

Published by CSRC Storytelling
Los Angeles, CA 90006

ISBNs:
978-1-955382-42-7 (Hardcover)
978-1-955382-25-0 (Paperback)
978-0-9891698-8-2 (Ebook)
978-1-6622687-7-9 (Audiobook)

Cover illustrations by Justin Benford.
Cover designed by Hampton Lamoureux of TS95 Studios.
First edition: July 2020. Second edition: August 2022.

prettydudesweb.com

Table of Contents

thots

Beauty is present in all creation, but the danger lies in the fact that we allow ourselves to be influenced by what people think. We deny our own beauty because others can't or won't recognize it. We try to imitate what we see around us. We try to be what other people think of as 'pretty' and, little by little, our soul fades. We forget the world is what we imagine it to be. We stop being the sun and become, instead, the pool of water reflecting it.
- Paulo Coelho, *Manuscript Found in Accra*

Sometimes, stupid and cute *are* enough.
- John Waters

Caught Gay-Handed

There's something anticlimactic about seeing a celebrity's dick, no matter how pretty it is. After all, dicks ("cocks," if you're the type, but you shouldn't be) are just a part of existence for nearly fifty percent of the human population. Whether it shows up in some award-winning film or in a grainy image from a paparazzo's hounding camera, it's the same thing so many other people have between their legs, made special only by the fact that if it belongs to someone else, we're not supposed to see it. When Sunji Spencer slings his in my face, he's no celebrity or larger-than-life personality. He's just a man, standing in front of another man, asking him to "check it out."

These aren't moments exclusive to my interactions with Sunji, who, it must be said, at this time of my knowing him is only considered a celebrity by a small sect of people who saw his infomercial with Rebel Wilson. It's me; I'm the common denominator. The escalation of initially innocuous situations irradiates my life. Not the nudity, specifically. As a photographer, many of my friends have ended up disrobed in front of my lens, per their own requests. Sunji's old roommate Ellington Gomez-Pacheco, currently on the couch next to me thumbing the shit out of a game controller, once paid me to take nudes of him for some girl. It should be said that it wasn't difficult for Ellington to persuade me to do him that favor, what with him looking like a cage-free, grass-fed, probiotic, non-GMO, organic full course meal. Rich in protein. A recommended source of Vitamin D. I mean—and I promise I don't talk about dicks this much in normal circumstances, but since we're on the subject—Ellington had a near-perfect genital set. His balls were even, almost youthful in the tautness of the skin, and his dick draped over them like a twisting balloon that was filled with water.

It must be said that I'm not into Ellington or his immaculate assemblage. I put a mental wall up when it comes to my straight friends. They're off-limits. Lusting over them is no good for either party. Besides, I'm typically an ass man. A leg man, really. And, despite his ardent claims to the contrary, I am not into Sunji Spencer at all, despite the proximity between his sticker and my sniffer.

In my defense, penises aren't sexualized to me. I can't even remember the first time I saw one. Eyes are sexual. Lips. Earlobes, sometimes. Calves. I'd rather men wear wide-legged pants or bell-bottoms than shorts because calves are so dangerous.

The first time a man's body became a point of wonder for me was the seventh grade, after my skinny friend Rafael got jacked over the summer. He flexed one arm for me and my eyes popped in conjunction with the peaking of his bicep. I begged him to do it again and he refused, which only made me beg harder. I'm sure that's the moment he verified my queerness, not that it changed our friendship. The summer before high school, his parents sent him off to a military school. When I realized I missed his body more than his conversations about Michael Bay movies, I got my first sneaking suspicion that I wasn't like the other boys.

In high school, I was cast in a musical with a senior football player named Lamaar, who was the first buff person I had ever met. Changing before shows, he would flex his chest when requested, with one of those smiles that was at once embarrassed and gratified, threatening to break his face wide open. We were double-cast as the Wolf in Stephen Sondheim's *Into the Woods*, though he dropped out of the show a few weeks before first curtain, allowing me to appear in the upperclassmen cast as well as with my sophomore peers. Again, I missed his body more than I missed his basso profundo. He had calves that spoke to me in all of my languages.

Even gym class didn't weird me out. We all showered with our boxers on. If I ever did glimpse someone's privates, there was never a feeling a shame or even desire. They were the things you pissed with, that's why you didn't just leave them out in the open for other people to see.

I do remember the first time I experienced a penis in a sexual connotation. Sex education. The video they made us watch with a camera inserted in a woman's vagina was quite anticlimactic, ironically. No thrusts, no visual context, just a single spurt. It made sex seem like the most unnecessary, messy thing. A gooey spurt, then a screaming baby pulled out of a gaping, bleeding hole nine months later.

To me, sexuality back then was like a blank page in a watercolor painting book. Some people had sexual awakenings that were pages with dots to connect or lines to color in. I would just wake up after vivid, detailed dreams about random male classmates and celebrities and my wet tool would tint that rainbow a little more each time.

I've gotten off track. I was talking about one dick, not all dicks, and definitely not watercoloring. But to give you the best context for why Sunji's bulldoze hose was so close to my nose, we'd have to go back a year and a half to my first week in Los Angeles. Specifically, the day I betrayed my ego and entered a public exercise facility.

• • • • • • • • • •

Two steps into the gym and I immediately knew I was doing something wrong, at least by LA standards. One look at me and everyone could see that I didn't frequent fitness centers. My hips were genetic, but the way my thighs filled my sweats was far more culinary than hereditary. To be fair, this was the time of year that patrons with pudge wouldn't be too out of place in the squat racks. It was January in Los Angeles; everyone would be posting stories to their social media pages from their gym of choice for the next few weeks. I knew, however, that if one look turned into two and they realized I swayed more than they might like and that I held my wrists in a certain way, then they'd think I was just there to scope out the hot guys mastering their roadmaps and dick skin.

That was something my old college roommate used to say, standing in the mirror and flexing, talking about "roadmaps and dick skin." Vascularity, I have since learned, is the appropriate term. Regardless, I didn't go to the gym for a veiny body. I just wanted to look good from any angle whenever someone captured me grooving to Selena.

I looked for the area where I would embarrass myself the least. If I went to a machine, the gym heads might not take me seriously. If I went to the barbell benches, I'd have to ask a stranger to spot me. The safest bet seemed to be the free weights.

I care about my fitness, sometimes. Honestly, the mood comes and goes. I'm very tall, in the six-four range, so I learned at an early age to not pay attention to the number on anybody's scale. Also, I don't put weight on my stomach, so I look good in most clothes since my flat stomach gives the illusion that I'm in some sort of desirable shape. In reality, I feel like I have the shape of a refrigerator, with just enough dimensions to keep it interesting. I'm hippy to a fault (my fault, specifically), but thankfully some of the curves have hit my ass in a desirable way.

To be honest, it wouldn't matter how many pounds I packed on. With my height, my face, and my stroke game, I'm top-tier gay outside of spaces like West Hollywood where the standards are more comical than desirable.

Two guys were doing pull-ups near me, one Black and one Asian, both shirtless. I paid them no attention at first, just like I ignored the woman who offered me her fifteen pound weight. I'm stronger than I look, lady, I thought. *Twenty* pound weights would do it for me.

I did a full set of reps on my own without anyone running over unsolicited to fix my form. As I rested, I gazed up at the two guys doing their pull-ups. Even with their faces twisted in concentration and competition, I could tell they were handsome. More noticeable were their abs, as their ribs stretched and their torsos tightened. The Asian one was dripping sweat and the Black one had switched to one-armed pull-ups and his abs were looking like biological cursive.

I was impressed. I decided to sneak a picture and send it to my college buddy LaMarjorie. She always sent me photos of the hot guys at her gym and I had never been in a gym to return the favor. My brand-new LA lifestyle was already paying off.

Click. Betrayed. Caught. Gay-handed. My silent mode was off and, worse, my phone was at maximum volume. The sweaty one dropped first, eyes pinned on me. Of course. The one fucking time.

"Did you just take a picture of us?"

My brain should have been working harder, but it seemed to have stopped entirely. "It was my text."

Sweat and Abs were approaching fast. I couldn't help but notice that Abs had the juiciest pecs. How was it possible for him to have abs like that, a waist that small, and giant tit-muscles all at the same time?

They were on me with a quickness. "Not cool, man," Sweat said. "Let me see it."

He grabbed my phone out of my hands. In my obsession with Tit-Muscles, I hadn't even locked the phone. Sweat's eyes grew wide and he showed the phone to Tit-Muscles.

"That is nice, dude," Tit-Muscles said. "The lighting. The contour."

Wait, what? They were impressed with the picture? Sweat looked as surprised as I felt and Tit-Muscles broke out into a grin that was even more beautiful than his body. He was perfect.

"Can you take another?" That was Sweat, giving me back my phone. Grin&Tit-Muscles looked at me pleadingly.

"Sure." I had died and gone to softcore porn heaven—well, I doubted there was any sex in heaven, with there being no expectation of physical forms after death.

Where was my brain going?

The two men began posing, each time more ridiculous than the last. A flex here, an ab touch there.

"Are you a photographer or something?" Grin asked as the three of us looked through the shots, deciding which ones I would airdrop to them.

"I went to school for it," I said.

"So, yes?" Grin stared at me and I couldn't tell if it was a statement or a challenge.

"Yeah, basically."

Grin nodded and Sweat asked, "What's your name?"

"Zario. Like Mario. With a Z."

"Who's Mario?" Sweat asked, and Grin, seeming to recognize the spacey look in his friend's eyes, immediately took control of the conversation.

"I'm Ellington. This is Sunji."

What a set of names. Soon-gee. I briefly wondered what the origin of that name was.

Sweat—Sunji—smiled conspiratorially. "He knows who I am."

"I do?" I felt a frown purse my lips. Had we met somewhere before? I was sure I would recognize someone as beautiful as either of these men.

Ellington sighed, speaking out of obligation. "Sunji's been in a few print campaigns."

Sunji seemed very proud. "Shoes. Cologne. College pamphlets. H&M." He held out his hand. "Sunji Spencer."

Now I perceived them in their fullness. Sunji had shoulder-length black hair, thick, with beautiful eyebrows. He stood erect, like a dancer, and when he moved, it was all unbroken motion, like an acrobat. Ellington had a similar frame, just with muscles rippling under his skin like he had been drawn by a comic book artist. No, that's not exactly it. He wasn't drawn the way those men drew other men—brick-bodied and thick-waisted. He was drawn the way those men drew women, with ridiculous muscles in place of ridiculous curves, a Dorito torso, and body parts that should have been out of visual frame drawing your attention away at all times.

I shook the offered hand, unnerved at the extended public attention I was receiving from two straight men and also freaking out because for a moment there, I was assessing the caliber of Ellington's dick print. My mind began to race. I had come here by myself. What if these guys were just baiting me? What if they planned to jump me in the parking lot? Why had I given them my real name?

"You okay?" Ellington asked. "Suddenly you look constipated."

"Could you two excuse me?"

I hid out in a bathroom stall for a good forty minutes before hightailing it out of there. In a just world, that would have been the end of the adventure.

I hopped on the bus determined to leave the concept of "gym" in the past where it belonged.. When I heard my phone ringing, I answered without looking at the caller, welcoming any distraction.

"Zario del Rosario."

I recognized the voice. "Hi, Alexander."

Alexander Erzähler was a college classmate I initially met through LaMarjorie during our junior year. We had shared plenty of experiences, but I was not expecting the call.

"Do you know why I'm calling?"

"I can't say that I do."

"You're in LA? You posted that you're looking for a place."

"Are you in LA?"

"Yes, and we're down a roommate. Do you want to come check it out?"

"What's the price range?"

"My landlord is cool. He can work with, like, whatever you can give, basically."

Less than twenty-four hours later, I was standing on a porch in North Hollywood, trying to remember all the things I could about Alexander Erzähler. He had been a serious gamer, and I think he had done it professionally since long before I met him. He was the youngest of several boys, and pretty mousy in personality. We had actually traveled to Europe together one summer, but even though I went on his dime, we barely spent any time together.

The house itself was unassuming. So many of the houses in this section of North Hollywood seemed far bigger on the inside than they ever looked on the outside. It was one story with a partially enclosed front porch elevated above a small front lawn. The steps were spacious enough for me to imagine entertaining company on them, in purely PG fantasies.

The door swung open and there he was, barely as tall as my tits and grinning liplessly. His blue eyes were endless and his skin was pale. I wondered if this was the first time he had been outside since he moved in.

"Zario del Rosario."

"Hi, Alexander," I said, moving in for a hug. Alexander didn't seem to understand, stepping aside to let me into the house. I didn't catch this in the moment, so I adjusted my attempt at an embrace.

"Oh," Alexander muttered, attempting to wrap one arm around me, ending up with it pinned between us. He let go of the door and awkwardly grabbed the back of my neck.

"Come in," came the delayed verbal invitation and I stepped inside.

"I brought my camera, if it's cool for me to take pictures."

"Don't fucking worry about that. I told the guys about you and you can move in whenever you want."

"Yeah, but they haven't met me."

"But I've met you," Alexander said with a self-important smile. "And my word goes a long way around here."

"Hey, asshole, open the window in the den. It smells like your taint in there."

Alexander's smile crusted over. "Zario, I'd like to introduce you to my landlord."

I looked up and felt all of my internal organs freeze into ice, save for my stomach, which was either plummeting toward my feet or rising in my throat.

"Zario?"

"Hi," I croaked as Sweat—Sunji—wrapped me in a hug. He smelled citrusy, and I briefly wondered if he was wearing perfume.

Away from the gym, with his muscles covered up, I was able to appreciate how beautiful he was. Some models look weird in person. Misshapen, or accidental. But he looked like God had worked on him in between churning out all of the rest of us, not putting him in the kiln until They were absolutely satisfied. His eyes crinkled with his smile, electric bolts of joy. His hair was an ebony black, darker and richer the closer you looked. In comparison, his teeth were impossibly white—the one thing on his face that probably wasn't natural.

"This is some type of destiny," Sunji said. "Alexander told us he had a guy from college and I imagined a scratching and burping motherfuck, but you are primo supreme-o, daddio."

I couldn't nail down the era of that slang, so I just nodded, my smile and feet still frozen.

"You guys know each other?" Alexander asked, his face drooping into a frown.

"This is the creepy kid from the gym," Sunji said brightly. "The photographer."

"I'm not usually creepy," I said feebly.

"Come check the place out. You remember the guy I was with?"

"Tit-Muscles," I nodded, and Sunji and Alexander both knitted their brows.

"What?"

I corrected myself quickly. "Ellington, right?"

"Yeah! He just moved out last week and you'll be taking his room."

"If it works out," I said cautiously and Sunji turned his brown open eyes to me.

"Why wouldn't it work out?"

Leading me through the house, Sunji laughed at about sixty percent of my dry humor, while giving me genuine, passionate responses to the forty percent he took seriously. He calibrated to my energy and vibe, which I appreciated.

I tried to map out the house as we talked. The entrance foyer opened into the kitchen to the left, where Sunji offered me a beer, then a cupcake he claimed to have made from scratch. The dining room was visible through the doorway on the right, where a stack of playing cards and board games were my first indication that these housemates were social. Straight ahead was the nicely-sized living room, with a wide window flooding the house with sunlight. The furniture, an unfamiliar shade of green that wasn't quite olive and wasn't quite mint ("mantis," according to Sunji), was clearly more for use than for show. The cabinets and tables were covered in collectibles, comics, and books, all in various states of handling and conservation.

My straight boy expectations were rewarded with Bruce Lee, *Speed*, *Romeo Must Die*, and *The Dark Knight* posters, but these were hung alongside a few unanticipated treats. An understated promotional *Aladdin* print was featured next to the door, and a vibrant, purple display for a Brazilian film *Orfeu Negro* had a prominent position near the television.

"What's this one?" I asked, pointing to a black and white Chinese language poster with the image of an embracing couple.

"*Comrades: Almost a Love Story*," Sunji replied brightly, before suddenly tearing up. "But it *is* a love story."

I gave him a moment, during which he audibly sobbed at least once, then he collected himself and showed me the two offshoots of the house beyond the living room. Down one hallway, the one ending with the den, were Sunji's and Alexander's rooms. The other hall led to two other bedrooms, one of them the recently vacated one. What quickly became a great mystery to me, however, was a giant, elongated two-door bathroom, big enough to comfortably fit all of the residents in front of its long mirror, with just one toilet and one shower.

"I've never seen a bathroom like this," I told Sunji, trying to figure out where the other door went. We had come in from the hallway connected to my potential room.

"Oh, that one doesn't open from the inside," he said.

"Is that a bedroom?" I asked.

"It changes. Like Narnia."

The rest of my questions received straightforward answers, and I answered Sunji's to his satisfaction.

I was able to pay the first and last months' worth of rent, and he said to just give whatever I could when I got booked for gigs.

In this moment, I think that's probably another layer to the whole "check out my dick" shit. I feel a little obligated. But there are worse obligations, I'm sure.

• • • • • • • •

It was just a few minutes ago that Sunji had walked into the permanently taint-scented den and positioned himself directly in front of the television, wearing nothing but a towel. I didn't mind this so much, as I wasn't one of the fellas using the flatscreen to play a game.

They're called games, right? Like sports, but virtual and without the athletic physical demands.

Anyway, Alexander was playing against Ellington, who had a key and was over nearly as much as he had been when he lived there. Neither of them appreciated the interruption. Ellington, being a fixer, spoke first.

"Did you lose something, Sunji?"

Sunji had the towel pulled away from his body, eyes cast downward. "I think I gained something. Can you come take a look at this?"

Sunji took one step and Ellington threw up an arm.

"Hey, hey, hey, no sir! Back it up."

"It's my balls, Ellington, not my dick."

"That distinction does not change my mind about looking down your towel at your wrinkly globes."

Sunji's mouth made a perfect circle as he took offense to this. "They're not wrinkly! My sack can barely contain them."

Alexander groaned, pausing the game. "Oh, God."

Sunji talks about the size of his balls more than I've recently talked about dick, if you can believe that. He talks about his nipples even more, which I don't understand, because his nipples are not, you know, special or anything.

"I think it's a knot on them or something. Jay…"

"Keep my name out of your mouth. Have Zario check. He's the gay one!"

That was Jay, another housemate, head on my thigh as he laid across the couch and crunched on a bowl full of carrots.

I looked up in horror. *No, no, absolutely not.* These guys pick the worst times to fuck up and tokenize me.

"Wayment. That's not how this works."

"It's why we keep you around, Zee."

This stung mainly because it came from Jay, even if I could tell he was just bullshitting.

"Not funny." I shoved his shoulder. He snorted, almost choking on his carrots and I immediately felt bad.

Sunji shook his head. "I'm not about to put my seed holsters all up in his face," he said, gesturing vaguely in my direction. "That's like offering vodka to an alcoholic."

"Oh, whatever, dude." I'm not positive what scoffing is, but I think I scoffed. "My penis passion is not dick disease. And nobody's checking for you. Firstly, you're a friend. Second, you are so not my type."

Sunji didn't buy this for a second. He never did. "But you were still sneaking pictures of me at the gym."

I shrugged, refusing this roundabout. "You and Ellington were strangers with nice bodies."

"That's what makes it creepy, Zario," Alexander piped up.

Jay sat up, unable to resist an opportunity to shut Alexander down.

"Shut the fuck up, man. Or should we talk about Ellington's 'Ass or Pass' album? The one in his phone full of women in the grocery store reaching to the top shelf?"

Alexander smiled. "That album deserves a Pulitzer."

Sunji turned to him. "Alexander?" with a nod toward his towel.

"Not unless you want me to take a bat to them or you're gonna pay me what a doctor makes to look at them."

Sunji had grown desperate. "Can one of you guys just check?"

I sighed, sitting up. "Show me."

Jay looked slightly annoyed. "This is an example of true friendship," he muttered, munching away.

Sunji and I said it at the same time. "Shut up, Jay."

. . . .

Jay is the housemate who's gotten under my skin since the day we met. I should be clear, he gets under my skin on purpose and I don't mind it, because it's him. It's symbiotic—I itch and he's got claws.

He's the roommate that Alexander had said was never around, the one whose room was down my hallway, but the morning after I moved in, there he was in the kitchen. He sat on top of the counter like a vagabond, legs spread like his dick needed airing out.

At first all I noticed was the meat—the pectoral cleavage displayed through the blue V-neck T-shirt and the bulbous biceps straining at the hem. He looked like the type of guy who enjoyed an extra meal as much as an extra gym session. He was Asian, but paler than Sunji. His eyebrows had a super villain arch and the eyes beneath them were permanently glinting, like he knew more secrets than you could ever reveal to him. He had large lips for such a small mouth, and his jaw was working overtime to destroy a bowl of noodles.

"Hi," I said.

"Hi." He looked me up and down, adding more secrets to his arsenal. "What's your name?"

"Zario."

"How do you spell it?"

"Z—"

"I'm Jay."

"Nice to meet you, Jay."

After a moment, I broke eye contact.

"You're gay, right?" Slurping noodles.

"Is that the only thing you've heard about me?"

"And that you take pictures of dudes in the gym. Because you're gay."

I can feel my face turning red. "Not because I'm gay."

Slurping. "Because you're a creep."

"Not that, either."

"It seems like it would be one or the other, if not both. Maybe you're a gay creep. A greep."

I was spinning. Jay didn't seem to be attacking me. He was almost teasing, but there was an intensity behind his curiosity, especially for a guy who was basically a stranger.

"I take pictures of moments. It's gotten me in trouble before."

"That was a moment, huh?"

"Yeah."

He chewed thoughtfully, never looking away from me. "That's bullshit."

"Excuse me?"

"That's bullshit. You want to be a voyeur and conceal it with the excuse of artistry. Just say you were being a creep."

"If I say I was being a creep—"

"Were you being a creep?"

"Okay, yes, I was being a creep, but I'm not a creep. I just had a creepy moment."

I noticed that he was chewing with his mouth open, lips drawing back into a smile.

"Was that so hard?"

He slides off the counter and I realize he's almost as short as Alexander. He grabs a bottle of vodka from the cabinet and tips it in my direction as he turns to go.

"Nice to meet you, Zee. Welcome to the house."

It became clear to me rather quickly upon moving in, that Jay did sex work. I was the earliest riser and I would often find Jay winding down from a long night with a drink, dressed in a button up and slacks, everything tight, everything hugging. The drink was a staple, whether he seemed loose or lucid. As we grew closer, he'd wake me up when he got home—four or five in the morning, if he knew I didn't have a gig—and make me do shots with him. I would accompany him to the ATM on more than one occasion, watching him deposit stacks of cash. Sometimes, there was lipstick on his collar. Once, there was lipstick directly over his crotch. Some mornings, he would go shower right away. We wouldn't talk much on those dawns. He'd get in his pajamas and disappear to his room, emerging in the afternoon set for a new night of unspoken adventures in K-Town.

At some point, when we became friends, we became best friends. Inseparable. From Alexander's point of view, that endeared me to Sunji. Both Alexander and Ellington claim that Jay was unbearable before I moved in. Some days, if I'm feeling frisky, I ask them why neither of them made Sunji more bearable.

• • • • • • •

That brings us fully to the present, with Sunji's waist at my forehead, towel open, his slinging cum pump failing to hypnotize me.

"Stop moving it," I command. Next to me, Ellington's laughing silently.

Sunji wasn't lying about his pendulous balls, undulating now between his taunt thighs. I'm struck for words. I look up at him and he looks down at me, giving me a wink before returning to being worried.

I wonder how he walks with those things swinging down there. I wonder how many children he'll have. He could repopulate the world with those things. I can't even tell what size his dick is, because nothing looks like a "normal" size propped between those. I force myself to inspect the primary point of concern.

Despite not getting a clear reading on his size, the shape is nice. Gradient coloring, healthy skin. A healthy hang, for him to be soft, with a good proportionality between length and thickness, despite Jupiter and Saturn crowding its space.

I say none of this, only, "Dude, I don't see anything irregular."

"You sure?" he asks, swinging his hips and making everything sway in front of me. I look over and see tears streaming down Ellington's face as he positively loses it.

"I'm pretty sure." Something misshapen catches the light. "Wait, what's that?"

I grab Sunji's knee with one hand and grip his opposite hip with the other, trying to stop all unnecessary movement.

Full panic mode now from above. "What? Whatwhatwhat?"

I peer closely. "Nevermind. It's just a vein."

"Can you touch it to make sure?"

"No!"

He swings his genitals toward me. "Can you touch it anyway?"

"How about I punch it?" I ask

He wraps his towel tightly, stepping back from the couch. I see the laughter in his eyes.

"You almost tapped my chin, you motherfuck."

I hate that their slang has become my slang, but friends develop a vernacular, a cadence.

"Can we get back to the game now?" Alexander asks, waving his controller.

"You know what? Let's go out," Ellington suggests, and I feel the excitement level rising around me.

He continues. "We haven't gone out as a group in months. Let's go. Pick up some ladies." He looks at me. "Or whatever."

"Oh, gosh, it's been ages since I've picked up some 'whatever,'" I say, drawing my top lip into my gums and blinking monstrously at him.

"That's not a bad idea," Sunji says. "I'm down for ladies or whatever."

"Or we could hang out here," I counter. "Play cards."

"Play with some dick tonight, Zee," Jay says, doing his open-mouth chew. "Don't limit yourself."

The truth is, I'm currently coming out of a pretty bad depressive episode and I can see now that they clearly had this planned already. There's no other reason Sunji would be getting in the shower so late in the day, and it's always odd when Jay is being social before sunset.

"If it's not popping, we'll come right back," Ellington promises. "In fact, let's go to WeHo. It's always popping in WeHo."

"Shit, I'll have to actually get ready if we go there," I groan. Partying with the gym and fashion queens in West Hollywood requires a certain level of Ken doll cosplay.

"Alexander will come, too," Sunji says. "Right, Alexander?"

The gamer nods. "Affirmative."

"All right, sure," I say. "I'm down. Just, promise me no drama tonight. No shenanigans."

"We are civilized beasts," Jay says.

"You guys know what I'm talking about."

Sunji shrugs. "That wet t-shirt contest last time wasn't our idea."

"Yeah, and we won anyway," Ellington adds, "so it worked out for everyone."

I shake my head. "You won, and there was no prize."

"Zario." Ellington has a soft smile on his face. "It was fun. That's the goal. Remember?"

"He doesn't remember fun," Sunji teases. "Do you think he had fun with Shane as his boyfriend for so long?"

At the mention of my ex-boyfriend, something inside of me is wrung out. I catch my breath.

"Alright, okay. You're right. Let's have fun tonight."

As the guys begin to scatter, Jay watches me, finishing the last of his carrots.

"What?" I ask him.

"We don't have to go if you don't want to. You know they want to see you back to normal."

"I am back to normal. Besides, it's obvious you guys had this planned already."

He chews. Mouth open. Smiling slowly. "You caught us."

"Real friends can't keep much from each other."

He grunts and stands into a stretch, his belly peeking above his belt. "That's why friends are better than lovers. Naked honesty."

I flinch.

"What the fuck was that?" he asks, looking down at me.

I drop my head into my hands, shoulders shaking with laughter.

"You said 'naked' and in my head I saw Sunji's junk again, swinging toward my face."

He shakes his head, moving down the hall toward the kitchen to wash out his bowl. "Is there a such thing as a wet nightmare? Because that's what you're going to have tonight."

I chuckle. "Erotic night terrors."

"Good one," he calls back over his shoulder.

I sit in the den alone for a few moments, resisting the impulse to disassociate. I can have fun tonight. I will have fun tonight. I might even compete in whatever spontaneous, free-spirited sexual objectification that arises . My eyes come into focus on a framed photo adjacent to the television on the entertainment center.

It's Sunji and Ellington, one of the photos I took at the gym on the day that we met. They both stare directly into the camera, pouting and flexing. Ellington was right. The lighting was on point.

I turn to go just as Jay returns to the doorway, finger pointed at me and eyes lit up in conception.

"Mr. Sandman brings you a cream!"

I stare at him blankly.

"You get it? Wet nightmares, erotic night terrors, and Mr. Sandman brings you a cream!"

I feign confusion, hoping for a specific response. It doesn't take much more back and forth (and several tentatively sung *bung, bung,*

bung, bungs) before Jay shuttles his hips back and forth and begins to warble in his baritone.

"*Mr. Sandman, bring me a cream,*
Make it the thickest that I've ever streamed…"

Ah, yes. I do remember fun. Too bad I'm not getting this particular fun captured with my camera.

The Curse

"Curses are real." Jay presses his palms onto the minivan's headliner. "I can prove it, but I really shouldn't have to. We've each seen how curses can impact someone's life."

"Here we go," Ellington mutters from the middle seat where he sits shirtless. ("You don't mind, do you?" he had asked the driver, who of course the fuck did not.) His freshly ironed button-up hangs on a hanger next to him.

Ellington keeps a stash of clothes in Alexander's closet, since Alexander cycles through the same few t-shirts and pajama pants. Whenever Ellington decides to stay over or ride out with us, he has nearly half of his wardrobe at his immediate disposal.

I'm in the back with Jay, sandwiched between him and Alexander. Jay's leg is thrown over mine and now he drops one of his arms on the seat behind me, leaning forward intently.

"I'm not being religious and I'm not saying that I buy into any of that mystic mumbo jumbo shit. You believe in blessings, right?"

"Of course," Ellington says. "I *am* religious."

"There's a balance, right? Good things happen, bad things happen. Circle of life and all that fuckshit. In fact, I'd take it farther. I say curses are usually disguised in the form of blessings. Take us for example."

"What, we're cursed?" I ask.

"Don't sound surprised. Think about it. We are the motherfucks who are the living proof that there's a cost to being a cosmetic genetic."

"A cost," I repeat.

"What's a 'cosmetic genetic?'" Sunji asks, sitting across from Ellington. If the driver had been attractive, Sunji and Ellington would have battled over the passenger seat. Instead, we are all grouped together behind her and the driver was probably better for it.

"A pretty boy," Alexander says. "Am I right?"

"Yeah, pretty boys," Jay says. "Or make it gender neutral. We call each other 'dude' all the time. Pretty dudes."

I turn to Alexander. "Is 'dude' a gender-neutral term?"

"You're asking too many questions," Jay tells me. "And, yes. How long have you been in California?"

"Don't call me pretty," Ellington says.

"You are pretty, though," Sunji responds. "So am I. Jay's not, so I don't know why he's saying 'we' and 'us.'"

"Take your boy Sunji Spencer here," Jay says to me. "If you wanna be real pretentious, the pretty dude species is *bellus abundantia.*"

"No one wants to be pretentious," Ellington interrupts. "Just you."

Jay continues. "Sunji is of the subspecies *adonis ignoramus.*"

"What does *adonis ignoramus* mean?" Sunji asks.

"All beauty, no brains," Jay replies.

"I resent that," Sunji says. "I've got brawn. See? You forgot one."

"That you do," Jay agrees, and Sunji grins.

"I'm a brawny *bellus,*" he says proudly, and I'm positive that Sunji's only going to take away mismatched parts of this conversation. I'm also sure that I hear our driver laughing up front.

"So, Sunji's a himbo," Alexander says. "No surprise there, but what about Ellington?"

Jay frowns, giving the illusion that he's deep in thought.

"Not to encourage any of this," I say, "but 'himbo?' Why do we gender words unnecessarily like that makes it catchier?"

"Calling him a bimbo insinuates that I'm feminizing him," Alexander says, "which in turn insinuates that femininity is a negative trait. Also calling him a himbo rightfully paints this entire conversation as the ridiculousness that it is."

I nod. "Fair." I silently offer him a breath mint. When he refuses, I make another offer, bugging out my eyes until he takes two.

Jay speaks now. "Ellington's subspecies is more familiar: *handsum harlata*. Still subject to the curse."

"You're calling me a man-whore?"

"That would be an insult to us whores," Jay says.

"A harlot is literally a prostitute."

"*Harlata* is Latin."

"*Harlata* is a word you made up."

"Then why are you offended?"

"Okay, then," Ellington says evenly, "what is my subspecies exactly? Colloquial terms."

I see a familiar glint in Jay's eyes when he replies, "Community dick."

Sunji's mouth makes that perfect circle as his eyebrows rise to meet his hairline.

Ellington breathes evenly. "Okay. Okay. At least you called me handsome."

After a moment, I remember to exhale. Sunji is whipping his eyes to me and I think he was expecting to witness a fight, as well.

"What about you?" I ask Jay. "What's your subspecies?"

"I'm *beefy beefiata*, or abrasive muscle, or—"

"You're basically an asshole," Ellington says.

Jay shrugs. "Hey, you call me an asshole, I become an asshole, so you're welcome."

"Karma's an asshole, too," Alexander says through a refreshing wave of mint.

"Alexander, I've got a subspecies for you: *aryan basic*."

"Okay, calm down," Alexander mutters, adjusting his glasses.

Jay leans around me. "You don't tell me to calm down."

"Wait, there's a flaw in your theory," I interrupt. "If we're cursed because of our looks, how does that affect Alexander? He lives in the den. He orders all his food through delivery apps. The only people he sees are us."

"You said it," Jay says, sitting back. "He avoids the curse by remaining single."

"And gaming," Sunji adds.

"And gaming," Jay nods. "Always gaming."

"Okay, do Zario," Sunji says, the only person buying into Jay's concept.

"Oh, I know Zario's," Alexander says. "*The bellus babyfice.*"

"Damn right. See also: homo-gay," Jay cracks.

Ellington nods as our driver pulls over into an alleyway, using it as an unloading zone. "See also: local Helen of Troy."

Sunji nods, turning to me. "You are a beautiful, beautiful man. I'm not into guys, but if I was, I'd be into you, you know what I'm saying? To the hilt."

"You say that like once a month," Jay says. "You should just fuck him."

"No, thanks," I say.

"Oh, you'd be thanking me," Sunji says, wiggling his eyebrows.

I glare at Jay, who shrugs and bites back a laugh.

We pile out of the vehicle and say our thanks to the driver. Ellington takes his electric pink shirt down from its hanger and Sunji slips on his leather jacket. I'm wearing pink, too, but mine is more muted than Ellington's. Jay's busting out of the blue V-neck he was wearing when I met him, and Alexander's shirt is blue and striped and wrinkled and definitely the best he can do. Four of us are wearing stylish black jeans and I'm happy with where mine cling.

"I feel like this whole conversation is why people judge you guys," Alexander says, picking lint from his khakis, which is like trying to empty a lake by spoonfuls.

"Ay, you're one of us by default," Ellington says, unbuttoning the top of the gamer's polo shirt. "You're white with blue eyes and abs. You're customary-hot. Taylor Swift wrote a song about you."

"'Style' is a song about white supremacy," I affirm. "Plus, Lorde's song 'Royals' is a song about cultural appropriation from an ally's perspective."

"I heard you playing both of those songs within the last week," Jay says.

"A bop is a bop," I say. "Don't come for me."

"You're problematic," Jay grunts.

"I won't deny it."

"Jiminy Cricket, Zee." Jay turns to Alexander. "We can't be judged. We're a product of our entitlement, not the cause of it. It's not our fault that people bend to our will just because our faces are appealing or our cum gutters are well-defined."

Ellington shakes his head. "What's a cum gutter?"

"No," I groan as Jay reaches around me, making a 'v' at my hips with his hands.

"These," he says to Ellington as we begin to clomp across the street.

"I don't have those," I say.

"Sunji won't mind," Jay purrs in my ear.

I pry myself loose. "Your fanfiction is uninspired."

The sign above our destination reads "The Ungodly Hour," but the neon in the 'u' has been burnt out for years and now everyone calls it "The Ungodly Whore." The guys love the Whore thanks to the amount of straight women who frequent the spot and also thanks to the amount of gay bartenders. So many of the bars and clubs in WeHo have straight bartenders, hired for their musculature and for being pleasing to the gay eye. The owners of The Ungodly Whore have more of a "for us, by us" mentality and hire mainly queer employees.

This works in the favor of someone like Ellington, who right now is flashing his commercial-ready grin at the bartender. Based on the flustered response, I'm sure Ellington is going to be drinking free for much of the night.

I begin to suspect that Jay's onto something with this curse thing as I watch the guys mingle. It seems like a self-replicating blessing to have good looks. It's pretty privilege, really, but the same mug that gets us into the VIP section also gets us into trouble.

• • • • • • • •

When it comes to examples of oblivious pretty privilege, Sunji's the lowest hanging fruit. Arguably that obliviousness destroyed his last relationship.

He had met Jerrica Yun on a modeling gig. She was a climber and he had just booked a guest star on a Ryan Murphy series, plus he had irresistible dimples when he smiled a certain way. Dating led to exclusivity and, before long, our main bathroom was her bathroom and we were just lucky to get to use it every once in a while. He cooked exclusively for her, which wouldn't have been much of a problem if we hadn't gotten used to him cooking for us. She didn't have a chance when it came to us liking her. It didn't help that she had particularly potent intestinal gas and she was a shady crop duster.

One day, as they were primping for a red carpet event, she hit him with a relationship pop quiz, Tamia style.

"Sunji," she asked while curling her hair, "where was our first kiss?"

"You should have run then," Jay would tell Sunji later. "You already failed if she thought a cross-examination was necessary."

At the time, Sunji was focused on his nipples. He tweezed them before every event, no matter the amount of layers he'd be wearing.

"On Wilshire," he mumbled, with his chin pinned to his sternum, "after we left the club."

"It was Runyon Canyon. Remember? Because your sweat got in my mouth."

He shrugged. "If you remembered, why did you ask me?"

She doesn't answer, volleying instead with another question. "Can you hand me my perfume?"

"Sure," he said. "Which one?"

"My favorite," she replied

He handed her one that he had bought her. Not her favorite. Another mark against him.

"There you go, babe."

"Thanks," she said dryly, placing it on the counter and sliding it against the wall.

"What are our plans tomorrow night, again?"

"We don't have plans tomorrow night, babe."

"Shouldn't we?" she asked him.

"Should we?" he asked her, looking up from his nipples.

"I guess not," she said.

He picked up his electric razor and started working on his pubes. "Sunji, nobody there is gonna see that much of us."

"You never know," he said, handing her the razor and staring pointedly at her waistline.

"Don't be disgusting."

"Babe, your Venus flytrap is turning into a little shop of horrors, if you know what I mean."

She broke up with him on the way back from the event, counting his faults as he sobbed. The next night would have been their one-year anniversary.

The Pretty Boy Curse. Fatal when you're an asshole. Even an accidental asshole.

• • • • • • •

"Are you drinking tonight?" Jay asks me. He's got three beers in his hand and I know he's going to drink two of them if I don't take one from him.

"No, I'm good," I say.

He chugs one, his Adam's apple practically galloping.

"You've got skills," I tell him.

"You have no idea," he says, looking out over the dancefloor. "You're not dancing. Are you gonna come sit?"

He points to where Sunji's secured the five of us a table.

"I might dance a bit."

He stares at me for a moment, smirking. "Okay. You know I was kidding about Sunji wanting to fuck you, right?"

"I'm not even thinking about that."

He waves a beer at me dismissively as he goes to join the model.

• • • • • • •

It makes complete sense that Jay would be the one to introduce this concept of a beauty curse. It's probably the only way he can make sense of what happened in his former relationship.

If Jerrica Yun was vapid, Callie Reynolds was shrewd. She was the type who always knew where the cameras were. She was a social media influencer, so it was likely she had paid to ensure the cameras were there in the first place. She picked up on our looks, our coughs, and our silences to the point that we could only talk about her when she wasn't around. And she made sure to always be around.

What I remember most about Callie was her hair. Not exactly her real hair, just whatever hair she was wearing. I had only seen her real hair once, as far as I know. It was a glistening afro that make her look like an umber angel. I asked her why she wore wigs when her own hair was so amazing and she told me that her hair was too good to be shared with everyone. The gaze she gave me was withering and I never saw her real hair again.

Jay gave me all the details about the day they broke up. He was blindfolded and handcuffed to his bed frame while she straddled him in lingerie. Next to the bed lay a feather boa, a bowl of ice cubes, and a spray can of whipped cream. She covered his face with kisses and stroked his chest with the ice. As his moans grew louder, she sat up.

"I can't do this anymore, Jay."

"Wha?" He rotated his hips, yearning still. "What are you talking about?"

She plopped the ice cube in his mouth to shut him up. He chewed it furiously.

"You. Me. This! I mean, even when you moan it's like one of those Herbal Essence commercials."

"Babe. What?"

He often mentions to me how maddening it was to not be able to see her in this moment, to read her expressions. I tell him that's probably how she wanted it.

"You're just so fucking pretty! Like, can you not?"

"Why do I feel like you changed the channel on me just now?"

She took a slow breath. In, out. "You remember when I posted those pictures of us at Disneyland right after I had gotten that spa treatment?"

"No?"

"All the replies were thirst posts about how good *you* looked and how great *your* skin looked. Even my father posted a paragraph about the part in your hair."

Jay struggled with his blindfold while trying to sit up. Callie shifted her weight forward from his hips to his torso to keep him down.

He grappled with the handcuffs, his wrists and ankles rubbing the fuzz from them. Callie, in an effort to distract him I've always thought, started kneading his chest.

"Shit," she said, "even your tits are bigger than mine."

Jay says he started moaning again and that his erection, which hadn't entirely deflated, began pushing against Callie's lace, and that's when she got off of him.

"That was it," he told me later that night. "She just lifted into the air and was gone."

"I'm done," she said, and he heard her putting on her jacket. "I'm so done."

Frantic, he cried out, "Babe! Callie, can you unlock the cuffs, please?" He yanked harder on his restraints. "And we can talk about whatever this is? Babe? Babe, there could be an earthquake!"

Jay is deathly afraid of earthquakes. He'll own up to it, but it's obvious anyway. It shows up in moments of extreme stress. I think it's his deep-seated fear about life on the west coast. He's from the midwest. Michigan, I think.

The kicker? Callie posted about the end of the relationship before she even left the room. Over three thousand likes before she got to her car.

When you realize you should have left months ago. #iaintsorry

I think she had it waiting in her drafts.

• • • • • • •

We give each other crap for not liking each other's partners, but when the breakups come, we all feel validated. That may or may not be fair, as most exes seem terrible once the relationship ends.

"Zario?"

Speak of the motherfucking fuckhole devilfuck.

I turn to see the only other guy in the club as tall as me. His skin is golden beige, his shoulders strain at his shirt seams, and his eyes are devouring me with a fervor. It's not lust that brings a smile to his pink-brown lips. It's the allure of scandal.

"I haven't seen you here since World War Shane!" he says, full Regina George.

"Hi, Patrick," I say, hoping I'm as casual as he is slimy. "I haven't seen you here since I started looking exclusively at things that were worth my time."

Ellington steps between us, appearing from nowhere. His eyes are flames, pinned on me, but his energy is directed to Patrick.

"Zario," he says brightly. "Come on. Groove with us, man."

I look and see Alexander, bless his soul, doing a rhythmless bounce and flop, which I think is supposed to be a come hither dance. Ah, yes, his finger is curling repeatedly in my direction. As I head toward him, Ellington turns back to Patrick.

"Get the fuck on," I hear him say.

Then I feel Ellington's hands on my hips as he guides me closer to Alexander.

It's like one of those scenes from any gay movie where the main character and the closeted guy get shirtless together on the dance floor, but this is no movie. I mean, out of all the dudes, I feel like Ellington's the one who would go for me if he wanted to experiment. That said, I'm positive that, out of all the dudes, Ellington's the least likely to experiment. He's a sexual being, sure, but he's one hundred percent straight. That said, I throw it back on him as hard as I can and make sure to give as good as I get.

After the song ends, Ellington abandons us for a beautiful blonde in a skintight black dress. Frankly, I'm surprised he lasted so long without a woman in his orbit.

"That was Patrick, right?" Alexander yells over the music. I nod.

Watching Alexander bop to Beyoncé, I think about how distinctly un-sexual he is. It's easy to overlook his attractiveness when he doesn't bother to refine it in any way. But Ellington's right. We live in a world where white is still the accepted default, and Alexander has luminous blond hair and seven-dimensional blue eyes. He doesn't try because he doesn't have to try.

I see some of the local queers staring at the two of us with envy. They'd probably have more luck with him than I ever would. If

Ellington is one hundred percent straight, Alexander's at least eighty, but I'm positive Alexander would go for someone more stereotypically effeminate than myself if he decided to explore his options. Jay would likely go for someone Black or Asian, like all of his girlfriends. And Sunji, well, I'm pretty sure Sunji "experiments" on the regular (this is as-yet unconfirmed), so I'm probably not his type, otherwise I would have gotten an invitation by now, especially with all the fucking he was doing after breaking up with Jerrica.

Sunji and Jay are across the room and having a terrible time.

"Where are the girls at, man?" Sunji asks, after striking out with a few. The girls here are as likely to be lesbian as they are to be male-attracted.

"It's a record, you know," Jay says. "Four of us are single tonight."

And he's right. This is my first night out since my breakup—what Patrick so cleverly called World War Shane. And before that, Jay was still with Callie, and even further back, Sunji was with Jerrica. Hilariously, the only one of us still in a relationship is the one currently slobbing it up with a girl on the back wall of the bar.

Almost at that exact moment, she pulls away from Ellington, looking much drunker than she did when they started kissing. She presses her pointer finger into his chest.

"But I thought you were gay?"

"What the fuck? If I was gay, why would you be kissing me right now?"

"Exactly," she slurs, and walks away.

In less than ten minutes, we're all outside the club waiting on our rideshare home.

"Seriously, though," Ellington asks me. "What about my outfit is gay?"

Jay snorts. "You're wearing it."

"Maybe it's the curse," I say, half-jokingly.

Sunji points at me, nodding with far too much enthusiasm. "Maybe!"

Alexander, as always, has far more detail than anyone asked for. "Actually, have you guys heard of Jo B. Paoletti? Her research has led to the belief that prior to the currently held traditions of blue for males and pink for females—"

Sunji interrupts him. "Guys. We're all going home alone."

Alexander wags his head from shoulder to shoulder. "Technically, we're going home together."

"Fuck," Ellington says.

I grin. "There will be absolutely no fucking."

Jay looks at me, humored and annoyed simultaneously. "Well, *darn*."

The Dudes Make a Bet

"How do you guys escalate every single thing?" I ask, pacing back and forth in front of the dining room table. "I don't need any help getting a man—and, even if I did, four straight dudes are the last people I would consult on the subject."

On the ride back home to North Hollywood, our conversation careened from Ellington's shirt, to Jay's ridiculous curse, to my status as a newly single gay man. This latest turn has proven most engaging of all, to my annoyance and now detriment. Even inside and a round of drinks in, it doesn't appear that the subject will be changing anytime soon.

"Come on, Zario! Four straight *pretty* dudes." Sunji gestures to the present bodies as if they were produce. "Who else pulls proper punani like the guys in this room?"

Jay nods in agreement. "We get offered pussy and bussy! It's that Pretty Boy Curse."

Alexander snorts as he sets a deck of cards on the table, crossing his legs on the chair underneath him.

Ellington looks up from his comic book. "What is 'bussy?'" He buries his face back in the pages almost immediately, muttering, "You know what? Never mind." His face twists like he's just tasted too much garlic. "Damnit, now I know."

Jay cackles. "And you'll know forever."

"Fuck you," Ellington says.

His offending shirt is fully unbuttoned, allowing his gleaming brown muscles to menace me with an air of superiority as he sips a glass of wine that inspired an acrobatic eye-roll from Jay when it was poured. Jay, it should be said, had goaded Sunji and Alexander into whiskey shots and all three of them are now downing beers. I'm enjoying a lemonade in lieu of enjoying this discourse.

"I just want to clarify," I interject before those two can start up again, "I'm not trying to get bussy."

Sunji leans in, flipping a replica batarang between his fingers. "Can we burn that word? Like, figuratively? And never use it again?"

"I'm not looking," I remind them. "Not even for a hookup. Shane really fucked me over."

Jay stares at Sunji, delighting as always in boosting an irritant. "Bussy that's burning is bad bussy."

"Let it go," Ellington says to Jay, who begins shuffling the deck.

At the same time, Jay switches to another thing he delights in.

"You fucked yourself over by going after a married man," he says to me, and the wind is punched from my lungs. "You can get everything you want, whether it's good for you or not."

Alexander interjects from the floor. "Hashtag: Pretty Boy Curse."

I do my best to wipe the image of Shane from my thoughts. His smile, his eyes, his honeyed skin. Newly annoyed, I ignore Alexander and address the asshole I call my friend. "Fuck you, Jay." Realizing quickly I have nothing more I want to say regarding my ex, I return to the situation at hand. "And regardless, when I start looking again, I'll be looking for a relationship. Not booty."

Jay shakes his head. "It's obvious you don't know how to choose a good dude."

The next words tumble from his mouth like lightning striking a stone tablet.

"We should choose for you."

That fucked electric current passes between all of us and I know something's shifted.

Ellington speaks up first. "Oh for sure!"

Ellington agreeing with Jay was like the opening of one of the seven seals. I intensely dislike this biblical energy.

"There's a guy in Business Law with me who'd be perfect for you." He's scrolling through his phone's contacts.

Sunji nods, his expression thoughtful which was scary in its own way. "I'm surrounded by the gays at my casting calls."

The gays.

Alexander spouts, "Pretty Boy Curse!"

The gays.

Jay sits a little taller, adjusting his antenna of aggravation. "Hah! I know his type better than any of you."

Ellington finishes his glass of wine, eyes leveling with Jay's. "Always running your mouth with nothing to back it up."

Jay laughs, a practiced one that is a laugh in look and sound only. "What are you talking about? You're only thinking about a sexual partner, whereas I'll get him a real partner in life."

"Like a dog?" Sunji asks, pulling his hair up into a ponytail.

I see that Jay and Ellington have taken something they agree on and still managed to turn it into a pissing contest. I need to shut this down quickly.

"Are we playing cards or not?"

Jay begins to deal. "If he picks your dude," he says and my head spins, "you get fifty bucks and I'll clean your apartment for a month."

Not a contest. A bet.

Alexander, now. "Don't believe that. He hasn't done a single dish since I've known him."

"Truth," Sunji says. Then, "Zario." He holds out his phone to me, unbuttons his shirt—always six buttons, exactly—and strikes a casual pose with Ellington's wine bottle and glass. I take a few photos, inspect them, then hand the phone back to Sunji for his final approval.

"He'll be cleaning my apartment, trust," Ellington says. "In one of those little french maid outfits with the lace."

Jay grins. "Well, if he picks my dude, I get fifty bucks and you've got to let me pretend your pad is mine for four consecutive weekends."

Ellington's bravado drops. "Fuck outta here." He taps my foot with his and I don't understand why. Only when he nods at the table do I remember the cards.

That's right. We're supposed to be playing a game here while they play one with my romantic life.

Jay grips the back of my chair with one hand, spreading his legs until his knees almost line up with his hips. They're marking territory and I'm the houseplant. "Now you're realizing which head you were thinking with. I mean," and now he touches the corner of his mouth with his tongue, "if I wasn't getting any from my girl like you—"

Ellington pours himself a new glass of wine. "But you don't have a girl right now, do you, Jay?"

"You're mistaken, Jay," Alexander speaks up, placing one of his cards on the table. "Ellington's still getting plenty of it. Just not from Mandy. From Sunan."

"And the Jillian/Lillian twins," I say. I can never tell them apart.

"Oh, and that barista girl in Highland Park yesterday," Sunji adds. He looks at Ellington in pride and dismay. "Why am I just now realizing that these aren't only occasional slip-ups?"

"Fuck all y'all," Ellington says, his Texas drawl slipping out. He turns his glass, watching the wine swirl as he prepares a debonair lie. "I do what I do in order to keep my celibacy vows to Mandy."

I laugh. "Do you even know what celibacy means?"

"She and I are abstaining from sex as a couple. I'm not, as an individual."

Jay stares at each of us, his mouth forming unspoken words. Then, "Twins?" He looks at Ellington. "At the same time?"

Ellington's smile says yes.

"You tagged twins?" Jay repeats in shock.

Ellington sets his glass down. "There's gotta be guidelines of some kind if we're competing to get Zario the man of men."

"Are we still talking about that?" I ask. "I thought we were talking about your ho ass."

"This is beyond talk," Ellington warns. "Your love life belongs to us. We're gonna be gay matchmakers!"

Sunji shakes his head. "That sounds wrong. We're *matchmakers* who are *gay*."

"You corrected that wrong," I say.

"I agree with Ellington," Alexander says. "If we're putting indentured servitude like apartment cleaning on the table, this has got to be legitimate." He hops up from the table.

Sunji, preoccupied with uploading one of the photos I've taken to his social media pages, only half-hears.

"What is 'indented servitude?'"

I hold up my hands, putting a stop to the nothing that this is. "None of that matters because this entire escapade will never be legitimate. You guys are being ridiculous."

"Nonsense!" Alexander is back with a sheet of paper attached to a clipboard and he is scribbling furiously. "What do we say? A date a week?"

Jay holds up two fingers. "At least."

Ellington shakes his head. "One date a week. Gives him time to marinate."

Alexander nods. "Dope. Then first, The Choosing. We all draw straws to see what order we get to select Zario's dates. Whichever one of us gets the longest straw picks the dude that Zario dates last. The person who gets the shortest straw picks Zario's first date. Is that clear so far?"

"Who holds the straws?" Jay asks.

"Zario will. Next, The Dates."

I say, "Oh, see I'm not feeling the idea of paying for the dinner of four strangers, especially when I may not even like any of them?"

"Be positive," Alexander says to me. "And we pay. With cash or gift cards. And if you guys end up going Dutch, the rest of the money goes into the overall pool."

Jay sneers. "How much?"

"One-twenty per date? Appetizers, entrees, drinks, and dessert… Matters of the heart require time, plus the more food there is, in addition to the occasional glass of wine, now you've got room for a connection to develop."

If nothing else, I might get five delicious dinners out of the arrangement. "I'm warming to this idea."

Jay rises and heads to the kitchen. I watch him pull a box of hard spaghetti noodles from the cabinet. This train is a runaway. Nobody's even thinking about whatever card game we were supposed to be playing.

"Finally we have The Rankings." Alexander taps his clipboard. "Sex will have no bearing on the success of the date, so leave all the cock-eyed bandits at the gym where you found them staring at you."

Sunji nudges me under the table and I pinch him.

"Bitch!" he squeaks.

Alexander is focused. His pen moves as fast as his mouth. "If Zario is on a date with one of our choices and wants to fuck, Zario fucks. That does not mean Zario wants a second date. Zario needs a good man and that's the goal of this. We'll have a numeric rating system I'll whip up with Ellington—"

"Why you always volunteering me for shit?"

"—and at the end of each date, Zario will fill it out and we'll file it. That way each week his brain is fresh and we get truer results."

Jay is back at the table, breaking a few noodles up into pieces of varying length.

Alexander turns to me, his mechanical brain returning to flesh as he smiles.

"We're making this fun for us, but the end goal is that you realize how much better you can do. You're worth so much more than you seem to think. We all see that. You're the platinum peak, man. The diamond dawg. Fuck everyone that *can't* see that."

"You *are* the Pan," Sunji says, quoting one of our favorite movies.

"You *are* the Pan," Alexander agrees.

Ellington claps his hands together. "Well, on that inspirational note, I'm in. A buck-twenty for the date and fifty—"

"A hundred," Jay says, eyes glinting. "You got bread."

"—a hundred to the victor. And I'll add in four consecutive weekends of use for my pad. I'll trade with the winner and sleep here at Sunji's."

The two men hold each other's gaze until Jay finally says, "Good shit."

"And you?"

"I'll meet the moolah," Jay says, shrugging. "And I'll add a month of cleaning."

Sunji whoops with excitement. "I'm in, too, especially if I can see Jay wipe down a counter just once." He turns to me, gripping my shoulder in his hand. "In all seriousness, Zario, I know the ex-factor's a bitch to deal with. Two-twenty combined for the date and winner, plus access to my personal liquor collection for…two weeks."

I see Jay practically salivating. There's no way he'll lose now.

Sunji's back on his phone. "Eagle's gonna want in on this for sure."

Ah, yes. Eagle. The Dude of dudes and our next-door neighbor. Eagle never clubs with us, but is a primary participant in our usual antics.

"That's a guarantee, now that alcohol's involved," I say, realizing that no matter who wins the bet, I'm losing control of the next few months of my life.

Ellington and Alexander are cheering, "EAGLE!" as they are wont to do whenever the alpha is summoned. Jay is busy doing math.

"Oh shit! With all of us, that'll be five hundred in the pot! Where are we dumping the cash?"

"App it to me," I say, and each of them verifies in turn that I have their preferred payment app installed.

"Eagle can't make it tonight," Sunji says, reading from his phone, "but wants to offer two hundred on top of the date money in order to pick a week."

Ellington grunts. "That's not fair. Three hundred."

"Three hundred's fair," Jay nods.

I can't believe my ears. "You gents are monsters."

Ellington rubs invisible bills together. "Convenience costs."

Jay types on an equally invisible keyboard. "Hashtag: Pretty Boy Curse."

This is ridiculous. "There's no such thing!"

"Eagle's down for three hundred," Sunji says.

"Hell yes!" Alexander exclaims, scribbling furiously.

"Eagle also wants to know your celebrity crush, Zario," Sunji says. "It's me, right?"

"Mario Lopez," I correct him, and he drops his phone.

"I'm not typing that."

"But he's perfect! Fit, gorgeous, always grinding, into sports and the arts. If you're gonna have issues with my answers, why ask me any questions?"

"You know those famous people who aren't considered problematic because they stay just on this side of the line?" Sunji asks, sliding one palm against the other. "You can search all of the times Mario dropped hints that he's right here on the problematic side. Have Alexander compile a list for you."

"Sunji's almost famous," Ellington says, "so you know he knows shit we don't know."

"I am famous," Sunji protests, adding, "I told you guys about the infomercial I did with Rebel Wilson."

"Yes, and now I can't watch *Pitch Perfect* without hearing that story in my head," I groan. "You take the fun out of Hollywood."

Sunji thrusts his hips. "Then I stick The Fun all the way back in."

"Okay, I guess I asked for that." I say.

"To the base of my shaft," Sunji continues.

Ellington pours another glass of wine. He's going to be sleeping here tonight. "We get it, Sunji."

Jay places the spaghetti straws in my open palm. I adjust them, realizing that my participation gives this venture my blessing.

Jay perches across from me, reading my mind. "This is gonna work out so well for you, ya know. I took this girl to prom my senior year. Her name was Constellation, true story. I called her Connie."

Ellington puts up a hand to silence him. "These girls' names never matter and all their names are too wild to be true."

"I've dated wild girls!"

Ellington leans in. "I wonder—do they have made up names because you dated made up girls?"

I hold up the adjusted straws as Jay continues his story.

"My best friend picked her out for me and it worked out like a motherfuck. Been searching my whole life for a girl with better dick-throat."

I grit my teeth. Every time these guys compete to be some teen soap opera bachelor of the week, I get nauseated.

"You're going to hell," Ellington says.

"Me?" Jay's arched eyebrows rise to their peak position. "You tagged twins while your girl was at home with a padlock on her clit!"

Alexander, as impatient as I feel, speaks up. "Are we set?"

"All set," I say.

Alexander gestures to Sunji. "Landlord."

Sunji stands and approaches me with ceremony.

"May the curse be broken, boys," he says.

"Amen," Ellington agrees.

Sunji draws a straw.

Almost Nothing

There's a lot of talk about Shane, and rightfully so, but Shane isn't my first love.

There's my first crush, Harry from kindergarten, who was the same color of brown from his shins to his curls, who I would always offer my drawings to. There's my first sexual partner, Ernesto who liked to get drunk with me in high school, put his fingers in my butt while we jacked off together, then would send me Christian rock songs the next day like I was the lone sinner. There's my first almost, Brian Henry, the green-eyed half-Hawaiian who put his penis in my mouth when we were alone in the locker room and taught me with great care how to suck it. Nothing came of that, which was completely my fault. He'd invite me to parties that I would never attend. Senior year, he came out and then I made sure to stay away from him because I wasn't out myself yet. He got prom king and now plays for the Boston Celtics or the Atlanta Braves or something, so I truly missed out there.

My first relationship was in college, with Patrick Maandig, the tallest Filipinx I had ever met. He played football and took French with me. We became study partners and then fuck buddies over the course of the semester. In fact, that's how I met Alexander. Patrick and Alexander were roommates and the blond got an eyeful of Patrick getting an assful when he walked in after one of his night classes ended early. But I didn't love Patrick. No one could love Patrick back then, he was the stereotypical closeted jock, almost villainous in his performative homophobia. Fascinating in retrospect, considering his pendulum swing to the catty queer he now portrays nightly in West Hollywood.

In the impossible way that life lines up dominos, I met my genuine first love because of Patrick, and through Alexander. Alexander and I had a mutual friend, LaMarjorie, who had put together a trip to Paris, and Alexander had bought in for himself and his brother Aiden. Aiden decided not to go at the last minute, and since Patrick was going, Alexander thought it would be beneficial for all of us if I took Aiden's vacant spot.

It turned out that Patrick wasn't so keen on the idea. Looking back on it now, I think he had been planning on some Parisian dick, but at the time I naively thought it was something else. So I spent the entire plane ride and first day in the city begging him to talk to me, to explain his mood. I didn't really get to meet the rest of the folks on the trip until the first night.

LaMarjorie had arranged for us to have escargot immediately, "just to get that touristy shit out of the way." Alexander and I bonded over the fact that we were the only two who could not finish our plates. (Patrick finished mine.) The two of us went over to a smaller spot with one of LaMarjorie's classmates, Ryu Muraoka.

"I'm just still hungry," he explained.

He was a little taller than Alexander, Japanese, without an ounce of fat on him, which annoyed me. We were still at that age where guys like him could eat like me and still burn it all off just by walking to the corner. His eyes were glittering and brown, and his dimpled smile was crooked and wide.

Ryu had to listen to me bitch about Patrick to Alexander for half of the meal, then our talk turned to what we were most excited to do on the trip.

"I'm excited for the free day," Ryu said in his Japanese-accented English. "LaMarjorie's packed the schedule so full that I don't know if I'm going to do my own thing that day or just sleep."

Three days later, on the free day, I woke up and Patrick had already left our room. He didn't reply to my messages, so I went downstairs hoping to find him at the breakfast buffet, but none of our trip mates were there.

Girl's gotta eat, so I made two plates and sat down, keeping my eyes on the door.

When Ryu walked through it, he scanned the room and lit up when he spotted me. Waving, he came straight over.

"Everyone else is still asleep," he said, sitting across from me.

"Not Patrick. He's gone."

"How early did he get up?" Ryu asked.

"I'm not sure. Must have been pretty early."

A few minutes later, LaMarjorie joined us, talking a mile a minute while somehow polishing off an entire plate before Ryu had finished his first. At one point, she turned to me, waving a fork in my direction.

"Did Patrick make it back okay?"

"What do you mean? I haven't seen him this morning."

Her forehead creased with tildes. "Kennothy and I were coming back from the Latin Quarter like around one and he was heading out."

This was news to me. "We went to bed around eleven."

"Strange," she said. "Well, I'm off. Gonna bang a Belgian."

"You're going to Belgium?" Ryu asked. "Today?"

"No, I met a Belgian last night at a piano bar and I'm gonna go fuck him. Here in Paris."

After she left, Ryu turned to me.

"Are you okay?" he asked me. "Wanna go look for him?"

"I'm sure he's fine," I said, not sure at all.

"Did you two have plans for today?"

Come to think of it, we didn't. "Nothing serious."

"Well, I was gonna go do some solo adventuring, but you're welcome to join me," he said. "I usually just pick a street and start walking until it gets boring or scary. If you come with me, I think we could walk forever."

And we did. We stopped here and there for pastries, chocolates, and cakes. He wouldn't let me pay, which was bold. Even bolder were the shops and restaurants that served us, because he and I had matching appetites. We passed several spots that I recognized from movies he had never seen and he passionately informed me about a local political movement that was happening which I hadn't heard anything about. By the end of the night, we had reached some corner cafe, miles from the hotel, dancing our asses off to some unknown radio genie.

We ended up walking back to the hotel for reasons that weren't clear in the moment, and somewhere along the way we started talking about our families. His had moved with him to Georgia when he was nine. His father was a huge businessman, and his mother was poised to take over the company full-time, because his father had off-and-on health problems. I talked to him about losing my mother to cancer, which is something I never do. It was a long, brutal battle that she seemed to have won, before it came roaring back and snatched her from me in less than a month.

He had a way of looking at me like he was seeing my back and my front. He got my humor, but didn't think I was as funny as I thought I was. What was odd about this, was that he wouldn't even give me a laugh out of courtesy. He would nod casually, waiting for my own laughter to ebb.

I liked that. It was an unexpected version of candor that I don't think I had ever experienced before in my life.

We said goodbye outside of our rooms.

"Maybe they'll leave without us and we can sleep in," Ryu said when I reminded him of the planned excursions due to kick off in a few hours. "LaMarjorie likes to stick to her schedule."

"She'll send someone to wake you up," I told him. "I tried that trick already."

"Then we should get dressed as slowly as possible."

Our plan didn't work and, due to my exhaustion and the fact that Patrick would barely talk to me, the next few days of the trip were miserable.

He and I broke up on the plane ride back.

• • • • • • •

That summer, Ryu and I started following each other on social media, and he would send me things that reminded him of our walk in Paris, and soon we had fully fledged inside jokes and routines that would leave me cackling for hours. We started talking on the phone and he had one particular quote from *Beauty and the Beast* that he would squawk in the funniest way.

"Marie! The baguettes! Hurry up!"

We started making a list of films he needed to watch, starting with all of the ones I had called out on our walk. The list expanded quickly, evolving to just any movie he or I loved and the other hadn't seen. *Before Sunset. Charade. Daughters of the Dust. Presque rien.*

"'Almost nothing?'" I translated.

"That's what it means," he said. "I think the English title is *Come Undone.*"

"Poetic," I said.

He laughed. "It's interesting how things that are poetic in one language need to be changed in order to be poetic in another."

I flooded our movie list with the sequels I loved. I explained to him that for whatever reason, I had seen more sequels than I had seen originals. Or worse, I had finally seen the originals just to hate them. There's no proper way to enjoy the first *Terminator* if you've spent your entire childhood loving the fuck out of *Terminator 2: Judgement Day*'s Sarah Connor and those T-1000 special effects.

More sequels with overlong titles were tagged onto the list. *Back to the Future Part II. Free Willy 2: The Adventure Home. The NeverEnding Story II: The Next Chapter. X2: X-Men United.*

"We'll watch them all," Ryu promised.

By the time the fall semester rolled around, he had begun teaching me various Japanese phrases. I could greet him in Japanese and he would reply in French. "I'm working on the Spanish," he promised.

The day before classes began, we met up at a nearby park, and I watched him skip into a run as he rushed toward me, waving.

"Eh, guey! ¿Que onda?" The words came tumbling out of his mouth so fast, I could tell he had them locked and loaded.

I laughed as he gripped me in a hug. "It's nice to see you, guey."

He pulled away, his hands tight below my armpits. "I told you I was working on it. My Spanish."

"Yeah, but with who?" I asked, but he didn't hear me, going on animatedly about how excited he was to see me.

We picnicked like geeks and caught up on all of the things we had failed to mention in our other conversations. He was thinking of joining the family business and I had tried valiantly to grow a beard.

"Thursday night, my place," he said, when we were returning to our respective dormitories. "Foster, my new roommate, only has classes Tuesdays through Thursdays because he's got some girlfriend out of town. So, he's gonna be gone more than he's here."

"Thursday night, got it," I said.

"I'll make you dinner and we'll watch one of the movies on the list."

"Sure," I agreed, smiling.

He grabbed my hand. "A special night."

"The most special," I said, and he grinned that lopsided grin that took up half of his face.

• • • • • • • •

He picked one of the movies he had already seen, which I didn't think was entirely fair. I didn't complain, though, because the dinner he made was delicious and the movie, *Presque rien*, wasn't half bad. It was definitely one hundred percent gay, and, solely because of that, I was surprised that he had picked it.

About two-thirds into it, the two main characters fucked on the beach and I had to casually cross my legs to hide my dickening. There was no music scoring the scene as their naked bodies thumped against each other in the sand. Just heavy breathing, grunting, and the crashing of ocean waves. Ryu was next to me in his bed and had no visible reaction.

Of course not, I thought. *He's seen this movie before.*

"That was more intense than I expected," I said as the credits rolled.

He laughed. "You're shitting me."

"What?" I asked, laughing with him.

"It's a European movie. They're always so…" His eyes flew around the room as he mentally searched for the word. "Laborous."

"Laborious," I corrected gently.

He nodded. "Laborious. So long. So dramatic. So nuanced."

I knew what he meant. Scenes of unimportant characters holding long conversations. Scenes of important characters doing basic activities, or, worse, staring at something that may or may not be in frame. I was very American in my entertainment consumption. If there was a sequel where the two lovers were fighting off a town of zombies, even with a whack plot, I would have loved that more.

"At least this one was French," I said.

"What do you mean?"

"It was more than just drama. It was romantic."

"Yeah, I'm sorry," Ryu said, looking down at his hands.

I chewed on my lip, waiting for the rest. When it didn't come, I asked, "Sorry for what?"

I watched his arms helicopter around his body. "I meant for this whole night to be more romantic."

My hands pulsed hot, then cold, and I'm sure my face was changing color, too.

"This?" I croaked.

"Tonight," he said. "I'm bad at first dates, but if you aren't upset, I know I can make it up to you."

I stared at the television, then at him, then the television again. *Presque rien.*

"This was a date?"

Ryu's face fell. "Only if you wanted it to be."

"You never asked me out," I accused, and he made a face I had never seen him make before.

"I asked you out on Sunday at the park."

I blinked in surprise, sure I, too, was making new faces. "That wasn't clear that this was…" I shook my head, trying to get oxygen to the proper brain cells. "You like me? Like that?"

"I like you like that," he nodded. "I like you a lot."

I processed this, assessing the situation. "So this whole thing…" I wriggled my eyebrows. "You're trying to seduce me?"

"Don't be weird, Zario," he said, half-chuckling.

"I just mean… What if this isn't going as bad as you think?"

He blinked and I blinked and one of us flew at the other or maybe we both flew at each other and our lips pressed and then opened and then our hands were acting on instinct. Somehow we were ripping off each other's clothes and somehow I told him I was a virgin bottom and somehow my legs were in the air and I felt like the whore the preachers had told me all homosexuals were.

I couldn't bring myself to care about hellfire, though, because my entire body had finally found God's promise.

After putting on a condom, Ryu's hands gripped my waist, firm and guiding.

"Now push against it," he commanded me. And there it was. I felt him moving into me. It was a strange sensation, then it began to hurt. I cried out.

"Push against it," he said again. Then, in Japanese. "Like you're taking a shit."

I'm glad he didn't say it in English, because I might have laughed. But I followed his instructions, freaking out inside that we were going to have a very unsexy mess on our hands. The first time I topped Patrick, he and I made several mistakes.

He pushed into me further and I pushed back and the moment arrived when I knew that he was all the way in. I gasped, then I moaned and his hips began to dance with mine. Every nerve in my body added music to the percussion of his thighs as they slapped against mine. I was glad he wasn't thicker, because after a while it didn't hurt so much. Then it didn't hurt at all. And then it was just music. His lips were on mine, then on my chest, then on my swelling nipples. His fingers were in my hair, then my mouth. His eyes were in my soul. His dick was in my soul.

He gripped my shoulders; I gripped his ass. I somehow wanted more of him, if that were possible. He flipped me over, laying me flat on my stomach. His hands again. My hips again. Lifting me up just a bit. Legs on mine. Arms near my shoulders. And he entered me again. More of him.

"Fuck," he moaned above me, and I breathed the same into the comforter. And our rhythm returned.

Ryu had always looked at me like he was seeing all of me at once —the one person who made me feel naked wherever we were. And finally all of those viewing sessions were paying off. He understood my body like we had been lovers long before that night. He laid on top of me, covering the back of my neck and shoulders in kisses as he thrust into me, slower now, like each delayed squeeze of his hips was a detailed prayer. His hands slid on top of mine, fingers sliding between mine, bringing me into intercession with him. I felt his chest on my back, and I knew his hallowed petition.

Suddenly, "You're so quiet."

"What?"

"You're quiet. Is this okay?"

"This is great," I said, and I realized I'd been holding my breath. Instantly, I was breathing ragged and shallow. I was moaning. I was now anything but quiet.

"There it is," he said, with an exhale of relief.

He rearranged me again. I got on my hands and knees and he crouched on his feet, knees framing my ribs, and our lovemaking shifted into fucking. My own dick slapped against my lower abdomen and I knew I was close. Ryu grunted above me and I knew he was, too.

His fingers kneaded my flesh and he whispered my name. "Zario. My Zario."

I finished all over the comforter, the music inside and outside of me climaxing as I did. Only then did he pull out, flipping me over with one hand and removing the condom with his other. He barely got a single hand back in position before he shot ropes over my shoulder. One hand found my chest, gripping it without any sort of discretion, tightening and releasing synchronously with his alto bellows.

"Fuck, Zario," he said when he finally spoke again.

"You did," I giggled, my sense of humor returned.

He laid next to me, my humor always accepted, but never appreciated. I was reminded that he saw me in all of my intricacies, but I could never quite get a full view of him.

"I didn't wanna cum before you did," he said. "But you made it difficult."

I saw his legs were trembling, his ridiculous abs flexing in ripples. Patterns. Contractions.

I was amazed. "Are you still…?"

He nodded. "It might take me a minute."

I leapt off of the bed and knelt, taking his dick in my mouth. It was like electricity flew between us as his torso lifted from the bed. He said Japanese phrases I didn't know yet and his fingers found my hair again. After a few endless moments, he pulled me into a kiss. And he kissed me and kissed me and kissed me.

I can't identify when the kiss turned into a second round of fucking. I can't pinpoint when the second turned into the third.

We showered together, rubbing loofas and suds over each other's bodies. Laughing and joking, he dried me off as if he was studying my body again. It seemed at the time that he had mapped every freckle, every hair. All of my sameness was new under his hands. All of my oddness was revered.

He had a toothbrush for me. Told me to stay. He held me as I drifted away. When I woke in the middle of the night, he was still holding me and I breathed him, staring at nothing until I made out the shadows of the side of his ear. The shadows turned back into nothing and then I woke up and he was already dressed.

I was reminded of his beauty, with the eyes that sunk like amber and the mouth that smiled even when it frowned in concentration. I was still naked and I looked for my clothes. I was so hungry I could smell the greasy food I was craving. I told myself that I'd start a diet the next day, even though the night before Ryu had seemed to appreciate every inch of my skin and all that came underneath.

"How's your ass?"

I looked at him and he was grinning openly.

"Blessed," I said, and something happened in his face that was too quick for me to catch.

"LaMarjorie called. She wants us to go shopping with her. So get dressed as slowly as possible." I finished the last sentence in unison with him before I realized the changed context of our words. Then I added, "I'm starving."

Ryu placed a hand on his clavicle in mock dismay. "I am not an animal, Señor del Rosario. There are two double cheeseburgers and gooey fries on the table."

"Holy fuck, you're amazing."

I'm ashamed to say (but not really) that at least one of the burgers and all of the fries were devoured before I bothered to find my boxer briefs.

As we left his dorm, Ryu grabbed me by the hand.

"Spend the night again. Foster doesn't come back until Monday night. Stay the whole weekend."

I thought about his roommate being gone for four more days and I could feel the precum oozing in my shorts.

"Keep the double cheeseburgers coming and I might stay for a lifetime."

And again his face did something. It didn't change as much as it reacted, beneath the levels of skin and muscle and bone, some level where emotions wrestle with logic, there was a shift. Something taking a brief upper hand over the other, and he squeezed my hand, locked the door to his room, and led me down the hallway. We walked to the elevator, not yet falling, but going in that direction anyway.

• • • • • • •

The next Thursday, he met me outside of class and said, "Okay, tonight. Let me give you a better date tonight."

I smiled, gripping my textbooks and feeling like the straight white girl in every movie. "Okay, yeah, sure."

"I'll pick you up at six."

He did, in a nice suit with a dangling chandelier earring. He produced a large bouquet when I got in his car, full of flowers he had purchased, but arranged himself. He took me to one of the nicer Japanese restaurants downtown and ordered shōchū and appetizers.

"This is very Presbyterian," I said, and he didn't get it and I wonder why I said it. It was something from high school, a guy I knew was trying to say "patrician" at a fancy dinner and said "Presbyterian" instead and I had found it riotous. I made a face at Ryu. "You don't think I'm funny."

"Sometimes you are," he said, "but not usually when you're trying to be."

"I'll work on that," I mumbled.

"You don't have to," he said. "You make yourself laugh, and that's a great thing. Manifest your own joy."

Halfway through dinner, he clasped his hands.

"So, I have something I want to talk to you about."

"You can talk to me about anything," I said. "Sooner rather than later, because my anxiety is going to kick in."

"Not your anxiety!" he exclaimed. "It's nothing bad."

Whatever it was, he visibly lost his nerve when the waiter approached to check on us. We started talking about the movies we were going to cross off our list over the weekend and I nearly forgot about his announcement.

It took until dessert, and I started choking on my mochi when he said, "I want you to eat my ass."

• • • • • • • •

We stayed together so long that we got marriage-comfortable. Our heartbeats fell in sync. We named our hypothetical kids. He talked to me while he took a shit, which I *always* hated. We held hands in public. He got conversational in Spanish and my Japanese got so good that I could hop on the phone with his mother and chat long enough to make him nervous. On the outside we were deceptively simple. Within our relationship, it was intense. If I rolled my eyes, he wanted to know why. If he sucked his teeth, I challenged him. We never raised our voices, but we would go on lockdown, not leaving the room until we got things sorted out.

Ryu made me realize that romance wasn't cute. It was dangerous.

We looked at houses, considered our future. He was determined to make all the money so that I could focus on my art. I told him I was happy to pull my own weight. He said that was his job and he fucked me right there in the library study room he had reserved, pounding me until I was sure I felt his dick in my esophagus.

He topped that (heh) on our anniversary, when he took me to the beach and fucked me so good I still can't go to the beach without getting a hard on. I haven't bottomed since then, either, but he's the reason I still say I'm versatile. If someone could fuck me like that again, I'd be bottoming faster than celebrities forgive war criminals and racists.

• • • • • • •

"I have something I want to talk to you about."

I knew what it was this time. He was getting serious with this girl. Ryu and I had never officially committed to being anything more than friends, so when he started dating her, I didn't mind because he was still polishing my prostate multiple times a week. I don't know what I was telling myself.

Well, I knew what I was telling myself, I just can't believe it was working.

I figured he just wanted to be sure. I figured maybe a part of him was keeping up appearances. But I never felt threatened. He'd kiss me goodbye in front of her. He'd kiss me hello in front of her. If she was over for dinner, he'd hold my hand. He'd hold hers too, but I always felt like it mattered more with me.

Fucked up, yes, I see that now.

When he got the call that his dad was sick—really sick—he flew home, telling me he'd send for me. Weeks later, I saw her with him there, on his social media. Cooking with his mother. Walking on our beach. Crying at the funeral.

He didn't have to tell me. I knew. Everyone knew. We were done. Unpaired, disconnected. *Presque rien.*

Unpacking

Jay bounces his knee at a location in the NoHo Arts District that we have come to affectionately call "our" coffeeshop due to how often we frequent it. His computer sits open in front of him next to a bread plate covered in crumbs. His face is pruned with a perplexed expression.

It's a face I've seen him make a million times—he pushes his lips out so far that he almost becomes attractive. It just so happens that I'm not with him when he's making this face, but a stranger sitting nearby is enraptured by it.

This person is draped in brightly covered cloths, shimmering and patterned. Clunky rings cover their fingers and comfortable loafers adorn their feet. After exploring Jay's face for several minutes, the stranger returns to their coffee. Now it's Jay watching the stranger, mind racing.

After staring for far too long, Jay noisily begins to scoot his chair over to the stranger's table. Once he's directly in front of the stranger, he reaches for his computer and sets it between them.

"Can I ask you a question?"

The stranger looks up slowly, starting with Jay's elbows, then across to where and how his gut protrudes over his belt, then up to the curvature of his pecs, across his neck, then around his jawline, up to that memorized pink pout of his lips, his nose, his furrowed brow, then the fullness of his face. When the stranger speaks, their voice has a slow, southern drawl.

"I suppose."

Jay scratches his tricep. "What's a twink?"

The stranger sets their coffee down, leans all the way back in their chair, and crosses their legs. "Excuse me?"

"Like, in gay world. I'm trying to set my friend up on a date with a guy—he's a guy, my friend is—and I have no clue where to begin."

"And you're asking me…"

"I could just use some expertise with this."

Stranger gets it. They're amused.

"I see."

Jay points to his phone. "Twinks, otters, bears… I mean, Zario always reminded me more of a wombat, but that's not an option on this app."

"Have you considered asking this Zario? It's a whole new generation of gay out there. In my day, all we had were cougars."

"Cougars?" Jay's face prunes again. "There are gay cougars?"

"Absolutely. We called them rhinos. Or chickenhawks."

Jay stares down at his phone in amazement. "I thought you guys all wanted to be unicorns or something."

Jay thinks about the many cougars he's experienced in his life, and tries to imagine the male equivalent of that. Then he thinks of the times older men had propositioned him, not just in WeHo, but all over. For the first time in his life, certain aspects of my gay life don't feel as alien to him.

The stranger can't hold in their curiosity any longer. They lean in.

"So of all of your gay friend's friends, you're the one trusted to wield the selecting scepter?"

Jay laughs and shakes his head. "Oh, all of us are doing it. We're each finding him a man. We have a bet."

The stranger raises an eyebrow and Jay is quick to add, "Oh you're too old for him, no offense."

"Undoubtedly. I'm no spring chickenhawk." Chuckles. "Are you always this discerning?"

Jay smirks proudly. "Probably, I don't know." After a moment, he snaps his fingers in realization. "But I do know somebody who would know this shit. Thanks, man."

Now both of the stranger's eyebrows are raised. "Sure."

Jay closes his laptop and stands. "You want me to get you a danish or something?"

The stranger lifts their cup of coffee. "No thanks."

Jay sits. "One last question."

"Promise?"

"Why were you staring at me?"

The stranger takes a long sip before answering. "You have an interesting face."

"Oh," Jay frowns like he understands. "Like a cute face?"

The stranger laughs. "No. Like an interesting face. You have a lot of features that work on their own, but when they're all put together…" They lean back again. "It's interesting. Why do you ask?"

Jay sits for a minute, then grabs his computer. "No reason. Appreciate your help."

He exits quickly, not hearing the stranger's tickled reply.

"You're welcome."

• • • • • • •

Ellington has told me a few times what his startup business is, but I never remember. I do know it's doing so well that he decided to get a business degree, which causes quite a few heated discussions at Sunji's place, as Sunji thinks the degree is a waste of money ("You already have a successful business," is the typical argument. "What the fuck is school going to teach you?") and Ellington replies that his girlfriend wants a man with a degree.

Sunji loses the argument every time.

At the moment, Ellington is sitting on his couch surrounded by books, notepads and a few electronic devices. He's actually going over his conversations with Sunji in his head because in this moment, he agrees with his friend. In this moment, he hates school.

His door opens and two long-haired beauties walk in. The blonde is the girlfriend. Mandy is petite, with the largest blue eyes this side of anime. She toggles between bubbly and perky and is a lot to take. That would explain the expression on the face of the brunette.

Taller than both Mandy and Ellington, who are already tongue-slapping, the lanky brunette wears all black from hair tie to combat boots, outside of the white skull gleaming beneath the sheer shawl tossed over two shapely shoulders. This is Ellington's younger brother, Marshall.

"Your brother dragged me all over, but we finally found the proper wave cap for you."

Marshall's lips draw back to reveal his teeth. "She wanted to buy you one. Said she needed the 'experience.'"

"We went to Compton," she says proudly. "I bought a fish dinner from some church ladies!"

Ellington's eyebrows turn into tildes. "Babe, you can get wave caps at 7-11."

Mandy is still rhapsodic. "I asked for advice at a real barbershop."

Slowly, almost imperceptibly, except to his brother, Marshall raises one eyebrow.

"Again," he stresses, "she wanted to."

"Babe." Ellington places a hand on his girlfriend's knee. "You don't have to try so hard, k?"

Marshall hasn't moved from the door, and when he hears the voices in the hallway, he turns the handle, allowing us to pile in the moment that the two on the couch begin kissing again.

"Ew," someone says, and I quickly discover that person is me.

Jay, Sunji and I are dressed in workout gear and, to really set my outfit off, I cradle a basketball like I know what I'm doing. Whenever we hit the courts in Ellington's Burbank neighborhood, Sunji, Ellington and Eagle shoot hoops, Jay does court-side workouts, and I pretend to do whatever Jay's doing.

"Homie G," Ellington greets Sunji.

Sunji replies in kind. "Funky cow!"

"Let's go be athletic!" I cheer, trying to spin the basketball on the tip of a finger.

Jay grabs Marshall's shoulder, heading off toward the hallway. "Marshmallow, you got a minute?"

Ellington daps me, but stares after Jay. "Since when do you talk to my brother?"

Jay turns. "Since he got a minute."

"This is my territory," Ellington says, "and I will kill you."

Jay, walking backwards, mimes like he's urinating down the hallway.

"After I win the bet, all of this is my territory."

"Hey, there's a human at the center of that bet," I holler after his disappearing figure.

A voice, musical and flat at the same time. "Hola, Zario."

I smile and sit down next to the lady in our presence. "Hi, Mandy."

She leans in, eyes bright. "There's a new cashier at the corner store who I think might be a little—"

She dangles her hand limply from her wrist and I try not to flinch.

"And I'm pretty sure he's documented. His English is perfect."

My smile threatens to give way. "Thanks for thinking of me."

Ellington is collecting his study materials. "I'll be ready in a second. Eagle's meeting us there?"

"Like always," Sunji replies. "Hey, can I borrow a pair of compression shorts?"

Ellington shakes his head. "No."

"Okay, then I'm taking some."

Sunji runs down the hallway toward Ellington's room and Ellington gives chase.

I laugh until I feel Mandy's eyes on me.

"Zario. A bet? That's precious."

"It was their idea."

"And you trust them with your romantic life?"

"To a point," I say and it sounds like a question.

She smiles sweetly. "Let's unpack this."

We have not paired off optimally, I think.

Down the hall, Jay sits on Marshall's bed.

"You need my help getting Zario a man?" the younger Gomez brother asks, fingers flexing above his skyward palm. "I'll tell you the same thing I told my brother. Why don't we just go to WeHo and find the most damaged—"

"That's not helping anyone," Jay says brusquely.

"Sorry," Marshall says, anything but. "You know sister-friend loves drama. Why don't you make an online profile for her?"

Jay rubs his temples. "Can you stop calling him a her? And I did! But I'm not getting any hits."

Marshall sits next to Jay. "Show me."

Jay pulls out his phone and opens the app for Marshall, who lays a hand on Jay's shoulder as he leans in.

"Baby boy, baby boy! We got some work to do. What picture is this?"

At the very top of the profile Jay created is a picture of me in a rainbow Mohawk, laughing so hard that anyone would be able to count my cavity fillings.

"Zario at New Years! I think it shows his personality."

Marshall shakes his head. "Personality comes second. You gotta get them to swipe first. Have you ever used one of these apps?"

Jay pockets his phone. "The way I look? If I wanna get laid, I just walk outside."

Marshall takes a deep breath, exhaling as he realizes what helping Jay will entail. "Come by tomorrow. I got you."

"Thank you," Jay says as I walk, rather, I run in.

"Hey, Jay! Can we go? Mandy's asking me about places to visit when she goes to Cancún."

"You've never been to Cancún," Jay says, rising.

I nod. "We know that, but it's in Mexico. She thinks I was born there."

Marshall puts his head in his hands. "That girl thinks she's woke, but she stays sleepwalking."

• • • • • • •

When Ellington picked his brother up from the airport last year, he told us that it took him a moment to get used to Marshall's new look.

"Your hair's long."

"Only on the top," Marshall grinned, flipping his curls over his shoulder.

"How'd you get away with it? Papá would take me to the barber if he saw mine touching my ears."

"I'd tie it up on top of my head and wear a hoodie."

"During dinner?"

Marshall pursed his lips. "Elián, you know we stopped having family dinners once you moved to California."

Ellington pats the steering wheel. "Ah, out here everyone calls me Ellington." He cuts a quick gaze at his brother, self-consciously.

Marshall smiled. "Oh, you full-Black out here, huh?"

"I'm serious. And Dad only started calling me that because he could never pronounce 'Ellington.'"

"Well, I guess now's a good time to mention that I don't answer to Mars anymore. Full name these days."

"Full name?"

"You know what I mean. Call me Marshall."

"Do the hermanos call you that?"

"You know they don't. Caví calls me Mars like it's scripture."

"He's still devout, huh?"

"Painfully. And he and Alvera claim full Chicano, believing all of Papá's revisionist history."

"How? Caví's as dark as us?"

"And Alvera has your wash-and-go 4A hair."

"No you didn't say 4A," Ellington chuckled. "Look at us! Black and cultured."

"I'm trying to get culture," Marshall said, almost singing his words. Every syllable out of his mouth is an identifiable note on a musical scale. It used to piss their father off.

"You're not a mockingbird," Papá Gomez would say, usually punctuated with a backhanded smack. "Speak like a man." And Marshall spoke less and less.

In the car, he continued. "I want that California food culture. Burgers! Taco stands. Korean barbecue!"

"I cooked!" Ellington protested.

"I'll eat that, too," Marshall laughed. "What I look like?"

"You look like you don't eat anything."

"I can't keep weight on, you know that. I burn it off just thinking about exercise."

So over two double-doubles and animal fries, Marshall caught his brother up on life with their father, brother, and sister after the divorce. It was a well-spun comedy, out of a situation Ellington knew had become horror.

"Do you ever think you took the easy way out?" Marshall asked at one point.

Feeling his brother was being unnecessarily cryptic with the phrasing of his question, Ellington replied, "In what way?"

"You chose to be a light-skinned Black man and our other brother is gonna go through life as a dark Mexican."

Laughing, the older one said, "I think every day it's bravery to live in a body that's not white, but neither Caví nor I did anything heroic. I don't think we chose according to levels of oppression. I think I chose according to comfort and he chose based on the proximity he could have to whiteness."

Marshall's jaw dropped and he snapped his fingers like Ellington was delivering spoken word. "And he wants to be Dad. He's Papá hijo."

Too late he realized the implication that Ellington put distance between one half of his heritage for the same reason their brother embraced it.

"Are you gonna finish your fries?" Marshall asked.

Ellington slid his unfinished meal over to his brother. "Where do you put it?"

"My third leg," Marshall said, making eye contact with a cute guy a few tables over. Ellington laughed so hard that a piece of fry lodged in his nostril.

On the long drive to their place, the older brother entertained the younger with stories about Sunji, Jay, and Alexander.

"And there's a new one?" Marshall asked. "Who's gay?"

Ellington nodded, "Yeah, Zario. He's in my old room. You can't fuck him."

"That means he's good looking."

"No, that means you can't fuck any of my queer friends."

Marshall grinned wickedly. "So I'll fuck your straight friends."

"This isn't Copperas Cove, Mars. *Marshall.*"

"I was kidding. How many queer friends do you have?"

"Just Zario. But if I get more, they're off-limits, too."

"You think you'll get more?"

"If it keeps you from hanging out with some lowlifes, I'm gonna befriend every man-loving-man in Los Angeles County."

"It's just weird," Marshall says, staring out over the highway. "You didn't have any gay friends in Texas. Did you get a gay friend just because I came out?"

Ellington's laugh got caught in his throat like a gurgle. "You're not that special."

"But I'm special enough for you to move out of that house that you loved, with roommates that you loved, and for you to buy me a plane ticket to come move in with you when I have no job, no skills—"

"Is it suddenly a problem that I want to take care of you?"

Marshall was silent.

"What is it?"

"It might be a problem that you suddenly want to take care of me."

"I always wanted to take care of you," Ellington said quietly. "This is just the first time that I've been able to."

"You left me. With Papá."

"When I left, there was a family."

Marshall's jaw flexed. "Exactly."

Ellington looked over at his brother, then at his mirrors as he made a sudden exit off of the highway.

Marshall looked at the signs, confused. "I thought you said you lived in North Hollywood."

"I do," Ellington said, pulling into an empty parking space at the nearest gas station. He turned the car off and pulled the keys out of the ignition. "Let's go. Out."

Marshall raised his hands. "What?"

"Get out of the car."

They unbuckled and as Marshall got out of the car, Ellington came around the front bumper and gripped him in a hug.

"I love you, Marshall," he said.

"I love you, too," Marshall said, eyes flying around. "What are you doing?"

"I love you, little brother."

"I love you, Ellington. What are you doing right now?"

Ellington pulled out of the embrace, gripping his brother's shoulders. "What you and I are not going to do is have some kind of tumultuous, non-communicative, dysfunctional relationship. Okay? We're not those people. We've left those people behind. I'm not coming into this with any ulterior motives and you can't come into this with any hidden resentment. You can feel whatever ways you want to feel about me, and those feelings are recognized as valid. What you cannot do is toss out some passive aggressive barbs and half-realized conspiracy theories. If I fuck up, tell me you think I fucked up. I'm gonna do the same to you.

"I left because there was no future for me living that close to dad. I'm the oldest. If I stayed, the rest of you would have thought it was okay to stay. And it is not okay for any of us to stay. I'm glad mom got out. I hope hermana does, too. Caví won't, you know he won't. But the moment you could, I sent for you, didn't I? Tell me if that wasn't good enough. Make it plain how I screwed up. Right now."

"He didn't beat you like he beat me," Marshall said quietly. "Like he hated me."

Ellington searched his brother's face. From a distance, they look nothing alike, with Marshall all lithe and limbs and Ellington all curves and cuts. But their skin is the exact same copper gradient, their laughing smiles are exact duplicates, and they each have their grandmother's earlobes.

"He was scared of me," Ellington said. "He still is. You know the reason I didn't come back to get you? You know I kicked his ass the last time I was there, right?"

Marshall blinked.

"Of course he wouldn't tell you that," Ellington said, dropping his hands to look at his knuckles. "It felt good," he said softly. "I paid for it, though. I broke my hand."

Ellington looked back up at his brother. "Like I said. I always wanted to take care of you."

• • • • • • •

"So what are the rules?" Marshall had already put his clothes away, and now he was placing his trinkets around the apartment. Calaveras, refrigerator magnets, energy crystals.

Ellington dried his hands on a paper towel. "The what?"

"The house rules. For when I have a gentleman caller or you have some cheerleader."

Ellington groaned. "Romance remains in the bedroom. And whoever you bring home needs to be both of legal age and young enough to not be on Medicare."

"Brother, if I'm with someone on Medicare, I'll be at their residence, not here."

"Don't hook up with an ancient, please," Ellington said. "And if you do, just don't tell me."

"I'm kidding, brother," Marshall laughed. "You know I don't have sex."

"I keep a stash of condoms in the entertainment center," Ellington said. "All sizes. And loads of lube."

"Why all sizes?" Marshall asked, then gasped, placing a hand on his chest. "For me?"

"Just looking out for you," Ellington said. "Don't make a big deal out of it."

"I hit the jackpot with you," Marshall cried, gripping his brother in a hug.

"Ah, that reminds me," Ellington said. "Before my girlfriend gets here, I need to prepare you."

"Oh, Lord," Marshall said, stepping back with apprehension. "How white is she?"

Millennial Gay

When we return to our house from the basketball court, dripping sweat, Alexander is giving his best *Batman '89* Vicki Vale, feet up on the dining room table while he reads a copy of the *Gotham Gazette*, one of those promotional ones he got from some convention.

"Hello, legs," I say, knowing he'll appreciate the fact that I get the reference. Sunji slaps his feet off of the table.

"Hello yourself, Zario," Alexander says, folding the newspaper. "Inquiring minds need to know. Are you a bottom or a top?"

I blink. I think I forget to breathe. So I blink more until the sensation of breathing returns to me.

Jay, Ellington, and Sunji react with dismay, disgust, and confusion, respectively. I find myself smothering a laugh.

"Your dedication to this has no limits," I say.

"I'm in it to win it, motherfuck, like always. These jokers," his pen jabs the air in their direction like an accusatory sword, "aren't ready. So answer the question. Bottom or top?"

Alexander pulled the shortest straw. His choice for my next romance would be the first date of this bet.

Realizing that the more I avoid answering, the more this would seem like a taboo subject, I decide to put it out there. "I'm versatile."

Ellington is quick to interject. "You can't do that. That's like if someone asks you Pepsi or Coke, and you're the asshole that says some shit like, 'water.' Or, 'wheatgrass shots.'"

"I've never been that asshole," I say. "And that's totally not the same thing."

"Just rephrase the question," Sunji says to Alexander. He turns to me like he's hosting a family game show. "Are you, like, the man or the woman in the relationship?"

Here we go. I take a deep breath. "You have a brother, Alexander, right?"

He nods, the corners of his lips turning down further than should be possible. "Three."

"When two of you are out and you introduce each other to a new acquaintance, does that acquaintance ever ask, 'Which one's the brother and which one's the sister?'" I turn to Sunji. "Shane was the man in the relationship. I was also the man in the relationship. Because we were both men. In a relationship. You guys have to drop your heteronormative bullshit."

I see them struggling to process this. Ellington is inspecting the ceiling as if heaven holds the answers. When he looks at me, it's clear none were provided.

"So, any gay? Any gay will do?"

"Of course not," I say, wondering how he never talks to his brother about these things. "They've gotta be open about their sexuality."

Now Jay speaks. "And they've gotta be single."

"Of course."

"Shane wasn't either of those things."

Arrow. Target. I glare at him.

"You gonna keep bringing that up?"

He shrugs. "Jiminy Cricket, Zee."

Sometimes he is my nemesis.

Alexander's talking again and I give him my full attention.

"Shower and change, del Rosario. We've got work to do."

• • • • • • •

Alexander sits cross-legged on the counter where his notebook and several papers are spread about. Finished with my shower, I join him and take a look at the notes as he drones on.

"Dating, sorry to enforce the stereotype, is a game. But just like the games I'm an expert in, when you encounter a challenge, you have an arsenal of tools at your disposal."

"Is this necessary, Alexander? I've been on dates before."

"And your talents have got you here. Let that sink in."

He has a point. I listen.

"The trick to managing an arsenal is being able to select, in a moment, which tool or weapon to use."

I shrug. "Like?"

"Flirt with me."

He adjusts his position until his legs dangle next to me.

I drop his notes back on the counter. "This is obscene."

"Do it."

I sigh impatiently. "Do you have a map?"

Alexander tilts his head and bats his lashes in a poor imitation of someone trying to flirt. The mirroring isn't lost on me.

"No," he says. "Why?"

"Because I'm getting lost in your eyes."

Alexander gags so effectively that I take a reflexive step back. "That's a bomb. Why are you giving me bombs? Look at your arsenal. If this was League and the enemy has High Armor, get Last Whisper. But this is love so what are you going to do?"

I sigh again, more for weariness now than agitation. "What are my choices?"

"You're a millennial gay. Your choices should be second nature to you. What would you do in this circumstance?"

I think about this, the concept of being a millennial gay.

"I would call out the fact that I was just trying to get his attention with a crappy joke."

"Authenticity. Bold choice. Grab it from your arsenal and use it."

I take a deep breath, then talk to whatever man Alexander is pretending to be. "That was lame, wasn't it? In all honesty, I just needed an ice breaker and I do think you have beautiful eyes."

"I'm not feeling you right now, Zario. You gotta wield your weapon."

Okay, motherfucker, I think. *You want it? I'll give it to you.*

"Your eyes," I say, leaning in closely, pressing my palms onto the counter on both sides of Alexander's hips, "they remind me of this painting by this artist from Istanbul, Serhat Koçak. *Blue.* That's what it's called. It's full of prisms and depth and sharpness. It's my favorite thing to look at when I need a burst of the majestic. Well," I say, sliding my hands toward the edge of counter and ever so lightly tracing the edges of his thighs, "now my second favorite."

Alexander swallows. When he speaks, his voice cracks.

"That was good. We'll work on that."

• • • • • • •

"Let's talk skin."

Ellington has me trapped in our bathroom with an assortment of dermatology potions displayed on the counter. His jeans seem to be held up by only his ass, since they're slouching so low in the front that his abdominal v is almost a full on genital d. I wonder if they make low-rise underwear, because he never seemed like the type to free-ball it. I don't know when he took his shirt off, but I wish he would put it back on so my brain wouldn't go to these places.

"Skin?"

"That marvelous melanin. You got some."

"Some?"

He half-shrugs. "Not as much as I do."

I place my finger on an exfoliator. "It's like you guys think I'm the Swamp Thing or something."

"Like attracts like," Ellington says, looking at my reflection. "And I want you attracting nothing but the best, from here on out. You're a ten masquerading as a six most of the time."

"A six?" I feel my eyes leaping from my skull.

He points to the back of my neck. "When's the last time you tidied up your kitchen?"

My nose flares. "Point made. I'll get a haircut. But my skin's fine!"

I mean it. I lucked out without ever having bad breakouts, just a random zit every now and then. I never even got chicken pox.

Ellington is shaking his head. "We're not settling for fine. Texture, smoothness, firmness. Skin isn't merely a source of titillation and intrigue,"—he pops his pecs with each syllable of "titillation"—"but one of the most important organs of the human body!"

"Now I'm in science class."

"You're damn right," he says, "and I'm Professor Luminosity. Now if you want that guava glow, take notes."

After a detailed detour into tonics, creams and cleansers, during which I was instructed to touch Ellington's face and chest multiple times, I am sent on the conveyor belt to Sunji's room. To my dismay, he wears even less than Ellington.

"And some here," he says, squirting a fragrance on his hip bone before retying his towel. "And remember, I only use perfume. Use scents girls love and they'll flock to you."

"That's dope and all, Sunji, but I'm not trying to get flocks of *women*."

Sunji stands there for a moment. "That complicates things." He sits, pondering. "But wouldn't gay dudes dig perfume even more than chicks would?"

I shake my head no. "I'm pretty sure it doesn't work that way. Also, you should retie your towel."

As the days before the first date decrease, the dudes are increasingly encouraged and absolutely incorrigible. Ellington comes back over to give me the much-needed haircut, Alexander compiles a list of preferred dinner topics "among the gays," and Sunji loans me clothes for the dates, forcing me to model different outfit combinations.

"You know what would go good with that outfit?" he asks, once we settle on what I'll wear on my first date. "This underwear."

I look around. "What underwear?"

He points to his crotch, a shimmering black fabric with crimson letters stitched on the waistband. "This underwear. The way your waistline peeks when you move your arms? You'll want this brand to show. It's Maravilla. Plus, it's lucky."

"You wear Maravilla underwear? That's quality as fuck!"

"I know! That's why I only wear it on special occasions. I had a meeting today with a director about a part and I'm pretty sure I got it, so I don't need it any time soon."

I realize too late that he's stripping.

"I draw the line at pre-worn underwear, Sunji."

"But it's lucky! I wore it on my first date with Jerrica."

"It's nasty. I'm not doing it."

He stuffs the underwear into the pocket of the leather jacket I'm currently wearing. "At least have it on you," he says, and despite my best efforts, I see his unnaturally large balls swinging in my peripherals. "For luck."

With all of the straight boy hassle, I'm surprised that Jay doesn't have a lesson plan for me. In fact, he hasn't brought up the bet at all, aside from standing in the doorway on occasion to mock the others and wiggle his eyebrows at me.

This isn't to say that I am not actively learning things from him. I've always been the type to keep busy intellectually, especially with all of the free time I have between freelancing gigs. Jay's been teaching me Korean almost since I moved in.

The day Sunji gives me his lucky underwear, Jay is teaching me phrases. Something that I like a lot. *Manh-i, manh-i, manh-i.* Jay is leaning against my bed, clicking through the photos on my camera. I recline above him on my mattress, brain clicking through pronunciations and jaw movements.

"Good," Jay says, after tricking me into exclaiming my overwhelming love of penises in perfect Korean for the fifth time. "Let's take a break."

"Don't you have questions for me? About the bet?"

"No. I got this."

"You're so cocky," I say, realizing I've set him up for one of his macho retorts. I wonder if I did so on purpose.

Either way, he doesn't bite. "What I am," he says instead, "is honest and secure." He rises to sit on the edge of my bed. "You want a guy with thick lips."

"No Muppet slits," we say together. It's a mantra of mine.

"I don't know how white people do it. What are they kissing?"

Jay snorts. "Ask Alexander." He places a hand on my thigh. "You want someone with soulful eyes who doesn't skip leg day." His hand moves toward the inside of my thigh and I shove him off the bed.

"Separates the real from the fake." Spongebob Squarebodies, to paraphrase the internet's Patti LaHelle, are not my thing.

Jay turns and places his elbows on the mattress, propping up his head with his hands. "Someone cultured. Open to adventure." He flutters his eyelashes.

The dude has my entire list. "Ding ding ding."

He looks bored again. "I got this. Now move over."

He climbs back in my bed, saying another phrase in Korean. "*Jaja, deo.*" *Let's sleep a little more.*

This time, I fuck up the pronunciation—"*Jaji teol?*"—and he turns an appalled face toward me.

"That is not what I said, Zario."

"What did I say?" I ask, and he never answers.

· · · · · · ·

Ellington comes over to see me off. Sunji is making everyone else a dinner that I'm going to miss, and Jay is working out in the den as I announce that I'm leaving.

He joins us in the dining room and hands me my jacket. "Details."

"You guys picked the restaurant. Alexander picked the guy. You guys know more details than I do."

"Is he picking you up?"

"Rideshare."

"Same way home?"

"Yes. Don't worry."

He grabs my face in his hands, intense. "Remember what I said about earthquakes."

I most certainly will not. "Won't be necessary. I did use some of your cologne, though. That was helpful."

"The bottle shaped like a dick?"

I grin. "The bottle shaped like a dick."

Jay releases me, proud. "That's the stuff."

"Shoulda gone with perfume," Sunji says.

Alexander pipes up from his corner. "Natural musk is underrated."

"Text if you need resources," Ellington cryptically says, and I immediately think of his arsenal of get-out-of-dates-fast tricks.

Alexander catches this as well. "I know what you're implying. That I set him up with some weirdo hatchet murderer, but I didn't. He'll be fine."

Ellington, unmoved, repeats, "Text if you need resources."

"None of this matters, Zee," Jay says from the refrigerator. "Just go through the motions. I got this whole thing sewed up."

"The Uber's almost here," I say, not willing to start this debate again. "I'll see you Dolly Levis later."

I open the door and almost plow into a person who's standing directly in my path. I take a step back and then...

"Oh." It escapes me before I can stop myself.

In the doorway stands a beautiful woman, curly brown hair cascading around her smiling face.

"Hey, Zario," she says. "I came to christen your voyage."

Behind me, I hear the fellas yell in unison, hailing our alpha. "EAGLE!"

"Whattup, limp dicks?" she greets them, moving past me and raising a half-empty bottle. "I brought tequila."

Neighbors

On our second trip to Alexander's car to grab the bags of holiday groceries, she was standing on our porch, preparing to knock. What I remember about her that first day is her long, curly brown hair, falling freely around her face. She also had one of the most relaxed speech patterns I had ever heard, like her high never completely wore off or her drunk never completely kicked in.

"Hey?" Sunji said, stopping in surprise, causing Alexander and I to run into him.

"Hi," she said. "Sorry, uh. Happy Thanksgiving."

Sunji and I spoke together. "Happy Thanksgiving."

Alexander placed his nose in the air. "I am thankful for everything except this white man's holiday."

She looked briefly at Alexander and, making the right choice, ignored him.

"We're neighbors. My husband and I moved in a few weeks back… We cooked a big dinner for some of our friends, but the military base is on lockdown. Anyway, long story short, you want some kitchen food?"

Sunji gave a small smile. "We already have something planned tonight, but thanks."

I noticed something in her eyes that I would later come to recognize as desperation.

"Yeah, but I'm offering kitchen food. The main ingredient in those bags of shit you have is gonna be processed 'meat,' the type of which won't really be the kind it said it would be on the packaging.

Sodium content will be unnecessarily high, the oven will most likely heat it unevenly and you'll end up with burnt crisp just before icicle, plus the fullness will wear off before a drop of drool hits your pillow.

"Now, I know we haven't talked. Ever. And I know you've got those pretty girls and boys coming and going, so maybe you never had a need for any other company, but this is *my* need." She looked over the fence that separates our houses. "Plus, my husband made some mean steaks, because he has to have a steak on every holiday, so if you and I are ever gonna have beef, let it be only of this sort and come on over."

I looked over at their house and saw her husband—short, brown, and cute in that stuffed animal kind of way—staring at us through one of their front windows. Our eyes made contact and he actually *sneered* before pulling back into the darkness and drawing the curtains closed. It was very *Jane Eyre*.

"That man over there is your husband?" I asked.

"He doesn't seem friendly," Sunji added.

She looked at the window where he had been with a sharp gaze. "This isn't a setup." Her eyes, not at all softened, traveled to Sunji. "I've seen what you're working with, Mr. Window Fuck. You too," she said to me, "in a different sense. And the same sense, I guess. And neither of you will do much for me." She allowed herself to notice Alexander again. "I've never seen you before, but you're welcome as well. Steak. Company. I'll even send you home with a bottle of tequila, but that's it. I don't beg harder than this. So, we got beef?"

Jay stepped out on the porch behind us. "What's this about tequila?"

He shoved his way through us.

"I'm offering dinner," she began.

"And drinks," Jay finished. "Sounds good. What time should we be over with appetizers?"

And that's how our relationship with Eagle Diolosa began.

• • • • • •

Her husband Rockefeller was trickier to connect with. The base lockdown lifted before we made it over, so he called off our visit. Eagle personally delivered the news, along with two bottles of tequila. It was a nice gesture, but she had so efficiently filleted our own dinner courses through her descriptions that it was hard for us to enjoy our dinner without thinking of her eviscerating words.

Going forward, Sunji made sure to close his curtains whenever he was fucking someone against the window. I stayed in a minor panic while analyzing what she had meant when she said she saw what I was working with since my room was on the other side of the house, but after a while I realized she was simply referencing my sexuality.

The guys liked her immediately. It wasn't so much that she was a bro, because she refused to get involved in the heterosexual male shenanigans that Sunji, Ellington and Alexander, by nature of their nature, would devolve into. But she was most certainly a dude. She spoke our language, she watched the same things we did, she laughed with us, and she fought with us like an expert.

In friend groups as large as ours, bonding inevitably becomes stronger with some over others. Jay and I, for example, put each other above the rest. Ellington and Alexander have grown very tight without Jay there to breathe down Alexander's neck. Sunji was more of a wild card in the days before Eagle, and I can't even imagine what the group dynamics were like before I showed up. ("Easy," Jay says one night when I bring this up to him. "Before you showed up, we weren't friends.") Resultantly, I became Sunji's favorite and I found myself as Alexander and Ellington's second favorite. Alexander tried to turn us into a Musketeers trio, or "Sam, Dean and Castiel" which I had no fucking frame of reference for, but I could never get tight with Alexander because he would go on and on about subjects like "Sam, Dean and Castiel."

The problem was—is—that Eagle's arrival shifted the dynamics. Now Sunji had a bestie, and everyone liked—likes—her as much as me, if not more. I should have seen it coming. It might as well be scientifically proven that when a straight girl enters the ranks of a group of guy friends, the gay fellow falls on the priority list. Send a depressed message in the group chat (of which I have sent several) and her unrelated meme screenshot will get a reply first. Guaranteed.

It doesn't help that she's in the Air Force and regrets terribly the fact that she enlisted, so we get the cool military stories without having to sanction the fact that she's basically a cop.

She often reaches out to me, as if she senses my resentment. She offers for us to go out, "just the girls." The problem is that she's not feminine in the same way I'm feminine. She'll get her nails done, but she doesn't get pleasure from it. She's married, but she doesn't like to gab about men and romance and sex like I do. She likes those frenetic action movies that give me whiplash, and she tells the grossest stories.

It goes without saying that she's at the bottom of my personal ranking system.

My relationship with Rock, however, is a different case. Where Eagle is crude, Rock is just rude, and I have experience with that. It helps that he's hot in a Gael Garcia Bernal kind of way. He has strong features that aren't the typical Eurocentric formations, and his face is almost the opposite of symmetrical, but his eyes are lush, his smile (when you get it) genuine, and he has thick hair that I fantasize about gripping in my hands while I pummel his prostate. So yeah, I have the hots for Eagle's husband and maybe that is the true reason why I can't vibe with her. I can't be open with her about that, so it doesn't feel right to open up at all.

• • • • • • • •

Even though we weren't welcome at his place, we were never bothered if Rock was dragged over to ours by Eagle. This would happen most often on a game night, if there were going to be an odd number of players, what with girlfriends and boyfriends coming in and out and housemates going in and out with them.

One evening, the seven of us got on the subject of race while finishing up a round of Jenga. Alexander pointed out that those of us in relationships at the time were all partnered up with someone from another race. Mandy and Ellington, Shane and I, and the Diolosas.

Eagle, it turns out, was Latinx, but she hadn't grown up in the culture in the same way that I had. I didn't judge her for this (I judged her enough), but it was jarring sometimes when she wouldn't get a reference or understand a Spanish phrase. And her own Spanish was brutal.

"Wait," Alexander had said, squinting one eye until it was nearly shut. "Shane isn't Mexican, right? Have we talked about this?"

"I doubt he's Mexican," I said, shaking my head. I was cuddled up next to him, sitting out this round of the game, and Sunji was on his phone, updating his social media.

"He's gotta be Asian," Jay said. "No doubt."

"That brown though," Ellington said, taking an on-brand opportunity to disagree with Jay. "Are you sure he's not South American, Zario? He could be indigenous."

"I'm afraid to ask," I said. "I don't know how to bring that up. Usually you can just tell, you know?"

Sunji shook his head. "He's white, guys."

Jay's head dropped into his hands. "Sunji's wrong, guys."

"Only white dudes are named Shane."

"Noble point," Alexander nodded, "but he's hella brown."

"Hella," Eagle agreed.

Sunji put down his phone. "That's not a tan?"

Alexander chuckled. "If I could tan like that, it would be a super power."

Rock had been silent up to that point, but chose then to speak as if delivering the most obvious solution.

"He's Filipino."

We stared at him, registering his presence. Then, I asked, "How can you tell?"

"Have you ever heard of the phrase, 'It takes one to know one?'" He waved his forearm at us, showing off his tattoo of the eight-ray sun from the Philippine national flag. "We're so overlooked. We're the Greg P. Russell of Asians."

Greg P. Russell is a sixteen-time Oscar nominee without a single win, a record for the Academy. The fact that Rock knew this and casually used it in a conversation convinced me I could fuck him.

Jay also stared at Rock. "Pacific Islander isn't Asian."

"You know that and I know that, but they don't know that." Rock pointed at the rest of us with a circling finger.

"Well, we know that now," Ellington said. "So thanks, I guess."

"If you like this guy, just ask him. Get uncomfortable early. It pays off."

Sunji leaned over to Eagle and whispered, "Does it?"

She snorted so hard that the Jenga tower came down.

The First Straw

Eagle holds a teacup high in the air. "Obviously, we're drinking to your journey."

Sunji prohibits us from using shot glasses when we drink together, mainly because there was a huge skirmish when Ellington moved out over who owned what shot glass. There were detailed arguments about where and when glasses were purchased and whether or not there was sentimental value. The compromise was that once Sunji, Ellington and Jay settled on who owned what, they would each pack their glasses away to keep further battles from raging. Since then, we take all of our shots out of these delicate teacups Eagle gave us.

"They were my grandma's," she said at the time. "I told her repeatedly I wouldn't take them, but she shipped them to me when Rock and I got married. At least with you guys, they'll get some actually use and appreciation."

We have never used them for tea.

"You just want an excuse to drink," Jay mutters now.

"No, I don't," Eagle says, making a face, "even though there would be no shame in that. I drink to drink. I drink to think. I drink to stop thinking. I drink to make golf seem interesting or to get me through an episode of those bullshit sitcoms my husband watches."

"Let's do this quick," I stress. "My ride will be here, like, yesterday."

"Drama queen," Eagle says with a smile and in that moment I hate her.

"Let's see," she says, "a rhyming toast. To really make a production of it."

It's like she's aware that our friends are staging this ridiculous presentation, while ignoring the fact that she's enabling them further.

Jay, reading my mind, says, "You're worse than Ellington."

"Rhymes are tough," Alexander whines.

"Then you go first."

Eagle and Ellington, proving their like-mindedness, speak this in unison.

"Make it sound legit," Ellington says.

Again, I stress, "You guys are so extra."

Alexander tries. "Um, to the man, Zario. May your looks-to-age be resistant."

Sunji nods, then says, "May your wisdom and joy be perspirant."

I'm thrown by his word choice, but Eagle whispers in his ear and he corrects himself.

"Persistent."

Ellington curls his fingers into a loose fist, shaking his hand with a stiff wrist.

"May your stroke be ever consistent," he says, miming an ejaculation over the table.

Eagle's turn. "May your knowledge of tongues be efficient."

She draws out the word "tongues" and I wonder if all of my friends are deviants.

Jay has his line ready, having figured out his rhyme from the moment Alexander made his toast.

He lifts his cup and says, almost dismissively, "May this dude from the last fuck be different," and I know he's got a vision of Shane in his mind.

"To Zario!" Eagle says, moving her tea cup to the center of the table.

"To Zario!" my friends chorus, teacups clanking.

"To me!"

• • • • • •

The dudes had made this reservation at one of the nicer sit-down restaurants in town. It was close enough to the house for them to rush over if I needed anything, from a ride to any forgotten items, but I was pretty set. I had brushed my teeth, scraped my tongue, filed my nails, exfoliated, even put some light gloss on the lips. I was serving at my highest grade.

The restaurant was cute, too. Black and orange decor with gold and brown accents. I half-expected to see a salad bar, but the spot was a notch above that kind of service. The servers, dressed head to toe in black, move like agitated fish who don't stick to one spot for long.

A male server approaches as I confirm my reservation with the host. His skin is a rich, brown-orange (because I'm hungry, I think of hush puppies, but thanks to Rock, I can quickly surmise that he's Filipinx), and his pompadour towers impressively. He looks about my age, fresh out of college, maybe.

"I can take you over to your table, Mr. del Rosario. My name is Lando, like the best character from *Star Wars*. I'll actually be your server this evening."

I get his reference, because of course I've seen *The Empire Strikes Back* more times than I can count. I've seen the original *Star Wars* maybe once. *How you doin', ya old pirate?*

I follow Lando across the restaurant toward the windows with the best view. "Thank you."

"The other member of your party is already here," he tells me over his shoulder.

I had wanted to arrive first. Get my bearings. Oh, well.

"What is he like?" I ask Lando.

"Oh, you haven't met him before?" Lando replies. "He's nice. Seems nervous."

Alexander had told me this guy was a gamer, too, but not professional, so hopefully we won't struggle finding things in common.

When Lando and I arrive at the booth, my date pops up, smoothing down his shirt, which is already tight on his body and, I'm delighted to note, sheer.

"Mario?"

I dock him points. "Zario."

He shakes his head sharply. "Right, Zario. Hi, I'm Zick."

His lips are huge. Gigantic. I can't stop looking at them. "Zick?"

"I mean, Mick. You're Zario; I'm Mick."

I give him what I hope is an easy grin. "So you say."

His throat clenches and his eyes bulge. "I'm sorry?"

"What?"

"What?" He does a half spin, looking behind him then back at me.

"What did you apologize for?" I ask, and he seems to relax.

"For getting your name wrong." He makes a gesture for us to sit.

I take my seat and open up my napkin, placing it in my lap. "Just now?"

"Just when?" He looks up at me, and veins pop in his face.

"Would you care for something to drink?"

I jump at Lando's question, realizing he hasn't left. Mick's anxiety must be contagious.

My date has picked up the stack of notecards, and his hands tremble. "Hoikey-boikeys and fuckrabbits," he says, quite audibly.

Lando leans in. "Pardon?"

Mick looks up. "Water, please."

Lando turns to me. "For you?"

Mick looks back up, annoyed. "I said water."

"I meant for the other gentleman."

"Oh."

I smile apologetically. "I'll start with water, too."

Lando nods politely and leaves us, but I feel like he doesn't exactly want to. I see a smile curve on his lips as he walks away.

I turn back to my date. "Did you say 'hoikey-boikeys and fuckrabbits?'"

"Oh, geez. Yeah, sorry about that. It's just something I say when I'm trying to think happy thoughts."

"I have so many questions."

Mick holds up his notecards. "Me first."

• • • • • • •

I'm missing out on a game of darts. Sunji and Ellington are playing in the den as Eagle pours a set of tequila shots, Jay munches on a handful of almonds, and Alexander texts furiously on his phone.

Jay looks at the blond out of the side of his eyes. "Stop texting him."

"I'm not texting him," Alexander replies. "I'm texting his sister. Making sure Mick was in a good place when he left tonight."

Eagle looks up from the teacups. "In a good place? That sounds ominous."

"He gets really nervous before dates."

Jay's jaw tightens. "Nervous enough that you're nervous?"

"I could be setting him up on a date with the gay Oscar Isaac and I'd still be nervous."

Jay nods. "Fair."

Eagle sets the bottle down, signaling for the fellas to pick up their cups.

"Round three," she says, lifting hers high. The others follow suit.

"What are we toasting to this time?" Sunji asks.

"To getting drunk," Eagle says, affecting a slur.

"To Zario," Ellington suggests, "for taking the necessary steps to improve his life."

Sunji nods. "To us, for getting him off of his ass to take those steps."

Eagle accepts this. "To Zario and us."

They drain their teacups and Ellington smacks his lips.

"I'm proposing."

The stupefaction is immediate.

"Proposing to what?" Jay asks.

"To Mandy!"

Jay curls his mouth into a frown. "Proposing to that?" Then, after Alexander nudges him, "To her?"

Sunji waves darts in front of his face as if clearing mental cobwebs.

"Remind me," he begins. "Mandy forced you to make chastity vows when you started dating. You haven't even…tickled her fancy this entire time. And now you're gonna drop on one knee? Do you wanna fuck her that bad?"

Ellington motions for Jay to pour him another shot. "No guys, this is serious. I've never met a girl who's made me feel this way. She's the one."

Alexander grins. "Well, once you go white…"

The others look at him expectantly.

"I really thought one of you guys would have something ready," he mutters.

Jay slides Ellington's cup back to him. "What, once you go white, your friends will feel sorry for you?"

"You guys are mean," Alexander says, going back to his phone.

• • • • • • •

The questions come fast, but not at all loose. Mick sticks to his list of questions like a gay man sticks to his favorite homophobic gospel singer.

"How long have you lived in LA? Alexander said you were a photographer. What do you like to shoot? What are your hobbies? What's your favorite thing to do in the summertime?"

I do my best to answer each question before he rattles off a new one. It helps that he has those lips. I'm mesmerized watching him work them, whether it's to voice a new inquiry or his nervous pursing.

Then we get to the question I hate.

"Zario's such an interesting name! Is it short for something?"

I'm surprised he didn't lead with it, but he shuffles the notecards every third question to keep things his version of spontaneous.

"My last name. del Rosario."

"And what's your first name?"

I'm newly annoyed. "I go by Zario. Been called that since elementary school."

Mick doesn't catch my hint. "Why? Your first name must be terrible."

I laugh. "Famines, child warfare, and that turd-passing face Katy Perry makes when she tries to sing 'Firework' are things that are terrible. My first name is simply none of your business."

He blinks. Finally, message received.

"I'm so sorry, Zario."

I put the bitch back in his compartment. "It's cool, Mick."

"Mick is short for Michelangelo," he offers.

I grin. "And who is it long for?"

He blinks. "I'm sorry?"

"What?" If he's going to feign ignorance, so will I.

"What?"

No, he's genuinely confused. Unfortunate.

Beyond Mick's stumped face, I notice a man sitting at the bar, staring me down. He looks about my age, pan-ethnic like fast Diesel and furious Johnson. He smiles, and I look away. His lips are beautiful. I'm tempted to compare.

Mick shuffles through his cards again. I remind myself to focus on the lips at hand, not the two at the bar.

"Mick, put down the cards. Just talk to me."

Mick sets his cards on the seat next to him.

"We are talking. I know so much about you. Oh, man. I haven't let you ask me anything yet, huh? I should have made cards for that. Reminders, in between each one. Hoikey-boikeys and—"

Before he can finish this meltdown, I ask, "What exactly is a 'fuckrabbit?' Or a 'hoikey?'"

Mick stills. "Oh."

"Oh?"

"I have two sisters," he says, as if that's anybody's version of an explanation.

"Go on," I say, when I realize he isn't planning on elaborating.

"Will you excuse me?"

He doesn't wait for my answer, sliding out of the booth.

I stare after him for a moment, and Lando the server returns to the table.

"I just wanted to check in, Mr. del Rosario. Will you two be looking to order food anytime soon?"

Shit. We hadn't even ordered food yet.

"Um, I'm so sorry. Let me tell you what I want, and then when he gets back we can handle the second half of the battle," I tell him, placing my order. "He should be back from the bathroom soon."

Lando nods, his eyes laughing. "In the meantime, would you like me to refill your bread basket again?"

"Please," I say. "It's the only thing keeping me alive right now."

He nods. "Happy to do it."

As he walks away, the lips from the bar approach attached to a cute face and a body dressed in a vibrant suit with a patterned bowtie. Lips places a drink near my hands, so I touch his arm as he turns to walk away.

"Thank you," I say, genuinely appreciative. "I don't drink, though."

He's turned back to me, and now he gestures to one of his ears and shakes his head. I notice a hearing device.

He signs, "*Sorry.*"

I sign back, "*It's okay. I was just saying that I don't drink, but thank you.*"

Surprise spreads on his face as he watches me sign, and I see him calculating the level of my skill. He makes no mention of it, signing back, "*It looks like you may need to start drinking. Are you two even going to eat?*"

The audacity. I laugh and it feels good.

I sign back, "*If you know I'm here with someone, how are you bold enough to buy me a drink?*"

"*Because it's obvious that whatever's been happening at this table isn't going anywhere.*"

I smile, then sign, "*He brought notecards.*"

"*I saw.*"

I sign my name and he signs his, then provides his name sign. "*Wesley.*"

He continues. "*Now tonight won't be a total waste.*"

"*What do you mean?*"

"*You met me,*" he signs with a grin, dipping his upper torso to the side and pushing his opposite hip out just enough.

"*Nice to meet you, Wesley.*"

"Nice to meet you, Zario."

Wesley walks away and I watch him take every step. Every step until Mick steps into my line of vision, wiping his hands on his pants.

"There's a drink here for you," I say, pushing Wesley's drink toward Mick's side of the booth. Mick stares down at it as he sits. He stares for too long, unmoving. When he looks up, his eyebrows are knit together.

"I think I should be going."

"Oh, okay… Before entrées?" This fucker was dumping me on our first date.

"I'm making a fool of myself, Zario."

He's still speaking into his drink. I decide to encourage him.

"You're fine!" I lie. "I'm enjoying this." That part's the truth.

Behind him, I see Wesley leaving the restaurant and waving. Shit.

Mick is talking, finally looking at me.

"For the wrong reasons. Look, I think you're a great guy, and you're really attractive, but I shouldn't be dating right now."

Is this really happening? I can't tell if I ask that last question aloud, but Mick provides a bit of an answer anyway.

"This is my first date post-closet."

"Oh man, really?" It would be like Alexander to set me up with the first gay man he thought of. Or met. "I didn't know."

Mick is gathering his things. "I'd like a do-over sometime if that's at all possible. Maybe down the line if we're both still single?"

I nod. "Oh, for sure."

"Hoikey-boikeys and fuck rabbits!" he blusters one last time, slamming fists on the table.

• • • • • • • •

"And he left?" Alexander is shifting between incredulity and righteous anger. He pulls out his phone. "What the fuck?"

I collapse on the dining room table, arms splayed amidst the teacups and playing cards. Telling them the story had made it seem funny, but I had felt strangely emotional leaving the restaurant. I had felt an obligation to eat my meal (and, being honest, I was hungry as a motherfuck), and Lando had stopped by to chat me up a few times during my meal, but it still felt like failure. If this was my first step on the road to an attempted return to normalcy, I was in for a rocky journey.

Sunji is laughing. "Hoikey-boikeys and fuck rabbits."

"What even is that?" Ellington pats me on the shoulder. "Your life is a comedy, man."

"Ugh," I groan, turning my head toward him, "and this was just the first straw."

Jay winks at me. "Not the last."

Eagle points to herself. She's got next week's date. "Not the last. It'll get better!"

"It fucking better! No offense, Alexander."

He doesn't hear me, texting furiously.

Eagle stands and heads toward the door. "Gotta jet, fellas. Rock is texting."

"Tell the hubby we said hey," Sunji says.

"I'm not gonna do that. You guys never say hey."

"Wait, Eagle," Jay says before turning to me. "Zario."

Immediately, Sunji starts giggling and my antennae goes up. "Jay."

"Did Ellington tell you he's proposing?"

Now even Alexander is laughing, everyone with hands up to their mouths.

"To what? To *that*?" I look at Ellington in dismay. "Dude, do you love yourself?"

"Right?" Jay says, a booming sort of exclamation.

Ellington looks at me, daggers, swords, and more than a little hurt in his eyes.

"Y'all can be some real assholes, you know that?"

Americano

Alexander exits the bathroom at our coffeeshop, passing a table where two women—one long-haired, the other short-haired—are having an animated conversation.

The short-haired girl notices his shirt and speaks, rather, she crows.

"Rufio!"

Alexander stops and looks at her quizzically.

"Your shirt,"she says, pointing to the tri-hawked lost boy staring out from his chest. "I love *Hook*."

"Aw, yeah. Thanks."

"He was so cool," the long-haired girl agrees. "I wanted to be him growing up."

"Where'd you get the shirt?"

"I don't remember," Alexander says, thinking. "A con or something."

"I'm Ty. This is December."

The long-haired girl waves.

"Okay," Alexander says, mystified.

"What's your name?" Ty asks.

"Oh. Alexander."

Ty smiles. "Nice to meet you, Alexander."

Alexander stands for a moment, then lets rip a piercing crow of his own. He smiles his biggest smile then and walks away.

Now it is the ladies who are mystified.

At the register, Sunji orders and pays for his coffee. As he looks for us, he hears a familiar voice call his name.

"Sunji?"

His eyes grow wide and he looks around until he spots her.

Jerrica Yun. She stands a few feet away from him, now closing the gap, a gray blazer and pencil skirt, hair perfect, infomercial happy. She hugs him and he grips her back, tightly.

"Jerrica," he breathes, and they release. "How've you been?"

"Real good," she says, tossing her black hair with a manicured hand. "I've been seeing a doctor about my digestive issues."

"How's that going?"

"Nothing's changed! My farts can still clear a football stadium. But," she points to emphasize each word, "I'm seeing a doctor. That's half the battle."

Sunji spreads his arms. "What brings you up here?"

Jerrica lives downtown, though she does business all over. Still, it's rare to see her in our neighborhood.

"I got sick of sitting in traffic, so I decided to make a pit stop. The pour overs here could always improve my mood." She flicks a finger in his direction. "How have you been, mister?"

"Real good," he says, as his eyes begin flying around the coffee shop, looking for an answer that will impress her. "I've booked roles in about four features in the past few months."

"Four! That's impressive. You were always talented, though." She toys with her cup. "You know, I hated how things ended between us."

"You threw all of my shaving supplies in the toilet."

She sighs happily. "I did."

"You chucked my two hundred dollar perfume at my head."

She scribbles on a napkin, saying casually, "I can now genuinely say I'm sorry I missed."

She hands him the napkin. She's inked a date and a time. He recognizes the address as a beautiful apartment complex in Hollywood.

"Let's do a meal," she says brightly. "Bring your lady friend over to the new place I'm sharing with my man friend. And put the address in your phone."

Sunji is running behind mentally. "I don't have a lady friend—you have a man friend?"

"Don't lose that napkin!"

"Just give me your number!"

Jerrica gathers her things. "Uh-uh-uh! I changed it for a reason after that onslaught of unimpressive dick pics almost made me file a restraining order. You should have had Zario take those shots for you."

"I asked him. He said no!"

He did. I did.

Jerrica waves as she exits. "Enjoy your Americano!"

At this moment, where the rest of us are seated around coffee, tea, cakes, and quiches, I'm doing my best to reason with Ellington.

"Dude, you obviously aren't ready to propose. Marriage is more than a relationship status update. Don't commit unless you're ready. Shane wasn't ready."

This sets Jay off like a rocket. "Oh, God," he starts, and I genuinely don't know what I said until I see a familiar steam rising from his ears, "this isn't about Shane. And *you* were the mistress!"

"Wouldn't that make him a 'mister'?" Eagle asks, hoping to add some levity, but now I'm steaming too.

"Who knows how those gay titles work. I figured they were both, 'gurls,'" Jay says, rolling his neck and snapping his fingers.

Now I speak. "You're not funny, you sack of shit."

"Mandy's the one." Ellington is serious.

Eagle isn't buying it. "What makes you so sure?"

"What made you sure Rock was the one?"

"Lame deflection, and I'm not biting."

Ellington raises an eyebrow. "Okay, I'll answer first. She makes me want to be the man she sees in me. And because of her, I know I can be that man."

"You're on some Cameron Crowe shit with that," I say.

"*Aloha* Crowe?" Jay snorts.

"Or eighties Crowe?" Ellington asks.

Alexander shifts in his seat. "Or *Jerry Maguire* Crowe?"

I respond simply, "Yes." The guys always knew how to disappear in the minutiae at any given moment.

Ellington turns back to Eagle. "Your turn."

Eagle crinkles her nose. Shrugs. Plays with the hem of her shirt. "I'm not sure Rock is the one."

Jay's gaze sharpens. "You married him."

"Yeah. I did. And I think he was the one for that moment in time. And he may be the one at another, later moment in time. I just know he's not the one for all moments."

"Yeah," I say, "but you can't find the perfect person."

"I'm not looking for perfection. I'm looking for love."

Ellington puts down his coffee. "Oh shit."

"Well, my word choice sucks in the moment. I'm looking for compatibility."

My words come out before I can stop them. "Yeah, but Rock is so..."

She reads me. "Appealing? Charming? Consistent?" She shakes her head, curls leaping over her shoulders. "He's the guy I should be in love with. I'm just not most days."

Jay is shaken by this conversation. "I didn't know it was like that over in the Diolosa household."

Eagle shrugs. Her body continues making outward signs of her internal discomfort.

"It won't always be. When I say I'm looking for love, I mean that I'm looking for signs of it in me. Look, humans used to not live as long. And now we're expected to find love with someone and endure decades with them? I'm not convinced."

Alexander whistles slowly. "'Endure?'"

"What I mean is, humans change. Shouldn't our love?"

Sunji, with a legit reason for being oblivious this once, approaches the table with a huge grin. "Hey, guys!"

Jay looks him up and down. "Who swallowed?"

"Jerrica was here."

Ellington, again with, "Oh, shit."

"Fuck outta here!" Alexander looks ready to dash for an exit. "What's she doing on our side of town?"

Sunji shrugs. "I don't remember. But she remembered I like Americanos."

"And that's the reason the two of you didn't work out," Ellington says, tightening his lips in frustration. "She remembers everything and you remember nothing."

"Sunji can't help that he doesn't have the brain power to remember his own middle name," Jay says.

"I don't have a middle name!"

"You sure about that?" Jay asks, and suddenly Sunji isn't sure.

"You're a dick and a half," Alexander says to Jay.

"Maybe according to your scale," he shoots back. "Plus, women are engineered to remember those things. Men have been conditioned by centuries of hunting and gathering and being awesome so that they don't have to remember every anniversary of the first time they had cheddar popcorn."

"He's in one of his moods, guys," I say. "Just being contrariwise." Only I can make out the smile beneath his practiced smile. He loves stirring up shit. "Just because there are differences in gender doesn't mean there should be inequalities."

I get a text from Alexander. It reads:

contrarian

I make an annoyed face at his apologetic one.

Jay is responding to me orally. "Then men should get paternity leave."

Ellington slaps the table. "It's the twenty-first century, jackhole. They do!"

"I always find it fascinating," I say, "when another man of color doesn't understand a different type of inequality."

Jay almost flinches. "Don't make this about the bananas in your fruit stand, okay? Race is a made up social construct invented by Europeans because their original caste system did not organically enforce how much better than everyone else they assumed they were. Sexuality is a non-starter and women get paid even though their quality of work drops significantly once a month—not to mention during their pregnancies—and they uniformly get better opportunities because they have breasts than men ever do because they have dicks."

Ellington scoffs. "You're ridiculous."

"I'm ri-cock-ulous," Jay counters stupidly. "I just think sure—race is an issue, albeit an engineered one. These inflated gender wars, though, aren't worth the time of day."

Eagle leans back in her chair and it's the equivalent of a long drag on a cigarette. "Ah, so you don't want equality; you want privilege. You're discounting the fact that the reason you perceive breasts as such a strong influencer is due to the overwhelming presence of straight males—"

Now I interject. "Straight, cisgender, white males."

"Sorry about that," Alexander mutters.

Eagle continues. "—in positions of power in the workforce."

Sunji looks up from his coffee cup. "Are we still talking about Jerrica?"

Later, as we walk to our cars, Ellington holds me back from the rest of them. "I've known Sunji for a few years now. In all of that time, I've never known him to pine over a girl they way he pined over Jerrica."

"Are we absolutely sure she doesn't turn into an ogre when the sun goes down?" Jay asks, suddenly on the other side of me.

"He had this elaborate proposal planned before she dumped him," Ellington continues. "I know he still has the ring in his sock drawer. I actually prayed he'd get over her in time."

I watch Sunji literally skipping ahead of us.

"'In time' wasn't specific enough," I say.

They Call It Falling for a Reason

My second date is with this guy named Oscar, one of Rock and Eagle's Air Force friends. He's my height, which is already impressive, with russet skin and a wide smile. He eats quickly, which unnerves me, and then tells me he wants to take me dancing at The Ungodly Whore.

Two hours later, I'm sweaty, exhausted, and sore in places I can't be sure actually exist just yet. Oscar continues to dance furiously. He's shirtless now and he's so in shape that I'm less attracted to him than I was before. If not for his friendship with the Diolosas, I'd be thinking he's lied to me about his career and that he's actually a fitness model. After a moment, I accept that both things can be true.

"Can we sit? We've been dancing for a bit."

He grips my wrists, eyes pleading. "Next song? Next song!"

His shoulders lurch on the twos and fours and he throws his head back in ecstasy. This is why he's so in shape. If he dances like this on the regular, the only thing that will survive on his bones are these muscles.

"You're doing the ScarJo dance," I say to be funny, but he doesn't hear me. We haven't had much dialogue since we hit the club, and I'm beginning to wonder if this is all there is to know about him.

The song melts into the next and I'm ready to go nurse my feet.

"Oh, this is my song, Zario!"

They're all his songs. Each one his jam, his shit. I don't have much more energy for any of his shit, so I mutter, "Dance on, then," and hobble off the dancefloor.

"Come back, Zario!" he calls after me. "Don't you feel this rhythm?"

I want to feel my ass on one of these couches, and I find a free spot on one in the corner.

The moment I lift the weight from my afflicted feet, I hear a familiar voice.

"Hey, Zario!"

Thankfully, it's not Patrick. It's Rock, who is the person I've collapsed next to without even looking.

"Rock?"

Eagle leans around him to wave at me. "And lady friend."

"How's the date going, baby?" Rock asks.

Eagle looks out over the dancefloor. "Yeah, where's Oscar? We knew he'd try to get you here."

I point. "Don Henley wrote a song about her."

Rock laughs. "'All She Wants to Do is Dance?' Yeah, he's an alien life form if you give him a good beat and at least two notes."

"Go wear her out," Eagle tells him.

He rises. "Not likely."

As he steps into the gyrating bodies, I turn back to my neighbor.

"This is the guy so amazing that you chose him to go second?"

She shrugs. "I figured the bounce back from last week's travesty would guarantee a slam dunk."

"You know, Mick was sweet. I don't even know Oscar yet. He shoveled down his food and practically dragged me here before the last bite was swallowed."

"I owe you one," she says ruefully.

I laugh. "I mean, you're already out of four hundred and fifty dollars."

Now she groans. "This bet was the dumbest idea."

"Where were you when I was trying to tell that to the rest of them?"

"Rock actually was really invested in the idea. He worries about you. And since he thinks Oscar's amazing, he figured you would, too."

"Again, he might be." I catch glimpses of Rock and Oscar strutting and spinning to the music. "Wayment." I turn to Eagle. "What are you guys doing here? We can never get you to come to The Ungodly Whore!"

"Rock is trying to do this thing where he steps into my life a bit. He knows you guys always come here, so he figured he'd check it out with me."

"And then next time we invite you…" I say, understanding.

"Exactly. We come. Or he'll make less of a fuss if I go without him."

"Good luck with that."

She doesn't catch my sarcasm. "Thanks. Also, Sunji texted me that you were headed here, so Rock and I headed over. We figured we'd just hang out and uh…"

My jaw hangs open. "You guys are spying!"

"Like I said, bruh. Rock worries about you. I never know what to tell him. I wasn't around Shane much, but I know he fucked you over real bad."

"That's right," I muse. "You weren't there at the beginning. You know, I actually met him here. We broke up here, too."

She makes a hilarious face I've never seen her make before, part confused and part horrified. "Wait, here at the Whore?"

"It's my favorite spot," I say, grimacing. "Let's catch you up, girl."

We bend our heads toward each other and I begin to fill her in on all of the romance, all of the sex, and all of the drama that was my relationship with Shane Cortéz.

• • • • • • •

The thing is, before meeting Oscar, I had never encountered anyone who loved dancing more than I did. In college, I would go out Friday and Saturday nights and dance out all the alcohol I had drank while pre-gaming. In LA, I don't go out by myself, so usually whichever of the Dudes is single at the time is forced to roll out with me.

109

Alexander tries his hardest not to frequent the clubs, but we drag him along. It's almost always a guarantee that one of us is going to meet someone, so he's left to be the wingman for the other.

It was Alexander who was with me as I abandoned myself to the music on the night I was fated to meet Shane. Ellington had arrived with us, but disappeared with the first hot male-attracted girl he could find. I always have an extra condom on hand for him, because he's always in need.

"I'm going to the bathroom," Alexander hollered in my ear. "Do you wanna go with me?"

"I'm okay," I yelled back, feeling brave. "Just come right back or text me if something comes up."

"Five minutes, tops," he nodded, the strobe lights turning the fragmented blue of his eyes into a kaleidoscopic rainbow.

He moved off, bounding awkwardly to the music, and I wondered how many guys were going to hit on him before he got back. I probably should have gone with him for his own protection more than mine.

"Hey, Zario."

Patrick, materializing like the fairy's curse he is. He was stuffed into a one piece bodysuit, and he had boots up to his calves. I wondered briefly if he was go-go dancing before remembering the Whore has no dancers. This man just felt like wearing this out of the house.

I peered at him, feigning confusion. "How'd you know my name?"

"It's not that dark in here, bitch. I know you recognize—"

I wasn't listening to him. I saw a man swaying through the crowd. Based on his expression, I could tell he was perusing the setting and not heading anywhere in particular.

I grabbed his arm. "Babe!"

"Hon," the man said instinctively, and I couldn't tell if it was because he had learned to go with random stranger's flow or if he thought he might know me.

I reached out to him, my eyes bulging to indicate assistance. He nodded.

"The line at the bathroom was ridiculous," he said, leaning up toward me, and we locked lips. My hand traveled up his back as he pulled my hips closer to him. He was a damn good kisser, this lifesaver. At some point our lips parted and we were dancing together, in that intense way where the music becomes less important and instead it becomes about the vibe of the person across from you. By the time I remembered Patrick, he was long gone.

He was a great dancer, too, this lifesaver.

He pulled back suddenly, laughing as if realizing or fabricating the ridiculousness of the moment.

"I hope your boyfriend isn't jealous," I yelled into his ear over the music.

"What boyfriend?" he yelled back, laughing. "Are you and I over already?"

"I don't have much luck with long-term relationships," I said, twisting my mouth like I'd seen Alicia Silverstone do a million times. *Anything you can do to draw attention to your mouth is good.*

"Okay, then, let's see if this can last for at least ten more minutes, at least. I'll get you a drink."

"I don't drink."

Instead of the expected, "Really?" he held out his hand to me. "Then do you wanna accompany me while I drink?"

At the bar he asked, "So what made me 'babe?'"

"Oh, God. I used to date that guy. Now he carries a torch like it's the opening ceremony at the Olympics."

"That doesn't answer my question. What made *me* 'babe?'"

I shrugged. "You were there?"

"Ouch."

I looked off into the darkness of the club, pressing my palms into my knees while straightening my elbows. I felt my shoulders crack deliciously as I asked, "What made me 'hon?'"

"Oh, you hated that." He raised an eyebrow. "Let me see. In my head, we were a long-term couple."

"'Were' we?"

"I mean, we are? You tolerate my drinking and I tolerate your…"

"Weakness to fall for a guy I just met?"

He smiled. "I can tolerate that. I mean, as long as that guy is me, you just keep on falling."

Those days were full of foreshadowing.

Alexander was happy for me, but more appreciative of the fact that he didn't have to leave alone. Apparently Ellington had already fucked that girl somewhere in the club and was ready to go home. Shane said he lived far, so I accompanied him to a nearby hotel, between Sunset and Santa Monica Boulevards. He paid for the room, a nice one, high enough to provide a beautiful view of the quieting streets.

"It looks like the Los Angeles I saw in movies," I said. "Shades of gold. The first time I remember seeing the city was watching *Set It Off*. It looked like…is it too gay of me to say it looked like Oz?"

"I don't know," he said from behind me. "Is it too gay of me to have butt sex with another man for pleasure?"

I turned from the window and walked over to the bed. "I wouldn't say so, but if you have butt sex for any other reason and the pleasure is coincidental, then you're in the clear." I ran my fingers over the comforter. Smooth. That was going to make for a pleasant ride.

He was watching me with eyes that matched the view, glittering and dark all at once. After a moment, he took off his shirt and I caught my breath.

"Roadmaps and dick skin."

"What'd you say?" he asked, laying his shirt across a chair.

"Oh, your body." I pointed to his ridiculous torso. "You're all veiny and taunt."

He laughed, kicking off his shoes. "Should I apologize?"

"You don't look like you're planning on apologizing."

His socks were off. His feet were pretty. "I don't think you want an apology." He paused in the middle of unbuckling his belt. "But maybe we should be clear on what you *do* want. We can go slow."

"For who's benefit?"

He raised an eyebrow. "That's not your speed?"

"Not usually."

"Coulda fooled me."

He helped me realize I was still standing there fully clothed, so I, too, began to strip. He and I had danced so hard I had to peel my clothes off of me.

"You're upfront," I spoke through the fabric of my shirt. "That's my second favorite thing that I like in a man."

When I finally got the shirt over my head, I saw him standing on the other side of the bed, naked.

"What's your first favorite thing?" he asked me.

"That I like in a man?" I started taking my pants off. "Me."

His penis began to rise, the tip glinting with precum. It was slender, but not thin. Long, but not remarkable. It was cute, I thought.

"Do I look like a bottom to you?" he asked me.

"Any man with an ass is a bottom," I said, my own dick hardening. I don't know if I was longer, but I was thicker and I had become an accomplished wall destroyer since my relationship with Ryu.

Shane laughed, putting one knee on the bed. "That's poetry."

"You know…" I realized the words I wanted to say were going to make me sound very strange. "I didn't notice it until now, when you put your knee up like that, but you remind me of my first crush."

"Please don't tell me I look like a first grader."

I laughed. "No, he's an actor. Kenny Morrison."

He shrugged, not recognizing the name. "I'm guessing that's a good thing."

"Yeah, it is."

He beckoned to me and I joined him on the bed. Grabbing my shaft, he proceeded to possess me through my dick, his mouth claiming my spirit, his tongue making me speak in ones unknown to me. His fingers would return there and I'd have moments of clarity, then I would be absorbed back into the wetness and warmth. When my back arched at its highest peak and I began puffing out explosive breaths, he returned to my own mouth, where I received him with thirst.

I was grateful that he was a kisser. I'm a kisser; I could have kissed all night if that's what he wanted. Instead, I began to explore the temple of his body with my own hands of worship and mouth of devotion. I turned him over, pressing my face between the muscular mounds of his ass, licking and caressing the softness of his hole until he thrashed in rapture, his own prayers of thanksgiving being moaned into the sheets.

Then, inexplicably, there was a shift. A lateral movement from a focused, driving session of pleasure to a communicative experience. The typical questions and commands ("Do you like that?" "Yeah, right there!") slowly expanded into intercourse-aided discourse. We shared what we liked, what we wanted, what embarrassed us, and soon we were laughing and teasing each other.

Our dicks were allowed to soften as we stretched what might have been a spirited and memorable fuck into two hours of giggling, exploratory conversation, and movement. It wasn't foreplay; it was something completely new to me.

Once I put the condom on, we transitioned a third time. We took the knowledge we had gained about each other, infused it with the intensity we led off with, and cultivated a searingly thorough lovemaking session. Our flesh was complimentary, like his ass had been molded for my dick. He straddled me and I can't remember if he was slamming down or I was slamming up, but our hips kept clapping together as if magnetized. I adjusted him onto his side, thrusting as I held one of his straightened legs to my chest and every stroke was a fully engaged, spine-reaching sensation. I dripped sweat and he moaned in a pitch that steadily rose higher.

At one point, we were standing on the bed, him with his fingers splayed against the wall, me with my hands gripping his waist as I tried to pound him through it into the neighboring room. We were loud now, all exhales and exclamations with one flapping dick kept fully erect by another plunging one.

Eventually, I laid on my back and pulled him on top of me, linking my arms through his armpits as his shoulder blades pressed against my chest. We were in possession of each other now, each of us having seized the spirit of the other, refusing to let go without a blessing. I drove up into him, my muscles working on their own accord. Within a few thrusts, he sobbed and he released his anointing, blessing me while damning himself as he came. Almost immediately, I pulled out from within him, ejaculating up through the groove between his cheeks, fusing his back to my stomach and, like him, fusing my desecration with his consecration.

I won't say that I loved him then, but I loved what we had done together.

We laid there for a bit, catching our breath. Nibbling, licking, kissing. He wiped up my cum with his dick and I sucked it off of him. We were so spent that he stayed flaccid the entire time he cleaned me off.

"Now might be an awkward time to mention this," he said when he was done, "but my name is Shane."

I rose onto my elbows, my jaw dropping to the point I thought I might have a loose ligament somewhere.

"Holy fuck."

He nodded, grinning. "That's what I'd call it."

"No, I mean, how did I not get your name? Did I give you mine?"

He shook his head.

"Zario. Like Mario, but with a 'Z.'"

"Nice to fuck you, Zario," Shane said.

"Nice to fuck you, too, Shane," I replied, and we shook hands, laughing as hard as we had just made love.

• • • • • • •

"Do you ever think about the future?"

This was the kind of shit Shane wanted to talk about whenever we'd get high and fuck.

All of the first responses I came up with to say to him were movie related. There was the corrupt lieutenant in Burton's first *Batman*. There was wild-haired and wild-eyed Doc Brown. But I always tried to seem mature when I was with Shane. I could tell he was older than me, though I had never nailed down by how much.

"Not when I wanna think about the past," I said, gripping a pillow between my chest and my sheets. We had begun fucking at my place on a weekly schedule by this point, capping off nights and days of watching movies, hitting the Santa Monica pier, and eating all over LA.

A lazy grin stretched across his face. "Oh yeah? What, specifically?"

"Just the last hour or so."

This made him laugh. I laughed with him before he silenced me with deep kisses. I stayed face-down, though, so my penis wouldn't get any ideas. I was exhausted. Shane, laying on his back, was clearly getting excited again.

After a moment he said, "I looked up Kenny Morrison, by the way."

"Oh God, you did?"

"Why did you say I looked like him?"

I gritted my teeth. "It's not so much that you look like him. It's that you look like the grown up version of a character he played."

"Holy shit. You think I look like Atreyu?"

"I see the dismay in your face, but let me specify that I meant from *Part II* specifically. He's way more brown in that one."

"Well, yeah, because the guy from the first movie was just white. Kenny is part Filipinx, so we have that in common. I guess I can give you that."

"You're part Filipinx?" I asked, imagining Rock's version of an I-told-you-so.

"Oh, yeah, I'm full-Filipinx. What was Atreyu? He was supposed to be indigenous, right? But indigenous to Fantasia?"

A grimace and a smile fought on my face. "I actually know a lot about that. Too much, really."

I began comparing the films with the original book by Michael Ende, breaking down the characterization of Atreyu within the context of the novel. Shane was amused by this, and I was amused by him until he climbed on top of me and called me Falcor with a wicked smile.

I swatted at him.

"Come on, be my luckdragon," he said, and I felt his dick on top of my ass.

I didn't know what he was trying, but I knew I wouldn't like it.

"Get off," I said, bucking my hips.

"I gotta break you in?" he asked. "Is that in the manual?"

I turned my head and I think he saw the lightning in my eyes.

"Get off me," I said again, my voice deeper and somehow bigger than myself.

He rolled off of me, raising his hands in the air. "Okay, alright."

I sat up, feeling the heat crawling across the nape of my neck and behind my ears.

"I don't like being dominated like that," I said.

"You said you were vers…"

"I didn't ask for a conversation; I asked for you to stop."

His lips pressed tight. I hated when he did that, because they all but disappear.

"I think I have a job for you."

"I'm not sucking your dick," I said sharply.

He didn't speak for a moment.

"A client of mine needs headshots with a different look."

"Nice of you to think of me."

I hadn't meant to sound so salty , but I didn't regret it. He had always offered me things after sex. On most occasions, I had chalked it up to him being in a good mood or something like that. This time, it was clear that he was trying to make up for something that he wasn't quite sure he'd done in the first place.

"Look," Shane began," I don't know what I did just now exactly, but—"

His phone began ringing from inside a pocket of his discarded pants. He laid a hand on my shoulder, sighed, then rose to grab it. Looking at his screen, then back to me, he held up a finger.

"Hey!" He slid on a pair of pants and stepped out of the room. "I'm just out. I'll be there…"

My suspicions began that day, quickly exacerbated as it became clearer that Shane did not want us at his place.

At first, it was because his place was far, but we drove all over the county and he never complained about distance. Then it was that his walls were so thin and he didn't want his neighbors to complain. When I suggested that we didn't have to fuck at his place, it became about his invasive landlord and how there were renovations happening that would ruin our time together.

I bought it because I wanted to, not because he was great at selling it.

When we progressed to seeing each other five to six times a week, he would come over my place directly after work and we'd hole up in my room, usually stoned and fucking. We had gotten impossibly better since that first night, still exchanging redemption and damnation. We started taking preventative drugs and I began leaving my salvation inside him. After we fucked, we would eat, ordering food because Sunji was still dating Jerrica at the time, so he wasn't cooking for the rest of us. Then Shane would either leave or, if he had a few hours, he'd help me practice my ASL.

He had family members who were deaf, so he was fluent with signing. Thankfully, I could pick this up just as easily as I could with spoken languages and we were holding decent conversations.

One day, he got on a kick about us having children together. This wasn't a first for us, but it was a first in sign language.

"*I want three girls. We can adopt one, then you and I could each—*"

"*You can have the girls,*" I replied. "*I want one son. To carry my name.*"

"Your name? *What about my name?*"

I tried to sign, "*You have a white name,*" but based on Shane's expression, I must have gotten one of the words wrong.

"*WHITE.*"

"Ugggggh! *HARD.*"

"*So hard,*" he replied, but he wasn't referring to a difficulty. "I thought we were talking surnames."

I grinned. Shane flexed his fingers and I noticed a familiar golden band on his ring finger, which was an unfamiliar placement. It gave me a weird itch in the corner of my jaw.

"Isn't that ring usually on the other hand?"

Shane glanced down, glaring as if he'd been betrayed. It took a moment for him to relax his expression, and he chuckled before taking the ring off and moving it to his right hand.

"I must have been out of it this morning."

I scratched at my jaw. This was new.

"Shane?"

"We're separated."

He looked up into my eyes.

"Haven't been together in months. She and I—"

This lifted me straight off the bed and I pressed my back against the door to my closet.

"She?

Shane rose as if to console me, but I put my hand out to hold him off.

"Hey, hey," he spoke softly. "I was going to tell you, I just didn't know how. Please. Don't be upset."

My chest rose and fell as I took in oxygen, hoping that some of it would reach my brain.

"Upset? Of course I'm upset. You're a 1900s closet case and I'm an idiot for the ages."

He grabbed me, pulling me close.

"I'm not a closet case and you're not an idiot. Let's talk about this, babe."

We never talked about it. The truth can be a bogeyman and if you don't feel safe with it, you might be able to settle for being comfortable without it.

• • • • • • •

I saw Patrick's devilish, glinting teeth coming from a mile away. I had seen him a few times since the night I used Shane to avoid him, but ever since my relationship with Shane had become non-fiction, I didn't mind talking to him. Something about his barely concealed bitterness fed my spirit.

"Hey, Zario. Can I get you a shot?"

"I don't think so, Patrick," I declined sweetly. "I'm here with my boyfriend."

"Is that so? You two are still..." Patrick said, almost snarling. "Where is he?"

I felt a familiar warm arm drape across my shoulders.

"He's right here," Shane said, kissing me.

"Well, well, well," Patrick said brightly, raising his eyebrows. "Maybe I'll buy you both a drink. Shane, since you're dating Zario, I'm sure you're familiar with the rule of three."

Shane shook his head. "No thanks."

"I mean, babe," I said. "It is a free drink. Let Patrick be good for something for once."

Patrick laughed. "I guess it wouldn't be shade if I wasn't present to be cooled by the shadow."

"That's called a read, baby," I said to him. "There's no point in throwing shade at you because you wouldn't catch it."

"Oh, I caught everything you pitched," he said, eyes unblinking. "Remember?"

"Careful with the sports references; you might slip into your old persona."

"We wouldn't want that, would we? I'd be prime butch competition for Mr. Assjock of the Month here?"

Shane's arms slid from around my shoulders and he gripped my hand instead. When I looked at him, he was peering at Patrick, a twitch happening in his jaw that I was sure my ex could not detect.

"Look," Shane sighed. "I know I've made the mistake of being congenial with you, but since you've summoned me, it feels like the perfect time to level set. Now, I'm not into wordplay or this battle of wits you have going on, so let me tell you plain. If you fix your mouth to say something else disparaging about my boyfriend or dare to mention me again, I'm just gonna straight beat your ass."

The bartender dropped off the two shots Patrick ordered, eyeing Shane carefully. I smiled at him reassuringly before turning back to the men who flanked me.

"Heard," Patrick said. "Let's drink to that, Zario."

Minutes later, I was following Shane out onto the sidewalk in front of the club.

"What, Shane? Why are you acting like this? It was one drink. You had already made your point with him!"

He spun on me and I saw Sally Field in a black dress with a white handkerchief fluttering in her hand. *Are you high, Clairee?*

Something had definitely died.

"I'm sick of this shit!" he said to me, and our messy reality became very three dimensional and loud and the preening queens on the walk were staring.

"Oh?" I rushed to move in front of him. "You're sick of this? You don't think I am?"

He spun, down the alleyway beside the club.

"Whenever we're out, I'm sick of you flirting with everybody! Always!"

What the fuck? This was new.

"Wow. 'Everybody.' 'Always?' Hyperbole is not the only way to make a credible point."

"You know what the fuck I mean!"

"I don't know, and I don't appreciate you cussing at me."

"Oh, grow up."

"Where is all of this coming from?" In my head I could hear Jay talking about his last conversation with Callie. *Why do I feel like you changed the channel on me just now?*

"Taking shots with your ex? Being all flirtatious with him?"

I wanted to deescalate, so I pressed my hands together and touch my lips to my fingers.

"Is this because he's my ex, or because he had my attention?"

Shane sputtered. "Both."

We've moved away from the crowd and lines now, standing in the reflective liquids on the black concrete between the buildings, while employees on their smoke breaks pretended to ignore us.

"Can I not talk to people, Shane? Do you have to keep me to yourself? I can't keep you to myself."

I could see that stung. I meant for it to.

"Oh that's rich," Shane said quietly. "What did he mean by the rule of three?"

I inhaled sharply before I could stop myself. "That was before."

"Before what? Before me? I get that it was before me. I want to know *what* it was."

"Patrick and I used to have threesomes at the beginning of our relationship. Like all the time."

"He made you?"

I'm silent.

"You made him?"

"He wasn't crazy about it, but he did them because I asked him to."

"Why wasn't he crazy about them?"

"I don't want to talk about him, Shane."

"Why wasn't he crazy about them?" Shane asked me again.

I crossed my arms over my chest, feeling exposed. Feeling stripped.

I swallow hard. "They were women. We had threesomes with women. I was still trying to figure shit out, so I felt like less of an abomination if there was a woman in the bed with us. I could still spin it as an experiment. I think he held that grudge against me for the rest of our relationship."

"I can't believe you," Shane says, and the words sliced through the air and I had reopened wounds. "You made your boyfriend fuck women and you've got an issue with me having a wife?"

I came back roaring. "Those two things do not have an equal sign between them. You're fucking married! You're cheating daily with me, betraying some innocent woman who has no idea about us."

"Fuck you," he whispered. "You don't know my story."

"You need to face your shit, Shane, since you wanna talk your shit." I clapped my hands together, feeling rage I hadn't felt since I left home. "Let's go. Let's do this."

"Oh, we're facing shit? I don't know if you're up to the task. You're twenty-four years old, you can barely pay your bills, talking a big game about photography and artistry and career plans, when your photographs are so shit that the only jobs you get are the ones I have to beg my friends to give you! Face that."

Everything in me tightened and pulled. My nails dug into my palms as my hands squeezed into fists. My eyes grew so big that I was worried they'd roll out of my skull. My teeth clenched down too quickly, drawing blood from the sides of my tongue.

He shook his head slowly. "I didn't bring you into my life just so I'd have to deal with *two* bitches. Fuck that."

I felt the tears dropping down my cheeks from the physical pain and the emotional rage and I still couldn't close my eyes.

So I spun on my heels and marched back to the sidewalk.

"Zario," he called from behind me, but he wasn't following me. "Babe."

I couldn't stay and listen to any more. I refused to. The moment someone showed who they were, you had to believe them. You couldn't make the mistake of thinking it was a random one-off.

In that moment, Shane was possessive, judgmental, and verbally abusive, so that moment was the last one I was willing to give him.

Ellington and Sunji picked me up three blocks away. As soon as I got in the car, I fell apart.

• • • • • • • •

The weeks passed and a day came where the Dudes did what dudes sometimes have to do. They didn't tell me at the time, of course. I can't blame them.

Ellington was out on the porch relaxing, shirtless for the benefit of all the passing eyes. He noticed Shane before Shane noticed him, and he stood, moving quickly to the top of the steps.

"Hold up, man. I'm gonna have to ask you not to step on my friend's porch."

Shane looked up from the bouquet of flowers in his hand. Paused. "I'm here to see Zario."

Ellington waved him away with a dismissive hand. "I gathered as much. You can stay your drama-loving ass on the sidewalk with all the other weeds."

Shane took a step up. Ellington took a step down. Shane smartly didn't move any further.

"Can you at least tell him I'm here?"

"No."

"Can you—"

"Can you get off of my porch?"

The front door opened and Sunji and Alexander stepped out, trying to look menacing and finding different levels of success. Shane stepped back involuntarily, then held up the flowers.

"Will you give him these?"

"He's got better buds," Sunji said, scowling comically. "Us. Not because we're flowers. Because we're his friends. Like bud-dies."

Shane was already walking away. "I get it."

Alexander watched him leave, but spoke to Sunji. "Bud-dies?"

Jay was asleep when Shane came by. When he heard about it, he raged, as he's wont to do. He had an overabundance of opinions, thoughts, fists, but not the space to enact any of them. And that's when he decided to get me out of the bed.

"It smells like sharted dreams and cumdust in here."

"Go away," I shouted hoarsely from my bed.

"Rise and shine, Zario," he said, kicking his way through all the mess scattered on my carpet. "It's not good to wallow so long. Shane's a jackass, but you never should have dated him."

"This is why I said, go away. You don't get it."

"I don't get it?" He sat down next to me. "Actually, it smells like piss and tequila in here. Have you been pissing in here?"

I grumbled.

"What?"

"In the bottles. In the tequila bottles."

"That explains how you've been going so long without leaving you room." He said this softly and, even though he seems determined to avoid showing judgement, I felt ashamed anyway.

"I didn't want to see any of you."

"How'd you get the tequila?"

"I'd go out when you guys were at the gym and Alexander was gaming."

Jay nodded. "I'm surprised you haven't turned to jerky."

My cracked lips said otherwise.

"I got a heartbreak story for you," he said then, laying a hand on my thigh. "When I was nineteen, I met a girl named Hurricane. True story. I called her Ricki. I think we fucked within hours of talking. Sorry if that sounds crass. We met at the Promenade and talked so long, we decided to make it official and had a meal. Next thing I know, I'm walking her to her car then we're both in the car and... I mean, I already said it. We met again a few days after and the attraction was just as strong if not stronger.

"I found out she was married about two weeks in and I didn't care. He was some jag off in the Air Force and, man, she and I were feeling each other. So literally. She could do this thing with her fingers when she positioned them like this—"

He combined three—THREE!—fingers and started poking at my butt. Without going into too much detail, he definitely pinned the tail on the donkey, so I swatted his arm away.

"Is this just a tangent or are you torturing me to death?"

He was quiet for a moment. "She got pregnant. Her husband found out about us and beat her until she miscarried. I bought us tickets to Portland, and she promised to meet me at the airport. I got a text message from her instead."

"What did it say?"

"'We decided to work it out.' That's it. No disclaimers. No profession of love or shame. Just the perfect pocket encapsulation of what our relationship had always been and always would be if we had continued."

I heard something in his voice that I didn't recognize, and when I looked up, he was wiping a tear away.

He sniffed. "So. I know all about sharted dreams and cumdust."

He stood, holding his hand out to me.

"Let's get you out of this room, Zee."

• • • • • • •

I don't tell Eagle the details of Jay's story and I leave out Alexander's digital detective work where he verified that Shane was definitely still married and absolutely no divorce paperwork had been filed. I'm sure she's been filled in on the specifics of why the guys at home hate Shane, and besides, I'm losing my voice after hollering over the music for so long. I had never told her my side of things, let alone told her this much about me.

I do tell Oscar goodbye when Eagle and Rock offer to drive me home and I feel a small amount of guilt about leaving him once we reach our street.

"I hope Oscar gets home okay."

Eagle laughs as she parks. "He's gonna dance until they kick him out. I'm sorry that he was so oblivious to the fact that you weren't having a good time."

"He's gonna swear this was the best date of his life," Rock cackles from the backseat.

"At least one of us can say that."

"We showed up and made it better," Eagle says. "So technically, we win, right?"

I laugh and thankfully the Diolosas join me.

As we walk down the sidewalk, husband and wife linked at the elbow, Eagle turns to look at me.

"Is it fair for me to say that I'm still learning you?"

"Just like it's fair for me to say I'm not an easy course."

"I get certain chapters," she says, and I think about how we're not better friends.

"The Shane chapter makes everything that comes after pretty skewed, so I don't blame you."

"Yeah, but you're you. You're not skewed. You existed before you knew Shane."

"It doesn't always feel that way."

Rock speaks now, thoughtfully. "I believe that the specificity of your existence requires there to be a specificity in your intention."

"I don't have any sort of intention right now."

"Find some!" Eagle says. "And I don't mean in these booty boys we've been setting you up with. Individual."

Rock repeats, "Specificity."

Eagle nods. "Run away from all this if you have to."

Her husband squints up at her. "Run away?"

"Okay, my word choice sucks right now! I mean, go where the love is."

I look between the two of them. "I feel like I should be high for this conversation."

"Rock's high enough for all of us, trust me."

"She ain't lying," he says, giggling and hiccuping and still managing words.

"What's your real name?" I ask her when we arrive at the base of Sunji's steps.

"What's yours?"

"Hector."

"Shit." Her face looks like she just read a horrific news report. "I wasn't expecting you to answer. If I lose the bet, I'll tell you."

Rock's eyes have grown huge, and he makes a sound like, "Ooop!"

"You're definitely losing," I tell her.

Eagle laughs. "You better hope so."

We hug. Her husband and I bump fists.

"Sleep deep," she says as Rock begins to tug her away.

"Count your blessings instead of sheep," they finish, more or less in unison.

I walk up the steps reflecting on my dates with Mick and Oscar. When Shane left, it really felt like the end of my world, but as the old quote says, what the caterpillar calls the end of the world, the Master calls the butterfly. I wonder if all of this is my chrysalis.

I open the door and Jay is waiting for me in the hallway with a teacup, which means he was watching through the window as Eagle and Rock dropped me off. Sunji is juggling bananas to my left in the kitchen, and Ellington and Alexander are doing something weird and unidentifiable to each other in the dining room on my right. All four of them cheer when they see me and soon I'm buried in hugs and questions.

We spend so much time seeking out romantic love when so few of our amorous partners ever compare to the platonic friends who we keep close for years. Some friendships are ridiculously romantic and tender while others can be fiercely passionate and I have both in this house. I try to imagine finding someone who's going to defend my honor, nourish and nurse me, provide support, listen to my stories, check on me, and literally fight for me like each of these four will and do, even without request. I marvel at how they love me because they want to.

It's unfathomable when you reduce it to its basics. They've observed me and all of my idiosyncrasies and faults, determining through some independent system that none of my deficiencies are too much of an inconvenience.

I'm surrounded by an incalculable amount of love in this place and I am forced to confront the paradox that is platonic intimacy.

All that they give me is still not enough.

All-American

Jay pulls me between his legs so forcefully that I worry the counter's about to bruise my hips.

"You're lucky I put my plate down," I admonish him, holding my hands above my shoulders almost in fear of where they might land.

"Here. I'm not going to finish this." He forks a large chunk of shamrock-colored pork into my mouth.

"The color doesn't help," I say as I chew.

"The color does not help," he agrees, scooping more greenery onto his fork. "Here."

He crams more meat into my mouth, before finishing the last bit himself.

Sunji enters, shirt tucked, shirt only halfway buttoned. I know this look. It says, business, but look at my chest.

While I size up Sunji, he's doing the same to Jay and I.

"What are you two doing?"

Before I can step back, Jay locks his ankles behind my back.

"Zario was just showing me how easy it is for him to counter-fuck at his height." He starts to pant, lifting his hips and grinding away. To Sunji he asks, "You want to tap me out, butt-slut?"

I pry myself free and watch as Jay's face falls immediately into disinterest. From sixty to negative ten, with barely the shrug of a shoulder.

"Thanks for breakfast," I say to Sunji, pointing to Jay's empty plate.

Sunji's eyes brighten. "How'd you like the green eggs and ham?"

"The omelette was wicked," Jay says, belching an 8.7.

I agree less rudely. "Steamed rice and green pepper pesto filling, dude? That's a yes, a yep, and an absolutely."

The remarkable thing about Sunji Spencer is that of all the things his brain struggles to retain, he has no problem recalling every dish he's ever made or witnessed being created. Every time he cooks breakfast, it's something brand new or a delicious twist on a familiar favorite.

Jay, though, is notoriously picky. "Did you have to make the ham green, too?"

Sunji's frown deepens. "It's green in the book."

Jay sucks his teeth. "Yeah, but in real life, green ham looks…"

"It's green in the book."

"Got it."

"A doctor wrote that book, Jay."

"*Got it.*" He takes in Sunji in full for the first time. "Why are you dressed like you're going to go breastfeed a librarian?"

"I'm meeting with that director today over lunch. This is the look that says I can sell everything."

I can see Jay biting back jokes, and I'm impressed when all he says, "Fuck it up, yo."

Sunji juts out his jaw. "That's kind of a jerk thing to say. You should want me to do well."

Jay looks at me in confusion, then turns back to Sunji. "That's what I mean. Like, fuck it up. Shove your dick in. Full thrust."

Sunji's eyebrows rise in direct correlation with his level of being offended. "My talent got me this meeting, Jay, not my dick."

I lay a hand on Sunji's arm. "He means break a leg."

Sunji's face relaxes. "Oh. Thank you."

Jay is bewildered. "You get 'break a leg' but you don't get 'fuck it up?'"

Ignoring Jay, Sunji points to me. "Am I still dropping you off?"

"Holy shit, yeah! Give me five minutes. Lemme grab my camera."

"Fuck me later?" Jay asks.

"It's a date," I say as I run out of the kitchen.

I hear Sunji grumble to Jay, "That's the last time I make you a Beginner's Breakfast."

Sunji and Ellington have worked their connections to get me a gig with this podcaster who they know, a guy known for his blunt opinions and has apparently said some insensitive things about Asian representation and is now in essence doing an apology tour from his living room.

The drive to the podcaster's spot in Lincoln Heights is long enough for Sunji to share with me about the movie he's meeting about, but I don't retain much of it. Sunji, eternally hopeful, hasn't had much luck when it came to turning his good looks into acting gigs, and it's painful to see him get hyped for another project that might fall through like the others.

He idles in his car as I walk up to the giant metal gate of the apartment complex with my camera bag hugging my armpits. The bright, sunny courtyard of the complex opens up on the other side of the gate and I'm struck at how there are places like this in LA, with beautiful settings and architecture, and none of the residents enjoy it. Sure, they pay for the splendor, but they're either in their apartments or out and about at jobs or in traffic. It's backwards, really.

I stand beneath the giant letters spelling out "Puerta del Sol," and before I can scan the listed names and buzz the intercom, a balding Black man with a wild beard waves at me from the other side of the courtyard. He power walks to the gate, squinting at me.

"You're Ellington and Sunji's guy, right?"

I nod. "Zario."

"Great." He pulls the gate—the sun gate—open. "Kito. Come on in."

Sunji honks and Kito peers out to the street.

"Hey, sweetness!" he hollers at the car and Sunji honks again before driving off.

"What a great guy," Kito says, securing the gate. "Nothing between those ears, though."

He motions for me to follow him and we move through the courtyard's lush greenery and circular benches. The yellow building surrounds us, towering on all sides.

"How many stories?" I ask him.

He looks up, then around and I can tell he doesn't remember. "I think five."

He leads me to the elevator. "I would have just buzzed you up, but everyone gets lost their first time here, so it's easier for me to come get them."

In the elevator I ask, "How many other people are coming?"

"Three guys," Kito answers, looking over at me. "This'll just be some promo footage for me to shove up on my website and blog about later. Ellington gave me your rates. I'm surprised you weren't already booked, as good as they were."

I just smile. He doesn't need to know how my ex-boyfriend shook my confidence and now I am taking every job I can find in an effort to pay for classes and get better and better and even better still.

We arrive on the third floor and step into the hallway. After two turns, I'm already lost. I understand why it was easier for him to head down instead of have me come up.

"Wanna blaze up before the guys get here?" Kito asks me. "Talk existentialism and shit?"

I grin at the offer. "I'll pass. I wanna be good for the shoot."

"Getting high *is* good for the podcast," he cracks. "It's called *Kush Points with Kito*. It's lit."

Inside Kito's apartment, I spend several minutes staring at the artwork on his walls. One striking image of yellow, blue, black, and red depicts a large smiley face under a crown.

"That's a Basquiat," I say, impressed.

"It's a poster of a Basquiat," Kito clarifies, already lighting up. "That was the first thing I bought for this place."

"I don't recognize the rest of these."

"That's because I painted them. And I am no Basquiat."

"They're good!" I turn to him. "You're an artist?"

He chuckles. "That depends on your connotation. I make shit."

"You make good shit."

He exhales, grinning. "And that's why some people call me an artist."

The setup is simple: one table, four microphones, and loads of pot in the form of blunts, joints, bowls, and vapes. I turn down his second offer to partake, but I do accept a water. He leaves three separate times to bring the guests up, and I begin taking photos the moment the first one settles in.

His name is Gregory, and I recognize him as a one-time guest star on one of my favorite supernatural soaps, *Fang Wars*, where he played a student at an all-boys boarding school in Moonlight Cove that turned out to be a coven for hot, frequently-shirtless warlocks. I resist the urge to talk his ear off about filming for the show. Thai, lanky, and soft-spoken, he giggles at the weed and says he'll have a little once everyone else is there.

The second arrival is Elijah, who is Filipinx, packing a canister of edibles, and painfully attractive. At first I don't recognize him, but when he lists all of the series he's been in, I remember him from a few, especially his arc on *Fang Wars*. (He played a doomed vampire in love with a female werewolf, both of them on the run from Van Helsing's descendants and stopping in Moonlight Cove where the werewolf had family.) He winks at me, which means he's straight. He apologizes to Gregory because, he says, he's already faded.

Samuel is the last to get there and he's loud and quick-witted. He's also Filipinx and he tells me that he was a last-minute replacement for the East Asian Sunji, who had to pull out because of his meeting. Elijah and Gregory are trying to get the very role that the director seems interested in Sunji for. I get the feeling that Sunji's lunch is a legitimate big deal this time.

"So you got two Pacific Islanders here talking about Asian American representation," Samuel bellows to Kito, handing out beers from the case he's brought. "You're off to a great start."

They're laughing and joking like old friends within minutes, and by the time the THC and beers start hitting, they're on another level.

Kito's right. It is lit.

Gregory is speaking now. "They act as if our names are difficult to pronounce, but they can roll out a Schwarzenegger and everyone just adapts."

"White people have the funkiest names," Samuel adds. "Mia Wasikowska? Saoirse Ronan? Chloë Sevigny? And they get tripped up by Ki Hong Lee or Quvenzhané."

Kito shakes his head. "Why are we talking about white people? I'm trying to get the experiences of you as Asian actors."

"That's just it, Kito," Gregory replies. "Our experience is affected by white people. We're cast by white people. White people write the roles we play."

"And that's a problem," Elijah chimes in, "because white people aren't engineered to see us as peers."

"What do you mean, Elijah?" Gregory asks.

"In school, historical figures of color are taught and displayed as relics of a bygone era. Especially if they're American POCs. Mostly they're nameless, or they're filtered through the white gaze. So they see us as representations of said relics. Meaning we're not important or impactful because we're not *now*. That's why Hollywood has trouble recognizing or honoring us in contemporary roles. They can only see us as the help, or the immigrants, or shitfuck like that. And if a role is described as 'all-American'—"

Samuel shakes his head. "Don't even check for it."

"Don't even check for it," Elijah echoes.

"Cuz they sure as sin ain't checkin for someone with melanin in their skin," Gregory says.

"Kito," Elijah continues, "I can't even tell you what your struggle is, because that's not taught, so I'm immune to your pain and indifferent to your story. But we see white people every day on our screens and in our books. We're taught to identify with them and we spend the rest of our lives living with the repercussions of that."

Samuel points the vape in his hand. "You know, I disagree! Come on, Elijah, it's just entertainment. Instead of watching *Friends*, watch *Living Single*."

"That's just a life rule," Kito interjects.

"And now there's *Dr. Ken* and Hudson Yang's sitcom," Samuel continues. "And it's not like we don't have certain privileges of our own."

"To be fair, Samuel," Kito says, "having 'certain privileges' doesn't amend the fact that Asian Americans are underrepresented in media."

Samuel sets the vape down and points with both of his index fingers. "Follow me on this, Kito. We're all able-bodied straight males."

Gregory speaks now. "Eh…"

I pause. Samuel sucks his teeth.

"Oh, Gregory, come on. If you're thinking about Bryan Singer's pool party with all the dudes puckered and peckered, I almost got a role as an X-Man. I was too brown, though. I got kicked out, actually. To be honest, I hadn't been invited."

"Ew." Gregory's eyes cut to me. "I wasn't talking about Bryan Singer's 'private screenings.'"

Kito grabs his microphone, speaking directly into it. "Fellas, I'm trying to leave controversies in the past!"

"What I meant is," Gregory continues, "I'm not straight. So already your assumption of privilege is faulty. And why should we think that just because we have privilege in one area, we can't look for improvements in others?"

Elijah speaks now, seeming as if he's parachuted in from another plane of existence. "Because we've been fooled into thinking we an only focus on one act of injustice at a time. The gender wage gap, or gay representation, or the struggle of POCs. Also, I'm high as fuck right now."

"Yeah, I'm losing my grip, too," Kito laughs. "Let's wrap up with our final Kush Points. Elijah."

"If all the roles white people were getting were mass murderers and corrupt cops," Elijah says, "they'd be the first ones to jump on board with the concept of diverse storytelling."

"Gregory."

Gregory shrugs his shoulders just as I snap a photo. Definitely using that one.

"My revolution will be intersectional or it won't be my revolution."

"Holy shit," Elijah says in approval. "Put that on a shirt."

"Samuel."

"Final point?" Samuel asks. "We need an Asian *Living Single*. And cast me, dammit."

• • • • • • • •

Ellington waits on the sidewalk next to his car. There's movement in the passenger seat that comes from either Mandy or Marshall and I dread discovering which one it is.

Kito pats me on the back as he opens the gate. "Your shots were dope, man. Feel free to come back every week if you want. Let's make it happen."

I grin. A steady gig. No such thing, but it would be fun to pretend for a bit. "Yeah, man, that sounds cool. Thanks again!"

"Fuck, I meant to ask you on the way down, what did you think? Any thoughts?"

I wrap my thumbs around my backpack straps and bounce on the balls of my feet.

"I did actually. I think it's nice that you brought in men from the AAPI community and let them share their experiences, but I think you would have had a more well-rounded discussion if you had involved Asians who aren't male? Or cisgender? You had Gregory there repping for queer voices, but you didn't even know he was queer before he said it during the conversation. I think as marginalized men, we have a duty to step up for those who are even more marginalized than us. And if you're passing the mic, Kito, you're responsible for who you do and do not pass it to."

Kito's surprised expression has held on his face during my entire rambling speech and now he nods once, and blinks many times. "Well. I gotta process that. Thanks, Zario."

I smile uncomfortably, positive my return invitation will be rescinded.

Kito waves to Ellington, who tosses up a peace sign, then brings his fingers to his mouth and flicks his tongue between them. Kito doubles over with laughter as he heads back across the courtyard.

I bounce over to my roommate.

"Hello Ellington," I greet him.

"Wuzzup, sexy," he says, giving me a hug. "Wanna put your bag in the trunk?"

"No, it's cool."

"Hi, Zario." It's from the passenger seat. Marshall, thank God.

"Hi, you beautiful man."

"Stop flirting with my brother and get in the back," Ellington says, climbing into the car himself. "Wanna grab some burgers?"

"Yes! The answer is always yes."

I set my back on the seat be side me and close the door.

Ellington looks at his brother. "Marshall, you hungry?"

"We should probably get to Zario's place." The younger Gomez waves his phone at me. "Zario, check your messages."

I pull out my phone and begin scrolling. "Oh, God."

Ellington recognizes my tone. "A spider."

"Yeah."

To Sunji, spiders were from the fifth dimension of hell. A war had broken out at the house. Sunji, Jay, and Alexander versus what they claimed was a giant arachnid.

I skim over the group thread. "Sunji's trying to burn the kitchen down. Are you not getting these?"

"I muted the thread when Eagle and Jay started cracking proposal jokes yesterday."

I nod. It had gotten brutal, but I certainly had found the conversation hilarious.

Marshall is confounded. "Sunji hates spiders that much?

"It's not hatred," I say.

Ellington buckles in and cranks the ignition. He and I speak together.

"It's fear."

When we arrive at the house, Ellington knows better than to come in. He promises me an owed burger before he and Marshall drive off.

I'm the one that kills the spider—there would be no rest in the house until it was dead. Sunji drops the remains of the spider on the front porch.

"So all your friends will know," he says.

Jay peers from a position of safety over Sunji's shoulder. "Yeah, you eight-legged bitch."

Mac 'n' Cheese Nocturne

The black of pitch in my room is corrupted by a fissure of light and a body squeezes through the doorway. Seconds later, Jay whisper-yells my name and I'm lucid.

"What's up?"

"Genie just texted."

"Context. Or I'm going back to sleep while you go back to your Aladdin fanfiction."

Jay sighs, sitting on my bed, pressing his back against my thighs. I sense him playing with the corner of my comforter. "My cousin. Eugene. He's in town."

Jay's mentioned the cousin he was raised with many times in the past, though whenever he's ripped through town in the middle of the night, I've only found out about it the day after.

"That's great."

Jay doesn't leave.

"He's down the street, actually. I told him to come over. He's only in LA for a few hours on his way to Mexico. Sit with us, please?"

"Why do you need me?"

"Come on, Zario."

Too late I realize my question isn't exactly fair. We need what we need when we need it, and, as I friend, even sleepiness shouldn't have made me so resistant.

Jay sighs and offers an explanation anyway.

"I don't like being around family by myself. I usually have a girl with me when he pops in like this."

"You'll bring me Chego three times next week?"

"Deal. And tonight I already ordered your other favorite."

I sit up. "Jalapeño popper mac 'n' cheese?"

I can sense his smile in the darkness. "And Nashville hot chicken. You always forget about the chicken."

"Because I only care about the jalapeño popper mac 'n' cheese."

"For someone who only cares about the mac 'n' cheese, you sure do eat a lot of that chicken."

"Don't judge me."

"Well, get dressed because the mac 'n' cheese is getting here with my cousin in about fifteen minutes."

"Fifteen? And you're just now waking me up?"

"He just told me ten minutes ago! He called me to put in the order."

Now I sigh, laying back down. "Okay. Just let me find my brain and I'll be right there."

"Find your brain?"

I toss my hips, signaling for him to get off my bed, but he presses the issue instead.

"What do you mean, find your brain?"

"Fine. If you must know, I was having that dream I have about Rock, so my blood flow—"

"Got it!"

Jay hops off the bed. Another crack of brightness and he's gone.

• • • • • • •

The first time I ever found Jay attractive, like a "he could get it" attraction, was brought on by one of his mid-night moods.

A few months after I moved in, he woke me up after returning from an early night in K-Town.

"I just fell asleep," I warned him, but he leapt on top of me anyway.

"What do you have going on tomorrow?"

"Nothing."

"Then we got something going on tonight," he said shoving my face into my pillow. "Come on, let's drink my money."

It's as if he pulled me by the dick because suddenly we were in the kitchen, where he had shot glasses lined up on the counter, with two large glasses of beer waiting in the middle.

"You take each shot as quickly as you can, from the outside in, and you don't stop until the beer glass is empty."

I start counting the glasses. "You're trying to fuck me up!"

"Of course," he grins. "You ready? The drinks get stronger as you get closer to the center."

"Then I'm not ready."

"Why are you breathing heavy? Don't be so dramatic."

The first shot tasted like death, and went down like someone clawing to life for fear of dying. I knew that if they got stronger from here, I'd be pissing out my tastebuds within a few hours. But the next shot was smooth, thick and sweet, a perfect compliment. I watched Jay pacing himself with me, his cheeks pink. Of course he'd already been drinking. At least he hadn't told me to catch up because we both knew that would prove impossible. What would count me out on any given night would just get his engine revving.

The third shot was spicy, and I realized he had taken the time to mix these. The fourth shot tasted like nothing, while the final shot was thick like molasses, and left a flavor of rust and sap on my tongue. The beer was a fantastic chaser. We chugged, and there things shifted to my favor.

"How'd you drink that so fast?" he asked me.

"My throat opens and I take it. I'm gay," I laughed.

"No, that ain't it," he said.

I pointed. "You tried to kill me with that first one."

"Overproof. You're about to have a good fucking night."

Overproof? Holy shit. "And a terrible fucking morning."

"If you're awake in the morning, I didn't do my job."

"I always wake up early when I drink."

"Not when you drink with me," he said, and I was struck at how everything he said is like he's the troublemaking student in a John Hughes film. Though if he was Bender, the only person I could be is Duckie. Fictional cinematic history rarely made room for gay youth. Looking at Jay's face, hearing him shout some Korean at me—about how he's going to turn me into a real boy, which I think was heteronormative at best and homophobic at its worst implications—and me replying in Spanish—about how I'm a man, not a boy, and he's barely a sperm—I thought about the one time John Hughes gave a role of substance to a person of color. The world was better off without Long Duk Dong.

We weren't Bender and Duckie at all. We were Jay and Zario. Someone should have made a movie about guys like us.

He tried to wrestle with me, but I shut him down. I had my limits. That testosterone shit made no sense to me. Plus, all I'd have to do was sit on him.

He wanted to show me pictures next. "This lady" had taken them, and he wanted to know what I though.

I thought they were beautiful. They were a series of shots featuring Jay in a bathtub, soaking in milky, coruscant water, annoyed, amused, then adorned by ever-shifting iridescent bubbles. It was garish and dingy and simple, the way the foam gripped his hips while leaving his butt cheeks on display. How the liquid shifted back and forth from pearlescent to just murky. The froth was glittery, then oily, and back again. Here and there the body was out of focus, while the bubbles flared like a sequined disco. In each picture Jay took on a different persona, one of the endless facets of mood and energy that I had become acquainted with, if not accustomed to.

His body was beautiful, with his massive muscles coated in a layer or two of fat. He always has impressive dimensions, but never any definition—he eats and drinks far too well for that. He never calls attention to it, but it's apparent how he feels about his body whenever he gets around Sunji or Ellington. It takes a near miracle for him to even go shirtless around them, but in those pictures, he wasn't covered in anything but a diminishing amount of bubbles. No shame or self-awareness. Thinking in this one, telling a smutty story in that one, laughing and falling and concealing his dick in this set.

"You hate them," he said and I realized I hadn't spoken. When I looked up, it was clear he knew I didn't hate them. "Send them to yourself."

"What are you going to do with them?"

"Nothing," he said.

"Is she going to do something with them?"

"Oh no, I deleted them from her camera while she was asleep. I'm gonna delete these, too, but if you want them, get them now."

"Why'd you delete them?"

"I told her that pictures are extra and pay is upfront. And she got me in this bathtub and started taking pictures, so…"

Looking back on this night, I'm positive that this is the first time he opened up to me about his job, but I didn't ask any more questions at the time, sure that he'd shut down.

"If you want to take pictures of me," he said, pouring us each a large glass of milk stout, "you don't have to pay me."

"Good, because I don't have anything to pay you with."

"Don't be so sure," he said, grabbing for my tummy, and after the giggling quelled and the humor subsided, he was still holding me.

His skin, flushed from liquor and laughter, glimmered like the bubbles in the picture. I took in the sequined disco of his face, those impossibly plump lips, those eyes that were so warm on a face so practiced at being cold.

He had me gripped tight and I wriggled to get loose. He pulled me closer and then we were dancing. Reckless movement, liquored laughter, sequined disco. One of those inscrutable moments where a relationship became certifiable. Acquaintances became friends, friends became besties. Here was where Jay and Zario became Jay *and* Zario, his fingers into me, my steps moving his. Jay and Zario sleeping in late because we were up all night on some ill-advised adventure. Jay and Zario off exploring the K-Town spots that wouldn't close until four, or would serve us right at two just because Jay could sweet talk the owner, respectfully of course. Out riding in Jay's car because Sunji pissed him off big about something small. Locked in my room because we tried some new edibles and now the world was painted in neon for him and made out of vegetables for me. Jay and Zario after too many drinks or too much bulgogi or too many donuts. His fingers into me, his laughter tuning mine.

Our experiences were cinematic. There was Jay driving down Wilshire in his obsidian sports car, visible only when reflecting the headlights from the surrounding traffic, or the neon illumination from restaurant windows. There I was waiting on the curb outside of

LACMA, lit up by joy and backlit by the Urban Light instillation of street lamps, glad he was close enough to pick me up. Hopping in the passenger seat like that girl from any movie with a guy like that in sunglasses like his.

Our dynamic was torrid. He'd cuss me out over some argument I was having with Shane if he thought I was letting my boyfriend get off easy. Sometimes he'd see the tears in my eyes and apologize. He'd always apologize with words first, which mattered so much in the long run.

"I'm an asshole," he'd remind me, "but I'm not trying to disrespect your feelings."

Only then would he present an offering of some sort. A joint. A movie. A drive to some new escapade. It was easy to forgive him. And he'd always focus on me with his unique frown. The corners of his lips never dug down. His mouth instead would lift toward his nose and his extended chin would dimple.

"I want to understand," he'd say, when he knew I had anchored my emotions in the high of marijuana or food or the wind coming through the passenger window of his convertible. "What is it that I'm missing about him?"

If I was up to it, and I usually was, I'd explain it and he would listen, which was dangerous, because the moment I contradicted myself during a later conversation, he'd call me on it and that might lead to another heated discussion.

"You're settling," he said once. "You always settle."

I don't mean to imply that our heart-to-hearts always turn into head-to-heads. Most of the time they turn into food or drinks or a marathon of my favorite movie sequels. Sometimes we dance, sometimes we sleep, but we never move too far from the "we" that had been created.

Thinking back on that night in the kitchen, I don't remember getting loose from his grip. Maybe he never let go.

· · · · · · ·

Watching Jay pace the kitchen floor, I realize I've never seen him nervous like this. I've picked up pieces of his past, but only those he's laid down with bright neon signs that read "clue here!"

He's already buzzed up his cousin, who is due to have some containers of deliciousness in tow, so I rush over to help with the bags the moment the door opens.

"Genie!"

"Jericho!"

I feel the breath ripped from my chest. Genie is beautiful. Hair, body, face. Dimples. When he grins at me, I know instantly that he knows he's beautiful and he can tell that *I* know.

"Come inside, man," Jay is saying, as my mouth flaps like a fish. "This is my roommate Zario. Never sleeps."

Sure. "Nice to meet you."

Genie's brown eyes are warm and surging with an electric current as he cups my face.

"Hello!" he says right into my mouth and I gulp his CO_2. Turning to Jay, he adds, "This one's an upgrade, Jericho."

Genie empties the contents of sweating plastic bags onto the kitchen counter, but my eyes don't even travel to the awaiting goodies. I have completely abandoned my plan to help in any capacity. I might just look at him.

Jay closes the door and I lean in to whisper, "Can this count as a date?"

His eyelids lower and he whispers back, "No."

"But you'd totally win if he was your pick."

He replies with the Dude mantra.

"Fuck outta here."

• • • • • • • •

Unbeknownst to us, Ellington has implemented Plan: Perfect Proposal across town. He returns to his apartment with Mandy in tow after a meticulously executed date. As he hangs their jackets, she sets their bags on his couch.

"I haven't had a night this perfect in a long time," Mandy says. "You really outdid yourself, babe."

He shrugs. "I don't know. That night we saw Ghostbusters was pretty epic."

She grimaces. "You know I hate slime."

"Leave your mother's cooking out of this." He smiles as she hits his arm.

"You always have seconds."

"Because you're my number one," he says, grabbing her and twisting into a deep, wet kiss. She strokes his back as she pulls away to look into his eyes.

"Let's fuck."

Ellington doesn't even translate the words at first. When he does, all of his thought processes begin to work in opposition.

His mouth moves and sound comes out. "What?"

She's certain. Sure. Her eyes haven't left his face. "We've proven our love to each other. We've been patient. Dedicated. Monogamous. Now let's get dirty."

"Mandy, I..."

"Filthy."

He's panicked. "Tonight..."

"Tonight," she repeats, grinning. "I want you inside me. Jungle style."

Even though Ellington doesn't know what the fuck "jungle style" means, he quickly becomes just the latest in a long line of examples that prove straight men can only resist so much.

· · · · · · · ·

I don't mean to pick on straight men too much (not like it's going to affect them any, let's be honest). Besides, gay men like me are quick to fall into traps as well.

Genie, Jay and I have gotten much more comfortable around the coffee table in our living room, with bellies full of Nashville hot chicken, jalapeño popper mac 'n' cheese, and milk punch, poured with Jay's choice rum and a premium bottle of bourbon.

"It makes sense he doesn't talk about me," Genie says from the floor. "He feels threatened. I mean, from the beginning we sucked the same titties. Not much has changed since then."

Also on the floor and opposite his cousin, Jay says only, "Oh God..."

"It was balanced though. We shared friends."

Jay shakes his head. "They were always your friends more than they were mine."

Genie leans toward me. "He was dating this girl named Chandelier, true story. He called her DeeDee and for similar and other obvious reasons I called her Double D."

"Behind her back," Jay adds. He breaks out into a wicked grin before touching his tongue to the right side of his upper lip. "Which was almost as nice as her front."

Genie starts telling a story about how DeeDee seduced him before he knew she had been sleeping with his cousin. "She dated us both for almost a full month before we figured it out."

I hug the cushions, enthralled. "Did you both dump her?"

Genie yields to his cousin and in turn Jay smacks loudly on whatever he's chewing.

Eventually he says, "We fought over who should dump her first, so both of us dated her for another month."

It's as if a rocket of laughter is set off up Genie's spine as his back arcs and laughter erupts from his throat, deep and thick, and his Adam's apple bounces across both of the hemispheres of his long throat.

Jay chuckles, eyes on his cousin.

Genie finally speaks, voice still cracking with cachinnation. "I felt that since he had gotten first dibs, I should get last dibs."

Jay throws a plastic straw at Genie. "There are no rules for such things."

Genie, dodging the straw, raises his hands in irreproachability.

"Well, there should be."

I look between them. "When was this? High school?"

Jay looks at me, eyebrows stitched together. "Three years ago."

Genie nods. "So, almost."

"But despite that, you guys are still close."

"There's a blood bond, sure, but there's a milk bond." Genie points to the drink in his glass.

"Kinda like a twin thing," Jay agrees.

"I can read him."

"And I can read the fuck outta him."

Pointing at each other across the table, they're like bookmarks. Genie's smile bringing levity to what feels like a darker source, while Jay's eternal frown masks the joy I sense from him having his cousin here.

"Whenever I swing through, I always give him a ring. One time I tried to sneak past and he called me."

"He was almost outta the San Fernando Valley, can you believe it?"

"I picked up the phone and he just said, 'Really? Fucker?'" Genie laughs, soul deep. "I can't stand this asshole."

Jay places a hand on my knee. "That's why I couldn't ignore his call this time. He'd know. Plus, I kind of wanted to see him."

Genie's eyes drift to Jay's hand. "Good to know it's possible for you to miss me."

"Naw, I wanted a refresher on how much better-looking than you I am."

Genie's eyes flicker, like when the brightness of a room changes so briefly that you can't tell if it was your imagination.

"Well, let's ask the expert," he says, and in unison they turn to me. Twin thing for-fucking-real.

"Expert of what?" I say, raising two unimpressed eyebrows.

"Which one of us would you date?" my friend asks me, in front of a complete stranger. "If you were DeeDee."

I lean back, hoping to disappear in the couch cushions. "Probably neither of you."

Genie adjusts the entire way he's sitting. I'm his full focus now, but it's for his cousin's benefit, I'm sure of it.

"Say you didn't know us," Genie says.

This is that bullshit.

"Which one of us would you want to date?" Genie asks.

Jay turns his body toward me as well, gas pedal stomped on. "Fuck a date. Which one of us would you want to sleep with? Get that Korean pipe all up in your guts."

He slaps his forearm into his hand, and his left eyebrow leaps up.

"I won't answer that, you fucking nasty ass."

Genie pats the air over the table as if calming a giant invisible baby. "Too far, too fast, cousin." His left eyebrow rises to match Jay's. "Throw us a bone, Zario, but not the kind Jericho was talking about. Which one of us would you probably look twice at while standing in line at the grocery store?"

I laugh, imagining either of them giving me this same energy as strangers in a grocery store.

"Am I still answering as DeeDee?"

"No," Genie says, "as you."

Easy. "Jay."

"Suck it, Genie. Why me?"

"I don't know," I lie. "You have an intensity about you that's, uh, magnetic, I guess."

Straight guys always do this. As if just any guy is attractive to their resident gay. Thing is, though, the guys who ask these fucking questions are usually busted, or I know enough about them to keep them from being even remotely attractive to me in any sober circumstance. But these two have the genetic pool of Korean Hemsworth brothers. I don't think I've ever seen smoother skin on anyone outside of Ellington. This slope is damn slippery.

To his credit, Genie won't let up. "Who's got the most intoxicating voice?"

"I mean, 'intoxicating' is such a strong word," I say.

"Answer it," Jay commands.

I lift my hand to ordain his cousin. "Yours, but that's probably because I don't hear it everyday." And yes, he sounds like his vocal cords drip honey, while Jay speaks like a hornet sting.

"Okay, who's got the best body?" Jay asks sharply, proving my point. They lean over the table in flattering positions, flexing.

Before they can get more ridiculous, I answer easily. "That's Jay."

"You sure about that?" Genie asks, removing his sweater.

Afraid that I gasped, I say, "Yes," as Jay rolls his eyes.

Genie smiles widely, his dimples diving deep into his cheeks, and shrugs. It takes a full moment for me to pull my eyes away from the curvature of his chest, the deep etches of his abdominals, the perfect spheres of meat trapped in his upper arms as they flex involuntarily.

Why is every night in this house like the beginning of a synopsis-lite porno?

When I do look away from our guest, Jay's eyes are pinned to mine before he too looks away.

I hear Genie ask, "Yeah, but who's got the cutest face?"

Jay twists his face into a comical supermodel pout. Genie furrows his brows and bites the insides of his cheeks.

"God. Neither."

"You have to pick!" Genie says.

"Well, Jay has the cheekbones, but you have the Mario Lopez dimples. So you win that round."

Jay moves on quickly. "Hair."

They start running their fingers through their hair and I sink deeper, in over my head.

• • • • • • •

Ellington's head is in other places, thrusting as if for an Olympic competition and sending Mandy into a delirious ecstasy. He had tried to eat her out for a solid set of minutes, but she was adamant that she wanted him to fuck her with more than his tongue.

It must be said that Mandy is not a virgin. Their abstinence hadn't originally started as some commitment addendum. She just wouldn't fuck him on the first several dates and when it came up in conversation, she acted like sex wasn't that important to her when it came to relationships and establishing a connection. All that may be true, but another truth is that Mandy is really good at what she does, and purring "Oh, Ellington," in to the pillow soon gave way to her own Olympic sporting disciplines like (wink, wink, nudge, nudge) equestrian jumping, pole vaulting, and rhythmic gymnastics.

Eventually, it's time for plunge for distance diving and also time for me to stop repeating his Olympic innuendoes. He lays her on her back and begins to plunge with an unrivaled speed and rhythm. Ellington doesn't mind artful, tender love-making, and he's quite skilled at it, but once he begins to orchestrate what he calls the "mac 'n' cheese nocturne"—named after the melodious and unbelievably intricate arrangement of noises he and his partner produce while slamming privates in his favorite position—his energy centralizes to plowing guts and obliterating walls.

"Oh, Ellington!" Mandy screams. "Yes! Yes! Yes!" And suddenly, her voice pushes out of her as if from the deepest portions of her diaphragm. "Slam me with that Black sausage!"

For a moment, he's thrown off of his rhythm.

What did she just say? he wonders. *Did she just? No… I've been watching too much porn while Django Unchained plays in the background. Shit. This girl has got me all the way turnt. You betta beat this shit up, Ellington. You betta show her how good this dick is—*

Aloud, he asks, "You like this dick?"

"Oh yeah, feed me more of that big, Black cock!"

Nope, naw she just did it again. The BBD shit, now was that necessary? This ain't no Mandingo dick! What the hell is she thinking right now?

"Babe, naw," he pants, "you're doing too much. Just call it a dick, baby."

"But it's so big!"

Hell yeah it is, he thinks. *I get it. I get that it's Black, too. And I know it's worth all these months of waiting…well on her part. But she don't see me over here saying, "wiggle that flat white ass" do she? Oh, she's so wet.*

"Yes, King!"

I'm hitting it right!

"Kong!"

Whathafu?

"Dong!"

"*I can't smash this anymore,*" he thinks, reducing all of his almost-fiancée to just her vagina. Then, "*Yes, I can. I can smash this forever.*"

That word. *Forever.* The girl he has envisioned spending the rest of his life with isn't even seeing him in that moment for who he was. She's created some Black male construct. She is realizing a fetish.

It's a terrible time for him to orgasm, but he comes anyway, his ecstasy battling shame and confusion.

"Oh yes, baby!" Mandy moans. "My ebony god. The Pipemaster."

He thinks about her stipulations. How she's mandated that he get his bachelor's degree before he can meet her parents.

This girl doesn't want me... She wants a back-aisle dildo with a wallet.

• • • • • • • • •

In the living room, we're doing a piss-poor job at staying quiet, which Jay suspected would happen. In the den, we'd be too close to the bedrooms, but in the living room, we were far enough away to prevent disturbing the house. We were spending more time figuring out what board games we wanted to play than we were actually playing any.

"I'm gonna go take a shit," Jay says, after we settle on Clue. I join them on the floor and begin setting up the board.

"Appreciate the knowledge," Genie says, as I disingenuously chirp, "Thanks!"

The moment Jay disappears into the darkness of the hallway, Genie turns to me, eyes deceptively muted.

"So, what's your deal? Jericho never lets me meet his friends. Just his girls, as some flaunting tactic."

"Really?" I try—and fail—to raise only my left eyebrow like they've been doing all night. "I don't typically get to meet his girls myself. I just hear the stories. Glimpse an occasional walk of shame."

Genie laughs, but it's protected. "How do you put up with him? You're a photographer? Are you all tortured artist and shit? Because my cousin is torture. And shit."

I laugh, unguarded. "You say that, but you care enough to swing by in the middle of the night just to yuk it up with him."

"'Yuk it up?'" he asks.

"Hyuck, hyuck, hyuck," I demonstrate, shoulders bouncing.

Genie nods, understanding. "There aren't enough people in the world who care about him like they should." The eyebrow pop. "That's you guys' deal, isn't it? Kindred spirits?"

I put my elbow on the coffee table and prop my chin in the presented palm. "You're so charming," I begin.

"Oh, *I'm* charming."

"And yet so nosy."

He grins, not disputing my words. I contemplate his theory.

"Maybe that's it. But greater than being spirit-kin, some souls are just spun from platinum, you know? Jay has one of those souls."

Genie stares off after his cousin. "He does. Not that he'd want anyone to know it."

In Korean I say, "He's the best."

His face turns strange. "What did you say?"

"Did I pronounce it wrong?" Or worse, I think, did Jay trick me into learning some offensive or disgusting phrase again?

Realization settles on his brow. "Oh, I don't speak Korean."

"Great," I say, feeling faintly racist.

"The family that adopted us didn't speak Korean. He taught himself how to speak it when we were in high school. He felt a need."

"I always assumed he was raised by your parents."

"We're both orphans," Genie says. "We got to keep our last names, though. Our parents are like Y2K race hippies. You should get him to tell you about them sometime."

It sounds depressing. "He taught himself Korean? That's pretty awesome."

"Don't tell him I said this, but everything he does is pretty awesome."

Jay comes back in before we get stuck in the sap.

"Tap out," I say, jetting off to the bathroom.

Genie turns to Jay with the same veiled eyes. "Your boy though. He's one of three, right? There's also the actor and the gamer that live with you? Plus the guy that used to live here and your neighbor that's named after a bird."

Jay smiles. "Eagle, yeah. You're not missing anything, though. Zario's the dude."

Genie busies himself with the playing cards. "What do you mean?"

Jay leans against the couch, staring at the ceiling. "He puts up with me, first of all. Calls me on all of my shit. And when he smiles from way the fuck up there, it's like moonlight or some shit."

Genie looks up with an amused smile. "What the fuck does that mean? You can see him in the dark?"

Jay meets his cousin's gaze. "Exactly."

"Bitch, we speak in metaphors now?"

"Shut the fuck up."

"I'm just saying, man… I used to think you had problems."

Jay snaps back, "What? What are you talking about?"

I return to the living room just in time to hear Genie respond quickly, "Sounds to me like you've solved them." Turning to me, he says, "Jay always wants to peacock and I've got delicious plums, so you can have Mr. Green, Mrs. White, or one of the other ones."

I grin. "I love sausage, so gimme some mustard."

Jay shakes his head at me. "Don't do that."

"Do what?" I ask.

"Don't let him do that to you; don't buy into that." To his cousin, he says, "I'll take Colonel Mustard because he's a badass, and Zario always wants to be Professor Plum. You can have one of the others."

I look between them, feeling a shift. Genie just smiles. "I'll peacock then. It's genetic."

• • • • • • •

The day Jay got me out of my bed after my Shane breakup, he pushed me into the shower and cleaned up my room. Only later did I realize what an undertaking that was. The half-eaten sandwiches. The opened bags of stale, uneaten chips. The empty liquor bottles and beer cans stashed around the room. The bottles that had been empty before I filled them back up with piss.

When I came out of the shower, he had clothes laid out for me. A glass of water on my dresser. The window was cracked and fresh air was flowing through for the first time in weeks.

"I'm not going anywhere," I said, my anxiety rising in my chest like vomit as I stared at the clothes on the bed.

"We're not leaving the house," he said. "Drink the water."

Ellington had come by and picked up Sunji and Alexander. They were spending the evening out at the movies so that Jay and I had the house to ourselves. First, he got me to the kitchen where we ate cereal in silence. Then he got me to the den, where we watched *Back to the Future Part II*.

"I don't know how you like this shit," he grumbled.

Finally, he got me on the back porch to watch the blue sky turn purple and gold and black. The fresh air was heavy in a way I still can't explain without convoluted allegories. It was heavy like it was being given to me. Like the atmosphere was a personal gift.

Jay walked me back to my room like he was returning me home from a date.

"Maybe I'll see you tomorrow?" he said.

"Like I have a choice," I said, laughing, my throat still dry. My veins still dehydrated.

"Ah, good," he said. "You figured it out."

"See you, tomorrow," I said, moving to close the door. He put up a hand.

"You can't do this to me again, okay, Zee?" he said, blinking a noticeable amount. "You can't check out on me. This is a package deal. You're never in this alone. Ever."

"It's not your job to save me."

He smirks. "I know. It's more like a friendship liability. It's part of the contract."

"That can't be healthy."

He doesn't raise his eyebrow as much as he pops it. "We all have our vices. Love is one of mine."

• • • • • • •

About an hour after we play the last game and Jay walks Genie to his car, we wind down in the den, clearing the table of food and board games, but not the alcohol.

When Ellington enters the den, Jay is in a deeps slumber, laid out on the couch with his calves in my lap. I'm reading by the jumping glow of the television—some movie starring some actor named Chris and not deserving my attention.

Ellington whispers as his vision adjusts. "You still up?"

"Yeah," I croak. "One of us, at least."

Ellington sits, pouring himself a glass of bourbon. "Busy night?"

I chuckle sleepily. "Crazy night. You?"

Tears, unseen by me, stream down his face as he answers. "Same."

Enter Sandman

I've drifted off to sleep, Jay's calves cradled in my hands. The television's still on, now playing a film starring someone who used to be on a children's show (one that I loved back when I was its target demographic) and is faux edgy now. I look over and Ellington's asleep in the chair, one of his own legs swung over the armrest.

When he's asleep, you can see how young Ellington is. With his deep voice and debonair demeanor, it was easy to assume he was the oldest of all of us. He moved out on his own, was taking care of his brother, and was even considering marriage. But Ellington is younger than most of us—he entered college at seventeen and graduated three years later. As hard as that man fucks is as hard as he does everything. I don't think it's possible to catch up with him, when he's already lapped me.

I lift Jay's legs, moving beneath and around them to freedom. As I walk past his head, one of his hands rockets up and grabs my thigh.

"Holy fuck," I scream-whisper.

"What time is it?" he asks, opening one eye.

"It's almost five," I reply, prying his fingers loose.

"How long did you sleep?"

"Like, two hours, I think."

"Don't go to bed yet," he says, sitting up.

"Shh," I caution, pointing to Ellington. Jay looks, makes a face, then grabs the alcohol.

"You working tomorrow?"

Oh, fuck. "No, but I'm not trying to turn up tonight, Jay."

He ignores everything after the first word. "My room. We'll watch a movie."

He never makes a big deal about his bedroom, but Jay doesn't make a habit out of inviting the rest of us in there. I've been sent in there on occasion to grab an item or two, but usually that's his sacred pulpit, fit only for himself and the women he worships. I'm excited about the prospect of hanging out in his space though. It feels like the final frontier of our friendship.

"Lemme brush my teeth," I tell him. "I've got sleep mouth."

"Yeah, that's fine," he says. "Get comfortable."

Comfortable is an understatement. I put on my favorite pajama set with matching socks, and grip my stuffed animal, a blue-grey dog named Loonah, under my arm.

Jay opens the door in his boxer briefs. Looking immediately at the stuffed animal, he shakes his head.

"Don't bring that in here."

"What if we watch a scary movie?"

"You've got a whole ass man standing here and you think you're gonna need a plushie?"

Moments later, I enter his lair, Loonah-free. His room reminds me of a classy Vegas bar that Ellington took us to once. One of the quiet ones hidden on a floor you could only access from one section of another floor, and tucked away from the high traffic and thumping music.

Everything in the room is gray, black or burgundy, like the solid colors of the walls, or the curtain completely covering the wall that has his one window. His platform bed is inset between his cabinets, framed with embedded LED lights that illuminate his satin sheets.

Jay hands me a remote and tasks me with selecting a film from his extensive pirated library, currently displayed on his flatscreen. I sit on, then sink in, his bed while he retreats to his desk, rolling a fat blunt.

"Are you picking a scary movie?" he asks over his shoulder.

I click off of the *Scream* franchise, guilty. "No, I was thinking action. Maybe the only *Mad Max* we acknowledge—"

"Fuck Mel Gibson," Jay mutters, just before licking the tuck of the wrap.

"—or a John Boyega flick."

"Good options," he says, setting the joint aside. "You want some whiskey?"

"The sun is almost up," I protest.

"So?" he says. "You've gotta taste this."

"I really don't gotta," I reply.

He walks over to me holding a bottle of imported brown in his hands. "What if we're some kind of mythical gods whose celebrations bring the fires that light the sky into morning? What if we're the reason the sun even rises? Our light, our heat, our blood?"

He stumbles drunkenly into me and I steady him with a hand on his waist that he swats. He straddles my thighs and raises the bottle.

I stare up at him. "Are you writing poetry or fanfic, right now?"

On a typical, human level, nothing about Jay is comforting except his presence. He's still, like the surface of a river. You might mistake it for calm, but there are all sorts of battles raging beneath that occasionally erupt above. I've grown to be skeptical of his calm, and I suspect he knows this. He always seeks out physical contact with me, almost as a way of letting me know I'm safe. If the venom spews, it's never in my direction.

It's not just the act of touch, it's how he does it. Most of the time it's simple surface-to-surface contact, but on drunken occasions, like now, it's intimate. Tender.

He grips the back of my skull and gently tugs my head. "Open your mouth."

I obey and he pours in far too much. My throat doesn't betray me and I gulp it all down. It travels smoothly, and I only feel the burning after. I squint as my chest turns to magma and it races up to my forehead.

His eyes take in my face, as he absently traces my Adam's apple with his thumb. "There's the sun."

Three more shots. The entire blunt. A quick run to the 24-hour donut shop under a brightening sky and half a dozen donuts later and I'm asleep before John Boyega saves the universe, which I'm assuming is how the movie ends. I wake as the credits roll. Sitting up, I bump shoulders with Jay, who's been watching me at least the whole time I've been conscious.

"Your bed is so comfortable," I say, meaning it as an apology.

"The sun's up," he says, and for a moment I think he's still talking about me. "You can go back to sleep; I don't care if you stay here."

I stretch, but slumber has a tight grip on me. "You don't mind sharing?"

"As long as you don't mind me being naked."

This pulls me into lucidness. "You sleep naked?"

He raises the remote and mutes the television. "Don't you?"

He gets out of the bed and places the remote on his desk.

"I do, sometimes. But not with friends."

He turns back to me. "You can go to your own bed if it bothers you. This is my room. I do what I want."

"If you're not bothered, I'm not bothered," I say.

"Then shut up about it, Zee. It's only a big deal if you make it a big deal." He tugs at the waist of his boxer briefs. "Like this."

He turns back around to face the wall, pulling the shorts lower as he bounces his hips back and forth.

"*Bung, bung, bung, bung, bung,*" he sings, looking over his shoulder at me.

"*Mr. Sandman, bring me a cream,*

Make it the thickest that I've ever streamed..."

He pulls the underwear down just below his butt, wiggles his ass, and then covers back up.

"I don't have any dollar bills on me," I laugh.

"*Sandman,*" he continues, "*I'm so turned on,*

Don't have nobody that I can bone..."

He strips completely out of his underwear, tossing it into his hamper. Leaping on the bed next to me, his knees drive into the sheets and his arms punch into the air as his genitals swing in impressively balletic circular motion.

He bellows now, and I'm glad the others are on the opposite side of the house.

"*Please let loose my nightly semen,*

Mr. Sandman, bring me a creamin'"

He drops his hands, breathing heavily. I keep my eyes on his face, but it's a full-time effort.

"Can't get weirder than that, right?"

"I don't think so," I agree.

He's already knocking against his headboard, moving beneath the sheets.

"Good. Stop being anxious."

He leans over the edge of the bed and I can't see what he's doing, but the LED lights begin to dim until there's barely an amber glow. He drops his light controller and nestles into his pillows, face toward me. He throws his leg over mine and mumbles something into the pillowcase.

"I didn't hear you," I tell him.

Moving the pillow from his mouth, he says, "If you jizz in my bed, you owe me one hundred and sixty-five dollars."

"Where'd you get these sheets at? Orange County?"

"I got them at the mall, but you'll owe me one thirty-five for emotional damages."

"Well, no worries there. Unless your cousin pays me a visit in Slumberland."

He lowers his lids just enough for me to realize that maybe he doesn't want me bringing up his cousin after the night's weird tension.

"You know what's funny?" He chews on his tongue. "Genie thinks you like me."

I turn to the ceiling and guffaw.

"No bullshit," Jay says.

"What were his exact words?"

"Why would I make this up?"

I flex my jaw. "I don't think you'd make it up, but maybe you're interpreting it wrong?"

"I know him. I don't get him wrong. Milk bond."

"That's a gross fucking phrase, by the way, and, also, don't do this."

"Don't do what?"

"I don't play these straight games and you've got it twisted if you think I'm gonna go another round of 'Would You Fuck Me.'"

"That was Genie's idea."

"You could have squashed it."

He's quiet. "Did that make you uncomfortable?"

"Yes, the fuck it did."

"I'm sorry. You and I are always honest with each other, so I figured..."

"It's different. I don't know him." And before he can protest, I add, "I know. Milk bond."

"Next time, just pull me aside or whatever. Call me into the kitchen."

"Next time, don't trot me out like your token fag."

His face falls and I turn back to the ceiling.

"Hey." His voice is so thick and deep, it's like he croaks. "Zee."

He bounces his leg on mine and I turn to him with a labored sigh.

His eyes are taking in my face. "You know I don't think of you like that. You know that. I did some damage, okay, and I'm sorry. But you know my intention wasn't to hurt you, okay?"

"It didn't hurt me, it just annoyed me. Plus, I'm moody. My body is ten percent weed and fifty percent alcohol, thanks to you."

He grabs my waist. "Which fifty?"

I punch at him beneath the sheets. "An internal fifty. Don't grab me like that."

He lets go, then wiggles his fingers in my face. "I can dig for it."

"Why are you so gross?"

"I gotta match your expectation," he chuckles, and pulls his hand back beneath the sheets. "Guess where my hand is going."

I shriek in expectation. "No, Jay, stop!"

He shrugs. "Okay. I'm already there anyway."

"No," I whine, giggling.

"You always this weird when you're sleepy?" he asks, raising up from the pillow and lifting it with one hand where I can see the other one laying there innocently.

I've been pranked.

In all of our silliness, our legs have adjusted position. Our thighs touch and I avoid thinking of how close my leg might be to another part of him. He rocks my thigh with his.

"Goodnight, Zee."

"Goodnight, Jay."

• • • • • • •

When a man who currently identifies as straight first begins to seduce another queer man, it's incremental, but the out queer man can easily clock it. Each straight-identifying man has his own goals, of course, but the beginnings are almost copy-paste identical. A comment on how good another man looks. An "if I was gay" verbal fan fiction. A lingering touch. For some of these men, the goal is not the bed, sometimes it's merely to verify that they could, if they wanted to because they may want to with someone else. Many men are satisfied at various increments of knowledge. The response to that touch. The response to that late night text. Sometimes it's that authenticating blow job. But it's always at the benefit of the man who says he's straight and at the detriment of the man who is further along on that queer journey.

It's ironic, and tragic, that the out (and usually outwardly queer) party is the one that society deems as predatory, as that's not the story for so many of us. I talk to Marshall about this once, to compare experiences, and I regret it instantly.

"Do you think Jay is just trying to see how far he can get with you?"

Yes. "No. This isn't about him, just straight guys in general. They all do it."

"Gay guys do it, too," Marshall replies. "I think it's a guy thing. We have these egos that need constant stroking. Men always want to be wanted."

"I disagree. I get sick of men coming on to me when I'm just trying to have a good time, or order a coffee."

"Oh, sure we don't want unsolicited attention. But we welcome it when it's solicited it."

Our conversation drifts to rape culture and it's controversial overlap with gay culture. It's frustrating how often literal assault has been interpreted as acceptable. I have millions of stories, some worse than others, of men doing things to me in public and private places just because they think I am or should be sexually attracted to them.

Marshall has similar stories. "I read somewhere that sex through coercion is rape and I didn't—I couldn't accept that. I don't want my first time to be rape. I mean, I said yes. Eventually. But I felt... I felt the way I think I would have felt if what happened..."

He doesn't speak for a moment.

"Even though I said yes, as it happened I still felt that no in my spirit, you know. I gave him verbal permission, but I did not want it. And I had done everything I could to express to him how much I didn't want it. It's like, how many noes does it take for a man to just take the L? To just leave you alone? You can say a million noes and give one exhausted yes and that yes is all that counts."

"Was he older?" I ask.

Marshall correctly reads me. "You mean, was it statutory?"

"It's statutory for too many of us," I shrug, as if the lifting of my shoulders lifts the heaviness of the conversation.

"Was it statutory for you?" Marshall asks me, his way of avoiding his own answer.

"No, we were both in college."

His eyes grow comically large. "Your first time was in college?"

"Yeah, and then I quickly made up for lost time."

I don't tell him much more, which is fair because Marshall has things he doesn't tell me. Like the fact that Ellington knew about his first time.

It was with an older college guy that Ellington knew through local athletics clubs, Victor Ruiz. Victor had told a mutual friend, who in turn told Ellington, causing Ellington to check in on fourteen-year-old Marshall with a focused kind of attentiveness. The next day, Ellington had weekend passes to Disney World, two round-trip plane tickets, and a hotel reservation for two. He invited Marshall while he cut their middle brother's hair on their back porch. Carver was upset at not being invited, but Ellington promised he'd make it up to him.

Carver and Ellington had similar builds, and Ellington gave him a haircut that matched his own, maybe as as an outward expression mimicking the inherent closeness he had always held with Marshall. Then, late in the night, Ellington remembered he had a project due for his literature class. He begged Carver to go in his place, and they switched IDs so that there would be no weirdness with the plane tickets. When Marshall woke, suddenly he was going to Six Flags with his other brother and Ellington was staying behind.

Oddly enough, Victor Ruiz got curb-stomped that very weekend by someone who he later claimed to authorities was Ellington Gomez, which was not possible. Ellington Gomez was in Orlando, Florida with his brother Marshall, verifiable according to flight records, hotel check-in details, and even the name printed on the theme park tickets. Not once was it ever suspected to be the other Gomez brother, since everyone knew Carver was a pacifist. In fact, Carver had checked into a Motel 6 for the weekend to do some focused biblical readings, also verifiable thanks to the ID the hotel had on file.

The attack left Victor Ruiz with permanent injuries. Marshall never had to see him again.

This is the well I draw from when Sunji swings his balls in my presence or when Jay naps in my bed. I find myself looking for clues, for hints that they're nudging to see how far they can get me to go. But for both of them, it's very different. Sunji is positive he could, despite being completely wrong on that assumption, so he doesn't bother to prove it. Jay, on the other hand, is like a different side of that same coin. I think he knows that he could, that he really could, but he doesn't care.

It's comforting, really.

Platonic friendships can become paradoxically romantic, and I think if society weren't so inherently homophobic, men of all sexualities could have much more honest, open and healthy relationships with each other.

The Dudes Go to Church

Ellington calls me out of my dreams. It takes a long time for me to register this, because he's calling through the door to my room, but I'm not there — I'm one room over.

I untangle myself from Jay's legs, realizing too late that all three of them had been pressed up against me. I shuffle to the door and peek out.

Ellington is looking dapper as fuck in a black sweater that's pulled over a red button-up shirt and a black tie. Red windowpane stitching on cuffed black pants completes his look and I drool.

Not that he can tell, since I still have slobber on my face from sleep.

"Hey," I whisper and he spins. "Why do you look like you're going to church?"

"I am going to church." He peers past me, frowning. "Why were you in Jay's room?"

I step into the hall, pulling the door closed behind me. "He woke up last night and wanted to party some more and we didn't want to disturb you."

"Disturb me next time. I could have used a party. Wanna go to church with me?"

"It's gonna take me a while to get ready."

"That's fine. We can skip the eight o'clock and go to the eleven o'clock."

The eight o'clock? "What time is it?"

"Seven-fifteen."

"Oh, that's brutal," I breathe. "Do I have to dress like you?"

Ellington considers this. "Just wear the suit I got you for that 80s party."

"The white suit?" How dressed up is this church?

"Yeah," Ellington replies, unfazed. "Solid color button up. And I've got a few white ties in Alexander's room. Take a shower and I'll check on you around nine? We can grab breakfast on the way."

He walks away, bouncing like his ankles are springs. Meanwhile, I feel like the walking dead. I slide back into Jay's room, planning to catch another solid hour of sleep.

Jay is awake, sitting on the edge of the bed with his legs spread and his morning wood softening. He scratches at the head above his shoulders and that's where I train my eyes.

"Who was that?" he asks groggily.

"Ellington. He invited me to church."

He looks up like I've told him a joke. "Church? Are you going?"

"Yeah."

"Okay, I'll go, too."

"You don't have to."

"You say it like I don't know that. Church sounds fun."

"Church never sounds fun," I say, still pinned to the door.

"He goes to Black church. Black church is awesome. It's like going to a concert."

He stands, stretching, and I look over at his desk. "I guess I'll go get ready."

"Is it dressy?" he asks, scratching at his waist.

"Very," I say. "Ellington looks like he's about to hit a red carpet."

"I'll look better," Jay promises.

At nine o'clock, Ellington comes in my room with far too many white ties. He holds a few against my chest.

"Look at us," Ellington says, selecting one that accents well with my forest green shirt. "Beauty and the Beast. Of course, if anyone else calls you beast, I'll rip their lungs out."

It's one of my favorite *Batman* quotes, and we collapse over each other laughing. He begins tying the tie around my collar as Jay walks in, wearing tight blue slacks with a matching tie over a white button up. He's slung a shimmering black jacket over his arm, and as he gets closer I can see it's detailed with blue magpies that match his pants.

I whistle and Ellington turns.

"Where are you going?" he asks.

"To your church," Jay responds, knocking Loonah off my bed and sitting where she had been.

"You look like you're hooking."

"No, I'm taking the day off," Jay replies.

As we walk to Ellington's car, Jay nudges me.

"You haven't gone to church the whole time you've lived here."

I frown down at him. "What about it?"

He stares ahead as we walk. "How do you feel about God?"

"I don't know. How does God feel about me?"

"It seems like He likes you," he says, as we reach Ellington's car. "How so?"

He holds the passenger door open for me, grinning. "He gave you me."

I roll my eyes and he shrugs.

• • • • • • •

"Brother Ellington! So good to see you."

The pastor's name is Reverend Beverly, and he's a young-looking forty-something man, with shiny skin the color of rain-soaked sycamore. He moves up and down the church rows before the service starts, connecting with as many attendees as he can.

Too far from where we sit comfortably in the middle of our pew to feasibly shake hands with us, Reverend Beverly instead points at Ellington with enthusiasm.

"Thank you, Pastor," Ellington booms back. He motions to us. "These are my friends Jay and Zario."

Jay stands and offers a partial bow. "Jay for Jericho. Named after the wall."

Ellington sucks his teeth and I snort.

"Brother Jericho, Brother Mario, welcome to our church. And don't wait on Brother Ellington to bring you. You're welcome here anytime."

"That was church shade," Ellington says to me as Reverend Beverly walks away. "It's close to gay shade because Black gay people started it in both communities."

I laugh.

"I'm not joking," he says.

Sure enough, once the service begins, I spot them all over the sanctuary. In the congregation, on the usher board, and certainly involved with the music. The choir director I clock quickly. The organist, most definitely, and at least seven of the choir members, including the second soloist.

"That's cool that this church is welcoming to the queer community," I say to Ellington during what they call "the welcome," where far too many people rushed over to shake hands with Jay and I, while thanking Ellington for bringing us.

Ellington replies in my ear. "They're not out within these walls. Trust."

As the service trucks along, Jay enjoys the song service the most. He stands up during the first uptempo song and I'm delighted to see how percussive he is with his clapping. I don't know if he's vibing with the content of the lyrics, but he definitely feels the music.

On the third and presumably final song before the sermon, one of the choir members comes forward to a microphone. She adjusts the stole stitched on the front of her robe as church members yell out her name. I get excited, hoping this is the Beyoncé of the choir.

She speaks. "The Bible says, 'There's a commandment to bless.'"

Around us, people begin standing and exclaiming in anticipation. Whatever this next song is, it's a crowd-pleaser.

"'He has blessed me,'" the choir member continues, sounding a bit like one of those exciting televangelists, "'and I cannot change it.'"

The choir director sets a meteoric pace and the musicians come in, a richly composed burst of gospel, with the organ trilling through all of the instruments like a soloist.

When the woman at the microphone begins singing, though, the song turns over to her. Her voice tears through the room like a freight train, shaking me in my seat like I am a car in park as she hurtles uninterrupted down the track in front of me.

"God is not a human that He should lie,
He is faithful, He doesn't change His mind.
When He speaks!"

The choir comes in, like one massive, tridented harmonic voice, and I wonder honestly if this is how God sounds.

"He acts; I can't undo it!"

More people are standing now, and one of the queers across the aisle is clobbering a tambourine with jaw-dropping precision.

The lady at the mic continues the chorus. *"His promise!"*

"Fulfilled; I can't undo it!"

She sings another verse, before the chorus comes back around. They work the refrain for all it's worth and then launch into a bridge, modulating into a higher key.

"The Lord our God is with us!
His shout among us!"

I have no idea what it means, but I can tell it's scripture of some kind. I'm amazed that they can take the same book that has been used to do so much evil, been used to create so much ugliness in the world throughout history, and make something so beautiful and so… *immediate.*

The choir director waves the musicians off and they all drop out, save for the drummer, keeping steady rhythm with the kick drum on beats two and four. The choir keeps singing the bridge and again I think I'm hearing God's voice. After a few circuits—and these are some athletic vocals—the director quells even the choir and now it's just percussion.

"If you got it, put your hand on it," the soloist squalls, and the congregation creates something I've never experienced before.

An implausible symphony of handclaps fills the space. Each person is clapping their own complex rhythms and, multiplied by the hundreds in the sanctuary, the patterns alternate in primacy and synchronize. Across the sanctuary, folks are yelling out "Hallelujah!" and "Yes, Lord!"

After several moments of this, the vocalist starts humming and moaning into the microphone.

She sings again, a new vamp.

"He blessed me; I can't undo it.

He blessed me; I can't undo it."

The director brings the choir in, softly at first, and they echo her in their massive three-part harmony.

"He blessed me!"

"He blessed me!"

"I can't undo it!"

"I can't undo it!"

"He blessed me!"

"He blessed me!"

"I don't wanna undo it!"

"I can't undo it!"

"He blessed my soul!"

"He blessed me!"

"There's nothing you can do about that!"

"I can't undo it!"

This continues, with the vocalist ad-libbing and exploring new melodies as the choir sings a little louder on each loop. The director signals the organist whose fingers begin to dance on the keys. As the choir hits full volume, the director lifts his arms high above his head as if directly invoking the Holy Spirit. On the down beat, his hands plummet to his sides and the full band comes in.

This sets the soloist off, sending her roaring and spinning as the choir hunkers down on, ***"I can't undo it!"***

It's transcendent. Jay and Ellington are both on their feet, and I join them.

There's a call and response of *"Won't He do it!"* between the lady at the microphone and the mass of voices behind her and I find myself singing along with the choir while rocking back and forth. The room has erupted in a strange heat, and a woman two rows ahead of me is leaning so far back that she has to be supported by the congregants on both sides of her, one who is fanning her while also bouncing in praise himself.

At some point, the song ends, but the music and the praise haven't ended. The band has moved into a speedy, bass-driven instrumental and I realize that this is the thing I've seen adapted in so many films where a white person goes to a Black church. People are hollering, leaping. Some people are literally running laps around the church, shouting at the top of their lungs. A third of the choir is doing what I might call a two-step, but I can't quite tell what it is. It's a quick dance, but it seems to be limited in complexity to whatever is happening beneath their knees.

Reverend Beverly has moved to the podium in preparation for his sermon, quietly and calmly arranging his Bible, a handkerchief, and a small stack of notes. Out of some type of requirement, or maybe out of respect to the moment, he steps back, head down and hands folded, nodding to the music. Jay and I have sat back into our seats, but Ellington is still standing, hands waving, his own eyes closed.

I can't imagine this happening every week. I feel so recharged, but if I was one of the people doing cardio, I would probably have to take some weeks off to recover.

After a while, the strange heat pulls back and the preacher moves up to the microphone.

"If you will," he says, "turn with me in your Bibles to the Book of Romans, the twelfth chapter."

Jay pulls a Bible from the book rack on the back of the pew in front of us. He flips pages, moving his hands between us so that I can read with him.

Reverend Beverly intones that he will read the odd-numbered verses aloud, we will read the even-numbered verses, and the last verse of the chapter, verse twenty-one, we will read together. He says, "altogether," but I know what he means. We stand and recite the scriptures as instructed, the only variation being that he has us repeat the second verse straight out the gate.

And be not conformed to this world: but be ye transformed by the renewing of your mind, that ye may prove what is that good, and acceptable, and perfect, will of God.

As we take our seats, he says, "From these scriptures, I take today's message. 'Prove It.' Let us pray."

Throughout the prayer and the sermon, Reverend Beverly is a measured speaker, and the sermon begins like a college course. He's cross-referencing scriptures, making modern day correlations, and sprinkling in pop culture references to keep all of us engaged. I'm with him as he works his way through the chapter, until he gets to verse ten.

Be kindly affectioned one to another with brotherly love...

Suddenly, he goes off on a tangent, comparing kind affection and brotherly love negatively with men sleeping together. I get hot behind the ears, but I try not to react outwardly. The congregation around me is still in his corner.

I look at the choir members and musicians I've mentally outed and some of them nod and say amen along with everyone else, but two of them, one on the front row of the choir stand, are silent. Frowning.

The reverend's demeanor has changed now. He sounds like one of the uncles out in the yard during a barbecue, or one of the neighborhood guys you always see on the corner near the liquor store, talking story. His erudite delivery has been replaced with AAVE, further managing to push me out. He's speaking directly to certain members of a culture now, and due to the hatred in his words, I'm not okay with feeling excluded. I slide down in my seat.

It feels like he stays on the subject for far longer than the sermon's original topic calls for. He's trying to cover every talking point in the queerphobic bible, forsaking the one he's got open in front of him.

"You're a child!" he's saying now, and I wonder if even he knows where he's going with any of this. "How do you know what you want to sleep with?"

The affirmations being shared around me are even worse. It sounds like everyone is eating this up, but I don't look. I count the hairs on my right arm instead.

Jay's hand shoots up in the air, not in praise or accord, but in inquiry.

"Put your hand down," Ellington hisses. "This isn't Bible study."

"Yeah, that's clear," Jay replies, but he drops his hand.

I realize now that Ellington, too, had retreated into himself. Jay's action, though, has forced him to reengage with the situation.

"If you're living in sin," Reverend Beverly is shouting now, "you're going to hell. The Bible says it, and what did the song say, church? I can't undo it! I can't!"

Ellington taps my leg. "Come on. Let's go."

I give him the strongest side eye I've ever given anyone. "What?"

"We're not going to listen to this; let's go."

Jay nods his head in agreement, and both of them rise to their feet.

"Excuse me," Jay says loudly to parishioners seated between us and the end of the pew.

I'm horrified, but sitting still while my roommates leave without me is a worser prospect, so I stand, too.

I keep my head down, but I can feel the disapproving stares as we reach the aisle. The door leading out of the back of the sanctuary seems to grow farther away with each step until we suddenly reach it.

The female usher posted there hisses at us. "You're not supposed to walk during the Word."

I look over to where the other ushers are seated together and pinpoint one I'm sure is queer. He's got an apologetic expression that hardens when he sees me studying him. He adjusts in his seat, recrossing his legs and looking away. So gay.

"That's alright. Let them go," Reverend Beverly says from behind and above us. "Let them go with love."

• • • • • • • •

In the car, Ellington's face is stitched tight and even Jay doesn't speak, though his raised eyebrows tell me that he has plenty he wants to say.

"I didn't expect that, Zario," Ellington finally manages. "I'm sorry."

I look at him. "I don't know. Walking out mid-sermon was pretty badass."

"That's the guy who gives you your spiritual guidance, huh?" Jay asks, cheeks high as his face morphs into one of his antagonistic smiles. "No wonder you're so fucked up."

"He's never done that before. He usually, uh, limits his queerphobia to his prayers. Binding the demons of homosexuality and things like that."

"Every person in that church is fucked," Jay proclaims. "What he was saying doesn't even make sense! The title of the sermon was 'Prove It,' and then he offered no proof for all the bullshit he was shitting out of his shitty mouth."

"Homophobia is full of inconsistencies," I say, rolling the window down to feel something other than whatever it is that's been crawling on me since we left the church.

"So is religion," Jay says.

"I don't believe that shit," Ellington says, pointing both of his hands inward to his chest before returning one to the wheel. "You guys know that, right?"

"Oh, sure, you're just hypocritical in other ways," Jay says. "Fornication. Bearing false witness."

"You don't even have a moral compass," Ellington says, looking at Jay through the rearview mirror, "so don't come for mine."

"I bet you didn't know I grew up in the church," Jay replies. "I'm a believer, but I'm not a Christian. Christians can go fuck themselves."

"How are you a believer, but not Christian?" I ask, looking back at him.

"Didn't we all just have the same experience?" he asks, looking perplexed. "That shit's the fuck why!"

"It was good until then," I say to Ellington.

Jay leans forward. "You're friends with someone for five years and then you see them being crazy-fucking-racist to some other ethnic group. Do you give them credit for the five years or do you tell them to go fuck themselves for being racist?"

I stare out the window.

"Exactly," Jay says, leaning back. "Reverend Beverly can go fuck himself."

I've long learned that it's better for Jay to vent his anger like this than to sit on it, but even I'm taken aback by the venom. It makes me wonder why I'm not angrier than him, especially since it was my community that was targeted.

"Are you going back?" I ask Ellington.

"No," he says. "I feel like I betrayed by brother even sitting there as long as I did. I was just kinda hoping Pastor would move on."

"Same," I admit. "But silence is complicity, right?"

"And violent," Ellington replies. "I got y'all for dinner tonight; it's on me. I feel like I have the Christian version of white guilt."

I nod, remembering the feeling. "Catholics have perfected that."

· · · · · · · ·

I spend the night in Jay's room again. We watch *Grease 2* which leads him to tell me that he's picking the movie next time. Again he keeps conversation going with me long after I've indicated my level of sleepiness. I have to respond to him, because whenever I don't, he rubs my thigh with his own and it sets off things in me that have nothing to do with Jay and everything to do with my erogenous zones.

This means I'm forced to answer when he asks me, "How did today really feel?"

"What? Church?"

"Yeah."

"I don't want to say triggering, because it didn't send me spiraling or anything like that, but it definitely was the wrong kind of nostalgia. To be in an environment where I felt accepted and was starting to let my guard down and then..."

"Boom," he says, eyes closed.

"Boom," I repeat, closing my own eyes.

"When's the last time that happened to you?"

"I don't know," I say, and his thigh starts moving.

"Yes, you do."

"The other day, you started tickling me, and when Sunji and Ellington came around the corner, you pushed me away."

I can tell his eyes are open now.

"It was time for us to leave."

I open my eyes and see that I was right. "You shoved me to the floor."

He's silent.

"You'd be surprised how often you all do those microagressions, reminding me that I'm not exactly the same."

"None of us are the same."

"Don't do that. Don't trivialize my experience. I know what you guys do and I know how it makes me feel. And that's important. And it's important that you acknowledge that."

"You're right," he says. "I'm sorry. And I'm sorry for shoving you so hard. I won't do that shit again."

He's staring at my mouth, so I close my eyes again.

"I'm always amazed you put up with me. I'm kind of a shit."

I smile. "You are."

"You're brave dealing with all of this."

"It's not brave being your friend. It's natural. We fit."

"We do fit," he says, and he rocks our thighs to a brief rhythm. "I can't undo it."

Sufficiently Talented

I floss as Jay brushes his teeth. Eagle always stresses that there's a difference between being pretty and just being hygienic or, like they used to say, metrosexual.

"Look at how fucking pretty this asshole is," she'll say, gesturing to Jay. She's always dismayed that he doesn't have loads of hygienic weaponry, that his hair just falls like that, that his porcelain skin is natural. "He should exfoliate more, not because he needs it now, but because he'll need it one day."

In our bathroom, and in Korean, I ask Jay, *"How do I say, 'I'm nervous?'"*

He translates, then replies in Korean, *"Why are you nervous?"*

I'm back to English. "So far these dates are oh-for-two."

"You're set, though. Tonight is my pick. He's perfect."

"How'd you meet him?"

"I catfished him. Pretended I was you and joined a few dating apps. So many deviants. So many bots." His eyes grow clouded. "So many unsolicited penises."

"You impersonated me online? The fuck?"

"Yep. Narrowed it down to three guys, then I confessed, told them about the bet, and met with the two of them that were willing to prove that they were real."

Imagining Jay trying to flirt as me on dating apps was bringing a smile to my face despite my best efforts.

"I'm going to put you in friend jail," I say in an attempt to mask my amusement.

"They were great guys, both of them. But believe me, Iggy—tonight's guy—he's perfect."

"He'd better be amazing." In Korean I say again, "*I'm nervous.*"

Jay spits into the sink. "Do you think you're a twink or an otter?"

"A what now?" I heard him, but still.

"Body type. I said you were an otter after I looked it up. I think you're too tall to be a twink, plus you have a front tushie." He pokes at my stomach and, despite my dismay, I'm even more delighted.

Sunji enters, tweezing his nipples. "Guys! I know what I'm gonna do."

"Finally," Jay exclaims, turning away from me. "About world peace?"

He's still poking at me with his fingers so I shove him. "Sunji's dinner with Jerrica is tonight."

"Why are you going to that, again? Such a bad idea. You guys should have met for coffee or something. A public place. With witnesses." Jay grimaces. "And lots of oxygen."

"Well, you're going to go hang with Eagle and Rock," Sunji counters. "If there are bad ideas, I'll take mine over yours."

"So what's your amazing plan?" I ask.

"Halfway through dinner, just when she begins to realize how much she misses me, I'm going to accidentally spill my drink all over my shirt, forcing myself to remove it so that my abs and chest really seal the deal."

I decide to humor him. "What deal?"

"Her new man won't be able to measure up to me. It's a foolproof plan!"

"Nothing is foolproof to a sufficiently talented fool," Alexander says, entering.

"Amen!" Jay shouts.

Alexander grabs a roll of toilet paper.

"I owe you," he says to Jay.

"I know," Jay replies. "I've kept a list."

My attention is still on Sunji. "Isn't the focus on your looks the exact reason she dumped you?"

"It'll get her attention."

"Then what will you do with it?"

"What do you mean?"

"Exactly," we chorus.

Jay hops up on the counter, mirroring Sunji and looking at Alexander. "Where's the slut?"

"He's meeting us there," Alexander answers. "Said he was gonna pick up some sweets."

"That means he's bringing Mandy," I translate. "He's gonna use her as an excuse to leave if things get awkward."

"*When* things get awkward," Sunji corrects me.

"I wish I had a girlfriend to take," Jay says, turning to me. "Will you be my girlfriend?"

"How quickly you forget that I already have plans. Plans that you made for me."

Jay grins and turns to Alexander. "You heard it. That wasn't a no."

"In your dreams," I say.

"Promise?" he asks, grabbing my head and pulling it toward his crotch. I punch his dick, grinning as he falls against the mirror.

Alexander points a finger, bouncing it between Jay and I. "When did this start?"

I look at him confused. Jay and I have always roughhoused. "What?"

Alexander doesn't respond, but I see his eyelids drop a little lower.

"Is that what you're wearing?" Jay asks him, pointing to the wrinkled blue shirt Alexander had slung over his shoulder. It's the same shirt he had worn with us to the club.

Alexander turns his palms upward. "It's Eagle and Rock. Who am I trying to impress?"

"I can't believe you guys are going over there. Rock is so fucking weird." Sunji looks up from his freshly tweezed chest. "How are my nipples?"

• • • • • • •

Nearly an hour later, Sunji stands in the hallway in front of Jerrica's apartment, hair pulled back into a ponytail and wearing one of his least favorite shirts—perfect for a drink spill. He has it unbuttoned to the base of his sternum, but he decides going for the navel is better. As he unbuttons further, the door opens and a slender Chinese man with stylish, rimless eyeglasses salutes him with a glass half-full of red wine.

Sunji blinks in recognition. "Erwin?"

Erwin smiles. He's wearing black slacks, a yellow button up underneath a pink sweater, and a matching patterned tie. He steps to the side, gesturing for Sunji to enter.

"Hey, Sunji. Come on in. Jerrica's in the kitchen."

Sunji doesn't move for a moment, a sinking in his stomach. "How do you know Jerrica?"

"We're dating." Erwin waves with his entire arm. "Come in, come in!"

Shellshocked, Sunji manages to walk inside. Erwin closes the door behind him.

"Baby, Sunji's here." He pats Sunji's shoulder, eyes dropping to Sunji's exposed chest. "You look nice."

Sunji begins to button up his shirt as Jerrica rounds the corner, drying her hands on a towel. She wears a silk blouse pattered with oversized orange, pink and yellow flowers, with a yellow pencil skirt and pink heels. Sunji realizes with dismay that she matches her boyfriend.

"Welcome, Sunji! You know Erwin."

Almost accusatory, he echoes, "*You* know Erwin."

He turns to the man in glasses, taking in his rail-thin frame, hunched back, and fucking matched clothing. "And you know Jerrica."

They move into the dining room.

"I had my suspicions after hearing a story or two about you from Jerr-bear," Erwin says, looking at Jerrica lovingly. "I mean, how many Sunji Spencers could be out there who had done an infomercial with Rebel Wilson? And when Jerrica mentioned she had run into you, we traded notes and verified it."

"Kismet!" Jerrica beams.

"Kismet!" Erwin beams back.

Sunji tries to work a smile onto his face.

"I've only played Kismet once," he apologizes. "You'll have to remind me of the rules."

• • • • • • • •

The last time Sunji and Erwin had interacted, they were meeting each other face-to-face for the first time in a Little Tokyo eatery. Erwin, being an up-and-coming Asian American writer and director, was benefiting from Hollywood's current interest in the concept of "diversity" and was meeting with a few actors to potentially headline his upcoming feature that was being funded by some older white men who saw dollar signs.

Similarly, Sunji Spencer was teen soap-talented, with a look his new agent had excitedly called "ethnic." He was being sent out for every third and fourth male lead. They wanted him to learn martial arts, to open himself up for more culturally specific roles, but he refused anything that could potentially damage his face or his body in any way.

When Sunji submitted for Erwin's film, *The Triangle*, it was more than his name that had caught Erwin's attention. They agreed to meet, no handlers, no bullshit, and see if the vibe was right for the project.

"Thank you for bringing a printed version of your résumé," Erwin said, setting it to the side of his chicken katsu. "Interesting choice to include your different tan tones."

"I'm glad you like it!"

"Yeah, sure." Placing his elbows on the table and threading his fingers, he peered through his glasses at Sunji. "How passionate are you about acting? We've established that you're a successful social media model. And I saw you in that infomercial with Rebel Wilson."

Sunji nodded, beaming. "It went national."

"Yeah, you put that in bold on your resume. Why are you looking into acting at this point in your career?"

Sunji took a long sip of his water, cheeks pulling as he sucked on his straw. This was another tactic of his. Showing off the cheekbones while getting a feel for the sexuality of the person he was drinking in front of.

Smacking his lips, he said, "I gotta be honest."

"Please."

"The first time I saw myself in that Miranda campaign and I realized what the photographer saw and how he got it out of me, I realized how important what I did was to the whole picture. I used to think that modeling was just me being still and photogenic and getting a cute pic, you know?" Sunji struck a quick, impressive pose. "But there was something about working to realize a vision, not just a picture."

Erwin chewed this over, repeating, "A vision, not just a picture."

"Acting is like that. And I get to use more of myself. And get ugly."

"Do you get ugly?"

Sunji didn't think so, of course, so instead he offered, "I'll try really hard."

Erwin tried again. "What's your dream role?"

"I want to play, like, a homeless person, you know? Who's got a really tough life and is hated by his dad or something like that, and there's, like, a dead girlfriend because that's always killer. So I'm, like, mourning her and dealing with all of these obstacles and I still die in the end because life is just so hard."

Erwin sighed and adjusted his glasses. "I don't know why I ask actors that question. The answer always fucking sucks."

Sunji was taken aback. "You asked!"

Erwin nodded at this truth. "My mistake. Look, this is my feature-length debut as a director and writer and I've got a lot of fucking awesome people who are invested in this project, so I only want to bring in talented people who are going to enhance that energy and that dedication. Do you think you would be interested in being a part of this?"

Sunji nodded enthusiastically. "Sure. Is the character straight?"

Erwin paused, somewhere between amused and annoyed.

"Yes. Why?"

"I was just wondering," Sunji said, sipping more water. "The movie's called *The Triangle* and that's a gay thing."

"Have triangles been a gay thing since the nineties? It's called *The Triangle* because of their unhealthy obsession with their impending

Bermuda vacation, plus there's three of them..." His eyes searched Sunji's face, finding nothing satisfactory. "Never mind."

He pulled out his phone and his fingers moved quickly.

"I'll email you the full script and we'll hop on a call and discuss it? You down?"

"No, I'm up!"

Disregarding the boner that kept Sunji from standing to shake Erwin's hand as the director left, Sunji was up in a major way. This was the first time in his career that someone was taking him seriously as an actor. He was determined to do everything he could to not screw this up.

• • • • • • • •

Minutes away from screwing everything up, Sunji is doing his best to enjoy the dinner Jerrica has prepared. It helps that he doesn't have to talk, so he can just focus on the food as Erwin tells him about the short film that had gotten him his initial attention on the festival circuit, leading to *The Triangle*, which the director hoped would be his industry breakthrough.

"And the rest, as the white folks say, is Asian-American history," Erwin cracks.

Then Jerrica talks about the journey she's been on to clear out her "emotional garage," as she calls it, of all unnecessary hurt, anger, and feelings of inadequacy.

"Those therapy sessions really helped me embrace my body and all of the things others would call shortcomings. Like, I took a poo last year and killed one of our birds—"

"And she didn't cry."

"I wanted to," Jerrica says, wide-eyed. "I really did, because Buzz Beakyear was always my favorite. But it's a new me. It's Happy Jerrica."

Erwin, bringing his glass of wine to his lips, miscalculates the placement of his own mouth and tips the glass just above his chin. The dark liquid spills down his sweater.

He scoots back from the table and leaps up from the chair. "Well, shave a dick!"

Jerrica stands, yanking at the sweater. "Hurry, take it off! I'll pour water on it before it sets."

Erwin strips out of the sweater quickly, but the wine has already soaked through to his yellow shirt.

"Shave a dick," he says again, undoing his tie. Off comes the tie and then the shirt, revealing an immaculate set of abs underneath, the kind that some skinny guys have by nature of existing. Jerrica runs her fingers across them as she takes the shirt from him.

"Sorry. I'll go get another shirt," Erwin says, following Jerrica out of the room.

Sunji stares in dismay, brain racing at ten miles an hour. "I'll get another plan."

Erwin turns. "What was that?"

"What *was* it?" Sunji repeats.

Erwin stands for a moment. "Okay."

When Sunji doesn't respond—he just stares, his brain now just running in place—Erwin slowly turns again and leaves the room.

After dinner, Erwin heads to the bathroom to check on the clothes that Jerrica had left soaking. Jerrica begins cleaning up the table and Sunji attempts to help.

He's got one more hand he wants to play. A last ditch effort, because nothing is foolproof to a sufficiently talented—

"That's so exciting that you're going to be working with Erwin on his project," Jerrica says.

Sunji nods, doing his best to look troubled. "There's just one thing about it…"

Jerrica looks up, ready. "Just one thing?"

"Have you talked to him about the title? The title still confuses me. There's no mention of the Illuminati in the script."

Jerrica blinks. This wasn't what she was expecting. "Illuminati?"

He follows her into the kitchen with a stack of dishes.

"You know, the American kingdom Beyoncé rules with Taylor Swift. I got invited to one of their knighting ceremonies."

Jerrica shakes her head, frowning. "What does the Illuminati have to do with the title?"

"Because the triangle is the Illuminati's door to the other side where Miley Cyrus is the queen and not the jester."

"I don't know what the fuck you're talking about Sunji. It's called *The Triangle* because Steve and Matt both love Sierra, Sierra's obsessed with going to Bermuda, plus the isosceles theorem Matt obsesses over implies that the triangle is isosceles and the Illuminati only uses an equilateral triangle and," this next part she says with the fury of a Grecian goddess, "what the fuck is a knighting ceremony?

"I just think his audience will get confused. I think he should have done more audience research." He smiles now, leaning casually against the kitchen counter. "I'm really good at those things you know. Marketing. My socials are really jumping off—"

"Don't worry about the title, Sunji. Can you play this part?"

"Of course I can play this part!"

"Then why are you and I talking about it? I'm not producing this film."

"What happened to Happy Jerrica?"

"Normal Sunji showed up."

Sunji strokes her upper arm. "He can go away again if happy Jerrica comes back."

To her credit, Jerrica doesn't slam a single dish as she stops her chores and removes her gloves.

"Good idea. You should go."

She pushes him toward the door.

"I didn't mean to make you upset."

She puts a finger in his face, eyes crackling.

"But you did, Sunji. Erwin, *my boyfriend*, is a fantastic man and a fantastic director. This film is his dream and by fulfilling it, he's actually going to fulfill one of yours. So let him and don't fuck it up by spending your energy trying to impress me. Nothing about you impresses me."

They reach the door and she raises her hands to the ceiling.

"Somewhere in you is a good person, but I keep losing him all all of this..." She waves her hand at him. "This predictable prettiness you have going on."

Sunji smiles, never missing a compliment. "Thank you."

She rolls her eyes. "I'll let Erwin know you have an early morning gig or something. Four features, right? Isn't that what you said?"

He realizes now that she didn't buy his lies at the coffee shop. "Jerrica…"

"Good night, Sunji. It was almost nice seeing you again."

The Eagle Stirs Her Nest

Eagle's night begins in her kitchen, browning ground beef and ripping lettuce. She originally wanted to do something more muscular, like scallops or pork belly, but her husband had balked at what Eagle had considered a relatively modest price tag.

"Tacos," Rockefeller had said, and that was that.

In truth, Rock and Eagle are maybe testing the limits of what they are willing to put up with from each other. He finally agreed to have us over, over a year after she first started asking. It was never the right time for him, then he deployed, then he eventually ran out of excuses.

There's a reason they say be careful what you ask for.

Eagle checks her phone while finishing with the meat. "The guys are heading over."

Rock salutes her with his beer. "Let the orgy commence!"

Eagle sprays him with water from the sink. "Passive aggressive commentary not required."

She dries her hands and he grabs a spoonful of butter from the counter, dumping it down her t-shirt. He's laughing. She isn't.

"Payback's a bitch," he says, and the doorbell rings.

Eagle scoops the butter out of her shirt. "You're a fucking bitch."

"I'll get it," he says.

She looks up at him standing still. "The door?"

"The butter."

She wearily rolls her head from one shoulder to the other, shaking the butter from her fingers into the sink.

"Seriously, Rock, you always do too fucking much."

"Chill out." He still hasn't moved, watching her dig around for more butter. "You were gonna shower and change anyway. I tell you what, if it bothers you so much, I'll give you a ten minute head-start to suck my dick. I'll even pull it out for you."

The doorbell almost seems louder.

"Just a minute!" he hollers, unzipping his pants. "Or fifteen."

She stares up at him through her curls. "Get the fucking door."

Rock frowns and nods as if he understands. "Rain check."

He leaves the kitchen and Eagle begins to search for something messier than butter.

Rock opens the door with a nonplussed expression, which matches Jay's indifferent stare. Alexander smiles brightly.

"Hello, Jay," Rock says dryly. "Alexander. Welcome."

Eagle sneaks behind Rock, not greeting her neighbors as she grips the waistband of her husband's pants and underwear. Yanking the clothing back, she empties a bottle of chocolate syrup—cap removed, of course—all over his ass. Rock's greetings turn to gurgles as he stands frozen in shock. Eagle gleefully shakes the final remnants out of the bottle, then releases her grip, clenching his butt with an extra firm set of squeezes.

Rock finally speaks. "Come on in, fellas." He starts waddling away, two streaks of chocolate sauce following behind. "I gotta go scrub my nubs real quick."

Eagle watches him go. "He just shit himself. He does that sometimes." Then, brightly, "I've gotta mop this up, but you two make yourselves comfortable!"

She only briefly glances at them before hollering after her husband, "Oh, babe? Head-start not required. You get to suck, because mine is bigger."

The guests stand in the doorway, not moving.

A little moan escapes Alexander's throat, and he manages to speak, quietly. "What have we done?"

Jay shoves him through the doorway. "You know what? I changed my mind. This is gonna be awesome."

The next time the doorbell rings, Jay and Alexander are playing with glass shakers and some salt they've spilled on the table. Eagle calls from the kitchen.

"Can one of you get that?"

"Yep," Jay says, rising.

When he gets to the door, he opens it and stares up at a smiling Oscar.

"You must be Alexander," Oscar says, adjusting his messenger bag and holding out a hand to shake.

Jay looks down at the hand, then back up at Oscar. "Only if he won the lottery."

Oscar squints, as if trying to make out new features on Jay's face. "Oh, you're Ellington."

Jay's jaw clenches and Oscar is close to death. "Who are you looking for? Because I think you have the wrong house."

Before Jay can push Oscar off of the porch, Eagle walks up, drying her hands on a towel.

"Oh, hey, Oscar," she says with no discernible excitement. "Come on in. Rock's showering."

Jay closes the door behind Oscar. Eagle watches him size up Rock's friend and mirth returns to her voice.

"Jay, this is Oscar. He was my pick for Zario's date."

"Oh," Jay says, the worst kind of recognition in his voice. "The *dancer*. I heard you had a good time."

Oscar nods with enthusiasm, hitting a quick shuffle step. "We did."

Jay raises his lips to his nose in mock confusion. "'We?' No, that's not what I said. Because that's not what I heard."

Eagle begins to push Oscar down the hallway, shooting gleeful eyes in Jay's direction.

"Let me introduce you to Alexander," she says to Oscar, "the friendly one."

From upstairs comes a muffled call.

"Oscar?"

"Yeah!"

"Come up!"

Oscar shrugs at Eagle. "I'll be right back, I think."

Jay watches him go, a vein near his eye pulsing.

Eagle is apologetic. "Rock invited him."

"I thought this was our night. The Dudes vs. Rock."

"The Dudes *plus* Rock," Eagle revises. "And I had to compromise."

"That's bullshit," Jay says.

Eagle sighs. "You're telling me."

Upstairs, Oscar enters Rock and Eagle's bedroom. Rock is getting dressed. Laid out on the bed next to him is the outfit that Eagle plans on wearing.

"Did you bring it?"

Oscar nods. "If I was gonna make an 'emergency stop,' I could have just grabbed a dish while I was at the store."

"Fuck that. She wants to do work, let her do all the work. Hand it over."

Oscar hands Rock a spice container of cayenne pepper from his messenger bag.

"Do I even want to know?" he asks.

"Probably not," Rock replies, "but you will."

Rock takes Eagle's red lace underwear and lightly lines it with sprinkled pepper.

"God," Oscar says, placing a hand over his mouth. "You two are something else."

• • • • • • •

When Oscar and a freshly scrubbed Rock join Jay and Alexander at the table, they're locked in an intense conversation, leaving the other two bewildered and trying to keep up.

"But the exercise didn't have to go on for those additional six hours if they weren't trying to get the squadron another shot to redeem themselves," Oscar is saying. He punctuates every other word with a strange head sway that Alexander finds himself mirroring.

"He's just a dick," Rock responds. "They extended it so that he could look better, not the squadron."

"No, Captain Shithead's an asshole, but I think it was the last straw."

The doorbell rings.

Rock leans back in his chair, turning his head toward the wall and bellowing from a deep place. "Just a minute!" He winks at Oscar. "Hold that thought."

Once Rock is out of the room, Jay leans in toward Oscar.

"Is there a distinction to you?"

Oscar looks at him warily. "Hmm?"

"I'm assuming you wanted to contribute more than redundancy to this goddam fascinating dialogue about Captain Shithead. So what's the distinction for you between 'dicks' and 'assholes?'"

"What do you mean?"

"'He's a dick.' 'No, he's an asshole.' What's the difference?"

"There's no real difference, I guess."

"Hmm."

Jay is all but spitting fire. Alexander glances between the two nervously.

Jay begins. "I dated this girl named Tabernacle, true story. I called her Tabby. She had this brother who was a real dick, and I'm allowed to say that, because as an asshole myself, I can make the differentiation. So one day, I, the asshole, confront the dick, right?"

Rock reenters the room, talking over his shoulder.

"No, it's perfectly fine! The more the merrier! Eagle's finishing getting ready."

Alexander, Jay and Oscar look up as Ellington enters the room, arms linked with Mandy.

"Hey, guys. You know Mandy."

Jay breaks out into a wide grin. "This is turning into quite the party, isn't it?"

"Goofy," Mandy laughs. As she passes behind Jay's chair, his smile falls.

"What's on the menu?" Ellington asked, taking his seat across from Alexander. Mandy settles in between him and Oscar.

"We're having tacos," Rock says, taking his place at the head of the table.

"¡Arriba!" Mandy exclaims, shaking loose fists as if waving tiny flags or maracas.

Ellington points to Oscar, but looks at Jay and Alexander. "Who's that?"

Jay shrugs.

"Ellington," Rock says, "this is Oscar."

Oscar offers his hand to Mandy. "Hi."

She shakes. "Hello."

"You went on that date with Zario last week."

Oscar nods. "Yeah, he's great."

"He is," Ellington says and it sounds like a threat.

Oscar drops his hand.

"Rock, get your chocolate ass in here and help me bring this food out," Eagle calls from the kitchen.

"Oh, we can help," Alexander offers.

Eagle pops her head around the corner. "You're our guests. Keep your fucking asses in the fucking seats. It's called hospitality. *Rockefeller.*"

"Coming, dear," Rock sings.

After the first round of tacos, Mandy's face is flushed.

"So spicy. Where's the ladies room?" she asks Rock.

"We have a bathroom," Rock says. "Down the hall."

Mandy rushes away from the table. Eagle, too, is sweating, shifting in her seat across from her husband.

Ellington waits until he hears the bathroom door close and grins toothily at their host.

"Yo, Eagle, this place is pretty nice. You outdid yourself on those sautéed vegetables. Is that a picture of Rock with Peyton Manning? I'm pretty sure Mandy's a racist."

After a brief silence, Rock reengages Oscar in their exclusionary conversation and Ellington shares, as briefly as he can, the craziness that has become his relationship with Mandy. He's gone from wanting to marry her to trying his best to rid his life of her.

"That's some fucked up shit," Jay muses.

"Your eloquence astounds." Ellington stares at his plate as if the patterns around the edges are going to rearrange themselves into something solid. "Until that moment, she was perfect."

"Perfect for what?" Jay asks. "I mean, you said it yourself that you were her trophy dick."

"And you've been giving that dick to everybody," Alexander says.

"Everybody," Eagle repeats.

Jay whispers, "Community dick."

"Is it possible she was some type of trophy to you?" Eagle asks, gyrating slightly in her seat.

Ellington looks from Eagle's face to her overactive hips.

"Are you okay, Eagle?"

"Fine. Perfectly fine. Just feels like my cooch is turning into lava."

She stands and heads toward the kitchen, pausing momentarily to grind against the doorframe and throw a dagger stare toward Rock, who—it is now obvious—is purposefully avoiding her stare.

"You have to remember," she speaks again, loudly, as if to Ellington, though her eyes are drilling into the back of her husband's head, "everything that goes around comes back around harder and stronger."

Her hips lock and release as she grinds harder, sweat pouring down her face.

Mandy returns, her pace slowing as she passes Eagle.

"Oooh, are we playing charades?"

"Love," Rock says sweetly, turning to look at his wife. "You okay?"

"Whoo," is all Eagle can manage as she sweats. "Whoo." She thrusts. "Whoo." She glares.

"Babe," he begins innocently, "maybe you should go scrub *your* nubs?"

Her eyes gain a focus beyond description. "What did you do?" she hisses.

Rock shrugs. Eagle hunches her shoulders, curls falling into her face.

"Would you all excuse me?"

And with the posture, hair, and lurch of a fairy tale witch, Eagle disappears up the stairs.

• • • • • • •

Eagle comes downstairs in her third outfit of the evening and wordlessly glides into the kitchen.

"So, I tell him to get on his face and he drops and starts to push. I tell him I can't hear him counting, so he begins: 'One, ma'am. Two, ma'am. Three, ma'am.' So I kneel down and get right up in his face and say, 'Do I look like a fucking ma'am to you?' And he goes, 'Sorry! Sorry! One, ma'am-sir! Two, ma'am-sir!' And I'm trying my hardest to keep a straight face, right? Like, kid is about to shit himself. So I say to him, 'What the hell is a 'ma'am-sir?' And he goes, 'Sorry! Sorry! One push-up! Two push-up!'"

Oscar laughs while the rest of the guests stare dumbfounded.

Mandy turns to Ellington, growing excited. "Is there a camera somewhere? Is this for a streaming show?"

Ellington pats her leg. "Baby, I don't know who this is for."

Eagle returns now with two bottled sodas. She hands Rock one.

"Truce?" she asks and he nods. When she passes behind Alexander on her way to her seat, Alexander reaches for the other soda and she swats his hand.

"Reading my thoughts!" Rock exclaims, unscrewing the bottle top. Soda erupts from the bottle in burst of fizz and brown syrup, spraying his clothes and his face. The shock of it causes him to jerk the bottle, causing even more to spill out all over his shirt.

Eagle calmly unscrews her soda. "Oh. *That's* the one that fell."

Rock bolts from the table. "Do you know how long it took me to get my hair like this?"

"Dry it off; it's fine," she calls after him. To everyone at the table, she says, "Part one of a three-part attack. Wait for it."

A minute or so later, a sudden, odd sound comes from upstairs.

"Was that a thud?" Mandy asks. "Is he okay?"

Jay shakes his head. "Sounded like a 'poof.'"

Eagle sips her soda gingerly. "That sounded like part two."

Upstairs, Rock is coughing and sputtering, then the air fills with cuss words.

Eagle grins. "Flour in the hairdryer. I learned that one at summer camp."

"What's part three?" Oscar asks, and Eagle's face tightens.

"Like I'm going to tell you."

Rock reenters, white powder caked on his face and throughout his hair. The heads at the table move in unison, following him as he marches back to his seat, carefully lowers himself down into his soda-spattered chair, and gingerly folds his cloth napkin.

"I yield," he says quietly.

"Oh, it's too late, bruh," Eagle replies. "Demolition in progress."

"How did this start?" Mandy asks, but Ellington shushes her quickly.

Rock blinks, flour falling from his eyelashes onto his shirt. "Anyone down for a board game?"

Alexander looks at Ellington, then Jay. "I think…"

"For sure," Jay replies quickly.

Ellington stands. "Yeah. Let's go, Mandy."

Eagle grabs at arms and waist, but her guests are evacuating. "Stay, fellas!"

"Fucks no," Jay says as they all move down the hall.

"Zario's almost home," Alexander says in a small attempt at explanation.

Mandy bows apologetically, as her boyfriend says, "Mandy has an early morning."

The Dudes move quickly, vacating the space.

Oscar alone sits at the table with the Diolosas. "I could be down for a board game."

Rock doesn't even bother. "Goodbye, Oscar."

His friend nods and hurries out of the room .

The thing is, Eagle hasn't told the complete truth. Part three is contingent on Rock making one final move in their demeaning game of chess, a move Eagle has no doubt he's going to make.

"Can't you give me a hint?" he asks, pacing, while she cleans up in the kitchen. He's made himself another taco.

"Maybe this is it," she says. "Maybe the plan is to keep you waiting on another shoe to drop when there are no more shoes in the sky?"

"Where does that phrase even come from," Rock screeches. "Why are there all those shoes in the sky? Besides, if that was the case, you wouldn't have just put the thought in my head."

"Well, you asked for a hint," she shrugs.

His eyes fly up to the ceiling. "Is it a shoe?" He looks down at his feet. "Itch powder or something?"

An hour or so later, Rock is gripping the toilet seat with both hands, the last traces of flour on his face shuttled away by rivers of sweat as he takes a shit of epic proportions. He realizes in the moment that Eagle added a laxative to the taco ingredients just before shaking up his soda. She knew his hungry ass would be eating more at the end of the night, instead of helping clean.

He reaches for the toilet paper only to find a thin sheet remaining on the roll. He kicks at the cabinet doors beneath the sink, only to find it devoid of the tissue they typically keep stashed there.

"Babe? Babe!"

Eagle lays in the bed, headphones cranked up and a pack of ice resting on her crotch. Her face is serene, Rock's cries unheard.

Beneath her, under the bed, sit twenty-two rolls of toilet paper.

How We Break Our Lungs

My night begins with Lando, who ends a conversation with his coworkers the moment he spots me entering the restaurant.

"Mr. del Rosario. Welcome back."

His hair seems higher. His eyes are laughing at something and I instinctively grab the bottom of my jacket, tugging it until I feel it melted to my shoulders.

"Hi, Lando. And you can just call me Zario."

He grabs a pair of menus. "You know, I wasn't scheduled to work tonight, but I switched some shifts around to make sure I was here to take care of you."

"That's kind of you," I say, both grateful and surprised.

I follow him toward the familiar booth.

"I assumed you wanted the same table."

"I'm not picky, really," I say.

"Yeah, but these guys who call and make the reservations for you sure are. They say, 'the best spot in the house,' and this here is the best spot we have. And, truth be told, you're getting the best service with me. That's why I have to be here."

I sit, smiling up at him.

"Admit it. You're just curious to see how tonight goes in comparison to the last two dates."

"They *are* dates!" He claps his palms together and I wonder if he's won a bet of his own. "And the word you're looking for is 'nosy.' I'm nosy and I'm invested. Is tonight a new guy or one of the previous two?"

"A new guy." I'm trying to figure out if he's being intrusive or conversational, and I conclude that it's a tightrope many servers walk.

He laughs. "I'll be back with the usual. Water with no lemon."

When Lando walks away, I think about something Eagle says occasionally. "Zario's one of those guys who never seems to realize how good he has it. Or when someone is really into him."

I briefly wonder if Lando might be flirting with me, then I dismiss it. Even if he is flirting with me, some straight guys just like to know they could if they wanted to. Like Jay and his cousin. The motherfucks.

I notice a hand waving at me from the bar. It's gloriously, unmistakably queer Wesley. Brown skin, bow tie, those lips. I love when lips are still plump even when the smile stretches from ear to ear.

I realize my thought process. Lando, Wesley. Neither of these guys are my date, but here I am, walking over to the bar anyway.

"*You're back!*"

"*Do you live here?*" I tease.

"*At this bar? No. At all the bars.*" He points to a sign. "*Tuesday night is happy hour. You just happen to show up here on Tuesdays. How was the big guy from last week?*"

"*You saw us?*"

"*Tuesdays! And you two were in and out so fast.*"

I catch the implication and exhale. "*We went dancing.*" To avoid elaborating further (again), I sign "*It's good to see you again, Wesley.*"

"*I know it is.*"

I laugh. He's serious, though. I take a mental note. Folks tell on themselves early. He could be foreshadowing an ego problem.

He gestures to the wall of bottles behind the bar before signing more.

"*Still not drinking?*"

"*Still.*"

"*Another date? With or without notecards?*"

He's got jokes tonight. "*Yes, another date. With guy number three.*"

"*You're very social.*"

I can't tell if it's a judgement or not. "*My friends do this.*"

He sips his drink, forehead knotted.

"Your friends set you up on dates? Do they dump their exes on you?"

"Oh, no," I say aloud. Horrified at the concept, I clarify. *"All of my friends are straight."*

He stares at me for a moment, and I worry I fucked up my signing.

"Really?"

The way his chin sinks into his neck, I realize he's incredulous.

"Pretty sure," I reply.

"Isn't that weird? Being the only man's man? Risking attraction to someone you can't have?"

This strikes me. For a moment I think of Jay, Rock, then Lando. But attraction is controllable. It's not love. Besides, what was the alternative?

I sign, *"I avoid most girls. Not trying to be a token accessory."*

"Preach," he grins. *"But what about a supportive gay environment where people love you for who you are?"*

"I have that with my dudes."

He tries again. *"A supportive **gay** environment."*

I don't have an answer to this and he clocks that fact quickly. He pulls out his wallet and hands me a thick, orange business card.

"In case this date doesn't work out."

I glance at the card briefly before pocketing it. Wesley West. It's like the alter ego of a superhero. He grins slightly.

"Wish me luck," I sign.

"Good luck, Zario."

I return to wait at the best seat in the house, sipping on the lemon-less water Lando provides for me. Being gay for me is etched into my essence. It is as grafted to my existence as my race, my culture, and my love of coconut brownies. Having gay friends, though, was never really an option for me. The town I grew up in is small, conservative, and violently homophobic. Still. In college, the other gay kids were either closeted or competing for some prize of obnoxiousness.

It's possible to be a part of and apart from communities. It's easiest to understand this in relation to white gay men. They have an unattainable—and unwanted—perception of the world around them due to their particularly calibrated combination of oppression and privilege that makes empathizing with the things they claim as "culture"—Lana Del Rey, Ryan Murphy shows, swearing they have an "inner Black woman"—nearly impossible. Even though I benefit from being cisgender and male, I still don't feel comfortable in majority queer spaces. I still worry that my queerness is expected to be performative, overtly feminine, with a vocabulary laced with the latest terms and phrases, which I never know.

I blame the heteros. Before I get the opportunity to muse over why I'm right to blame the heteros—and I know I am—I realize someone is speaking my name.

There are a pair of shoes standing at my table. Out of those shoes, rippling like a beanstalk, are two of the most impressive calves I have ever seen, the kind that Richard Bruce Nugent once called "muscular hocks." They're coated in a golden-brown sheen of skin, covered above the knee by a pair of piped shorts. I don't notice his torso because once his face hits my peripherals, I am bewitched and I cannot look away.

He's gorgeous. His eyebrows are thick, his brown eyes are shining, and he's got a Cupid's bow cresting atop his full, pink lips. He has a mole like a tattoo in the center of his top lip.

"Zario, right? I'm Iggy."

To be honest, most of what follows doesn't linger. We order food, though I'm not sure what or how much I enjoy it. We share stories, but I can't say which ones or how the dialogue transitions. Then he gets around to the question I hate, and my memory begins to log the night again.

"So, 'Zario.'"

I hear it in his inflection. I've had enough experience to know when the question is about to come.

He twists his mouth to one side of his face. I notice the acne on his cheeks. He's so beautiful. I wish he would just stick to the fun stuff, but he continues, "May I ask?"

I raise my fork and cobbler falls back onto my plate. When did we get to desert? "Everybody does."

He leans back, rubbing his hands on his thighs. "Born with it, nickname, or something else?"

"My last name is del Rosario."

"Ah. Got it. Okay, you can ask me—fair game."

Oh, turnabout. I mull this over. "Ignatius?"

He chuckles. "No. My last name is Iglesias."

"Ooo. I like that." Zario Iglesias. Zario del Rosario-Iglesias.

Wait. I look at him and I realize he's Filipinx. Like Shane. That's unfortunate. But Shane did not have Iggy's face. Or his calves.

Iggy's laughing now. "Ignatius is a new guess, I've gotta say. My mom calls me Armando, though." He waves his hands with stiff wrists as if he's playing invisible bongos. "And that wasn't my slick way of trying to find out what your mom calls you, either."

"That wouldn't have worked," I say. "My mom's dead."

"Oh, man. So sorry."

I shrug. This line of questioning always gets here eventually, so I figured jumping to the destination was the best way to move past it. "She was listening to praise and worship, and when they said, 'lift your hands in the air,' she did."

His brow creases and he plays with his straw. "Forgive me for asking, but how exactly did that kill her?"

"She was driving on the 405. My mother was an idiot."

It takes him a moment. "You're lying."

I grin and I know the sadness is seeping out. "Only partly."

"How did she really die?" he asks softly.

I look down, but all I can see are the doctors, the screens, the neon line that suddenly went flat. I hear myself screaming for Dad who had just went to the vending machine. "Be right back," he had said, and on that queue everything had turned to a horror movie. I feel the wall. I always feel the wall. The subtle bumps of paint, sliding beneath my hands as I collapsed to the floor. Why did he fucking ask about my name?

"I don't like talking about it."

"Okay. My bad. You wanna get out of here?"

I look back up in alarm. "Oh, did I ruin dinner? I'm sorry, I—"

He holds his hands up, shaking his head, just as alarmed as me. "No, I just know of some awesome places we can check out. I know about this bet, and I'm not going out like a punk. So let's do this."

This raises my heart rate and my antennae. "Go where? I'm not trying to dance all night."

"Dance?" He throws his head back and the most musical, bouncing laughter bubbles out of his torso. "No, I'm a terrible dancer. This is the one dance I can do."

He begins to gyrate his shoulders, upper arms pinned to his side while his forearms flop beneath the table.

"Wait, what is that?"

Iggy stops, laughing. "Exactly."

"Was that some weird zombie-style novelty dance?"

"It was the Harlem Shake!"

"Oh, well, in your defense, anyone who does that dance right, still looks like they don't know how to dance."

I drop a fat tip for Lando and we head out.

· · · · · · ·

One ten minute car ride and a five minute walk later, I'm sitting with Iggy on a blanket in Griffith Park. I can see the road, which I appreciate, but I already started sharing my location with the guys the moment we left the restaurant. The sky is endless above us, and the trees are giving us space, watching from their silent orchestra around us.

"This is my favorite spot to be in all of LA." He points. "In January, Orion's up there. Ouch!"

It was his idea to play the slap game, but he's losing so bad—and I have a heavy hand, I've been told in far less PG circumstances— that I'm starting to feel sorry for him.

"Let's play word association," I suggest, as he rubs the back of hands on his thighs. "You've got me up here in the wilderness away from everybody I know and love, so I should figure out just how crazy you are."

"Shoot."

"Okay, um… Sky."

"Heaven," he says dreamily.

"Night."

"Boogie."

"Boogey?"

"Not like the boogeyman. 'Boogie Nights?' Heatwave." He sings. "*Whoa-oh-oh.*"

I shake my head. I don't know the song.

"Problem," I say.

Iggy responds immediately. "Solver."

"Okay, you go because I'm about to vomit up all this Cute in my mouth."

"Fine," he says. "Mouth."

His mouth is luscious, I think.

"Dick," I say, which is far worse.

He laughs, so I laugh.

"And there goes the Cute," I say.

"Have you ever noticed how white guys call it a cock all the time?" Iggy asks me. "Like, exclusively."

"Have I? 'Oh, yah, I want your cock,'" I pant. "Feed me your hot, neon pink cock.'"

Our laughter subsides into giggles.

"We derailed my round way fast," Iggy says. "There's no coming back from dick and neon penises. You go."

I can't think of a word, so I cheat. "Mouth."

"Smile."

Ugh. He's a dreamboat. "Dick."

"Grayson," he says, and now he looks at me—like really looks at me. "Do I have you feeling some kind of nasty way up here? Because that wasn't my intention at all."

"No, no, things are funny in my head and then I say them." That's almost true.

"Are you sure they were funny in your head?" he teases me.

I give his chest a soft punch. My hand lands on his shins, fingers on his calves. I wonder if I'm as slick as I think I am.

"You get the last word of the game," he says. "Go."

"Life."

Immediately, he says, "Kiss."

I lean back and remember I'm not in a chair, lurching forward again in an effort to avoid losing my balance. "Geez. Kiss?"

"I'm not pulling a, a you. The Sade song popped in my head." He sings. "*You gave me the kiss of life.*"

"Oh yeah, I've heard that song."

He doesn't reply right away, just stares at me as if waiting for me to say more. When I don't, he says, "I didn't mean for my lack of vocal ability to ruin this conversation."

"Hey, I ruin dinner; you ruin conversation," I laugh. "No, if anything, it was my dang dirty mind doing a good job of it."

I mull Iggy's words over for a moment, staring up at the sky, wondering where Orion is when he's not here.

"That's an interesting concept. 'The kiss of life.' People talk about that as if it's a one-sided thing. But there are moments when you have the opportunity to kiss life back. And those moments—you gotta have excitement. And openness. And no entertaining of fear. And like any good kiss, you can forget to come up for air. And sometimes because of the kiss you…break."

He was following me before that last part. Now he frowns.

"You break? That sounds painful. What do you break?"

"Your lungs. But it's really life breaking your lungs, because you can't breathe and,"—shit, I shouldn't have started talking—"the grip of that kiss doesn't make it easy."

Somehow Iggy's got one of my hands in his and he's pressing the tips of my fingers one by one. "Am I wrong to think that the solution would be to stop the kiss?"

"Of life? I'd prefer to break my lungs. How do you un-kiss life? Should you? Once you know how good it feels?"

"So, pain… due to pleasure?" Iggy asks me and I return to the stars.

"They're not sold separately."

He gently lays my hands back in my lap. "Are you sure about that?"

I don't have an answer.

• • • • • • • •

He walks me toward our house. If I didn't ruin our conversation in the park, I certainly ended it.

"Thanks for walking me home."

"No problem at all. This was a blast. The whole night."

We've reached the stairs and I stop on the bottom step, turning to face him with my hands jammed in my pocket. Now I'm the girl in those movies, but I'm towering over my date instead of matching his altitude.

"I'd love to see you again," I say, wishing I had hair to toss out of my face. Why do I always turn into the woman in any movie? "If I'm not breaking some kind of rule of the bet, that is."

"That's right," Iggy remembers, "I'm one of five. Well, at least I hope that's the current ranking."

Over Oscar and Mick? Abso-fucking-lutely. I say, "Thanks for being cool about this whole thing. And being cool in general."

He raises his dense eyebrows. "Cool is something I'm not usually called."

"The usual is rarely worth consideration," I say, and I realize which girl I am. I'm Anne Hathaway. What the fuck is wrong with me?

Abruptly, he says, "Well, goodnight."

No, I'm definitely not Anne Hathaway. I blink. "Goodnight, Iggy."

He walks away backwards.

"You have my number."

"I do."

He nods, and turns, moving quickly down the walk.

I turn, slowly heading up the steps. Somehow I had fucked this up. I don't know how, but it's clear I fucked this up.

"Zario."

I turn to see Iggy running back.

"Excitement," he says, stepping onto the stairs.

"What?" That sounds like something I should remember.

He takes another step toward me. "Openness."

"Okay…" I think I'm tracking.

Now he's on the step directly below me, and I don't understand why anyone ever says they want to be tall.

"No entertaining of fear."

"None," I say and he joins me on my step, still short.

"This is how we break our lungs," he says, and he kisses me.

I drown in that kiss. When we come up for air, I grip his chin and drag him back under with me. Our lips match, our tongues dance, our lungs burst, and still we plunge deeper.

• • • • • • • •

Alexander and Jay watch us through the window like creeps.

"Oh shit, motherfuck," Alexander says. "You won."

Jay pulls away from the window. "Yeah."

"Do you think their stubble makes kissing better or worse? Maybe it serves as a reminder that they're kissing a man. Maybe it comforts them."

Jay tugs at Alexander's shirt. "Ask them. Let's do a shot."

That's where I find them when I dance into the kitchen, doing my best *Singin' in the Rain* Debbie Reynolds. Again, I'm the girl, but her joy is so unchained and fresh in that movie that she's the only one I could be.

"Hey, guys!"

Jay holds up a teacup. "Shot?"

"Tonight? Maybe."

Jay pours. Alexander looks surprised.

"You must have had a great night!"

"What about you guys? Where's Sunji?"

"He's got some girl in his room, smashing her brains out. He didn't really talk to us when he got home." Before I can ask, Alexander adds, "*Not* Jerrica."

"So his night probably didn't go too well. What about Eagle's dinner?"

Alexander gives a diplomatic smile. "We just lived through it, and barely. Can the recap wait until tomorrow?"

I chuckle as Jay slides the cups to us. "Sure."

"To an eventful night." Jay holds his teacup in the air and ours meet his there.

"To an eventful night," Alexander says.

"To a wonderful night!" I cheer.

"Meh."

We drink and Alexander heads to the den. I hop on the counter as Jay begins to rinse the cups out in the sink.

"Have you ever met somebody who challenges the way you see the world? Who challenges the way you see yourself?"

Jay glances at me. "Yeah, I have."

I laugh. "Okay, you're making fun of me. I tell you this. I think you may have won tonight."

Jay's eyes are back on the cups. "Yeah."

I realize Eagle's dinner must have been far more difficult than I realized.

"Get some rest, bb," I say, dropping back to the tiled floor. "I'm going to sleep in my bed tonight."

I don't remember getting there. I'm sure I danced my way beneath my sheets. I do remember the dreams. Iggy joined me there and we dared Orion to look away.

The Coincidental Fantastic

"You should talk to her."

The suggestion comes from a young woman standing behind Eagle in line. Eagle turns, face flushing.

"I'm sorry? Oh, no, I wasn't—I was just admiring her hair. Wondering what treatment she uses."

Across the coffeeshop sits an Asian woman with long black hair. She reads a book while spinning her coffeecup absently on the table. Eagle had been admiring more than her hair.

"She watches you, too, you know. I should know, I'm her friend." The woman offers her hand. "Ty."

"Next?" the barista calls, giving Eagle her necessary excuse to turn away without making a new acquaintance.

Alexander returns from the bathroom, nudging in next to Eagle. "What are you getting?"

"Same thing I always get. You know what you want?"

"Oh, I got mine. Plus, I have no idea what I'm gonna get."

"You've tried everything on the menu."

"Almost," Alexander says, stepping back.

Ty looks over at him, her smile taking on a bashful shade. "The White Velvet's really good."

"It has a weird aftertaste," Alexander says, dismissing her suggestion without even looking at her.

She arches an eyebrow. "Have you ever ordered from the secret menu?"

Now he looks, intrigued. "They have a secret menu?"

"Ask for the Red Pot Pop."

"What?" His eyes bug out of his head. "They have potion pop? How'd you find out about that?"

"How do you *not* know about it? You're always in here with your awesome shirts that imply—well, how much of a nerd are you?"

Eagle turns a withering gaze on both of them. "Oh, he's the ultimate nerd. He games. He's pro."

Ty lights up. "You're a gamer?"

Eagle waves her receipt at Alexander. "I'll be waiting over there while you do whatever this is."

Alexander nods at her, turning quickly back to Ty. "Mobas are life!"

Eagle saunters away from them, pulling up a chair at a table next to the long-haired reader. She watches as the woman turns the cup in a slow circle, doing her best to make out the name scribbled on the side.

The voice rolls in like a wave, husky like Jessica Rabbit. "It was a green tea latte."

Eagle, with wide eyes, looks up into the face that is cooly regarding hers. *She watches you, too, you know.*

Eagle consistently appears to be the only one of us dudes who seems to have everything figured out. The honest tea is that when it comes to herself, she's just as clueless as the rest of us.

The woman tips her empty cup toward Eagle. "I drank it too fast and now I'm just trying to keep my hands busy."

Eagle's eyes grow wide. "What? Oh, no, I get the green tea myself. Does your cup say, 'December?' That's your coffeeshop name?"

Eagle spends countless hours waiting on coffee, hearing the most obtuse versions of customer's names. The number of syllables doesn't seem to matter—everyone's name ends up twisted beyond belief like a game of Telephone, but only between two people.

"I use June," she says now. "Which makes me think this moment is some sort of cosmic punchline."

December smiles at "June," her eyes flitting occasionally from Eagle's face to the rest of her.

"I have a friend who refers to it as 'the coincidental fantastic.' What's your real name?"

"My government name's shit, but everybody calls me Eagle."

They shake hands, and Eagle can't figure out who's hand went out first.

"December," the woman says, setting her book down. "That's my government name. Swear on my birth certificate."

"Really?" Eagle scoffs, then quickly adds, "Unique names are cool."

"Don't give it that much credit," December chuckles. "It's just the month I was born in. My parents have no imagination. What about 'Eagle?'"

"Oh, that's a long story. But let's just say I love my country." She holds up a fist. "*Murica.*"

The barista calls. "June? Iced latte?"

They both look toward the counter.

"Well, it was nice to meet you," December says, tipping her cup once again.

Eagle nods, shifting in her seat in preparation to stand.

"You know what? Wanna meet me here tomorrow for lunch?"

December doesn't blink. "Let's do dinner. I know a spot."

"Tell me what it is; I'll find it." Eagle panics. "Oh, geez."

December laughs. "I'll be happy to give you directions, instead. Give me your phone."

Over at the counter, running simultaneous to this new development, Ty and Alexander are raving to each other about their favorite players in a recent tournament.

"I have a tourney later on today, actually," Alexander says proudly. "I'm Thundereye13."

"Oh, I've heard of you," Ty says with genuine recognition in her voice. "Are you doing a LAN party?"

"No, just me at my place. You wanna come check it out?"

She nods and waves her phone. "Drop me your contact."

Alexander pulls out his phone. "Sure. And just hit me up around one. I live near here."

"Cool. Me, too!"

Alexander points to her phone as his contact comes through.

"Alexander."

"Ty."

"Ty," the barista interrupts, "your drink's been ready. And you wanna take this one over to your friend's friend? Hers has been ready, too."

"Sure," she says, lifting both drinks off of the counter. She smiles at Alexander. "See you later."

He nods stiffly and steps to the counter to make his order.

"I wish I could get a girl like that," the barista says to him, staring after Ty.

"Me, too," Alexander replies, before ordering a Red Pot Pop.

• • • • • • •

Sunji, Ellington, Jay, and I stand in front of the full-length mirror at a gym that's new to us. Technically, it's new to everyone, since it just opened a week or so ago, and we're taking advantage of the low traffic to do what dudes do.

Ellington kneads his chest. "Do you think there's a such thing as areola reduction surgery?" He looks up, pinching his nipples. "Not that I think I need it or anything. Just curious. These things are like a second set of eyes."

Next to him, I push my pelvis forward, attempting to slim my profile.

"My frame looks like I was engineered to have children. I have the hips of a birthing goddess."

Beside me, Sunji flexes his jaw. "I think the area between my lip and chin is shrinking. Is that a thing that can happen?"

Jay is just staring at himself, shifting his shoulders gradually to create new silhouettes. When he notices us staring, he frowns.

"What? I'm perfect."

I roll my eyes and follow Ellington over to the training area where we're supposed to meet our new group trainer, the famed (at least, according to Ellington) Mr. Seventeen.

"Ay, Ellingtwat," Jay huffs, catching up with us. "Why do they call him Mr. Seventeen?"

All Ellington says is, "You'll see."

We don't have to wait long. While stretching, I take notice of a man walking over to us with swagger like a rich kid who thinks he's talented at whatever job he was just given. From a distance, he looks completely nude and I'm wondering exactly what kind of fitness center Ellington has brought us to.

Understandably, Sunji cannot process this. "What's wrong with his penis?"

"That's not his penis," I say.

"Sure looks like one," Sunji says.

"Well, it *is* a penis."

We're both right. Mr. Seventeen arrives in front of us, rippling muscles on every inch of his short body. What Sunji and I have been calling his penis is actually a graphic on flesh-colored boxer briefs— the crown jewels of Michelangelo's anatomically correct David.

David wished he had this guy's dimensions. Then again, David probably wouldn't be standing in front of us with another man's dick on his dick.

"I know what you're thinking."

From behind me, Jay says, "You couldn't *possibly*, my dude."

One by one we stand as the half-naked man continues his well-rehearsed opening speech.

"How does he do it? The physique! The motivation! You want to be like me! You want to be me! You wanna be all up in me! And that's a natural reaction to someone in my peak condition. Today you will have the option to be like Mr. Zach Seventeen."

Zach. Anyone with that name was trouble. I learned that from *Saved By the Bell*.

I lean over to Ellington. "Is he serious?"

Zach hears me and walks over.

"Am I serious?" He circles me and I instinctually want to call him a bitch. "I'm as serious as something very important that happened to you that you don't let people make jokes about." He pauses long enough to create a type of anticipation in my spirit. "Like those hips."

I decide there's no harm in actually calling him a bitch, but all I can do is gasp before he moves on.

"We're gonna get started! But first I'm going to go put on clothes now that my point's been made. I wouldn't want to intimidate you further. Give me like ten, okay? Sometimes my hoodie doesn't go over my head easily. And sometimes my compression shorts don't go over my ass."

He walks away, and I gasp again.

He's got the juiciest ass I've ever seen in my life. Like, a peach come to life, wobbling back and forth on his muscular legs as he stalks away.

His legs. His calves. He's definitely going to be trouble for me.

I lean back into Ellington's ear, suddenly self-conscious.

"Is there a such thing as hip reduction surgery?"

• • • • • • • •

When Zach returns to us, now semi-clothed (he's wearing shorts), he leads us through a buttload of group exercises. He's the real deal. After a few sets I can tell how he's got his body and I can officially say I don't want one like his if this is the cost.

He splits us up, with Sunji and Jay doing a set of exercises, then switching with Ellington and I. I think the goal is to keep us engaged as neither duo wants to fall behind and have the other two waiting and—gasp—*resting*.

While doing overhead shoulder presses or some other exercise with a name that's a combination of a body part, a position, and an activity, Ellington keeps whipping his head toward me with an immoveable smile on his face.

"What do you think?"

"I think," I say between gasps, "that he's trying to kill us."

Ellington sets his admiring gaze on Zach. "Dedication. Determination. Discipline. Dat jawline."

I turn wild eyes to Ellington. "How are you breathing and talking at the same time?"

Ignoring me, he proudly announces, "This is the guy I picked for your date!"

"What?" Jay's eyebrow goes up, quite frightening with all of the blood vessels in his face bulging from the workout.

Sunji's eyes are equally wild. "That's not fair!"

Ellington shrugs. "We never said that these dates had to be blind!"

Jay rakes his eyes across our trainer. "At least if Zario's sore the next day, I'll believe whatever answer he gives."

Zach walks over to us. "If you four have enough energy to talk, you have enough energy for another set! Let's go!"

• • • • • • • •

"Welcome to my office," Alexander says, leading Ty into the den.

"Oh, it's nice in here!" she says. "Your roommates are okay with you doing your tourneys out here?"

"Yeah, I mean, it pays the bills," Alexander shrugs.

"I have to play in my room, otherwise it's a whole house meeting."

"You live with your friend from the coffeeshop?"

"December? Oh, no, I live with these movie industry guys."

"Actors?"

Ty settles onto the couch. "Writers."

"Ugh, the worst." Alexander tests his headset. "What's your name? I meant to ask you."

Ty makes a face that he can't quite read. "I'm Doomerang."

He stares at the inside of his eyeballs for a moment.

"You're Doomerang? You're top-ranked. You've beaten me a hundred times."

Ty smiles. "You always make me work for it."

"Did you know—?" he begins to ask.

She shakes her head quickly. "Not until today at the coffeeshop when you told me who you were. Just a touch of the coincidental fantastic."

"You said you heard of me. You didn't tell me you had kicked my ass."

"I don't like to lead with that," she laughs. "Then I'd never get to know people."

Alexander pauses, then nods. "I can understand that. You're not a backseat gamer, are you?"

"I'll just watch and cheer," she says.

"No, I mean, you can be a backseat gamer if you want to. You're fucking Doomerang."

Once the tournament begins, she's selective with her advice. He's quite good on his own, but as they near the end of the tourney and his work becomes sloppy, her suggestions become more forceful.

"You gotta go for it now," Ty says, "because you may not get another chance."

Alexander understands. "I got this, bro."

She arcs and eyebrow. "I'm not your bro."

"I know. Of course. I mean…" Alexander looks away from the screen and it's clear that he hears her on every level. "I have enough bros."

He jumps on her like a cricket. She squeals in surprise, then leans up to kiss him. Her hands start exploring his body and he reaches to take off her shirt.

"Wait!" she yells and he pauses, his arms wrapped around her waist.

"I'm sorry. I just—"

"No, you're fine," she says, reaching around him to the computer. She inputs a combination quickly and he wins the game.

"You're the best," he says.

"You're about to find out."

• • • • • • •

Ellington drops us off and Sunji and I leave Jay at the bottom of the stairs.

"Just bring me water, soap, a hand towel, last night's leftovers, and a pillow just in case," he moans, moving his legs stiffly.

"I'll come back in ten minutes if you're not inside by then," I tell him.

When Sunji and I walk into the house, it smells like sweat and spit and something Sunji calls "snatch."

When he closes the door, it alerts Alexander, who is lying completely naked and completely satisfied on the couch in the den. He realizes that he has maybe a minute to get dressed if we come directly back there to check on his game. Less than that if one of us has a funny story to tell him. Normally, a quick change wouldn't be too hard for him, especially since he doesn't wear underwear.

Today is different though, because Ty is also quick with putting on clothes, and Alexander is forced to watch in horror as she smoothes down his t-shirt and tightens the cord on his pants.

She must have grabbed the first things in reach because he can't even find her clothes. He wonders if they were buried between the cushions.

The moment Sunji and I enter the den, he dives to the floor.

"Hi," she says, not quite preventing us from stepping fully into the room. "I'm Ty."

I don't recognize her, and Alexander's shirt doesn't register, but I know those pajama pants.

Sunji, of course, notices nothing right away. "Hi, Ty. Did Alexander win the match?"

"He did. Yep." She's breathing heavily and nodding too much.

Behind her, on the other side of the couch, Alexander tries to slide toward the far side of the couch without moving too much, but, as he arcs his back, I see ass.

"1300 points to Gryffindor or whatever?" Sunji's asking. He looks at me then, noting my expression, turns toward the couch right as Alexander pops all the way up, hands on his genitals, side-stepping awkwardly toward the door, toward us.

Ty, not realizing this, is staring at the ceiling as she recounts each minute detail of the game. She trails off as Alexander lurches past her, moving between Sunji and I.

"Congratulations, Alexander," I say, as Sunji grabs a handful of naked ass. Alexander swats at his arm and Sunji nut-checks him.

I turn back to Ty as Alexander's whimpers fade into his room.

"Would you like something to drink?" I ask. "Or a toothbrush?"

"I'm fine," she says brightly, her face flushed to a brutal shade of red. She spins, going back to grab her actual clothes.

Sunji looks over at me, expression completely serious.

"We gotta burn the couch, you know that. We gotta burn the whole damn den."

Pleasantries (ICU)

Ellington jogs through the park, thinking about how much broader the footpaths would be at his favorite spot in Copperas Cove.

Noticing a girl stretching along the side of the trail, he rips off his shirt, tosses it on a branch and jogs backwards to offer her a better look.

She smiles at him and he recognizes her now. Her hair is cut close to her head, but the rest of her has been preserved in the sleekest of amber.

"Callie?"

"I thought that was you, Ellington. How are you?"

He bites the inside of his lips. "Single."

She laughs at first. "That's not what I asked."

When Ellington is zeroed in, there's absolutely no protection. He smiles now, megawatt.

"How've you been?"

"Good. Just trying to hold on to my summer body through the fall."

"I see you. You still *thicc*, though."

She blinks. Lets his words hang until they sound awkward to both of them.

"What is this?" she asks.

"What do you mean?"

"We've shared almost a full ten seconds of pretend pleasantries. That's a record for you and I."

Ellington did one of those frown-smiles, where all of the muscles in his face aim for a frown, but his lips still go for the smile. It ends up looking like a joker's pout, but like everything on Ellington, it worked and it worked well. "I just saw you and wanted to let you know that you look good."

"I know I do and I didn't ask." She looks at her watch. "I need to get my workout in."

Ellington's tongue massages the backs of his upper teeth. For her imagination.

"Don't be like that."

"Be like what?" She laughs again, but the timbre is different. "Suddenly we're having small talk? You didn't have shit to say to me when I was with Jay."

"Because you were with Jay! That's my boy."

"You two don't even like each other. And besides, are you saying I'm not worthy of conversation or basic recognition when I'm seeing someone who isn't you?"

"I'm just saying hey."

She sighs, no longer entertained. "No, you're trying me right now. Any possibilities that there were between us—"

Alexander runs out of the woods up to Ellington. He stops, catching his breath and wiping his glasses on the one tiny dry spot on his shirt. Placing them back on his face, he looks to see who Ellington's chatting with and his expression sours.

"Ew. Callie. I mean—"

Her voice is dry. "Hi, Alex."

He waits. She raises her eyebrows.

"Xander," he prompts.

Ellington smacks Alexander's chest with the back of his hand, with the skin, fabric and sweat combining into a mighty *THWACK*.

"One more lap." He then turns back to Callie, sure to let his pecs jump a few times. "So you were talking about… possibilities?"

• • • • • •

A few miles southwest, Eagle approaches December in the coffeeshop with a green tea latte in her hands and remorse on her face.

December doesn't look up from her book, but she speaks.

"You stood me up." She says this factually, and that digs into Eagle more than any chiding or histrionics would.

Eagle sighs. "I'm married."

This raises December's head.

"*You* asked *me* out."

"I'm horrible."

December returns to her book as invariable as an animatronic. "Maybe you should wear both of those facts on a sign around your neck to save the rest of us the trouble."

Eagle sits across from her.

"Do you want to know why I joined the military?"

December turns a page in her book. "No. I don't."

"It was late one night, just sweltering in the 626. I don't know, maybe the air conditioner had broken down. It was the summer after high school graduation and I was up probably texting someone and catching up on *Fang Wars* or something. My mother, who always stays up late, went up to the attic in her nightgown. Well, when she was coming down the stairs, a bug—she swears it was a roach— apparently fell into her bosom, so she ripped off her nightgown, pawing at her naked breasts in either panic or Satanic ecstasy."

December holds up a hand, her mouth pulled tight.

"Why are you telling me this?"

"I mean, she was really having a go at them, and I stared in horror as they were just slinging around and basically defying gravity. She's shrieking and cussing up a storm. *¡Oh mierda, me tiene! ¡Me tiene! ¡Ayuda!*

"So here's my father, running to the rescue, in a leopard print thong—I found out later that Mom had gotten it for him for Valentine's one year—and he grabs my mom, wrestling her to the ground. Now both of them are flopping around and it's battle of the titties and I think my dad's are winning."

December is laughing and trying her hardest to stop.

"And here comes Rascal."

"The dog."

"Our heroic pet of seven years, and man was he excited. He hops onto Dad and starts to hump Dad's leg. Just going to town. And I'm still frozen at the TV. Horrified. And Dad's swatting at Rascal and Mom's boobs just aren't giving up the ghost. And there I am, still not knowing about any bug, not knowing what the fuck is going on and I knew then that I had to get out and I had to get out fast."

December's smile fades. "This is your thing, isn't it? You talk until people stop paying attention to your actions. You weave distraction."

"There's a point to this."

"Doubtful."

Eagle tastes the words before she says them. "Sometimes life throws crazy shit at you and some things become clear because of it."

December leans in. "So in this historical parallel, am I your mother, your dad, or your dog?"

Eagle sits for a moment, then instinctively runs her hand through December's hair.

"You're my realization. Throughout all the crazy shit, this right here makes sense to me."

December grabs Eagle's hand and looks at it, holding it and not speaking. After a moment, she releases, grabs her book, and stands.

"Let's go," she says. "Let's see how long this continues to make sense."

December walks toward the door and Eagle stares after her.

Then, after another moment of realization, she scrambles frantically, one woman following another out of a coffeeshop in North Hollywood. Nothing to see here.

• • • • • • •

"Why didn't you bring Zario?" Genie asks the question to his cousin, settling into his seat at the table.

Jay shrugs, squinting over the menu. "He's getting ready for a date tonight."

"Oh, really?"

"I didn't realize you liked him so much," Jay says, putting the menu down. "I'm gonna order for us, okay?"

"Sure," Genie agrees, sliding his menu across the table. "And I never get to meet any of your guy friends. I assumed they'd all be shitstains."

"Like your friends?"

"Whatever," Genie laughs. "You don't like my friends because you don't like people. You were never really good at making friends. That's no secret. So this surprises me."

Jay leans back in his chair, one arm on the table and the other on the back of his seat. "In what way?"

Genie exhales. "I was gonna ask you to come home with me. Pack it up and ditch all of this."

Jay jerks his head back, frowning. "Why? I'm happy here."

"And that surprised me."

"It did?"

Genie cocks his head, wondering why his cousin is being so obtuse.

"When have you ever been happy before? Like, seriously happy?"

They're interrupted by their server, and Jay orders their food and drinks.

"Soju?" Genie asks after their server steps away.

"You don't have to drink any," Jay says, his eyes refocusing. "What did you mean last time, when you told me it seemed like I had things figured out?"

Genie replicates his cousin's earlier head jerk. "When did I say that?"

"Like, literally two weeks ago."

Genie shakes his head. "I don't remember that."

"Don't give me that shit. What the fuck do you remember, then?"

"Look, I'mma be real with you. I miss you."

The server returns with two glasses and a bottle of soju.

"*Gamsahamnida*," Jay says, nodding to the server.

Genie presses on. "If things ever get bad here, or you get bored... do me the favor. I'm used to your heartbeat."

Jay begins pouring the alcohol. "Move to LA."

"Nah, I'm working."

"*I'm* working. So." He slides a glass of soju to his cousin.

"I know." Genie's not willing to argue, but he slides the glass back. "But if."

Jay nods, downing his soju. "If."

● ● ● ● ● ● ●

After an afternoon of lovemaking, conversation, and some of the best green tea she had ever had, Eagle gets ready to leave December's apartment. As she goes to set her teacup in the sink, her muscles randomly spasm, and the cup flies into the edge of the basin, shattering.

"Oh, shit!" she says, watching the pieces clatter next to the drain.

"What happened?" December asks, walking up and peering over.

Eagle hunches her shoulders, looking for something to scoop the fragmented glass into. "I'm so sorry!"

"No, it's fine," December says, already fishing the pieces out of the sink. "I'll do something with these."

"What do you mean?"

"I dunno. A bird feeder? I mean, I can make something. A mosaic, stained glass… A kaleidoscope if I'm feeling up to the task." She looks up into Eagle's surprised face. "What? Even broken glass has a purpose. Even broken glass can create something beautiful."

Eagle follows her to the door. "Yeah, I guess those are things that are beautiful in spite of having broken parts."

December shakes her head in disagreement. "They're beautiful because of their broken parts."

The Pasadena streets where December lives are quiet. As they walk to Eagle's car, December fills the silence and Eagle realizes with a heart skip of joy that December is unsettled.

"I wish you could have stayed longer," she says to Eagle, "but my brother's going to be back soon and he's…" December presses her lips together in thought. "He's a menace. So I don't want you judging me by him."

Eagle laughs. "Well, I told you about my crew. I don't want you judging me by them."

They reach her car, but stay on the sidewalk, framed between a palm tree and a brick fence.

"I don't know where this goes from here," December says, her forehead creasing in concern, "but tell me it goes somewhere."

"It does," Eagle nods. "I promise."

She leans over and December grabs her face. They kiss gently.

"Excuse me."

They turn to find two men looking to pass.

"Sorry," December says, stepping back and pulling her hair back behind her ear.

Eagle's locked eyes with one of the men, and one of those eyes is tweaking.

"Excuse me, *ladies*," Jay says.

"Jay," Eagle chokes out. Her eyes almost spin in their sockets when she tries to look at Eagle. "This is, uh…"

December holds out her hand. "Hi, I'm December. Eagle's told me a lot about you."

Jay shakes, but his head is shaking slowly and he doesn't speak.

Genie raises his eyebrows. "Eagle!" He grabs Eagle's hand with both of his. "So nice to meet you. I'm Jay's cousin. Eugene."

He turns to December, who Jay has now stepped back from.

"Hi, December. Eugene."

"Hi, Eugene."

"We gotta get going," Jay speaks now, feigning apologies. "I told Genie here I was going to take him to karaoke and the room's on reserve."

As he brushes past her, Eagle reaches an arm out more as a flailing than a reaction. Maybe it's a prayer.

"Jay!"

He yells over his shoulder. "We're already late. But I see you!"

December watches Eagle's face, darting from her pulsing temples to her tweaking eye.

"Well, it's going somewhere now," Eagle says, unsure of where.

Healthy Competition

I wasn't prepared for the multitude of topics Mr. Seventeen could cover in a short span of time. He was similar to Mick, except he didn't really need me to participate in the conversation at all.

"Zario. I dig that name. I like how it fits with mine. Zach and Zario, like a set, right? My last name is Largaespada. Means "long sword". I know you knew that, because you speak Spanish. But isn't that great? Free advertising. The dating scene here in LA is like a non-factor, you know. Either you're just fucking or you're two close friends who realize you've been accidentally dating for five years."

We haven't even ordered appetizers. I'm zoning out and in.

"Seventeen reps. Isn't that crazy? Like the magic number. I could write a book, but nobody would believe it. Just seventeen reps!"

I nod wearily and wonder if this is the first date I drink alcohol on. Hard liquor, straight up.

"The self-titled album is definitely a better album, but *4* had the best jams."

Just as Zach begins singing "Don't Hurt Yourself," a new voice rings on Zario's ear.

"Zario?"

I look up to see the lanky figure, the golden brown skin, the slight twitch at the corner of a mouth.

"Gregory? Hi."

I stand to shake his hand, but he goes in for a hug. It's awkward, but we settle on patting each other's biceps.

"Yo, there have been so many think pieces sprouting up about the podcast. Your awesome photos are all over the blogosphere. I had to come out to my mom. As a weed smoker."

I laugh. "I hope I didn't cause too much trouble."

"Never," Gregory says, implying something I can't quite grasp.

He pulls over a chair and sits.

"Have you been here long?" He looks over at Zach as if just noticing him, the same way the popular kid in class notices a classmate just to bully them, endorsing an unnecessary hierarchy. "Hi."

Zach is grinding his teeth. "Hi."

They don't bother to shake.

"Not too long," I say. "Just drinks."

"Well, let me get you your next."

Gregory signals the waiter.

"No, you don't have to do that," I protest.

Gregory's eyebrows knit together. "I insist."

Zach shifts in his seat, nervously looking just below my eyes. "So how do you two know each other?"

"I photographed a podcast Gregory was a guest on." I smile at Gregory, remembering. "You know Sunji Spencer, right?"

"Of course!"

"That's my roommate."

"I know." He turns icily to Zach. "And how do you know Zario?"

"I'm a certified personal trainer," Zach says, impossibly nasal. "Professionally known as Mr. Seventeen. Zario's been seeing me for about a week or so now."

Gregory takes Zach in.

"You started working out after you realized you weren't getting any taller, didn't you?"

This hits me as hard as it was meant to hit Zach. I open my mouth, but Zach is quicker.

"I believe healthy living is important if you value your life." It's a harbinger. "When's the last time you worked out? Middle school PE? A few games of four square?"

Gregory's nostrils flare, and I imagine blue fire pouring out of them. All he says aloud is, "I have a high metabolism."

I speak now, beginning to understand.

"Do you two know each other?"

The guys speak in unison. I hear "You could say that," on top of "Not anymore," and I'm gobstopped.

"Oh. Well…" I look between them, then turn my most remorseful expression toward Gregory, who is still glaring at Zach. "I'm on a date tonight, so…"

"Yeah, could you excuse us?" Gregory says to Zach. He turns to me, mirroring my apologetic face. "I didn't realize I was running late enough for someone else to try to swoop you up."

"Late?"

"We're on a date," Zach says with no shortage of pride.

Gregory shakes his head, turning back to Zach. "I'm afraid you're mistaken. I was told by Sunji to be here at 8:30 tonight."

"Oh," I realize. "This isn't Sunji's week. I'm supposed to be on a date with Zach tonight. Next Tuesday must be our…"

It's obvious that explaining away the confusion isn't going to do me any favors in the moment. Fucking Sunji.

Zach smiles, vindicated. "Sorry about the mix up, Gregory. But feel free to stay if you want."

Gregory crosses his arms. "Excuse me?"

"Excuse you?" I parrot Gregory, staring at the trainer.

"Healthy competition is nothing to be scared of. He's deciding between us anyway." I swear Zach pops his pecs. "We can just save him a week."

"You could save him a week by leaving right now. Or would you prefer instead to do it in the middle of the night, Mr. Seventeen Seconds." Gregory turns to me, tossing his bangs. "He's a thrust and bust."

"I had work the next morning!" Now Zach looks at me, too. "And I know tantric. He's just trying to be witty."

"Guys—"

"He doesn't know tantric; he read a book. Once." Gregory turns back to me, gaze softening. "You wanna get out of here? There's a million better places to be and a million better things to be doing."

Now Zach makes a counter-proposition. "I'll take you to the falls. Gregorqueen over here would always run out of breath before we reached the top."

The actor snaps back. "Yet in any kitchen you walk into, you can't reach the top shelf without grabbing a step stool."

"At least I know what to grab to get the job done. You couldn't properly grab a wrench, a dick, or a personality."

"You want to talk to me about personality when your entire existence is based on a two-digit number? Did you pick seventeen because that's as high as you can count?"

I need to find a happy place. I need to hoikey-boikey and fuckrabbit myself out of here and quickly. Apparently what I do instead is scream. This works in my favor though, as it shuts them up.

"Zario?" Gregory reaches over to place his hand over mine, but I'm pulling away from him, from this table, from everything.

"No. Nope." I stand. "You guys were doing just fine without me."

Lando intercepts me as I leave the dining room. "I heard you scream. What can I do to help?"

"I'm not coming back," I say sharply. "Can I pay, please?"

He holds my gaze for a moment, worried, but silent.

"Actually," he begins, motioning for me to follow him to the register, "the owner's brother covered all of you meals here."

I blink. "The owner's brother?"

"Wesley West? You were talking to him last week? At the bar."

"I remember," I say.

Lando's peering at my face like he's looking through it. "So if you'd like to actually get something, we can make it for you to go."

"Can I get two meals?" I ask him.

He laughs. "Absolutely. What would you like?"

After I order, I glance back over to the table I abandoned. Even though I shouldn't be, I'm surprised to see Zach and Gregory making up by making out. Their tongues are darting in and out of each other's mouths like they're playing badminton with each other's tonsils, their hands are beneath each other's clothes, and the entire booth is rocking.

Lando follows my gaze. "It'll take fifteen to twenty minutes if you don't want to wait around."

"Thanks," I wheeze.

I hurry outside, pressing my palms to my eyes in a belated attempt to scratch the sight of Zach and Gregory from my memory.

Fuckrabbits.

. . . .

The hostess has my order ready when I return after a pleasant scenic walk around the local shops. Because I'm a glutton for punishment, I look over at the booth. Both Gregory and Zach are gone, thank goodness. Then I realize that they're probably on their way to have a make up fuck and I'm less grateful.

"Is Lando still here?" I ask the hostess. "I just wanted to say thank you."

"He's clocked out after you left," she tells me. "He was staying over to take care of you."

She's giving me one of those appraising looks that rides the line between curiosity and suspicion and I wonder if she and Lando have a thing. I want to assure her that I don't have a thing for her real or desired man, then I wonder why I always assume that the women I encounter are on the opposing side of a war.

I wonder why I live on a battlefield.

Outside, I send the *"**come get me**"* text to Ellington I should have sent fifteen minutes ago. I look up at the darkening sky and search for the premature stars. A voice floats in the air, reedy and honeyed.

"Why? Why do angels fall?

Are they letting go of heaven?"

Intrigued, I follow the song to an alleyway that separates the restaurant's grounds from an elevated stretch of grass that maybe at some point was intended to become a park. Directly above the short staircase leading to this grassy oasis is Lando, the source of the vocals. His back is to me and his forearms rest on a metal railing as he continues to sing.

"Are they letting go of heaven or learning how to fly?"

I walk up the steps and linger at the corner of the railing. He looks over at me, smiles, and takes a drag on the joint in his hand. A backpack sits at his feet alongside a longboard splattered in soft neon colors.

"I thought all waiters in LA were wannabe actors," I say, "but you sing?"

Lando cocks his head to one side. "Fuck yeah, I sing." He exhales slowly, hazing the air between us. His body must be fifty percent lungs. "And I'm not a wannabe anything."

He offers the joint to me and I decline.

"You sing in your spare time?"

"I work two jobs right now," he says, pointing over his shoulder to the restaurant below us. "I try to *live* in my spare time."

I join him at his spot on the railing and he looks…well, Ellington would say he's looking upside my head.

"Speaking of getting your life," he says, "are you doing poly now? Or was that mess inside just an attempted threesome gone wrong?"

Oh, fuck. I wonder what he thinks. I realize I care. "Ugh, 'that mess inside' was two dates scheduled on the same night. And with guys who know each other, apparently."

"Exes?"

I nod. Again he offers me a hit and I wave the joint away.

I feel like I should explain. "I associate weed with sex."

Lando finishes off the joint with another long drag before flicking it over the railing. "You're something else, you know that?"

This bitch. "Are you always this free with your opinions?"

"Oh, my bad!" He looks genuinely apologetic. "I'm not trying to be rude. You just struck me as the sort of person who can handle candor."

I laugh, mostly to put him at ease.

"You don't even know me," I say.

"But I'm right," he counters with conviction.

He's right. I turn my head toward the street, checking for Ellington's car.

Lando asks, "You getting out of here?"

"I think so."

"Me, too." He begins to unbutton his shirt. "This was a long day. Fuck."

He drags the last word out like he's fingering it. I flush, maybe at the phonetics, maybe at the skin, and I look away.

"Thanks for staying late, by the way." I raise my bagged dinners appreciatively.

"Oh, Kelli told you?" He grins. "You're the bright spot of my week."

The blue above is turning to a purple-black and there are more stars blinking on. I start counting again to keep my eyes occupied.

Lando chuckles, observing me with interest. "You okay? Does skin embarrass you?"

My hands move, making empty motions in equally empty air. "I was just trying not to, you know…"

"Trying not to what? If you're not gawking or drooling, then we're good."

He pulls a fresh t-shirt from his bag. Pink.

"Actually, you can gawk a little. Shit. Boost a motherfucker's confidence."

He pulls the shirt over his head and I find myself glancing at him. Even with Lando's version of permission, I feel depraved.

You truly belong here with us among the clouds.

"I'm just careful," I say.

"Yeah, about that," he says, placing a floral-patterned ball cap over his Johnny Bravo hair. "'Careful.' Why aren't you hitting up the clubs like a normal guy would? You're what, my age? We young! That babyface should get you a free drink at least! It already got you free meals, thanks to Wesley."

I pull my bottom lip back. "I don't really drink in public."

"Shit." Every cuss word out of his mouth is like foreplay. I might just be horny. He looks at me, no doubt wondering how I ever have fun if I don't drink or smoke weed.

"So these dates," he continues. "Controlled environment. Selected men. 'Careful.' What exactly are you getting out of this?"

He's too nosy. "What exactly are you getting out of caring?"

He rocks against the railing. "You're a nice guy. I can tell because you looked away when I took my shirt off. I said to myself, this man is a product of Obama's America."

The laughter that follows is bittersweet, but he still hasn't gotten an answer from me, so he persists.

"Serious question. Your friends. Are they trying to fix something or create something?"

"Fix something."

"And you, are you trying to fix something or create something?"

"I'm trying to fix something, too."

Lando isn't like the other men in my life. His gaze is open, pleading almost. "What's broken?"

I look away. "I don't really know."

"Then how are you going to fix it?"

What a question. He checks his phone, then looks back up at me.

"You got someone coming to get you?"

"Yeah, my—"

In an instant, Lando's somewhere else in his thoughts and his schedule, swinging his bag over his shoulder and grabbing his board. He hands me his phone.

"Good," he says, not brusque, but beyond our current conversation. "Give me your number. We'll get together sometime and I'll show you how to stop being so damn careful."

"You sound like Mercutio. And that sounds like a bad idea." I type anyway.

"They said the same thing about segregation, Romeo. And women's suffrage—even marriage equality. But at some point you have to go all in and let life take its course." He takes his phone back and points it at me. "You know what happens when you let go, don't you?"

"Yeah, you fall your ass down," I laugh.

He begins trekking across the grass, walking backwards for a few steps to hold my gaze.

"Do you?"

Espada

The thing about partners? They complicate things.

Mandy Bell is the worst kind of complication. We do not like her, and now her own boyfriend does not like her, yet somehow she's around more.

Today, she paces the living room on her phone while all of us— well, everyone except Ellington—play cards in the dining room.

Her voice carries. "I've been a faithful customer for years. I had the very first iPad! I got my parents into iPhones. And, as a loyal customer, I have to say I'm disappointed with Apple being unwilling to take care of something that is so obviously a manufacturing issue."

Eagle looks between us. "She spilled water on her computer. How is that a 'manufacturing issue?'"

"Alexander," Jay says in between popping walnut kernels into his mouth, "tell your boyfriend to come get his girlfriend."

Eagle winces.

I look around. "Where is Ellington? Are we down with free-range lovers these days?"

"Let me speak to your manager. What's your name? Let me speak to your manager, Roberta."

"I thought this whole bet thing was supposed to change our luck," Sunji muses.

"It's worked for one of us." I point to Alexander, who is squeezed into one of Ty's tops. Ever since that first tryst, his girlfriend seems to end up wearing his clothes more than her own, and he's found the weirdest way to adapt to this.

"Has it worked or have things just gotten worse?" Sunji points. "Look at Jay! When's the last time he's been on a date?"

Jay points a walnut at the actor. "Okay, fuck you, motherfucking fuckbag fucker."

Sunji prattles on. "Jerrica hates me now. Eagle—"

She raises a hand to silence him. "Eagle is happily married."

Jay snorts and Eagle snaps her head in his direction.

"Okay, sure," Sunji says, rolling his eyes. "We can pretend. And look how Ellington is dating that Daughter of Eve."

Vague memories of Tilda Swinton wearing a lion's mane, then William Moseley in battle armor, circle at the edges of my thoughts.

"That—What?"

"White women brought the world the first sin," Sunji says matter-of-factly. At our expressions he continues. "Eve. Made of bone."

Eagle leans in. "Elaborate, please."

Jay collapses the cards in his hand. "Can we not entertain this?"

"We shouldn't," I say, "but also…"

"Eve was made from rib bone, so she was white, cuz bone—duh. Adam was made of dirt so he was brown, cuz duh. This is why men of color always chase after white girls. And that's why I stay away from them. It's all there in the Bible."

Eagle holds his gaze. "Is it?"

"Yeah!"

I laugh. "Fuck outta here."

"Where'd you read that?" Eagle asks. "The Book of Yeezus?"

"No, Eagle, it's Old Testament. Genesis."

Eagle places a palm on the table between them, raising her head to the ceiling.

"I root for you, you know. But you make it hard."

Ellington walks in, half out of his jacket and entirely out of breath.

"Hey, guys! Sorry I'm late."

Alexander walks past him, saying quietly, "You smell like sex."

Ellington replies, just as quietly, "Shut your breath cave. Where's Mandy?"

From the other room, Mandy shrieks. "I. WAS TOLD. BY APPLECARE—!"

• • • • • • • •

Going back to the gym is weird for a few reasons. First, obviously, is the fact that it's hard to ignore Zach since he is our trainer. Despite this, I do my best. I only pick up weights after seeing the others do so. I ask them questions about the set or form or the amount of reps, and if Zach has notes for me, I stare at one of the others until they repeat it to me.

Childish, maybe. Petty, absolutely.

Second, Alexander and Eagle join us. Alexander has decided to get into shape for Ty, despite the fact that she has voiced no complaints. This means that he's doing far less than us, while pretending the entire time that he's actually keeping up with us. He gets winded during our warmup sets, he can't do a single pull-up, and the tire flips him. Eagle's presence is more curious. She is always down to meet us at the park or on the courts, but she has an aversion to gyms. I've always figured it's because she's weak or…like Alexander, quite frankly, but she surprises me by keeping up during the entire workout and that's when I see it for what it is.

Eagle's comfortable in this setting because there's a group of us with a dedicated instructor, so she doesn't have to worry about some random guy coming over to mansplain a machine or offer to spot her while angling for her number. Besides, we're an imposing group of motherfucks. Most men assume Eagle is with one of us, so even if they feel like they can compete with one of us physically, the odds that they'll have a shot when compared to the group of us make those chances slimmer than a pinkie. Additionally—and this I don't register until halfway through the workout for reasons that will be clear shortly—she has an extra safety net with our trainer being gay. Zach and Eagle talk about her body goals openly, she doesn't mind him adjusting her form, and they erupt into random gigglefests.

I resent this, and it's enough to make me start pulling away from her again.

The third and most surprising reason things are weird today comes from Jay, who at first appears to also be bothered by the connection Eagle and Zach are making, but as our training session stretches on, I discern that he's legit beefing with our neighbor. They're snapping at each other and there's no underlying humor. It's like they woke up with sudden, intense hate toward each other. Because of this, ignoring Zach's suggestions and racking higher weights, picking the advanced form options, and by the end of our workout, his limbs are actively rebelling against him.

He lays inside the tire, twisted at the waist with his legs splayed in opposite directions. His face is flushed and his hair sticks to his drenched forehead. Every few moments he makes a noise not unlike a big cat in the wild looking for their missing cub. In this case, the missing cub is his dignity.

Eagle walks over to him, offering her hand, but he waves it off.

"I'm good." He makes a noise like his internal engine is stalling. "Just stretching."

I watch this while ordering food from my favorite wing spot.

"Yeah, the thirty-six wing family pack. Lemon pepper, pineapple and habanero, barbecue bourbon and chipotle lime. And can I substitute the french fries for loaded potato wings and the pasta salad for the baked beans? Thanks." I turn to the guys hunkering against the wall with me. "Any of you guys want something?"

"Not me," Ellington says from the corner. "I've got to meet with an investor."

"I gotta see what the wifey wants," Alexander says, and even Jay gags.

"Ugh," Eagle says, sitting next to him. "You guys are one of *those* couples."

Sunji props an arm up on his knee. "I didn't even know you guys were official. Is it serious?"

"I always figured you were gay," Eagle said.

"What, just because he was single?" Ellington asked.

"I just get gay vibes. You know what I mean, don't you, Zario?"

I cut my eyes to her as I disconnect my call. "I have no idea what you guys are talking about," I lie.

"Hey."

Zach stands above me, his shirt pulled up over his chest to let the heat from his core dissipate. I try not to roll my eyes.

"I've got a pump going."

Now I roll my eyes. "Excuse me?"

"Think we can shoot some things? What's your rate?"

"I didn't bring my camera."

"I'll wait for you."

"But you've got your 'pump going.'"

"I can get it back."

Sunji leans over and places his chin on my shoulder, taking in Zach's bulge. "I bet you can." He flicks his tongue.

"I gotta eat, too," I tell Zach, shrugging Sunji off.

"Yeah, I heard you ordering wings. I've got wings." He pulls the shirt off completely, posing and grunting out words. "Obliques. Serratus. Latissimus dorsi."

I exhale. "Where do you want to shoot?"

"We can shoot here. There's a studio in the back."

"Pick me up at three."

Zach grins, but it falls when he looks at Jay's crumpled body.

"Seriously, dude, you're going to have to get up before the owner comes over here."

. . . . . .

Zach locks his car and motions for me to follow him up an outside staircase that leads to his second story apartment. The shoot went well and I was tired of pretending that I wasn't at least curious about sleeping with him. It's been a while since a man has shown such an open, direct attraction to me, and I know he's not a complete douchebag, so…

"I thought about you all night after you left the restaurant," he said.

"Lies you tell. Weren't you getting busy with your boy Gregory?"

He begins unlocking his door. "I promise you, once he gagged the first time, I remembered why we didn't work out."

I stop at the top of the stairs.

"Okay, we're done here."

"Why?"

"Because I'm remembering just how much of an 'espada' you are."

"I'm a sword?"

"No, you're a dick."

"I'm honest. It keeps my mental health in check. And I honestly feel bad about how that night ended. For both of us."

He steps aside, gesturing for me to enter. I don't move.

"You just wanna fuck me."

"Who wouldn't?"

Honest, indeed. Besides, why else would I have come here?

"What about romance?" I ask, but even I know it's a weak detour.

"There's no linear pattern," he shrugs. "I've broken up with guys before we even started dating."

I walk past him into the loft. I expect a buttload of gym equipment, but instead there are posters of classic paintings, loads of books and magazines, and a peppering of art deco furniture. Of course. He works out at the gym for free—he doesn't need to cram any of that into his apartment.

"The relationships I had like that were closet cases," I tell him.

"Exactly," he says, locking the door behind us. "I hope my kids never have to deal with that. Closeted dudes are the worst."

"Most of my relationships have been with closeted guys. My first boyfriend and I were both closeted when we met."

He takes my jacket. "Really?"

I think about Patrick and gag a little. "I mean, he's a full queen these days, but back then he presented himself as a straight basketball player. The night I first realized he was into me was completely random."

"That's wild," he says, hanging my jacket by the door and I realize he's not listening to me. "Make yourself at home. I'm going to slip into something more comfortable."

I watch him walk away.

There's a picture of Zach posing at the Hollywood Sign. I remember telling Shane that I had never figured out how so many LA locals got within shooting distance of that sign. I had tried several times when I first moved. We had only been officially dating for a week or so when he surprised me with a hike where we got some great pictures of it.

I don't realize I'm crying until Zach comes out of his bedroom stark naked.

"Oh shit," I say, drying my eyes.

"Are you crying?" He rushes over to me to rub my shoulder.

"It's nothing. I just…"

"Hey, no pressure. We can talk, we can carb-load. I've got some cocoa and hazelnut spread. Whatever you want."

"I just…" That spread sounds good, actually. "I had a moment."

"The basketball player? You really loved him, didn't you?"

I don't bother clarifying. "None of that matters. I'm here with you."

"So, what do you feel comfortable doing?"

I'm impressed at how sincere he is. Aside from his exposed dick swinging next to my leg, he doesn't seem to be focused on sex at all. And this is what makes up my mind. That and the fact that the last person I fucked was Shane. It's time I made some new memories.

We begin making new memories right there on the floor of his loft. For all the talking he's prone to do, he's quiet when I first begin to drive into him.

"Is this okay?" I ask him.

"Yeah," he rasps, grabbing my own ass to pull me deeper. "It's good. Don't stop."

I'm not used to quiet sex, but I have nothing else to say. I place a foot next to his ribs and use the leverage to increase my pace. I slam my hips forward and he gasps, reaching to grip something, anything. Our skin slaps, our flesh warms, and our breaths increase.

He starts to push back against me and I'm grateful to realize that Zach is a power bottom. He starts putting that ass to work, voracious to a point that I'm shocked he stays so quiet. We maneuver through a few positions, all right there on his floor, beating on the rug, beating up his guts.

It's not long before I'm collapsed on a chair above him, spent and feeling the best kind of disgusting.

Pretty Dudes

He speaks, his face still on the floor, his juicy booty still airborne. "I'm a terrible trainer. You weren't supposed to do any cardio this week."

Hazelnut and Cocoa

Ellington is patting a rhythm on the steering wheel when I get in, a shower and half of a bowl of pasta later. I required the former and Zach insisted on the latter.

"You didn't want a rideshare?" he asks as we drive.

"You're closer," I say, buckling the seatbelt.

"Wanna crash at my place?"

"No, Jay and I are working through a movie watchlist."

"Man, fuck Jay."

"Why don't you guys like each other?"

"What? I don't have a problem with that bitch. How was your date?"

I wobble a hand back and forth. "Eh. Did you break up with Mandy?"

He shakes his head. "I avoided her. I still can't. Did you ever think that dudes could feel this sexually violated?"

I hate myself for chuckling. "Yeah, actually."

Ellington gives me a questioning look, then exits the freeway.

"There's a spot up here with some good drinks. This seems like a story to tell over drinks."

Now I'm shaking my head. "You know I don't like drinking in public."

"I'll fuck anybody up, are you shitting me?" His laugh aches more than it froths. "Who do you think I am?"

We settle in at a quiet bar, one of those spots that seems to sprout up almost like they're located in the Twilight Zone. It's one of the reasons I'm glad Ellington has adapted to the Los Angeles culture of knowing locations almost purely by their proximity to certain streets and highways. We may not know exactly where we are, but we'll never be lost.

There are only a few customers here, but the crowd is a nice mix. I'm comfortable, and after a few sips, I tell Ellington a story that he's heard before, but only in pieces. Being roofied. Being assaulted. Escaping. Trying to communicate the situation to the cops, then to my father after dropping out of school. Moving to Cali because of how far it felt from my rapist. How far it felt from the person I used to be.

"Alexander doesn't know this?"

"We weren't that close at school. Senior year we weren't really seeing that much of each other, anyway."

"I'm sorry that happened to you, Zario."

I drain the last of my drink. Every time I tell this story I expect relief, but the same rotting hurt inside me just fills the space right back in. Like puss returning to a popped pimple or blood returning to a wound when a scab is ripped off too soon. It's always too soon. It scabs, but it never heals.

"Sometimes I think that's why I stayed with Shane as long as I did. After knowing his deal, I mean. Married with a wife. A closeted guy who loves me is still a guy who loves me, not a potential predator at a club or a bar, waiting to hook me." I feel myself shaking. "Shane's hook was already in. I was safe."

"In what way?"

"The passion in those cases is qualitative," I say. "I get to choose how I'm used. I prefer my victimization to be solely emotional."

Ellington stares at the top of the bar, face tightened.

"Dang, Zario," is all he says.

I try to wave the concern away. "I know I'm fucked up. I'm pretty sure there's no more normal for me. In some way I'm going to be settling for some replication of normal the rest of my life."

Ellington downs his drink and signals for another one. "Do you think that's why I'm having trouble breaking up with Mandy? Her hook is already in?"

"Maybe."

"I don't mean to suggest our situations are…"

"All trauma is valid," I say.

He repeats me. "Trauma."

It occurs to me that Ellington had allowed himself to feel the effects of what Mandy's words had done to him without qualifying what those effects were.

"Do you think that's what it is?"

"Maybe." He groans, and it turns into an undoubtedly orgasmic moan. My eyes shoot around the bar, but apparently he's not as loud as I feel he is. "The sex is really good though. It sucks that I can't enjoy it unless I somehow have her mouth occupied."

"You're still having sex with her?"

"Well, yeah, now that she's serving, I'mma eat."

He's unbelievable, but it can't judge it.

After a moment, he asks, "Have you ever had a lover who was only with you because of…"

"The Latin Lover thing? Oh God, I usually try to suss those dudes out on the dance floor. Some people only see tokens."

"I didn't think about it so much before, but now, I mean… I say something funny around you guys and I wonder if I'm cooning. You say something funny and you're…"

I nod. "Being sassy."

"Sassy. Ooh, I hate that word."

"I fucking hate that word."

Ellington gently shakes the ice in his emptied glass. "I walk by cars on the street and people lock their doors. I pretend not to notice, you know. I catch myself speaking softer because as soon as I raise my voice, people interpret it as a violent act. I smile more so that people don't assume I'm an angry Black man. Being Black is passive! It's just melanin, just the fucking skin I'm born in. It's passive in every shade. But my very existence is construed as aggression. You know what that's like."

I blink. "Being Mexican?"

He shrugs. "I mean being gay in straight spaces. Straight people react funny when they find out you're queer. I've seen it happen. To you and to Marshall."

He's right. "Sometimes I don't mention my sexuality just to see how homophobic somebody will turn out to be. I walk stiffer in unfamiliar neighborhoods so that the swish doesn't attract unwarranted attention. Even around you guys—I try not to look at you too long for fear that you'll think I'm catching feelings."

"That part," Ellington says, nodding. "And we don't help with our teasing."

"Eh, it's part of the code."

"Says who? You know, I had a guy who I used to call my friend who always had to crack one Black joke. Like some kind of mental icebreaker. I called him on it and he started arguing with me, telling me that he's not racist because he's my friend and I told him, you're white in a white-majority society. You can't help but be racist. That's why I say I *used* to call him my friend."

"White dudes are the worst."

"The worst."

"Alexander's cool, though."

"Yeah, because he does the work. He's always trying to be better. To learn. To grow. You wouldn't believe how openly queerphobic I was before Marshall came out. And I kept thinking, if he was anybody else, if he wasn't as secure in himself as he had been the moment he entered this world, I probably would have had him scared shitless to come out."

"I can't imagine not knowing Marshall was gay."

Ellington wobbles his head back and forth. "I mean, I knew, but it was different before he said it, you know? Like, maybe I could ignore it out of existence."

"If Marshall's like me, we thought the same thing."

He sighs. "Us straight dudes can suck sometimes."

I nod. "Allyship is tough. Us non-Black POCs can be tragic at times. I loved my mom, but she was anti-Black as fuck. And it took me some time to reconcile that."

I had stupidly repeated some of my mom's views to a few acquaintances at college who got me together with a quickness

The bartender drops off Ellington's new drink. I turn down his offer to bring me another.

"I'm sorry," Ellington says later, finishing his drink. "I'm just feeling hella Black today."

"I noticed. And don't apologize for it. I'm feeling hella gay."

He gives me one of his side gazes, where his chin locks into his shoulder and his torso twists just so.

"I appreciate you, Zario."

"I love you, Ellington."

He grips me in a hug. "I love you."

He lets the bartender know he's ready to close his tab, then returns to his thoughts. I watch the creases struggle to take hold on his smooth, blemish-free forehead.

"Did something happen today?" I ask.

He shrugs. "This girl I was with…"

"Not Mandy."

I'm surprised this makes him smile.

"Not Mandy."

• • • • • •

He doesn't tell me it's Callie. He doesn't tell me many specifics. Maybe he's embarrassed.

Callie was embarrassed as she put her shirt on. "I don't want you thinking I do this a lot."

She said it more to the wall than to him. He looked around for his boxers, debating if he should take a shower or put on enough clothes to walk her to her car.

"That you do what?"

She turned her face toward him. "Pick one. This hookup culture thing we just did. This ex-boyfriend's dude thing that I just did. Fuck to Chance the Rapper. You know that album is basically a gospel album, right?"

Ellington laughed. "Sex doesn't bring you closer to God?"

Callie bit her lip. "This did. But again, I don't usually do…this."

"That's fine. I don't usually do dark-skinned girls."

Her face thundered and he panicked. "I was joking."

"That shit wasn't funny." She stood then, grabbing her purse. "I'm gonna go."

"Really?" Ellington leaned back on his elbows, sliding his legs apart to give her a dick panoramic. "I thought maybe we could go for round three."

Callie pulled out her phone and he instinctively began to cover up with the sheets.

"Nah," she said, holding back a grin as Ellington angled away from her phone. "My self-respect is starting to think I made a mistake."

She had made it to the door before Ellington—having found his boxers—grabbed her arm, causing her to drop her phone.

"Shit, sorry," he said, bending to pick it up for her.

She glared at him. "I knew I should have tied your ass up!"

Ellington rose slowly, eyes pinned on her phone screen. "You were posting about me? Already?"

"Give me my phone," she said calmly, though she was snatching at it.

He held it above his head. "Tell me you weren't posting about me."

Her hands went to her hips and exasperation went to her tone. "It's wrong to look at my phone."

He handed it over, laughing. "The screen was up!"

Callie rolled her eyes. "Goodbye, Ellington."

"What's your main platform?" he asked her.

"Why do you care?"

"Because you were posting about me. Maybe I'll go check it out."

"I wasn't using your name."

She moved back toward the door and he scooted past her, leaning up against the wall as she gripped the door handle.

"If I scroll through your timeline, will there be posts about Jay? To your…"

She sighed, not turning the handle. "Fifty thousand."

Ellington whistled slowly. "…fifty thousand followers? Who you were about to herald my considerable skills to? And who you undoubtedly complained about my friend to? And probably posted pictures."

"Nuh-uh, I don't do that. I've got pictures of Jay's ass, but he knows about them and I'm never going to post them. That boy has a great ass for an Asian."

Ellington shrugged. "I've got an ass."

She made a noncommittal noise.

"I do!" he said. "Remember the things you were doing to it?"

As Ellington imparts this section of the conversation to me, I have to literally bite my tongue. I've seen Ellington's ass, and it's nice or whatever, but Jay's has the kind of shape that only happens when a guy does squats and also eats whatever the hell he wants. Thick, plump, solid. I sip my water and let my friend continue.

"I didn't use Jay's name either," Callie said, stepping back from the door and staring directly at Ellington. "But I doubt that's going to stop you from finding my account and doing some detective work."

"Fifty thousand, huh? You're pop culture."

Callie blinked. "What? What do you mean?"

Ellington's business sense had been enabled. "With a reach like that? You can influence the corners of the earth with a tweet. What's your market?"

Callie feigned ignorance. "Market?"

"Callie." He didn't buy it.

"Kidding," she said, raising her hands in defeat. "I have a plan."

He reached for her hand. "Tell me. Come on, I'll make you some tea and fix you something to eat."

And he listened. She understood her audience. She also understood the specs, the algorithms, and the moving targets of the zeitgeist. He had many thoughts, but he just listened. And tea and a massive salad turned into round three and then she got serious about leaving.

"I've never been asked to wear a mask before," he said, removing the rubber pig half-face from around his head. "I thought it was gonna be creepy."

"But it's not, right?" She grinned as she stuffed the mask in her purse. "It helps that your mouth was free."

He touched his jaw. "I need to rest it, now."

This time the walk to the door was without incident.

Until, "Why did you date Jay?"

She turned to him, her brown irises floating in a sea of jolted white.

"Oh, my God. Why are you thinking about him again?"

"I'm just saying. Was the relationship real? Or did he just fuck you out of your writer's block?"

"I take offense to that!"

"I think it's a fair question."

She pointed at him, bouncing the finger at her knuckle. "I don't like the implication. What Jay and I had was real. Just the timing…"

Ellington shrugged. "Did you fabricate the breakup?"

"Who do you think I am? One of those white writers who makes up tragic survivor stories just to hit a follower count or a bestseller list?"

"I don't know who you are," Ellington said.

"That's your fault," Callie retorted. "You and your boys were on the basketball court that day, and I was looking to talk to you, but Jay saw me and wanted me. You started paying attention to some other girl and I figured, 'What the hey?'"

Ellington fought back a grin. "You were trying to get at me?"

Callie laughed. "I wasn't into him at all. But we talked, then he showed me what he could do when we weren't talking. Fucked me out of my name, really, and every language I know and I was sprung for a while. My feelings matched his. But I came down to earth. He wouldn't admit it, but he came down, too."

"So…" Ellington raised his eyebrows. "He fucked you outta your name and I fucked you to God."

"Uh-uh, I'm not comparing," Callie said, though she clearly was doing just that. "I'm not trying to fuel the fire of whatever rivalry you two have going on."

"What are you talking about? Jay's my boy!"

"You two don't even like each other!"

"I don't know why people say that. We're in the same circle. It's a siblingship."

Callie's eyes returned to the door. "Which is why I should be leaving."

Ellington stared at her, and his smile began to open up his face. "But you're not."

"But I'm not," Callie nodded, still standing in front of him. "You shouldn't want me to stay."

"I shouldn't," Ellington agreed, shaking his head.

"But you do."

He stepped closer. "But I do."

Callie swallowed hard enough that he could hear it. "If I stay, it's more than just…"

"I know."

Their foreheads pressed together.

"You do?"

"I know."

Then they spoke in unison.

"We won't tell Jay."

• • • • • •

It takes me a moment to process the parts of the story he's told me. "So, you and this woman spent the night together? Doesn't Mandy have a key?"

"She's out of town."

I exhale forcefully, my lips making an embarrassing sound as the air pushes through them. "Oh, Ellington. That's dangerous."

"I'm worried, though. She's really great. But I don't remember the last time that I dated a Black girl. Like, what if this is just my reaction to Mandy going full Kard—"

253

"Ew, don't summon them. And it probably is," I say. "You should let us meet this new lady. You know we'll all hate her and then you can have justification to dump her."

"Why are we so weird about that? When is the last time we approved of anyone's girlfriends? Or your guys?"

"I'm working on a theory about that," I say. "When I perfect it, I'll let you know."

Ellington grins as he pays the tab.

"That reminds me. Did tonight help me win?"

"Nah."

"Okay, then tell me one thing. Do I need to kill Mr. Seventeen?"

"I mean, if you want to. But he was a perfect gentleman."

"Okay, last question." Ellington manages to dismount from the stool in the smoothest way possible. I'm annoyed. "Are you done so soon because it was only seventeen pumps?"

I follow him to the door. "You're gross."

"That was Marshall's question. He's been dying to find out!"

"Then Marshall should go on a date with him."

"No, because then I'd definitely have to kill Mr. Seventeen and then I'd be proving all those racists right."

When we hit the sidewalk, Ellington turns to me, grinning his Cheshire grin. "I've gotta say, man. I was worried about you back there."

"In the bar?"

"No, I mean, what, just two months ago, before we started the bet. I've never seen someone depressed like that. Alexander takes medication for his. I was trying to convince him to help me drag you to the doctor."

I shake my head. "I was just drinking too much. That's never the right solution for me, anyway. Only brings bad things. Slightly related: Have you heard of hazelnut and cocoa spread? Zach had some."

"Ooh, foreplay."

I spread my arms in disbelief as we reach Ellington's car. "I had never heard of it."

"Really?" He flicks his finger between the two of us. "That's you and me, baby. Hazelnut and cocoa."

• • • • • • •

I make the mistake of telling Jay about this new discovery while we're queuing up *Gremlins 2: The New Batch*. His room has become a nightly thing now. If he's not out, I'm in. Tonight, he's already gotten me to take three shots of vodka with him. His argument was that I had already been drinking with Ellington, which was fair. At least here I was already home. He rolls, he showers, then we watch.

"Yeah, hazelnut spread." He looks up from his rolling. "What, you've never had it?"

I toss the remote down on his bed. "How is this a thing? More specifically, how have I survived without lathering it straight onto my hips?"

"What's your obsession with your hips?" Jay asks.

"They're like thirty percent of my body," I say, frowning down at them.

When I look back up, Jay's abandoned the weed and is digging around in one of the cabinets next to his bed. I watch mesmerized as the blue of his boxers stretch against his backside. Maybe I'm extra-horny because of Zach, but I realize just how much more of an ass Jay has than even our trainer. It's because he's taller than Zach, so it takes up more space.

"I think you have one of the fattest asses I've ever seen."

"Don't objectify me. You were doing fine objectifying yourself."

I lay back on the bed. "What are you looking for?"

"I've got some of that spread stashed in here."

"Ew. I don't want your sex garnishes."

"Oh, my God. No." He turns around with a small, wrapped jar. "I got a gift basket from my parents. It was crackers and cheese and shit, but I never opened this. Shit usually tastes like melted candy bars."

"Okay, now you're making it sound amazing," I say as he sits down next to me, unscrewing the top.

"I promise that wasn't my goal." He looks inside the jar. "It looks all waxy."

"I think you have to mix it," I say.

He holds up his hands, his fingers fluttering while he grunts. This is how he freezes when something in his thoughts is just out of reach. "Toothbrush!" he says, and he's back to his cabinet.

He pulls out a brand new, sealed toothbrush, one of the ones he keeps stashed for whenever a girl sleeps over. Ripping open the package, he dips the handle in the brown mix and stirs thoroughly.

"Here," he says, bringing the toothbrush handle to my mouth.

I lick a little off the handle and the sweet, only slightly nutty flavor spreads across my palate. It's creamy, and surprisingly thick.

"What'd you think?"

"I don't know, it was gone as quickly as it arrived."

"Well, finish this," he says, spooning—toothbrushing—the full glob into my mouth.

As I work my way through the flavors, Jay tosses the toothbrush into his tiny trash bin and dips two of his fingers into the spread. He holds his fingers in front of his face, watching me swallow.

"Okay, that was good."

"Yeah? Here," he says, and I barely have time to open my mouth before his fingers come rushing in. At first I'm trying to get all of the hazelnut and cocoa, then I try to make sure I'm not leaving his fingers wet with saliva and I realize I'm sucking his fingers. I release them apologetically and his eyes peer into me.

"Well?"

"It's good," I say. "It's really good."

"Good," he says, and he dips back into the jar. He places a hand on my back as he thrust his fingers in. I try at first to suck his fingers the way a bro would and I start to chuckle because I know I'm being ridiculous. I give up trying to suck in any respectable manner, and begin to suck like the hazelnut ho I am. When I release his fingers, they're clean and I can finally get out a full laugh.

Before I can protest, I see him coming at my face with another glob. I open my mouth obediently, feeling slightly delirious and I don't know if it's because I'm breathing too heavily while working my way around Jay's fingers or if it's the vodka. I put a hand down on Jay's thigh to steady myself, and I feel his stiffening penis against my fingers beneath the nylon of his boxers.

"Oh, sorry," I begin, but he rams another dose into my mouth.

"Just suck," he says, his voice sounding strange. His hand goes from my back to my waist. I lay my other hand on his knee. His breathing grows shallow as I l go from licking to sucking and Jay unmistakably moans, his fingers thrusting across my tongue.

He breathes my name and it sounds like a prayer. I turn toward him and our faces challenge each other, flushed red and pulsating with a strange heat.

His mouth sits open and my left hand begins kneading against his thickening. His hand that was on my waist now grips my ribs before dropping swiftly toward my own-

"Zario!" rings down the hall and I push Jay away, leaping up from his bed in the same moment.

"Shit," I hiss. I look at Jay and he begins to screw the top back on the jar, demeanor so cool that he almost looks bored.

Sunji calls my name again so I go to the door. He's standing at the entrance to my room with Ellington, who nudges him and points to me.

"See. I told you."

I look back in the room and Jay's at his desk, taking a huge swig of vodka and swishing it around his mouth.

"I've got a gig for you if you can go right now! Elijah's starring in this music video and they need a photographer on set right now. Their last guy got the stomach flu or something. Can you come?"

Jay nudges me, suddenly at my side. "It's cool."

"What were you guys doing?" Sunji asked and Jay opens the door a little wider.

He's got his towel slung over his shoulder. "Movie night. Cool kids only."

"But we can put it off," I notify Sunji.

"Yeah, *Gremlins* can wait," Jay says, and I think he's smirking and my brain begins to race, wondering why he'd be smirking right now.

Sunji waves me forward. "Well, let's go!"

As I pass Ellington, he points at his mouth. "You've got something there on yours."

"Oh, thanks," I say, rubbing at my face with the back of my hand. Hazelnut and cocoa. Sunji follows me into my room to help me grab all of my equipment, leaving Ellington and Jay in the hallway.

Ellington points to Jay's boxers. "You, too."

Jay looks down to see remnants of the spread smeared over his crotch.

"Shit," he mumbles.

When Jay gets out of the shower, Sunji and I are long gone, but Ellington's waiting for him in the hallway, leaned against the wall and swiping through his phone.

"You're still here?" Jay asks, walking past him.

Ellington looks up. "I wanted to talk to you before I headed home, if you had a moment?"

Jay shrugs. "Sure, what's up?"

Ellington is smiling widely. They both know that he knows it's intimidating, meaning it's a tactic and Jay immediately bristles because of this.

"Do you remember what it's like when you're learning how to swim, and there's that one kid—maybe it's you—who panics and grabs onto the nearest body, almost drowning you both as you flail? Kicking each other's legs and shit?"

"Yeah." Jay chuckles a little. "That *was* me, actually."

Ellington nods, still smiling. "I bet. And what's the secret to 'not drowning' for everyone? The trick that the swimming instructors tell you."

Jay frowns, leaning his shoulder against the doorframe. "You kick on your own."

"Exactly." Ellington's smile fades. "You kick on your fucking own."

Jay looks around. "Wha——"

Ellington points his thumb in the direction of my room. "We've just brought that boy back from the brink, and he's out here swimming with us again, and now you wanna jump on his back because you suddenly realized you're in over your head?"

Jay's nostrils flare and he stands up straight. Ellington, rising from the wall, mirrors him.

"Hold up—"

"I'm not stupid, Jay. And as much as I love you, I guarantee I will fuck you up if you even think about making all of your mistakes on Zario just like every other man he's been with has. Kick on your fucking own."

Jay doesn't speak, despite Ellington's silent dare for him to do just that. When Ellington doesn't move, he turns, opening the door to his room, and slamming it shut.

Ellington stands there for a moment, realizes his fists are clenched and relaxes them. When he turns to go, Alexander stands at the other end of the hallway in the living room with his gaming headset on.

"Is everything cool? I thought you left."

Ellington smiles briefly. "Just had to talk to Jay real quick. Goodnight, man."

"You wanna stay and play? My tourney's finished now."

Ellington shakes his head, brushing past him. "I'm not playing games right now."

This Immediate World

The next evening, Eagle comes over and Jay is sitting on our front steps, deep in thought. He moves over to let her pass, but she sits down next to him.

"Can I help you or something?" he drones.

"We connected," she says, after a moment. December and I. Emotionally. Intellectually. It's not just… You know."

"I don't know. And I don't care."

"Liar. You care more than most of us."

"Look, what you got going on is none of my business, Eagle."

"I know. I just thought that because we're friends, we can talk about these things."

"We're friends, but we're not that close, all right?"

"We're not? You're always bringing me tuna melts, right when my period becomes unbearable."

"Coincidence."

"You had me talk to that girlfriend of yours about her brushing hygiene. Remember? Cuz Zario chickened out. What was her name… Moni?"

"Oh, yeah," Jay grins. "Desdimonifah."

"With the Janet Jackson cheekbones," they say together.

"And," she continues, "there was the time you got stung by the jellyfish and I pissed on you because Sunji said he wasn't kinky like that and Alexander was having 'performance issues' and then you started to cry—"

"All right, all right," Jay woofs. "We're close."

"Feel free to call me on my shit, Jay. You used to."

Jay purses his lips. "This feels different."

Eagle chuckles. "You're telling me!"

He looks at her now, for the first time since that day on the sidewalk. "You know how you said what you have with her is more than just…"

"Yeah. I mean it."

"That doesn't matter," Jay says. "Even if you just wanted to fuck her because you liked fucking her, that's your right. The issue is that this isn't just about you and her. It's about him, too."

Eagle sighs. "I know. I gotta tell Rock."

Jay plays with his shoelaces. "You thinking about marriage counseling?"

"I'm gonna divorce him."

Jay glances at her in surprise.

"I told you," she says. "She strikes me like lightning. Rock is like a drizzle on a foggy day. He's everywhere, in everything, but what's the point, you know?"

"I don't think I get you," Jay says carefully.

"Look," Eagle says, slinging an arm out. "We're not in this life long. All we have is this immediate world, and I think that if someone or something comes along and extends that horizon for you, why wait for another sign or for some checklist to be completely ticked off? You run to them. We're a species of runaways. We weren't created to stay. Everyone tries to fool us into thinking that we should be content growing mold."

They sit in silence.

"You liked Moni, didn't you?"

Eagle nods forcefully. "She was hot."

"So was her breath. So, are you a lesbian?"

Eagle mulls this over. "Probably. I was never really into anybody before Rock. He could make me laugh and shit and somehow he convinced me to marry him and separate and become a military wife. Some of that was military culture, you know. Everyone gets married. And fast. But December… I mean, I'm not thinking about marrying her or anything, but whatever we have is worth…"

"Exploring?"

"Sitting in."

Jay smiles softly. "I hope you're right."

"Shit, me, too."

Jay stops fiddling with his laces. "I wanna talk to you about something too. Someone. Just between us."

• • • • • •

The next week flies by. My work on set with Elijah leads to consecutive gigs over the next several days, and Jay and I don't see each other for those days. It's easy for me to default to thinking that he's avoiding me, but it's me who's out of the house twelve to eighteen hours at a time.

The first night I have off, he's working, so I send him a message asking if he'd be up for a movie the next night. He texts back immediately.

Sure.

I exhale, then spend the night catching up on all the sleep I've missed.

• • • • • •

Jay and I finish *Gremlins* at two in the morning and it takes me until three in the morning to talk him out of making a donut run. In exchange, I have to do three shots of whiskey with him. He often tells me drinking is Korean culture and, for the sake of his liver, I hope so.

"Are you going to make up your date with that actor?" he asks me on shot number four.

For a moment, I think about Elijah.

"Oh, Gregory? No. Absolutely not."

"I still can't believe you went through with this. I'd never let those fools pick out dates for me."

I laugh. "Oh, come on. It would be easy."

"For you. It would be easy for you. Can you imagine the kind of girl Alexandouche would pick out for me? Or which hole with two legs that Ellington would pull from his contacts?"

"Have you had sex since Callie?" I ask. "I mean, for fun?"

"You mean, am I dating?"

That's not what I mean. "Yeah."

"No," he says, shaking his head. "What about you? Just Zach?"

"Just him," I reply.

"You don't sound too enthused."

"I like having a connection with somebody. He was just some body."

"I feel you."

As he pours a fifth round of shots, I sit on the edge of his bed, bouncing one of my legs.

"Hey," I begin, "about last time. I hope I didn't freak you out or—"

He looks over at me, shrugging. "It's whatever; we were drunk."

"We're drunk a lot."

He turns, handing me my shot glass.

"That we are," he says, smiling. "So what, you want to stop drinking?"

"No, I just…" I don't know what to say, so I toast with him and take the shot. Now the words come to me. "What did you think about it?"

He shrugs. "It was sensual. And I like chocolate."

I scoot over to my side of the bed, annoyed. "Okay, bitch."

He matches my movement by walking up to the edge of the bed, both empty shot glasses in his hands.

"What do you want me to say?" he asks, his face sincere and his tone casual. "I got a dick. You made it move. I responded. Do we have to write a blog post about it or something? I'm cool. Are you cool?"

No, I'm infuriated. I never understand how straight guys can be so casual about explicitly sexual things in private and then freak out about the smallest queer-esque displays in public.

"I'm cool," I nod.

"No, you're not. You wanna smoke?"

"I said, I'm cool."

He's got that same knowing smile on his face that he had the morning I met him. "Okay, then."

He strips out of his tank and begins to put up his whiskey. "What do you think it would be like if we were together like that? All the shit you forgive about me now would really piss you off then, huh?"

"What do you mean?" I ask wearily, staring up at the ceiling.

"You wouldn't let me tease you so much, I think. You'd take it personal."

I disagree. "I'd be the same. I'd just be blowing your back out twice a day."

"Twice?"

"I'd have the access," I shrug.

He laughs. "Yeah, I guess you would." He wipes down the glasses, staring thoughtfully at his floor. "I dunno, I don't think it would work."

"Then why'd you bring it up?"

He stacks the shot glasses next to his liquor.

"I just don't think I'm your type. I'm not brown."

"Remember when you went down the list of things I look for in a guy? Brown wasn't on that list."

He's smiling thoughtfully when I look over at him. "Fair."

I know what we're both thinking now, that he checks all the other boxes. I decide to spin this around on him.

"I'm not *your* type, though."

"You?" he asks, stripping out of his underwear. "What are you talking about? I don't have a type."

"Yes, you do," I say as he lifts the covers and joins me in bed. "Asian or Black, big lips, big hips, big eyes, big ass."

He laughs. "Okay, some of those things are on my list." He looks at me, his laughter subsiding. "You have some of those things."

I freeze for a moment and notice something pulsing in his irises, almost supernatural. I blink and it's still there. Tonight might not have been the best night to get drunk with him.

He reaches over and taps my dick with the back of his hand. "You come with extra, too."

I grab his arm and he grabs my other arm with his free hand.

"I'm just saying that's not on my list," he laughs.

"You want to talk about curses?" I ask, as we lie in stalemate. "That's my curse. My face is fat, so my skin is smooth. My lips are large, so they're perfect DSLs. I've got the cupid's bow, so they don't look like I pumped them full of filler, either. And my eyes are fucking Bambi eyes, with these long, thick curly lashes. I've got these physical traits are typically associated with women. They appeal to a lot of men, especially guys who aren't comfortable yet with their own sexuality."

I hold his stare. If he wants to play this game, I've got my playbook on deck.

"You forgot something," he says, almost choking the words out through the drowsy drunk.

I swallow. "What did I forget?"

He releases my arm and grabs at my waist. "The hips."

I swat at him and he blocks it, so I go to pinch him and he grabs at that arm.

"You almost got my dick!" he screams and I laugh. I wrestle to get loose and he flips me on my back.

"I'm about to get your dick for real," I say, raising my knee warningly, but he sweeps an arm underneath it, lifts both of my legs and flips me over again.

"You ain't got nothing, bitch," he crows.

With my chest flat against the bed, I raise my hands to push myself up, but his hands grab my wrists and he pins me flat. He rests one forearm on my upper back.

"I think *I* got something, though," he says, smacking my butt with his free hand and grabbing at my waistband.

"Okay, I'm done," I say.

"Tell me I won," he laughs.

"No," I say, shrugging him off. "I'm done. Don't pin me down like that."

I feel my hands shaking.

"Hey, hey, hey, I'm sorry. I'm sorry." He grabs my hands. "I'm sorry, Zee."

Bringing me into him, he leans back against his headboard and braces me between his legs. His arms cross my chest and he holds me as my tears start to fall.

I think about the pulsing in his eyes and I think about his dick, which I can feel soft against my spine and I think about the last time I was pinned down and wonder if there's any way to ever feel okay.

To his credit, Jay doesn't talk any more, and doesn't try to make it better. He just holds me, lacing my fingers in his, and soon we sleep.

He wakes me, maybe an hour later, and I feel him lifting me off of him. Freed puddles of sweat begin trickling down my back.

Jay props me up, holding me with one arm and using his legs and a fist to maneuver around me like I imagine Tarzan would.

"You're hot," he explains, and he unbuttons my pajama top. "Here."

I watch the perspiration drip down his moon-shaded chest, pooling on his nipples. Reaching with my thumb, I glide my finger through the rivulets, letting the sweat coil into my palm.

"Your arms," he says, and I hold them in the air as he pulls the top loose.

His hair lies damp and segmented on his forehead.

"You're so sweaty," I say, wiping his forehead with my other hand.

"No shit," he says. "That's why I had to get you off of me."

He dabs my skin with the cloth of my pajama top, then tosses it to the foot of the bed.

"Lay down," he says softly, and I lay back on the bed as he adjusts his sheets over us.

For a moment, he's directly on top of me, palms on both sides of me with his hips between my knees. I register it, but I'm not sure he does, as he taps at my leg and rolls over next to me the moment I move it.

I wake up again because of him, but this time it's intuitive. My eyes open and he's on his side, hugging his pillow. Watching me.

"What?" I ask.

"Nothing," he says, and I can feel the alcohol swirling in his words. It's the same alcohol swirling in my thoughts.

"You've dried off," I say, like it's an achievement.

I reach for his bangs and he catches my hand, laying it on his cheek. Still watching me. We lie like this for a while, sharing space in each other's eyes.

I think of all the barriers we've broken as friends. I think of the comfort zones he's eased into and all of the protective bubbles he's invaded and I wonder how much intimacy we can have as friends while still calling it friendship. Whatever it is that he and I share deserves its own classification.

When he moves my hand to hold it against his chest, I recognize now, blazing through the alcohol and the drowsiness, what's happening—what's going to happen. He knows the breaks are cut, but he's waiting on me to press the gas.

His nipple is proud against my palm. Again, I rub my thumb across his chest, this time getting a feel for his shape, his texture, his responses. After a brief exploration, I lean over to take the nipple in my mouth.

I hear him laugh, but I use my wetness, the engulfment, this warmth that stokes heat, I use all of this to knead him into exhilaration. His hands cradle my head as his breaths become shallow. I travel from that nipple to the other with a combination of lips and tongue.

He turns fully on his back now, legs spreading. I move with him, centering myself over him. His hardened dick leaves a trail of eagerness on my stomach, but I ignore this, giving his second nipple all the attention I had given the first. My hands press into the mattress as his thighs clamp against my sides. One of his hands journeys across my back, the other runs through my hair. He's moaning now, sounds I've heard from him before, but always through a wall.

I slide my right hand between his legs, cupping his testicles in my hand and gently alternating my fingers against them. I lift my head up and he stares down at me with an intimidating amount of desire. It's not just lust, though, that's giving his face the numinous radiation I detected earlier. His eyes are filled with an intense craving to know this moment, to know this experience.

I have to weigh my options immediately, before my brain becomes entirely compromised. I can do three things at this point. I can smile at him, return to my side of the bed, and go to sleep. If I do that, I run the risk of leaving him wanting and leaving the moment unconsummated, with roots exhumed that might make a home elsewhere. This could validate his earlier suspicion that he's not my type, and he might decide to share this sexual experience with someone else, if at all. I might wake up tomorrow, and every day after, wondering what exactly this moment was and what it could have become.

The next option is more fun. I could give him a blowjob, benefiting both of us, and we can chalk it up later to being friends who had a great drunken night. The trouble here is that I might suck the soul out of him, like I once had done with Shane, and tie his energy into mine like a leash to a dog or a wish to a genie. Based on my experience, so many men with dicks have a manual transmission. If you know how to operate their clutch, you can drive them as far as you want to go.

The final option is deceptively elementary. I can kiss him. It's a choice that is tied into the type of intimacy that Jay and I share. Kissing will most certainly lead to lovemaking—not fucking. We are far too connected to just fuck casually, meaning there would be no turning back for him or I, and in the unflattering light of sobriety, the only way forward might not be a path that we could take together.

It occurs to me now that I've taken all of the agency in this moment, going against the very pillars I uphold for love and sex. I have to let Jay make this choice. If he comes to his senses, which I honestly hope he doesn't, then we can laugh this off together. If he so much as mentions a condom, however, I'm hammering Morse code into his prostate with my multilingual dick.

"Are you cool with this?" I ask him.

"Yeah," he says breathlessly. "Whatever you want to do."

Seeing him fully hard is a wonder. He's got a pretty dick, thick and shapely. I kiss the head of it, then take the tip in before letting it plop out. Each time I return my mouth to it, I take more in until I've worked my way down to it's base. Above me, his shoulders have lifted off of the bed and he's wordlessly saying things that I already know. I work my magic on his shaft, then I make sure to give dedicated attention to his testicles. When I return to his penis, his hips rock into me and I grab his ass with my hands.

His ass feels so good in my grip, that it takes everything in me to not flip him over and dive on in there. If I eat his ass, I know I'm going to fuck him, and I cannot fuck him.

There is a fourth option circling my brain that I hadn't taken into consideration. In all of the situations I had presented to myself, I had either benefited by myself or had been at a disadvantage with Jay. But what if we come out of this and he takes the only advantage? What if he takes my soul in through his dick and I end up the husk, the leftover.

What if I fall for him?

"I'm gonna, I'm gonna," is all he manages to get out, and I remove his dick from my mouth, letting my hands finish the work during the few seconds it takes for him to make complete good on his partial word.

I rise to my knees, smiling. I'm sweating again and so is he. He reaches into one of the drawers that frame the headboard and tosses me a towel to wipe up with, taking one to clean himself.

"I'll be right back," he says, half-stumbling, half-leaping out of the room to go piss.

I look at the stains on his sheets and tell myself, *We'll be cool tomorrow. We'll be glad this is all we did.*

Jay walks back in, so naked, so pearlescent. His cheeks, the ones on his face, are red as he breaks out his liquor again, rum this time. He fills two shot glasses and jumps back in the bed, spilling a little.

"Shit," he says, handing me the one that has the most rum left.

I take it and toast with him. It goes down smooth, and I'm grateful.

"How do I thank you for that?" He's got a wry smile on his face. "Want me to buy you flowers?"

I roll my eyes. "No, just don't ask for a repeat."

"Dammit, that was my next question," he teases, taking the empty glass and returning to his desk.

"That was a one time deal," I lie.

He turns around to me and his face falls. My heart follows suit.

"This is probably isn't the best timing," he says, "but, uh…"

I turn over so I don't have to see him when he says it. "If it's bad timing, save it."

"No, uh, can you get up? Just like, *two* minutes, I swear. I gotta change the sheets."

Bedfellows

When I wake up, the bed is empty. I look around for a moment, then figure Jay must be in the shower. Music is blasting from the front of the house, funky horns and sexy guitars. This is strange enough that, instead of going to my room, I head down the hallway.

The portable speakers are in the living room, blasting The Gap Band, but there is no evidence of life there except for the raised blinds. When I hear the clanging of pots, I walk toward the kitchen.

I pause in the doorway, because nothing I see makes sense.

Jay and Sunji are cooking and dancing, singing along while they whisk and chop and shred an assortment of foods. They look almost like friends. Sunji spots me first.

"It's not a real breakfast," he warns me. "We're making delicious foods that technically shouldn't exist."

"Abominations." Jay winks at me. No weirdness. "Go wash your hands and get in here."

In the amount of time it takes us to play through the Wilson brothers' greatest hits, we make and devour some amazing fusion cuisine. Spinach artichoke wontons, terimayo Japanese hot dogs, curried tahini pasta salad, enchilada meatballs, and—my favorite— black bean jalapeño popper egg rolls. My tastebuds have never been so overwhelmed this early in the morning.

Even with all of those vibrant flavors, I still taste him. I feel him, too, because he keeps one his legs against mine beneath the table.

Only when we're packing up the leftovers do I think to ask about Alexander.

"He spent the night with his 'wifey,' so I figured it would be a good time to do something for just us," Sunji says as he loads the dishwasher.

"And the other motherfucks," Jay says, packing up containers for Ellington, Eagle, and Marshall.

Just over Jay's shoulder I see the front door open. Alexander walks in with Ty's bags, and she's right behind him.

"Ty!" I say it for the benefit of the other guys, but I hope it passes as a greeting.

Sunji spins. We chorus.

"You're back!"

Jay half-grumbles, half-yells, "How fucking lucky are we?"

Ty peers in the kitchen as Alexander awkwardly balances her things. "Ooh, what are you cooking?"

"Cooked," Sunji gives an apologetic smile, popping his dimples. "So, it's not fair to tease you since you're not having any."

"But it looks like you guys have loads of left—"

"Does it?" Sunji asks. "Does it look like?"

Ty sees this for what it is and pulls Alexander back from Sunji's antlers.

"We'll get pizza," she says, leading him out.

Sunji and Jay sneer at their backs, and I, bending to peer pressure, do the same.

• • • • • •

Marshall pokes his head in my open bedroom door, all curls and bangles.

"Is my brother here?"

I look up from my camera and set it next to me on the bed.

"No. I haven't seen him in a minute."

He walks in. "You sure? I hear sex happening down the other hallway."

Nodding, I say, "That's Alexander."

Marshall looks like he's waiting on a punchline. "Alexander? Really? With another person?"

Jay walks in, rubbing sleep out of his eyes. Getting up so early this morning is taking its toll on him, but he lights up when he sees Marshall.

"Whattup, Marsh Swallows?"

"Have you seen my brother?"

"Nope. Did you ask Mandy?"

Jay sits at the foot of my bed, rubbing my legs. I scoot away from him, throwing my legs over the side of the bed.

"He broke up with her last night," Marshall says, "or he was going to. That's why I'm trying to check on him, but he's not answering his phone."

Jay's eyeing my shirt. "Zario, give me your shirt."

Annoyed, I strip out of it and he snatches it out of my hand, putting it on. His attention quickly goes back to Marshall.

"Break up with her?"

I ask Marshall, "In what language? Every time I see him, he smells like sex. I think he's going strong with Mandy."

Jay points to near omnipresent sound of Ty and Alexander's bed-squeaking lovemaking.

"Speaking of sex, that's fucking disgusting."

I correct him. "That's *fucking*. I don't know if you can remember back that far, but that's what you and Callie were like all the time." I look at Marshall, elaborating. "She used to make him oink like a pig."

"Oversharing," he says, while Jay grins.

"Tell me about it," I say, and Jay begins oinking, moving his hands across the bed toward me.

I hit at him once he reaches my thighs.

Marshall looks between us, then exits wordlessly.

"Move," Jay says.

"Why?" I ask.

"I'm gonna take a nap."

I smile a little. "You're bed's like ten feet away."

"If I go there, you gotta come with me."

I make a production of sighing, and I move to give him the bed.

"No, don't get up," he says, laying down and pulling me toward him so he's sandwiched between the wall and I. He pulls my stuffed animal from beneath his stomach and tosses poor Loonah over to the corner of my room. With one trusty leg thrown over mine, he's asleep in seconds.

• • • • • •

"I think we can do great things!" Sunji hasn't stopped talking for a solid three minutes. "Like Michael B. Jordan and Ryan Coogler! I can be your muse. But instead of Rocky, we can do a James Bond spinoff. I always wanted to be a Bond Boy to some hot Janet Bond, maybe James's half-Asian daughter or something. I came up with a couple of great Bond boy names, too! Willie Hung. Flexxx Majestic. Lord Bone-aire. Goody Thicknut."

Erwin hasn't moved since he sat down with Sunji at this Little Tokyo bar, a frown etched deep into his face.

All he says now is, "You're an idiot."

"Okay that last one was pushing it, I know. Maybe just Thickums Goodnut. Or Octocox. Dr. Octocox. Oh shit, we could do the next Spider-man reboot! Can he be shirtless?"

Excited, Sunji sips on his water and pics up a menu.

Erwin is exasperated. "You think I brought you here to talk projects? I want to talk about what happened at dinner the other night."

Sunji raises his eyebrows in surprise. "Oh, I'm sorry I left early. My roommate caught one of the plagues." He shrugs. "I'm a terrible liar."

Erwin signs heavily. "Sunji, I feel disrespected. Beyond any disrespect I've ever experienced before, and I sit in rooms with old, out of touch white dudes daily. I feel taken for granted. And all of this is sad because I think that—despite the weird inner-workings of your brain—you are one gorgeous, talented actor."

"I'll take 'pretty' over 'gorgeous.'"

This puts Erwin at a boil. "Look, Sunji. You came to where I live and hit on my fiancée. You tried to get my fiancée back."

Too late Sunji realizes that Erwin knows.

"Our history is complicated," Sunji tries to explain. "My roommate Jay didn't like her right off the bat because their names were so similar—"

"Tangent! Come on, Sunji. I knew who you were the moment you auditioned. Sunji Spencer. That name? That career? I've heard about you for months. The man I had to be better than. And I considered you for the role in spite of your history with Jerrica. Before that dinner, she and I talked about it openly. We were both cool—cuz love, you know? But to throw that back on my face? Her face?"

Sunji frowns. "She never let me put it on her face. Is that what she told you? Wait, does she let you put it on her face? You know, that's fair because she let me put it in her butt and after, like, the third time, she said she was never letting anyone do that again, so at least I have that over you."

Erwin stands. "I'm going to punch you, Sunji Spencer."

Sunji laughs. "No, you're not."

Erwin punches Sunji off of his barstool. The model curls as he hits the ground, before unfurling and bounding up in one motion like a rubber toy. He heads to the first reflective surface he can find.

Erwin cradles his knuckles. "Shave a dick!"

Sunji, inspecting his nose, crows. "Dude! You could have broken my nose!"

Erwin tries to get a verifying look. "I was trying to. I think I got that out of my system though. Should I take you to the ER? Do you think you fractured anything?"

Sunji returns to his stool.

"You didn't hit me that hard. I'm fine."

Erwin leans in to get a better look. "You sure?"

"You sound hopeful, you fuck!"

"I'm sorry." He's not.

The bartender walks over to them, hands raised. "Fellas, I'm going to have to ask you to leave."

"Sure, sure," Erwin nods.

Out on the sidewalk, they walk silently side by side.

"Do you still want to be in my movie?"

"Do you still want me in it?"

"Only if you want to be."

Sunji shrugs. "I'll be in it if you want me in it."

"I don't *not* want you in it."

"Me, too."

Erwin offers his hand. "Okay."

Sunji, shakes. "Okay?"

Erwin shrugs. "Sure."

They stand awkwardly.

"Tell Jerrica I'm sorry."

Erwin glances sideways at Sunji. "She already knows you're sorry."

They step into a new bar and take their seats at a table, planning to actually eat food this time. Erwin watches Sunji mull something over in his brain.

"What is it?" he asks.

"I'm your muse, huh?" Sunji breaks out into a wide grin. "It's nice to be appreciated for what I have to offer."

Erwin snorts. "I doubt Coogler and Jordan started like this."

Sunji hands Erwin a menu, and now it's Erwin who's pondering something.

"…Janet Bond, huh?"

• • • • • •

Jay and I sit on the couch with Ty uncomfortably between us. I had eventually drifted off to sleep and Jay woke me when he climbed over me to go to the bathroom. Now we sat in the living room where I was editing photos from one of my recent shoots. Ty types on her phone while Jay mean-mugs her.

When Alexander comes down the hallway, he makes a pitstop in the dining room, where Marshall sits, still waiting on his brother.

"Hey, Marshall? Where's Ellington?"

"Haven't seen him."

Alexander nods. "He's probably with Mandy."

Marshall shakes his head. "No, he said he was gonna break up with her last night."

"Oh, then—" Alexander catches himself, chewing on his tongue for a moment. "I'm stumped."

"You're weird," Marshall corrects him.

In the living room, Jay speaks now. "Ty. What did you do before you met Alexander?"

"I run a gaming blog when I'm not competing," she replies, meeting his eyes.

"That's nice," he says, meaning anything but. "Where did you live before you started squatting here?"

"Is this how you are all the time?"

Jay shakes his head. "No, sometimes I'm a bit of a jerk."

"You seem pretty toothless, if you ask me," she says, standing. "Alexander, I'm gonna go."

Jay, speaking more to himself than to Ty, mutters, "Why bite when barking gets the job done?"

Alexander spins to his "wifey." "So soon?"

It's out of my mouth before I can catch it. "She's been here for three days. How is this soon?"

Without looking at me, Ty rises from the couch and heads down the hallway toward Alexander's room. I usually come off as the nice one, so my words may have hit her with more sting than Jay's.

Jay heads into the kitchen, his stinger still out.

"Alexander, is she gonna pay a share of the utilities?"

Alexander follows like a dog. "Why are you guys being so difficult about this? Didn't Callie, Shane, and Jerrica practically have their own keys?"

"Yeah," I say, "but she's—"

"She's a nice person, which is more than we can say about Jerrica. And you know I hate Callie with a passion. But I was always polite to them. You guys are nicer to Mandy than you are to Ty."

"I'm always nice to animals," Jay says.

"My point stands. I'm going to say this, and I really want you guys to listen without interrupting—"

He's interrupted instead by Eagle, who cradles a bottle in the crook of her arm.

For once I holler with the others.

"EAGLE!"

She takes a quick inventory. "Whattup, deep-fried foreskins? Tequila refill." Her eyes land on Marshall. "Whattup, Little Ellington? How is it that you are so much prettier than your brother?"

He tosses his hair. "Our parents got the formula right."

"You're old enough to drink, right?"

"In this house he is," Jay says.

Marshall looks into the kitchen at us.

"Wasn't Alexander saying something to you guys?"

"What?" Jay asks, while I question, "He was?"

Alexander gives a bone-weary sigh. "I'm so tired of you guys."

I press my lips together and take a deep inhale. "Alexander, you might be right about us being hard on Ty, but don't you guys think you're going, I don't know, too fast, too soon? You two are never apart."

Eagle enters the kitchen. "Are we talking about Ty?"

"Alexander's live-in girlfriend? Yes." Jay arranges teacups on the counter. "But I'd rather be talking about why we haven't taken some tequila shots."

Alexander's tiny chest puffs up. "I'm sick of your shit, Jay."

Jay's massive chest bumps into Alexander's chin. "I don't give a fuck, Alexander."

Eagle has taken our side, the right side. "He's saying it out of love."

"He's incapable of loving anyone," Alexander replies.

Jay is still pressed against Alexander, daring him with his presence.

"Thanks, doc. Next week can we talk about my childhood?"

I step between them. "Alexander, have my shot. Jay, yours is bigger. Can we chill?"

Eagle stares at us. "What is in the water?"

Marshall answers from the dining room.

"Tea."

• • • • •

Across town, parked in the alley behind Callie's apartment, Ellington is being smothered with breasts and he figures if he dies, he dies.

Callie is riding the fuck out of him in his backseat, her skirt and her tank top twisting around her waist. They've made a heaven of this particular sin.

"Callie," he purrs, then he growls it, then he moans it.

"Don't call me Callie," she says breathlessly. "Call me by my full name!"

"What is it?"

"Calligraphy!"

Ellington almost lifts her off of him to pull out. He doesn't, of course, but the thought crosses his mind.

"You're shitting me. Your birth name is Calligraphy. Really?"

"Yes," she says, her index finger tracing his jawline. "Your birth name is really Ellington?"

"Named after Sir Duke," he says, as sweat stings his eye. He thinks about wiping it away, but dismisses the thought. He's got optimal grip.

He begins moaning. "Calligraphy. *Calligraphy.*"

Callie follows suit. "Dukie, Dukie, Dukie, Dukie, Dukie!"

Now Ellington pauses. "Just call me Ellington."

She doesn't hear him. "Dukie, Dukie!"

Now he lifts her, letting his dick flop onto his stomach.

"No, really. That's not sexy."

She grins. "Sorry."

He looks over at his phone lighting up. Missed calls and messages from his brother and his girlfriend.

"Do you have somewhere to be?" Callie asks.

"Probably," he says.

"Yeah, me, too." She shakes her head. "We're not good together."

"Not beyond this," he agrees.

"The physical." She nods, leaning back. "What do you want to do?"

He answers with his tongue, and she responds to him the way he had hoped she would.

• • • • • •

At the Dude House, those of us not dating each other are relaxing in the dining room, one or two shots deep in. Marshall is engrossed in a book, Jay is determined to braid my leg hairs, and Eagle chats on the phone with Sunji.

"Oh, Sunji, that's a bummer. But maybe there's a lesson in this." I can almost hear Sunji whining a response. "I don't fucking know, it's your lesson," she says, now exasperated.

Alexander enters, marching up to Jay. Jay looks up slowly.

"I have a Dude Dare for you."

Jay smiles. "Oh, yeah? You wanna start this?" Jay asks Alexander.

"Sunji," Eagle says into the phone, "Alexander just challenged Jay with a Dude Dare."

"What's this?" Marshall asks, closing his book. "What's happened? What am I missing?"

I turn to him and explain. "Tandem Truths and Dude Dares. It's our super-trashy version of Truth or Dare. If Jay accepts, all of us roommates, Eagle, and your brother have to do three dares—*have to* —no matter where we are or who we're around. It gets messy. We then, um, attempt to purify with a truth-telling session next time we're all together. Usually gets messier."

This was an understatement. The last time we did this, Jay locked a naked Alexander outside on the porch and the neighbors called the cops.

"What are you guys?" Marshall asks, and we hear the judgement. "The Real Housewives of NoHo?"

Eagle eyes Alexander. "One of us."

Jay sits up, pressing his shoulders back and clasping his hands. "What's the dare?"

I grimace. "Are we really opening this can?"

Jay ignores me.

"It better be a good one."

"Oh it is," Alexander says, ensuring that it isn't. "I Dude Dare you to say something nice about every person in this house to their face."

In unison, Eagle, Jay and I ask, "Is this about Ty?"

"You are so sprung," Eagle says, shaking his head.

Marshall offers, "Girl."

"I accept this soft-ass dare." Disappointment lingers in Jay's eyes, and it takes everything in him to look away from Alexander. "Zario, your photos are so good, I'm sure one day you'll win a photo Oscar."

I press my lips together. "Okay, sure."

"Eagle, you always bring the right things at the right time. Specifically, this alcohol. Marshall," he thinks, then, "I like your earring."

"Aw, thank you," Marshall says, fingering the crystal fringe hanging from his ear.

Jay turns back to Alexander and a grin stretches so slowly across his face, even I'm scared.

"Alexander… I'm glad you started this game."

Ty, oblivious, enters from Alexander's room, with her backpack slung over her shoulder. Alexander grabs her hand.

"And Ty?"

Confused, she looks at him, then at Jay, who releases a deep sigh.

"Ty, I'm really glad you came into Alexander's life. You are super nice for putting up with us and, as he has no life and no money, I'm sure you can only be in this for healthy reasons. I hope good things for you both."

She blinks and for a moment I wonder if she's blinking back tears.

"Thanks, Jay!"

Alexander frowns thoughtfully. "Wow. That seemed genuine."

Jay wastes no time. "Alexander. I Dude Dare you. Do you accept?"

"Of course."

Jay lifts a bare foot.

"Lick it. Lick my foot."

I turn to Marshall. "See what I mean?"

Marshall and I agree. "Messy."

And then, in a moment I can never unsee, Jay stuffs his little piggies into Alexander's barely open mouth.

Dude Dares

Ellington takes a long shower. He typically likes to start with hot water after sex, to allow his body to process the sensations and to release any acquired tension in his muscles. He then switches to cold water, to spike his alertness and propel him into the rest of his day.

Today he leaves it on hot, allowing his blood to continue hurtling through his veins. It's his way of keeping the bodily surge that being with Callie provided him. Turning off the water, he dries off and wraps the towel around his waist. Sliding into his house slippers, he wonders why Callie has this effect on him. He's had great sex before —he's had great sex with Black girls before—so he couldn't put his finger on exactly what made her different, especially now. He likes her more than he's liked anyone in a long time. He was remembering how deep certain feelings could run.

He finds himself singing now, a song by a British R&B singer Callie had put him on to. He heads to the kitchen, starving. He doesn't feel like making anything, but he doesn't think there are leftovers so he might have to pick up food on the way to Sunji's place.

"Just came from the gym?"

"Fuck!" he yells in fright.

Mandy stands in the corner of the kitchen, a chef knife in her hands. Her bright blue eyes aren't blinking, and it looks like she's been crying.

Shit.

"Basketball court," he replies. "With some of the guys from class."

Her head moves, just a bit, and finally she blinks. "Not your boys?"

"No. Why?" He eyes the knife, thinking of how accessible his genitals are.

"Your brother's been calling," she says, turning and placing the knife down next to some sliced apples. "He hasn't heard from you since last night."

Ellington breathes a little easier. She was making a salad, it looks like.

"Yeah, he was hitting me up. I was gonna call him after my shower."

She doesn't even raise an eyebrow, though she's careful to stay inquisitive. "You didn't come home last night?"

He shrugs. "Got home late. Left early. Didn't get to see him."

This is too much for Mandy, and she breaks down in tears. Ellington rushes over to her, concerned. He slides the knife away from her.

"Baby, what's wrong?"

"I know what you've been up to."

Those seven words cut him like had thought the knife would. Mandy's head is in her hand, the other hand at her side with splayed fingers.

Her voice is choking, but she continues. "I've been trying to act like everything's okay, but I can't anymore. The way you've been so secretive. How nobody knows where you go. The afternoon showers. And then I saw and I wanted to act like I didn't, but I just can't live a lie anymore."

Ellington moves his hands to her shoulders, willing her to look up. He speaks deliberately. He has an arsenal of lies, and even though he's not sure which one is about to come tumbling out of his mouth, he knows it will be foolproof .

"Baby, I can explain."

"You don't have to. I accept."

Mandy holds up her left hand to reveal a diamond ring on her ring finger. The ring he had bought just over a month ago. The ring he was going to propose with the night they had sex.

His feet have grown roots. Mandy has become a chattering, leaping squirrel.

"I thought you were cheating, and I was going through your dressers just knowing I was going to find something left by some skank. And it turns out you've been trying to prep the perfect proposal! I wouldn't have believed it, except the last time I was over at your place I heard Zario and Jay talking about you failing to talk to me over and over again. Then I thought about that night when we had dinner and—"

"Mandy." He's desperate.

She's bouncing, pacing. "It all makes sense and I'm sorry I've been so in my own head and so unavailable when you were just trying to secure our lives together."

He's in a waking nightmare. "You found the ring."

She stops moving, and something registers in her face. "Of course."

She removes the ring, handing it to him with expectancy in her eyes.

"I know, I know, I messed everything up. Don't worry; I'll let you ask me. I told my sisters, but I won't tell my parents until you get to ask officially."

Feeling like he's on repeat, he says, "Mandy, I—"

Leaping into his arms, she covers his mouth with hers, then leaves kisses all over the side of his face.

"I love you so much! Yes!"

"Yes?" he confirms weakly.

"Yes!" she says, kissing him again, then kissing his neck, then his chest, and he feels her pull his towel away. "Let's celebrate with a swirl."

• • • • • •

"Nobody tell me what was in that. I think we may need to pump my stomach later."

I set a protein shaker cup on the table, depositing a spoon in it. Both are coated with a thick, unidentifiable pink substance that can now also be found in my digestive system. I hope I don't die in the next twenty-four hours. The pathologist is going to think I was killed by invasive psychomagnatheric ectoplasm. *Destroy me, yeah!*

Marshall and Ty are watching me with horrified expressions while Alexander, Eagle and Jay cheer wildly.

"You amaze me," Jay says, clapping my back.

"If you rock my torso again, some of its contents are coming right back up and all over this table."

"Trust," Marshall says. "It'll be less gross coming up than it was watching it go down."

Ty nods. "That was like a reverse childbirth, but grosser."

At the ringing of the doorbell, Marshall practically leaps from the table.

"I'll get it."

When he reappears in the dining room doorway, he's with the stunning woman from the coffee shop that only Marshall and I don't recognize.

Eagle's laughter fades.

Marshall says to Ty, "Someone's here for you."

"Hey, Cem!" Ty exclaims.

This is the first time I ever lay eyes on December, and I remember thinking she looks like the beautiful ice-blooded queens in countless fairytales. On closer inspection, I realize that her skin isn't so pale, but her hair is obsidian.

"Hey, Ty!" Her gaze lands on Eagle. "Guys."

I repeat Ty phonetically. "Hi, Cem?"

"December."

I don't know if she's elaborating for my benefit or correcting me for hers. I watch Eagle slide out of her seat like she's made of liquid and slip away toward the bathroom.

"You weren't answering your phone," December says to Ty, waving hers.

Ty points to the table in her own defense. "They're playing the most ridiculous game of truth or dare. It's all dares now and then they go full confessional later after making idiots of themselves."

I take umbrage at her word choice, but Alexander smiles up at December. "It usually turns into warfare."

"A bloodbath really," I correct him.

Marshall makes a face like something smells of rot. "To misquote the greatest series of all time, *Got 2B Real*," he says, "you all don't make no sense, no change, and no dollars."

I nod. "Yeah, this game makes us pretty white."

On cue, Alexander says, "What should Sunji's Dude Dare be?"

Marshall seems smitten with December. Jay watches them from across the table.

"Don't think I'm hitting on you," Ellington's brother says to our newest guest. "I'm really not. But you are gorgeous."

It's apparent that she doesn't think he's hitting on her, but she's definitely uncomfortable.

"Thank you. You, too."

She scoots away toward Jay and Marshall's face cracks.

I turn to Alexander, back on mission. "Sunji's with his director."

Alexander nods. "I know. He's gonna be in so much trouble."

Then his face contorts, like he's turning into Jim Carrey turning into the Grinch and it upsets me.

"I know what we should have him do."

• • • • • •

Sunji and Erwin are several drinks in, talking excitedly and sloppily. Erwin scribbles madly in a notebook.

"So with Eaton dead, Jane decides that partnering with Laong is the best way to take down WRAITH."

"So they sleep together!"

"Again?"

"Laong thinks it's love. He lets his guard down."

"Oh, that's good!"

Neither of them notice Rockefeller Diolosa enter the bar, walking right up next to Erwin. He signals the bartender, then looks past Erwin at his neighbor.

"Sunji?"

Sunji blinks, coming out of the world he's been drafting with Erwin. "Rock? Hey, man!"

Erwin turns, staring at Rock through his glasses. "Your name is Rock? Like a stone?"

Sunji clasps Erwin's shoulder. "Oh, this is my director, Erwin. Erwin, this is Rock, my friend's husband."

"Yeah," Rock scoffs. "Your friend's husband."

Sunji's phone chimes and he lifts it off of the bar, seeing my message to him.

I have a Dude Dare for you. Do you accept?

He doesn't even blink at my text. We've been down this road a million times. *Of course. What u got?*

In ten minutes, spill something on your pants, then find the smallest person you're having a conversation with and ask to borrow their pants. When they say no, act utterly offended.

Sunji blinks in disbelief. *What if they say yes?*

Then you must put their pants on.

Sunji begins to sweat, and our next message doesn't help ease his growing anxiety.

But cmon Sunji, who would say yes?

Sunji only knows one person outside of his housemates who would. *I'm with Rock, you assholes.*

Eagle's Rock?

Sunji grabs a napkin to pat at his brow. *....yes.*

Erwin is explaining the plot of their new idea to an intrigued Rock.

"It's a parody mockbuster, you see. Our hero is Jane Blonde, and she fights off Eaton Bush to get to and take down the evil organization WRAITH alongside her lover, the biochemist Laong Tung, who Sunji will play."

Rock leans down to look at Sunji, face morphing into a lip-pressed smile that hides his grinding teeth, but not his clenching jaw.

"Oh, Sunji, always gotta be the desirable one."

"Fiction is a form of truth-telling," Sunji shrugs. He unlocks his phone to look at his latest received message.

HAHAHAHAHAHAHAHAHAHA

The bartender sets a beer down in front of Rock, who is locked in on his two surprise companions. "I've always wondered what happens on Sunji's mysterious meetings."

Erwin adjusts his glasses. "Oh, this is the first meeting he and I have had like this."

"Are you the same director that's dating Jerrica?" At Erwin's nod, Rock picks up his glass. "Does that intimidate you, knowing that Sunji and your girl…" He flicks his tongue through the foam in his beer.

"Initially," Erwin says, as if they weren't just kicked out of a bar for fighting over her. "Wouldn't you feel inadequate having to measure up to that?"

Rock sneers in Sunji's direction.

• • • • • •

Eagle leans on the bathroom sink, taking deep breaths.

The second door opens—the Narnia door—and Eagle's eyes widen as she looks through the mirror at the intruder.

"I didn't mean to scare you," Ty says. "You okay?"

"That door needs a lock," Eagle growls. "Why are you in here? There's still only one toilet."

"December really likes you."

"I know."

"That's my best friend." It's a threat, almost.

Eagle shrugs. "I figured."

"Please don't break her."

"Break her?"

"She seems strong, but it's super glue. Loads of super glue. Applied by yours truly."

"I…I dig her too."

"I know we haven't really talked, but…"

"I get you. I feel the same about Alexander. I'm protective of him, and being in a relationship is new territory for him."

Ty scoffs. "I'm not gonna hurt Alexander!"

"Not on purpose."

"Touché."

They both put their heads down.

"But seriously," Eagle says into the sink, "do you have to shit or something? Because this is creepy."

· · · · · ·

Jay stares intently at an increasingly uncomfortable December.

"Is this as awkward as it feels?" she asks, hoping for an ally.

"Where'd your friend go?" he asks her.

"I don't know; I guess to grab the rest of her stuff."

Jay wiggles his eyebrows. "I meant your other friend."

"Well, that I just don't know at all."

Jay stares at the side of her face until she turns back to him.

"What do you do?" he asks.

"I'm an art critic."

"No, I mean," and Jay draws this out, "are you a bottom or a top?"

Ty returns not a moment too soon.

"Ready to go, Cem?"

"Beyond," December says, taking a look at her phone's screen. Smiling at what she sees there, she locks it and rises from the table.

"Bye, babe." Alexander goes to kiss Ty, but she stops him.

"You were sucking Jay's toes not even an hour ago."

"So good, I gave him a standing ovation," Jay says in my ear, hand on his dick.

"You're gross," I reply, waving to Ty and December as they exit. "Hey, by the way. Why did you ask me to give you my shirt?"

Jay's eyes rest on me briefly. My eyes, my naked chest, then back at the closing door. "To see if you would."

Eagle returns from the bathroom.

"Dudes, my place. Two hours? Truth sessions."

I turn to Alexander. "You're to blame for everything that happens from here on out. I just want you to remember that."

Eagle shakes her keys at me, and I'm vaguely annoyed. "We'll finally find out your pick for the bet."

I wave goodbye at Eagle. "See you in two hours!"

"Bring your balls," she says, exiting.

• • • • • •

Sunji stands in Rock's too small, too tight, and too short pants. Rock stands next to him in boxer shorts. Erwin approaches and all three of them are obviously tipsy.

"I can't feel my balls," Sunji moans.

"Don't use them for a change," Rock says.

Erwin grips his head. "We took too many shots. And we got kicked out again."

Rock laughs. "They're kicking us out because we drank the whole bar."

"No," Sunji says, "they're kicking us out because you're in your underwear."

"These are called boxer *shorts*." Rock grins. "They're decent."

Erwin pulls out his phone. "Am I getting the rideshare?"

Rock's drunken smile is his answer.

Sunji hands his phone to Erwin. "Can you get a picture of us? I need proof that… *this* happened."

"Okay. Say, 'Laong Tung.'"

"Laong Tung!"

Liminal Spaces

"Would you still be my friend if I looked like this?" Eagle asks, contorting her face until she's virtually unrecognizable.

Instead of answering, Ellington poses a question of his own. "Why are you in such a good mood?"

"Why aren't you?" she asks, and he makes a strange gargling noise in his throat.

The doorbell rings and she heads to answer it, walking comically. "Would you still be my friend if I walked like this?"

"Yes, and I want you to know that you're being ablest right now."

"Oh, shit, really?"

Eagle opens the door and Marshall enters, running through the Diolosas' foyer and into the living room, leaping into his brother's arms .

"Can we get a dog?" he asks. "And name it Loonah?"

"If you don't get your Black ass down!" Ellington drops the younger Gomez on the couch, then turns to the crowd of us entering the door. "Who gave him alcohol? Jay?"

Jay is still wearing my shirt, so I've made him give me one of his, and he has. My refrigerator frame fills it out differently than his shapely chest does, but we're the same size and, to my surprise, I don't look too bad in it.

There is a part of me that is harping on the fact that we've slept together now in both of the ways people can sleep together and today we're wearing each other's clothes and that part of me is definitely panicking. The rest of me doesn't have the emotional bandwidth to give a shit.

As he strides in, Jay shakes his head at Ellington's question. "It was the wingèd one."

Eagle flutters her fingers. "Guilty."

She closes the door behind Alexander and pitches her voice up, squeezing it through her nasal passageways.

"Alexander, would you still be friends with me if I talked like this?"

He's a diplomat. "I think so."

Jay is already at Eagle's coffee table next to Ellington, pouring shots with Eagle's liquor. Ellington hasn't taken his eyes off of his brother, who stands in the corner dancing to music the rest of us cannot hear.

"He's cut off for at least an hour."

I collapse on the couch beneath Eagle's stairs, marveling at the kind of house a military paycheck could afford. In the living room alone, there are two couches, two armchairs, a bookcase, three floor lamps, and the coffee table where the drunks are congregating.

"Shots," Jay barks. "Eagle?"

She steps next to him, clapping his back. "Already here."

Jay looks to me. "Zario."

I hold up my bottle filled with gin and soda. "I already have a drink." We began pre-gaming the moment Eagle left the house.

Jay narrows his eyes at me. "Asshole. Shots."

"Fine," I grumble, rising to join them.

Keys rattle against the door's metal lock. Eagle turns back, but it opens before she can reach it. Sunji walks in stiffly, and we instantly break into laughter at the sight of him still squeezed into Rock's pants. Alexander claps like a seal and Sunji bows deeply to his applause.

Jay waves him over. "Just in time for shots, Ludi Lin."

"Ludi wishes he had my nipples," Sunji says, rising up and taking careful steps toward us.

Eagle laughs uproariously at this, too loud, too hard, too genuine.

Sunji squints at her. "You got fucked *good*."

Rock stumbles into the house, pantsless, and Sunji's last words hang in the air.

"There's my favorite pumpkin spice latte!" Rock holds out his hands to his wife.

"Hey, Rockefeller."

She kisses him like she means it, and suddenly it's clear to the rest of us that she doesn't.

"I'm going to find some pants," Rock says, and he disappears up the stairs.

Almost as one person, we turn to Eagle.

"Sunji's right," I say. "You were all chipper when you left our place, like you had a dick appointment or something."

Alexander's talking over me, "Is that why you and Jay have been—"

"It wasn't Jay," I cut him off, because I would know. Also because, "He was with us."

Eagle's eyes switch to me, taking away the one plausible excuse she didn't even know she had. "Fuck, brah…"

"Hey," Jay pipes up, "it could have been me!"

"Was it Ellington?" Sunji asks. His face cracks open into an approving grin. "You slut!"

Eagle wrinkles her face. "Ew."

"Don't I have enough complications—" Ellington is saying when Eagle's comment registers. He turns to her. "Why, 'ew?'"

Alexander has begun his computations. "You don't hang with anybody else. Who else did you see today? It wasn't Marshall. It wasn't Ty."

"Turn him off," Eagle says, eyes bright. "Take out the batteries or whatever."

It's too late. "Are you fucking Dec—"

Jay makes a last ditch effort to save the day. "Despicable people? Disgusting people?"

Alexander's convinced and incredulous at the same time. "Does Ty know?"

My eyes grow wide. "That lady? December?"

December must have met up with Eagle after dropping Ty off, giving Eagle enough time to come back here and shower. It's clear to me now, though, understandably this time, Sunji is still catching up.

"Lady?" he asks. "Is she a hot lady? Anyone got pictures? What're her socials?"

Ellington shakes his head. "That's a slippery slope, Eagle."

She turns to him, eyes flashing. "You're the pot calling the kettle!"

"Well, not Black," Sunji snorts.

Ignoring him, Ellington responds to Eagle. "That's how I know it's a slippery slope! First hand experience! Again, why, 'ew?'"

"Community dick," Eagle and Jay say in unison.

"Yo, I own mine," Ellington says.

"You do *not*," Eagle fires back. "Otherwise you'd just be upfront with Mandy about wanting an open relationship."

Ellington widens his eyes. "I don't want an open relationship!"

"Then what the fuck is all of this about?" Eagle asks him.

"This isn't even about me, it's about you being the only person that got pussy in the last hour and you being the last person that should be getting any pussy at all!"

"This subject is off limits for the rest of the night, because," and now she suddenly remembers to whisper, "my husband is upstairs!"

"You gotta tell him, yo," Ellington shrugs. "Tandem Truths."

"Don't tie this into the game. This is my life!"

"It's Rock's, too," I say.

Eagle looks at me, but doesn't respond.

"Secrets don't say secrets," Sunji slurs. He's collapsed in one of the arm chairs and we notice with dismay that he's taken Rock's pants off.

Marshall sinks into the cushions next to me. "All this tea and we haven't even gotten to the rest of the game yet.

Jay speaks, almost dismissively. "It's time for that shot."

"I, for once, agree with you," Alexander says cheerily.

"I don't give a solitary fuck."

Jay passes out the shot glasses. Eagle finds a blanket to throw over Sunji, who cracks his knuckles. "All right, let's do this! I've already pledged my money, and also my liquor cabinet. Please, pick Gregory. He's sweet."

Ellington takes his shot early, then indicates for Jay to pour him another.

"I've pledged money," he says, "and my place on the weekends. Pick our boy Zach. He's...savory."

"I pledged the money and my Boba Fett Hot Toy," Alexander says brightly. "Pick Mick because it rhymes. And he's a cutie. You said so yourself."

Eagle exhales, clearly not in the mood anymore. "I pledged mucho money and the reveal of my government name. But don't pick Oscar. You deserve better."

Jay is annoyed by this entire process. "It doesn't matter what I pledged, because I won."

Ellington takes another shot and Eagle pinches him in annoyance.

"You don't know that," Ellington says to Jay, indicating for Jay to pour him a third.

Jay pours. "Anyone who thinks I lost, let's make it double for my trouble."

"Ehh, I saw that kiss between Zario and Iggy," Alexander says. "I'm not doing it."

"Double," Ellington says.

"Double," Sunji agrees. "But the same goes for you."

Jay settles into the chair next to me. "That's easy."

"I wouldn't be too sure," Sunji retorts.

"Well, I'm as worried as you are intelligent."

I nudge Jay. "Stop being a dick."

"I thought you liked dicks," he whispers into my neck.

"That joke gets old," I say, scooting away from him.

"There's a bit too much subtext going on here," Eagle snaps.

"Girl, keep up!" Marshall squeals. "This is barely even subtext."

Ellington raises his glass. "All right, drama queens, can we toast? To the bet."

We finally toast, thankfully with no attempts at poetry, then Ellington, Jay, and Sunji send their additional funds to me for the pot.

Jay takes my glass for a refill and I protest. "I just had one."

"This is a chaser for that one," he replies.

When Rock comes back downstairs in a fresh pair of jeans, we've launched into the truth sessions, since we were pretty much in the thick of it anyway, thanks to the revelation about Eagle.

She's at the end of the second couch, cozy with Ellington and Alexander. Rock does a quick inventory and finds his place mirroring her on the couch with Marshall and I.

"What are the rules?" he asks.

Marshall responds, "You just ask someone a question, anything, and they have to answer it truthfully."

"Got it," Rock says, and he jumps right in. "Sunji? Who in this room would you fuck?"

Sunji looks around. "In this room?"

"Yep."

"Anybody?"

Rock spreads his hands. "No judgement."

Sunji nods. "Then I would totally tap my own ass."

Jay rises, crossing the room to give Sunji a high five.

Rock blinks. "What?"

"Nobody does it better! I donate five hundred dollars a year to this great non-profit, Clone S.C.A.M."

"You realize what that spells?" Ellington asks, but Sunji doesn't hear him.

"I'm very pro-cloning research. It's a life mission. I gotta fuck me before I'm fifty." He looks at Marshall. "That's around the time that age catches up to us Asians and we look ninety-five for the rest of our life."

Alexander is lost in the possibilities. "Dude, you're, like, asking for a Jurassic Park of humans. Imagine if all clones start living twice as long as normal humans. We would become inferior. So they'd start rounding us up into age camps—"

"Zario," Sunji says, sparing us from more of Alexander's musings, "who in this room would *you* get busy with?"

"He's gonna say my husband," Eagle says dryly.

I nod sheepishly. "Rock." Despite the events of the last twenty-four hours, it's not technically a lie.

"Yeah, that tracks," Ellington nods.

Marshall isn't convinced. "Rock?"

"Shouldn't I be at the top of that list?" Sunji asks me. "You don't have to be embarrassed."

"Sunji, I keep telling you, you're not my type."

"I'm every man's type. Lots of women's, too!"

"No. You have slender calves. You know beefy calves are my jam."

"And Rock's calves?"

Rock lifts his leg high in the air, grabbing it with both hands. "Sculpted by God's favorite artists."

It goes on like this for a while, giving answers to questions that don't matter, while pretending they're the most important things we will ever discuss.

I try to take things deeper. "Sunji, if you could change one thing in the world, what would it be?"

True to his nature, Sunji barely thinks. "That's easy, Zario. I'd make you guys happier. I have five of the best friends in the whole world and I don't understand why you guys aren't the happiest dudes alive. We got money."

"True," Ellington nods.

"We look good."

"Also true," Jay agrees.

"We got ride-or-dies."

"So true," Alexander says, nestling into Ellington, who pats the gamer's head in response.

Sunji opens his hands, palms upward. "Why aren't we happier?"

We sit in this for a moment, then Jay shrugs.

"We're entitled sons of bitches."

Eagle echoes him in agreement. "We're entitled sons of bitches."

"And in order to stay rulers of this microcosm," Jay continues, looking at Eagle, "we stay in this tiny little lane of life. We don't break out. We stay because it's comfortable. It's cush."

Alexander shakes his head. "Maybe for you. I'm not happy—yet—because I'm learning how to be happy."

Eagle points her finger at him. "I agree with that. Learning how to be happy."

"She's drunk," Rock says, shaking his head.

Ellington makes a face. "I think happiness requires no limits. And I'm learning how to be limitless."

I realize I haven't spoken up yet. Happiness. Such a concept.

"I don't think I've ever been happy?" I make it a question to soften the punch. "Not like, you know, beyond a party or a birthday. Shit like that. So, I don't miss the absence of it."

"You've told us your depression feels like an absence," Eagle says.

"Yeah, of all emotion. Like, I'm not sad or angry, I'm just a blob, I guess. The absence of happiness is just the luck of the draw."

This is exactly what I don't want to happen. Just because I'm not accustomed to happiness doesn't mean I am depressed all the time. Jay's watching me and I look away. I know that if I smile, he'll think I'm disguising something. That's the rule. If I'm happy, I'm masking something. If I'm upset, then I'm depressed. I can never just be. They always worry about me.

Jay plays with the arm of his chair, looking up at me without raising his head.

"Ayo," he says, "if a girl asked you for just the tip, would you do it?"

I roll my eyes. "No."

Alexander directs his question to Jay. "Where's the craziest place you've ever had sex?"

"Callie and I fucked in the middle of the dance floor once at this club in Florida. It was some big holiday weekend and we just kind of went for it."

"How?" I ask.

"She was wearing this turquoise dress. Lots of people saw what we were doing, but nobody really cared."

"I'm adding that to my bucket list," Sunji says, practically drooling.

Jay's eyes light upon Ellington. "Ellington. Who's the last person you hooked up with?

Ellington looks away. "Nah, I ain't answering that."

"Dude Code, pretty boy: you can't break the established rules just because your closet is oozing with fresh skeletons."

Jay's eyes are unnaturally bright and Ellington's are darkening.

"Chill, man. Ask me something else."

"I knew it!" Jay snaps his fingers. "You're still fucking Mandy."

This obviously isn't going to end well. "Yo," I caution, "let it go."

Jay is a steamroller. "Man, you really don't love yourself!"

Ellington sits back, danger looming. "It really pisses me off when you guys say that."

"One of us has to be willing to tell the truth in this game. If you don't answer, conclusions are formed based on the known information. And we all know—"

"It was Callie." Ellington says this with resignation.

I try to turn to Jay, but it's like the seconds have turned to hours and I can't move fast enough. No one's speaking. No one's moving, but I know Jay's erupting.

Ellington's voice comes through. "I've been seeing her for a week or so."

I finally get my head turned all the way. Jay is sitting straight up, shoulders toward Ellington.

"You're fucking my girl?"

Ellington shakes his head. "You guys haven't been together for months."

Sunji wrinkles his nose in disgust. "You guys are nasty rabbits."

Feeling attacked, I sit up, and Jay and I speak in unison. "I'm not fucking anybody!"

Jay's attention is back on Ellington. "Why would she even scratch you?"

With relish, Ellington replies, "Hashtag pretty boy curse."

"You motherfucker."

"Dude Code: You wanted an answer."

"Dude Code: You don't fuck some other dude's girl!" Jay's forehead wrinkles and he looks around in exasperation. "It's funny. You guys call *me* the asshole."

Ellington rolls his eyes.

Jay raises an eyebrow. "But I guess you're not an asshole. You're not shit, either."

Alexander seems to have shrunken into himself.

"I think the game's over," he says.

Ellington is still leaning back into the couch cushions. "Nah, I wanna keep playing. I'm having fun."

Sunji cuts his eyes between Ellington and Jay. "This is fun?"

I interrupt, staring directly at Jay. "I'm grabbing water. Anybody else want some?"

Jay waves me off.

"I'll come," Marshall says, and I enter the kitchen with the only person who doesn't benefit from a break in the game.

I grab two bottles of water out of the refrigerator. Marshall leans against the counter, watching me.

"Your boys."

I hand him a water. "Your brother."

"I know." He taps my arm with the back of his hand, the one gripping the water. "Hey, between you and me. Truth or dare."

"Truth. That's the name of the game right now."

He steps closer to me.

"Out of all those men, Rock is your number one choice?"

I begin a neck roll, but don't commit to it, so all I do is push my head forward and waddle it a bit.

"I wasn't lying! I haven't been able to shake those feelings since I first saw him."

"Jay, tho…"

I flush, feeling my face prick as if hundreds of pinheads are trying to break free.

"Do you see how he's acting? How is that attractive?" As my friend, Jay was borderline embarrassing tonight.

"Do you see how he uses those hips? He didn't learn that from dancing. I don't know how you do it with these straight boys."

"You're talking about lust, and what you do is just put up a mental block."

I feel like a hypocrite as the words come out of my mouth. I stare at Marshall's beautiful, unblemished face. Here, in front of me, is a single, attractive gay man. Out like a motherfucker. Why are guys like Marshall so impossible to find in the real world?

This is the real world, I think.

"Don't kiss me," he says matter-of-factly.

I take steps back that I don't remember having taken forward. "I wasn't going to."

Eagle walks in. "Is there any more water?"

I hand her the water in my hand and turn back to the fridge. Behind me, Marshall begins to laugh. A rib-rocking laugh.

"What?" I ask, turning.

Eagle's eyeing him, too, and he crosses his arms, looking deep into my eyes like he's found Waldo.

"That's one of your problems."

Problems? "Enlighten me."

"You don't know how to be friends—I mean true friends—with anyone else who's gay. They're either an enemy or a future erotic memory."

"I know gay guys," I say, waving a hand while locking my elbow against my ribs as if I need protection from this read. "I mean, I really know them."

"'Them?'" Marshall and Eagle ask together.

"In any group of them, the overlap caused by fucking each other—"

Marshall shakes his head. "That's a stereotype."

"Maybe. But I'm not dedicated to the d."

"Why not? There's a difference between a drug and a vitamin, and vitamin D is necessary. Look at me. I get mine, but I don't crawl for the dick. Dick is everywhere. Dick is a renewable resource. Naturally occurring and all that shit."

I roll my eyes.

"Are you a self-hating gay guy?" Eagle asks me. "Or even a self-disliking gay guy?"

"Oh, my God," Marshall says, eyes widening. "That's exactly it. You've been sipping that Diet Homophobia."

At this subliminal suggestion, I return to the refrigerator and grab a bottle of soda. "It'll make a better chaser than this shit."

"Maybe you just need a seasoned old queen to give you perspective," Eagle says as the three of us return to the rest of our friends.

"Maybe so." I turn to Marshall. "Do you have anyone like that who you can talk to?"

"You," he says, and runs before I can smack him.

"This is bullshit," Jay says the moment we return to the living room. "Let's stop prolonging my inevitable crowning as matchmaker extraordinaire."

I raise my hands in control or defeat, I'm not sure. "Let's do this. Very soon one of you will be receiving a sizable donation."

Sunji, Jay, Alexander, and Ellington look at their phones expectantly. I tap my screen and a cash sound effect chimes from one section of the room.

Jay whoops as the rest of my friends drop their phones in disappointment.

Alexander frowns. "Figures."

Jay raises his hips in the air, swiveling and gyrating in loud ecstasy.

"I'm rubbing my chode on all of you right now!" he exclaims.

Eagle's eyes are on me. Steady. Curious. There's so much to her that I still don't know.

"So, what's the next step?" she asks.

My mouth rises to my nose. "What do you mean?"

"Well, the purpose of the bet was to change the course of your romantic life," Alexander reminds me. "What you do after this decision is pretty important. You finally get to move out of this liminal space you've been in."

"Liminal space?"

Jay hits me, grumbling. "Why would you even ask him to clarify anything?"

"Technically you're having a liminoid experience. Liminal spaces are in-between spaces. A spot not intended for stasis, but for traveling through. Literal examples are like hotel hallways, especially at night. Empty parking lots, especially at night. Empty school grounds, stairwells, train tracks. In *The Twilight Zone*, Rod Serling says—"

"Hold on the dissertation," Sunji interrupts, turning to me. "He's right."

"How can you be sure?" Jay mutters.

"Call Iggy," Sunji continues. "Ask him out on a date. Get him to change that name."

"Invite him dancing!" Marshall squeals.

Ellington hops on this. "Tonight."

Jay clears his throat. "Nah, Ellington, that's not happening."

"I'm drunk," I protest to the room.

This is the wrong thing to say.

Eagle, Ellington and Marshall all scream, "Tonight!"

"You've got the liquid resolve," Ellington explains. "If you don't do it now, you're going to talk yourself out of it."

Jay shakes his head like a magic 8 ball sits on his neck.

"Look," Ellington says to him, "you can be pissed at me all you want, but he's fine."

"He's drunk. That's not the same as fine," Jay counters. "And I don't need your permission to be pissed at you. But karma is a motherfucker, motherfucker."

"I'll go with him," Marshall offers. "Be his wingman."

Jay turns to Marshall, face serious. Tender, almost.

"He doesn't drink. Not without us there." Now he turns to me, saying only, "Jiminy Cricket, Zee."

I nod. "I got you."

"Chill, Jay," I hear Rock say, but I hold Jay's gaze. "Let the man have some fun!"

"You good?" Jay asks me.

"I'll have Marshall. I'm super good."

He smiles, taking me at my word. "You gonna break the curse tonight, Zee?"

I roll my eyes. "For the last time, there's no such thing."

"In that case…" He holds out a fist. "Prove me wrong."

We bump fists.

"Eagle broke the curse today."

At first, I don't even hear Sunji. Then I register the sharp intakes of breath, the shifting positions.

"Broke what?" Rock asks, and I wonder if I can reach Sunji in time.

"The curse!" Sunji repeats, but it's the alcohol talking.

"How did we? No we didn't." Rock's mind is racing, eyes locked on Sunji's, with every other pair in attendance ever-widening. "Unless you mean you helped her."

"I think you guys are talking about two different things," Alexander begins.

Eagle is peering at Rock. "What did you just say?"

Sunji raises his arms in mock surrender. "No one slept with me. I meant that girl!"

Rock turns from Sunji to his wife.

"What girl?"

Marshall's smile falls. It's no longer fun-messy for him. He looks at me and I know he's remembering the other word I used to describe our self-flagellating game.

A bloodbath.

Where the Music's Strong, the Drinks are Loud

The club I choose is on a rooftop. I figure the perfect spot to reunite with Iggy is one of the few places in Downtown LA where there's nothing between us and the stars. There's a shallow pool, music that always pumps louder than necessary, and overpriced, but delicious food.

Once Marshall and I get in the rideshare, it becomes clear to me that I'm in no position to be out and about, which means that Jay is right, but nobody wants him to be. Ellington's brother is happier to be with my drunk ass than back in the middle of whatever's going down on our street. Once I hit the dancefloor, however, it's almost black humor that we ever believed Marshall would be able to keep up with me.

After a few songs where I'm the Oscar to his me, he follows me to the bar where I take a shot that does not go down easy.

"Slow down there, cowboy," Marshall says, gaining some points for actually looking concerned.

"I'm just trying to get rid of the nerves," I gasp out.

"By hacking them all up?" Marshall queries, clapping to accentuate his words.

"One more and then I'm good."

"Okay, but this one's on me," he says and I briefly wonder what it is he does for work.

"One more round," he says, spinning—never turning!—to the bartender. Looking at me he asks, "Did you douche?"

"I don't bottom first," I tell him. "If at all."

"Why do you make these rules?" he asks me. "Do you just want to see what a guy will put up with in order to be with you?"

I body roll away from him and his questions.

"I'm sorry, I can't hear you over all of this *me*."

. . . .

Eagle refuses to fuss at Sunji and she refuses to argue with Jay. No, she's not going to talk about it with them. No, she's not going to come spend the night. No, she's not even going to come over for drinks.

She gets them off of her porch and sends them back to our place where Ellington's waiting for them after seeing off his brother and I. Sunji waves forlornly, but she doesn't see, staring off down the street at the normalcy that's forever lost to her.

After several minutes, she walks back inside and sees him sitting on the stairs in the dark. She closes the door and walks to the base of the steps, looking up at him.

"I knew something was going on," he begins, taking careful pauses, "and if it was Sunji, I could have understood. I was ready to deal with it because he's a model or whatever. But a woman? I had Alexander pull her up and that is a gorgeous, smart intelligent woman. Who's taller than me! I mean, I thought that I made up for my height with my skills in the bedroom, but there are obviously certain things I'm sure she can do for you that I can't. But Eagle, I love you. I've loved you for so long and I gave everything for you." He's sobbing now. "I started manscaping for you and that shit's itchy when it grows back in, because my pubes are so coarse, and—"

Eagle, dismayed, holds up a hand to stop him. "Rock."

He sniffles. "I'm sorry."

The more emotional he gets, the more she feels herself shutting down. She wills herself to stay open for him. To stay available.

She has to talk. "I don't know what's wrong with me, Rockefeller. Nothing's wrong with you. I just realized that something was missing and whatever it was, she had it. She has all of it and I don't understand why that is."

He's incredulous. "She doesn't have a dick, Guadalupe!"

Eagle flinches at her first name. "Turns out I didn't miss that so much."

His face has fallen as far as it's physically capable.

"And you want me to live with that?"

He stands, and she hears the keys jingle in his hands.

"I'm going to Oscar's. Maybe I'll fuck him, see if I miss vagina."

As soon as the words are out of his mouth, his entire face curdles.

"Will you be back tomorrow?" she asks.

"We both know I will," he rasps, walking past her, careful not to touch her. "Sleep deep. Count your blessings instead of sheep."

He turns around when he gets to the door.

"This thing you and those fucks next door are always talking about? It's not a curse. It's privilege. You look the way you look and you get to do whatever the fuck you want to do and the universe is always like, shit yeah, go ahead! And you trample on everything. Anyone. And things might turn bad for you for like a day, but there's always something else, someone else, willing to be trampled just because of how aesthetic your physical features are. It's privilege."

He puts his hand on the knob, and now he speaks to the air, just in case his wife wants to hear. "I'm not willing to be trampled anymore."

• • • • • •

"I thought you didn't drink."

I roll my eyes, wondering who this is, policing me all the way across town. "Why does everyone suddenly care?"

I turn around and see no one looking in my direction. I look back at the bartender, but she's not paying any attention to me.

"Down here, Romeo."

Lando drifts in the pool, grinning up at me.

I smile back. "Mercutio! Oh, my God, hi!"

I walk over to the edge of the pool, holding up my drink. "Tonight's special. I picked."

Lando dips his chin, eyebrows lifted. "You decided to go with the two exes, didn't you? Going full poly. Nothing wrong with that."

I laugh, and shake my head. "Firstable, no. Secondish, the muscle dude—"

"Zach, the short shorty, right?"

"Zach wasn't half bad," I say more wistfully than intended.

Lando's eyebrows rise even higher. "Did you fuck him?"

My face gives it away and Lando whistles.

"Is that who you picked?"

I shake my head. "I picked Iggy."

Lando looks around. "I don't see him."

"He's late. Who are you here with?"

He turns back to me, grinning. "Myself. Just the way I like it.

"Can't you be by yourself at home?"

Lando jerks his head back, looking me from heel to crown. "You want me to leave or something?"

"No!" I curse myself for my drunken abrasiveness. "Um, you want a drink?"

He raises his own.

"I'll take a dance, though."

I feel like we're already dancing. "After you dry off, sure. I'm gonna go make a phone call."

"Go by the bathrooms," he suggests. "It's quieter there."

• • • • • •

Four missed texts and a voicemail.

"Hey, Zario. It's Iggy. I was texting and I guess you haven't gotten them yet. They've got, like, four lanes closed and traffic hasn't moved in, like, twenty minutes. It looks like I'm not making it. I'm sorry, man. I was excited to see you tonight.

"Let's meet tomorrow? After your hangover wears off? Text me. We'll break some things."

The message repeats in my head long after I lock my phone screen.

"Shit," I say into the night.

Lando, acceptably dry, approaches with his drink.

"What's wrong?"

I wave my phone. "He's not coming. Stuck in traffic. Some accident or something."

"That sucks. Want a pick-me-up?"

"After I finish this one, I'll probably lay off the drinks for a bit." Especially because for a moment I thought he was inviting me to lift him into the air. I could probably fuck him silly in that position. I hate it when my brain goes there.

He's straight, I remind myself.

He holds up half of a capsule. "I'm not talking about a drink. A little ex-tra."

I've had Ecstasy before. That seems safe.

"Why not?" I say, popping it in my mouth and washing it down with a sip of my drink.

"Atta boy," he says, and my dick jumps.

He pops the other half in his mouth, then freezes. "Fuck."

"What's wrong?" I ask him, worried because the other half of that pill is already being broken down in my system.

"I didn't mean to take this. I already had two. Three always sends me over."

"I'll take it."

Lando flips it across his tongue. "You sure? It's already got my slobber on it."

"I'll take that, too," I tease.

For the time it takes a wave to crest, he watches me.

"Make it cute," he says. He leans over and sticks the pill in my mouth, followed by his tongue. At first, I pull my own tongue back, but he seeks it out and I realize his intent is to make out with me.

It lasts long enough for me to forget who I am.

He pulls away, slowly, eyes on mine.

"You're lucky," he says. "I like kissing."

"You're lucky," I reply. "I'm good at it."

"You're drunk," he says, smiling distantly.

"Off of kisses."

"Lightweight," Lando teases. "I have a high tolerance."

I lean back in for another and he laughs, putting both of his palms toward my chest. "Chill." He plops the drink straw back into his mouth.

"Are you fucking with me?" I ask him.

"I'm only bisexual in the northern hemisphere, Zario, sorry to say."

"Then what is all this? You and me?"

He turns to me and his voice barely has any inflection. "Oh, my God, are you in love?" Then, "Don't make it weird. We can have fun, but don't make it weird."

I chuckle disbelievingly. "Right, okay."

I'm not even upset with him, really. What was it Jay had said to me the night they manifested this bet? I can get anything I want, whether it's good for me or not. Apparently, I wasn't satisfied sharing an increasingly carnal bed with my best friend, now I was trying to be Lando's gay boy exception. I was ahead and I wasn't quitting. The brakes were cut, but I had turned onto the highway.

Lando is watching me. "You need tonight, you know that? You still haven't learned to let go."

Marshall turns the corner, eyes flitting from me to Lando.

"Zario, you good?"

"Marshall, this is Lando. He works at the restaurant where I had all my dates."

Marshall nods frostily and Lando ducks away.

"He gives me bad vibes," Marshall says, watching Lando weave through bodies toward the bar.

"He's a bad boy," I say.

"What about Iggy?" Marshall asks me.

"Oh, he's not coming. I just got a voicemail from him."

Marshall looks genuinely sad for me. "You okay?"

"Yeah, I mean, Lando's here. I've got you. The music's good. Let's have a good night."

• • • • • •

"How old's your friend?" Lando asks me later when I join him at the edge of the pool, rolling my pants up. "He looks young."

"Yeah, he gets in everywhere though, because he looks like that."

"Was he one of the guys who set you up on those dates?"

"Oh, no," I shake my head. "That was his brother."

Lando raises his eyebrows. "You all run in a pack, huh?"

I nod. "A pretty pack."

"I bet you guys are a trip," he says, looking around furtively. He pulls something out of his shirt pocket and plops it on his tongue.

"What's that?"

"It's not Ecstasy," he warns me.

"I'll try it," I say, realizing that I'm acting hella reckless.

He reads it for what it is. "You just want to kiss me again."

"Don't feel special—"

He moves quickly and our tongues are dancing.

When he pulls away, the entire rooftop feels like it's shifted. "With a tongue like that, you could convince me to do all the drugs."

"That's kind of problematic, isn't it?" he says, looking out into the club.

It's not really popping tonight, and I realize I don't even know what night of the week it is. Marshall is standing near the bar being hit on by some older white guy, so I figure I can stay a little longer.

"What was that, by the way?"

He looks over at me. "Acid."

My face heats up. "Acid?"

He smiles. "Don't be scared. Take the trip."

I don't know how to explain my worries to him. With my cut breaks, this trip is fated to end in a crash.

Almost like he hears me, Lando adds, "Buckle up, baby. You're in for it, now."

Letting Go of Heaven

Jay smiles down at me, eyes turning in on themselves until they're brown spirals boring back into his skull. I take deep breaths as he lays his hand to rest on top of mine.

"You wanna go someplace else?" he asks, his mouth red like berries, wet like jam.

"I'll go wherever you want me to go," I tell him, my own mouth filling with the seeds of him.

Jay laughs. In the next moment, it's Lando there and he's laughing with me and at me all at once. I'm horrified at this change and I don't know who I'm seeing versus who's actually there. I don't understand why I'm thirteen floors in the air in the middle of this city.

"Then let's go," Lando seems to be saying to me. "I'm starving."

I swear… I'm sure… "I'm tripping."

"Yeah, you are!"

We talk over each other. Actually, he sings.

"*Un-pour the rain. Let the wind catch you.* It's some good shit."

"Whatever you gave me is," I swallow and I feel like there are levers and pulleys and metal chains in my throat, "like, opening up like a sealed chest. I'm kind of anxious and at the same time I have no fucks to give."

"Fucks are so unnecessary, why give a single one?"

I focus on the words like they're manifesting in front of my face and then they are, ornate and artisanal.

"Lando, I should probably go home now. I don't feel okay anymore."

"Oh, fuck. What is it?" Now he's worried. Too worried.

"Medically, I think I'm fine. I just feel like my demons are loose."

He sits down and takes my hand. "Any other time, that would sound badass."

Marshall walks over to us.

"You're sitting over here with your head in your hands like you're sloppier than Joseph," he says, handing me a glass of water.

"I'm leaving," I tell him, and I hear my words slurring.

Marshall's eyes cut over to Lando. "With?"

Lando lets go of my hand. I stare at him a moment but I can't find him. Shane is next to me, and I feel the sensation of him letting go of my hand over and over.

I stare down at my hands and there are so many hands letting go of mine. Ryu's hands. Patrick's hands. My father's hands.

"I'm leaving by myself. Do you want to stay?" I don't look up when I speak, but it's Marshall I'm replying to. I'm ignoring the rest of them

"I'll call my brother," he says, pulling out his phone.

"He's been drinking all day." I don't know if I say this to protest or to perform.

Nobody is holding my hand. My hands are empty.

"He never gets drunk," Marshall tells me, dialing. "He filters alcohol like a Brita."

I stand as Marshall gets on the phone. Maybe I just need to throw up. Maybe I just need to splash water on my face. I walk toward the bathrooms, but the ground is coming toward my feet too slowly.

I reach for it with my empty hands, and Lando reaches back, or Shane does, or Iggy does, but they don't catch me in time and my feet are in the sky, thirteen floors above the city and now all of me is empty.

· · · · · ·

"What did you expect?" my dad asked.

I was standing in our living room, two years ago. The house felt smaller, maybe because my mass was finally catching up with my height. Maybe because I had forgotten how the wooden paneling on all of the walls sucked the light in. I often wondered how mom could deal with being sick in a house that never aspired to brightness.

The darkness was on me then. I stood in front of my dad, aware that my toes were turned in the same way they always did when I knew I was in trouble.

I told him that I wasn't going back to school. I had just told him why.

He put his book down and wearily removed his glasses.

"You decided to embrace that lifestyle, Hector. You know how they are. Predatory. Perverted."

"Papá, I didn't choose anything. Being gay is just like being Mexican. There's a culture, but it's just who I am."

His eyes are wide. "It's not who you are, mijo. They walk naked in the streets. They fuck their cousins. They fuck the children in their neighborhoods and in their schools."

I shake my head, refuting this generalization. "Where are you getting this from, papá?"

"I'm saying that community creates a haven for those deviants. Let me ask you again, what did you expect?"

My father never raised his voice. In all of my years walking this earth, I had never known him to shout or scream. That was what made conversations with him so one-sided. I would succumb to mammoth displays of emotion while he would offer nominal displays of sympathy. Insufferably calm, collected, and coldhearted, he made me look the irrational fool.

"Papá, I'm here telling you that I was violated, and you're telling me that I deserved it?"

He rubbed his temples, loading bullets into the chamber of his words.

"I used to wonder what I did that was so wrong, so hateful that God would take her from me the way that He did. I prayed and I asked Him and I was told to wait on my answer. Now I have it."

My breaths came sharp and quick. There wasn't enough oxygen in the room. I couldn't think.

"Are you saying Mom died because of me?" My voice cracked and I could feel myself trembling just as hard as I had been when waiting in the police station just a month before. "You're saying that God gave her cancer and then she died, all because I'm gay?"

"Mijo, I forgive you, just like our Father has. And maybe this new thing has happened so that you would return home to me, your earthly father, just as our Heavenly Father wants you to return to him."

This rotting, soulless piece of shit. "I was raped so you could have some help paying the bills?"

He adjusted in his chair. "You know that's not what I'm saying, Hector."

"I know exactly what you're saying, Dad. I'm not coming back here. For a second, yeah, I thought maybe, but you've shown me that's impossible."

"You always have a home here," he said, voice still level, face still relaxed, "as long as you're living right. We can move forward as a family."

I realized that the darkness here, the darkness that I felt—he had put it on me.

"You're not my family," I spat at him, and a few months later I was on a one-way flight to California.

Fuck him.

The Depths

The Dudes do what dudes do.

Alexander meets Ellington and Sunji at the curb and I don't hear much of what happens as Sunji and Alexander carry me, stumbling, drunk and crying, into the house. I know Jay's pacing, also drunk.

"How is he?" he asks.

"Drunk as fuck," Sunji replies as they lay me on the living room couch.

"I wanna die!" I sob, and at the moment I mean it.

Jay turns on me. "Why the fuck, motherfucker—we talked about this! You know you shouldn't drink without us! What the fuck did you expect? A gay homecoming?"

"I'm sorry, Jay."

Hearing these words partially deflates Jay's anger, but not soon enough. Sunji walks past him to go pour a glass of water for me.

"Jay, step outside and take a few breaths."

Jay follows him to the kitchen. "Nah, I'm good. What do you need me to do?"

"I need you to step outside and take a few breaths. That's what I need you to do." Sunji has filled a glass, and heads out of the kitchen. Then, like the flip of a light switch, he spins around and nearly levitates into Jay's face. "What I want to do is tell you to fuck off, but I'm sure it'll come out something like 'Fuck off you selfish asshole and get yourself the fuck outside before our conversation continues with no need for words.' You've been a shithead all day, so let me remind you that this isn't the fuck about you or the fuck about your ego or the fuck about—"

Sunji catches himself. Now it's a glare off.

"Think about somebody else's feelings for once, Jay. He's supposed to be your best friend."

Sunji turns again, and heads toward my bedroom. Jay stands in the hallway for a moment, then spins on his heels, punching the wall as he leaves the house.

Eagle passes Jay on the steps. "He's inside?" she asks.

Jay nods.

"And you're outside."

Jay glares, and she steps past him.

Inside of myself, I am screaming. Sunji climbs onto the couch with me, gripping me tightly and rocking me with fervor. Alexander stands above us, worried.

"Fuck life," someone says, and it takes me a while to recognize my own voice.

"It's okay, man," Sunji is saying. "I got you. I got you."

At some point, Eagle enters. I hear her tenor as she talks to Alexander on the opposite wall. "Oh shit. What do you need me to do?"

Alexander shakes his head. "We got him. You take care of whatever you've got going on."

Eagle watches me for a moment, pain in her face. Then she's gone. It hurts more than I expect.

"I'm going to kill myself," I think, not realizing I'm saying it aloud. "Tonight." Screaming it through sobs. "Solve everybody's problems."

From above me, Sunji. His fingers in my hair, another palm tapping my waist. "I would very much appreciate it if you didn't do that. I love you too much to live without you, Zario."

"You'll get used to it," I mumble.

"I don't want to."

I fall asleep and he holds me still.

• • • • • •

While I drift in and out of consciousness, Alexander takes over for Sunji, holding me and rolling me over whenever I need to vomit. Then, strangely, starts telling me about his night. He does this, I think, more to keep himself awake than to actually communicate anything, but on varying levels, I hear him.

He talks to me about his brothers, about Ty, about what it was like being Patrick's roommate. He shares with me about how scared he was when I sunk into my depression after my breakup with Shane. How he feels responsible now, because he feels like tonight is his fault.

Ellington parks his car and he and Sunji talk in low voices in Sunji's room. Marshall sits undetected in the dining room, concerned that if anyone sees him, they'll transfer their worry for me into anger at him. The thing is, Ellington's not angry with his brother; he's shaken. Everything that had happened to him that evening, from Mandy forcing his proposal to Eagle's hookup confession and especially to Marshall's phone call from the club… The world is spinning like a room does to its drunken inhabitant, and he needs to put his foot on solid ground. He needs a point of focus.

Ellington subs in for Alexander, and he, too, begins sharing his thoughts with me, his growing affection for Callie, his history with his brothers back in Texas, and his excitement at how much I had opened back up to all of them when the bet started. He confesses to me that when he drops his brother off at their apartment, he's going to go spend the night with Callie, not to sleep with her, but just to be with her. She's become his point of focus.

They cycle like this. Eagle returns because she can't sleep, and she makes sure that I drink a little water every time I wake up. Sunji comes back in to send her home as the brothers leave and our house begins to fall asleep.

They all detail multitudes of stories to me, some mundane, some fantastical, some that I'll never repeat, and some of which I've detailed here. They show me, subliminally, the broken parts of themselves, the shifting nature of our existence. They detail a new beauty to me, one that I can only receive in my current, broken state.

Some of Eagle's words linger long after she's returned next door.

They're beautiful because of their broken parts.

• • • • • •

I wake on the couch in a sweat, but I feel far more lucid than the last few times I've come to. My stomach feels settled and the room is sitting still, finally at rest for the night and I appreciate it.

I sit up. My mouth is dry. Sunji is stretched out on the floor beneath me, still fully dressed, completely unconscious.

That changes the moment my feet hit the floor.

"Where are you going?" he asks through his haze, gripping the back of my legs.

"I'm just going to the bathroom," I tell him.

He rubs my calf in approval and I shuffle out of the living room. As I walk down the hallway, I see light shining across the floor from the crack beneath Jay's door.

I knock on the door and, after a moment, it opens. Relief is washing over Jay's face, but he doesn't speak, he just pushes the door all the way and I walk in.

It looks like he's in the middle of getting dressed, wearing his best slacks and a tank top.

"Going somewhere?" I ask him. He would know the only spots in town still open at this hour.

"Going anywhere." He sits on the floor, his back pressed against his bed. "There's no happiness here. Eagle and Rock Diolosa. They're supposed to be the peak, you know? The ideal. The destination. I don't know why the fuck I had them on a pedestal, man. This California air is toxic."

He trails off and I think he's lost in thought.

"Are you going to sit down," he asks now, "or am I going to keep talking to your knees?"

I take a seat next to him, rubbing my hands across the hardwood floor. "Are you still angry?"

"I'm like the Hulk. I'm always angry."

I laugh. Jay doesn't. He reaches over and rubs my scalp instead. It takes everything in me to avoid purring.

"Did you throw up?"

"Yeah, outside the club. And here."

"Good. You thinking clearly?"

"For once. You?"

He looks away, dropping his hand from my head.

"20/20, Zee."

I reflect on the night. "Iggy didn't show up. But this guy was there who I know from the restaurant. And then—"

"We don't have to talk about it." Meaning he doesn't want to.

I let silence reign.

"Are you gonna sleep?" I ask him eventually.

"Truth? Or dare?"

"Me? I pretty sure the game's done."

"Truth or dare." It's no longer a question.

Fine. I'll play along. "Both."

"I think you should run away with me."

His words enter the air and there is no room left for any other sounds. Everything is muted, and suddenly the scents are sharper. The bourbon on Jay's breath. The vomit on mine. His cologne, the same one I wore on my date with Mick. My sweat. How have we fit together all this time without having any matching edges?

I look at him. His expression is serious.

"Run away with me," he repeats.

It's both a truth and a dare. I'm not sure what's gotten into him so I turn away.

"You're making Sunji-sense right now."

"We've got nothing going for us here, Zee. Just ex-loves and ex-jobs and this fucking-ass, stupid-ass, bullshit-ass pretty boy curse. Got the whole region smelling like sharted dreams."

"And cumdust," I remember.

"And cumdust." He says it again, "Run away with me."

"Where would we even go, Jay? Some stupid *Harold & Kumar* adventure? Find some happily ever after?"

"Any ever after. And fuck *Harold & Kumar*. We could go to Portland. DC. Happy sometimes, sad sometimes, angry sometimes, but I tell you what."

I look at him, annoyed. "What?"

"I'll be with you every step of the way. You're Timberlake; I'm Timbaland. Or, who is Sunji always talking about? Coogler and Jordan. When did any other future sound so good?"

I reflect on this. "I never thought that when I had my 'Defying Gravity' moment, I'd be the Galinda."

Jay's turn. "What?"

"Did this Callie thing get you that bad? You always get like this over the girls you date."

"This isn't about Callie. This isn't even remotely—" He's spitting. "Man, fuck her. And fuck Ellington."

"In fact, you're saying it'll be you and me until, like always, you find another girl with those eyes you like or an ass you like, or that legendary 'dick-throat'—"

He's talking simultaneously. "Like always? Oh, I won't have time to look. We could go to Nashville, or Atlanta. Zee!"

I look at him now. It feels good to see him, the real him. No one else is taking his place, not Shane, not Lando, not Wesley, not Ryu. I don't want to see anyone else.

"You've got those eyes I like," he says. "That ass I like. And that legendary—"

"Easy," I say. "I was serious when I said that was a one time thing."

"You're still not listening to me. Sure, you have a few random reasons not to go. But what are your reasons to stay? What's keeping you here?"

I stare into this face that I love, Jay's face, and I explore the depths and finding myself in all of them. He has been falling and sinking long before I realized I was, too.

This is why he didn't want me to go out with Iggy tonight. This is why I had tried so hard to replace him with Lando. Now all of that has failed.

I have to be sure. It's a night of recklessness, so I don't think about it too hard, I just lean over and press my lips gently to his. He waits long enough for me to grow anxious, then he returns the kiss, his hands wrapping around my waist as mine grab his head. A serious of heavy, solid kisses, then his mouth is open and we slip into each other.

He pulls away suddenly, wiping his mouth with a small grin.

"What?" I ask.

His shoulders start shaking as he fails at fighting back a laugh.

"The vomit," he says, pointing to my mouth.

"Holy shit," I say, laughing, too. "I'm sorry."

His laughter fades and he looks at his watch. "Go pack, Zee. We're leaving before sunrise."

• • • • • •

It's weird, you know. There are times when it feels like life is falling apart on you, but, for all that falling, it turns out that things might just be falling into place.

We've stuffed the backseat and the trunk full of suitcases and it's madness, I know, because I'm sure neither Timberlake and Timbaland nor Harold and Kumar connected like the two of us. Like Zario and Jay.

Jay drives as the radio bumps between us and the road. A diva genie sings "*I wanna move like the air tonight. I wanna be free.*" And I feel free.

The next day is sure to have worry and chaos. We didn't leave a note or anything. Jay wasn't going to and when I considered it, I didn't know what I should say.

I wanna be free.

Just before taking the ramp onto the eastbound highway, he turns to me. At first I hope to see him grinning like a Cheshire cat in the midst of new wonder, but that's not Jay. He's a sober receiver. He stares at me with a calm, serious face and this assures me that he's content.

We merge onto the freeway; the city and its woes are at our backs. The distant mountains lay in wait and he looks at me again, like he wants to make sure I won't vaporize when we cross over the city lines.

Whatever he sees in me now brings a slow, lopsided smile to his face. He speaks and everything inside of me is set right.

"There's the sun."

The End*

* Continue the story your way.

Find out what happens when Sunji and Alexander wake up in the Dude House with two less roommates in *Pretty Dudes: The Sequel.*

or

Find out where the road takes Jay and Zario in *The Walls of Jericho Kim.*

or

Revisit the events of this book from Alexander's point of view in *Sired.*

Acknowledgements

I'm eternally thankful to the God who created me, especially for making me Black and gay.

The world has shifted drastically, not only from the moments *Pretty Dudes* was first manifested, but from the moments I first began adapting the scripts into prose. This book began before a pandemic and was completed during a revolution and I've been homeless the entire time. It absolutely would not have happened without the efforts of physical and emotional cavalries.

Thank you to the folks who believed in me before I believed in myself, especially Matthew Elam who's been in my corner since *Power Rangers*. Elton Keung, thank you for the recurrent stimulation. To my platonic intimates Tanner Herring, Marc Hightower, Dillon Meredith, Jason Wilbanks, Katori Brown, Manny Shih, Shaun Lau, Aria Song, Ariel Landrum, Dante Fernandez, Joe Brennan, and everyone who checked in on me before and during this process, I thank you for carrying me across this finish line.

A dedicated moment of appreciation to Gerry Maravilla and Steven Yee, who were present at the session that started it all and are therefore indirectly responsible for all of the creative trauma I have brought upon myself in the years since.

Thanks so much to the pioneers of screen and page, who gave me representations of myself long before I knew who I was, including James Baldwin, Patrik-Ian Polk, E. Lynn Harris, Essex Hemphill, Oscar Micheaux, RuPaul, and Marlon Riggs. Special thanks and love to Tarell Alvin McCraney and Barry Jenkins for giving me a pristine mirror during a time I least expected it and needed it most.

Thank you to those who sheltered me—Vista, Sylmar, Reseda, Glendale, and Apartment 210. To Trey Randol who holds space in his heart and lets me curl up in there on occasion.

Thanks to my betas, Matthew, Rhys and Vinnie.

Thank you, Heather Matarazzo, for helping me realize my story was running from the telling. Thank you, Andrea Lee, for just texting me back when my wheels were spinning in the mud of artistry. Thank you, Dickie Hearts, for pushing me to do more with what I've been given.

Special shoutout to my sisters Khacey and Gabby who reminded me how much I love books and always drive me to be a better person. I have to thank my brother Travis for thinking I was funny and being the Ellington to my Marshall.

Thank you to the amazing fans of *Pretty Dudes*, who laugh, cry, and kiki with us. Thank you for your love and your patience. You keep me going.

I'm appreciative of everyone who said no—those who said it was too gay, those who said it was too straight, also too Asian, and not Black enough, and, ugh, not white enough. Sometimes naysayers can be right and y'all were not.

I am indebted to the amazing, sprawling cast and crew who brought the Dudes to life in their first incarnation. My eternal gratitude to our season one leads—Bryan, Xavier, Tae, Kyle, Yoshi, and Olivia—who put flesh on sketches and blood in ink. Holla, holla at Kelsey, Marc F., and Cesar cuz y'all fuck wit me.

Gravity is a force, not a foe, and this book is for everyone who falls, everyone who leaps, and everyone who trusts enough to let go. Together, we can change the world.

So, what the fuck are we waiting for?

CHANCE SION-RAIZE CALLOWAY
July 3, 2020
chance@prettydudesweb.com

About the Author

CHANCE SION-RAIZE CALLOWAY is the author of several novels and book series including *The Charismatic Chronicles*, *The Never Novellas*, and *The Gay Man's Guide to Heterosexual Weddings*. Calloway founded CSRC Storytelling for printed media in 2012 with a passion for creating and promoting stories that change how people see themselves and the world around them.

In 2015, Calloway created the digital series *Pretty Dudes*, serving as showrunner and director for the LGBTQIA+ dramedy. Calloway and the series have picked up numerous awards, including Show of the Year at the 2017 National Youth Pride Services Awards. *Pretty Dudes* is currently available through Stoopid Ambitious, a streaming service and banner Calloway created as a hub for innovative and inclusive works by independent filmmakers with voices overdue for amplification.

All of Calloway's most recent projects—including this very novel— have been produced during the onset of the COVID-19 pandemic, in spite of his ongoing struggles with chronic homelessness. In the face of personal, global and systemic challenges, Calloway continues to focus his efforts on advocacy and change through art.

chancecalloway.com

"We are the motherfucks who are the living proof that there's a cost to being a cosmetic genetic." Cast members Xavier Avila, Yoshi Sudarso, Olivia Thai, Bryan Michael Nuñez, Kyle Rezzarday, and Tae Song photographed by Jeremy Perkins in downtown Los Angeles for the first season of *Pretty Dudes*.

"May this dude from the last fuck be different." Alexander (Rezzarday), Zario (Nuñez), Ellington (Avila), Eagle (Thai), Sunji (Sudarso), and Jay (Song) toast to Zario's return to the dating pool.

About the Show

A group of friends in one living space—it's been done before, but never like on *Pretty Dudes*. The boundary breaking and award-winning* web dramedy created by **Chance Calloway** is a show willing to look at race, gender constructs, sexuality, and all intersections of life in a comedic examination of what it is to be a millennial in today's America.

The series boasts an inclusive cast of actors portraying an equally inclusive and intersectional array of characters, including **Bryan Michael Nuñez** (*American Vandal*) as Zario, **Yoshi Sudarso** (*Power Rangers Dino Charge*) as Sunji, and **Xavier Avila**, whose performance as Ellington is his award-winning† acting debut.

Pretty Dudes exists to show the world the way it truly is, in humor and in heartache, with love despite our differences and hope despite our circumstances. It expresses, in front of and behind the camera, that we see ourselves best when we dare to see each other. Available through the Stoopid Ambitious streaming network, the series continues the hilarious story of Zario, Ellington, and their vibrant spectrum of friends.

Follow *Pretty Dudes* on social media @PrettyDudesWeb.

PrettyDudesWeb.com

** Show of the Year, 2017 NYPS Awards*
† Best Performance, 2017 NYPS Awards

More from CSRC Storytelling

Magna Releases

Beyond Passing: The Further Writings of Nella Larsen
Nella Larsen

Passing
Nella Larsen

The Princess and the Goblin
George MacDonald

The DOUBLE BOOKED® Collection

Alice's Adventures in Wonderland
Through the Looking-Glass

Cane
The Conjure Woman: Uncle Julius and His Stories

A Christmas Carol
Marie and the Nutcracker

Desiderio
The Veil and the Shade

Man Cub: The Complete Mowgli Stories
Rikki-Tikki-Tavi and Other Tales from the Jungle Book

Peter Pan
The Never Boy

Shadows Against the Dark: Collected Tales of Horror
The Turn of the Screw

The SHADOWS UPLIFTED Anthology

Volume I: Black Women Authors of 19th Century American Fiction

Volume II: Black Women Authors of 19th Century American Personal Narratives & Autobiographies

Volume III: Black Women Authors of 19th Century American Poetry